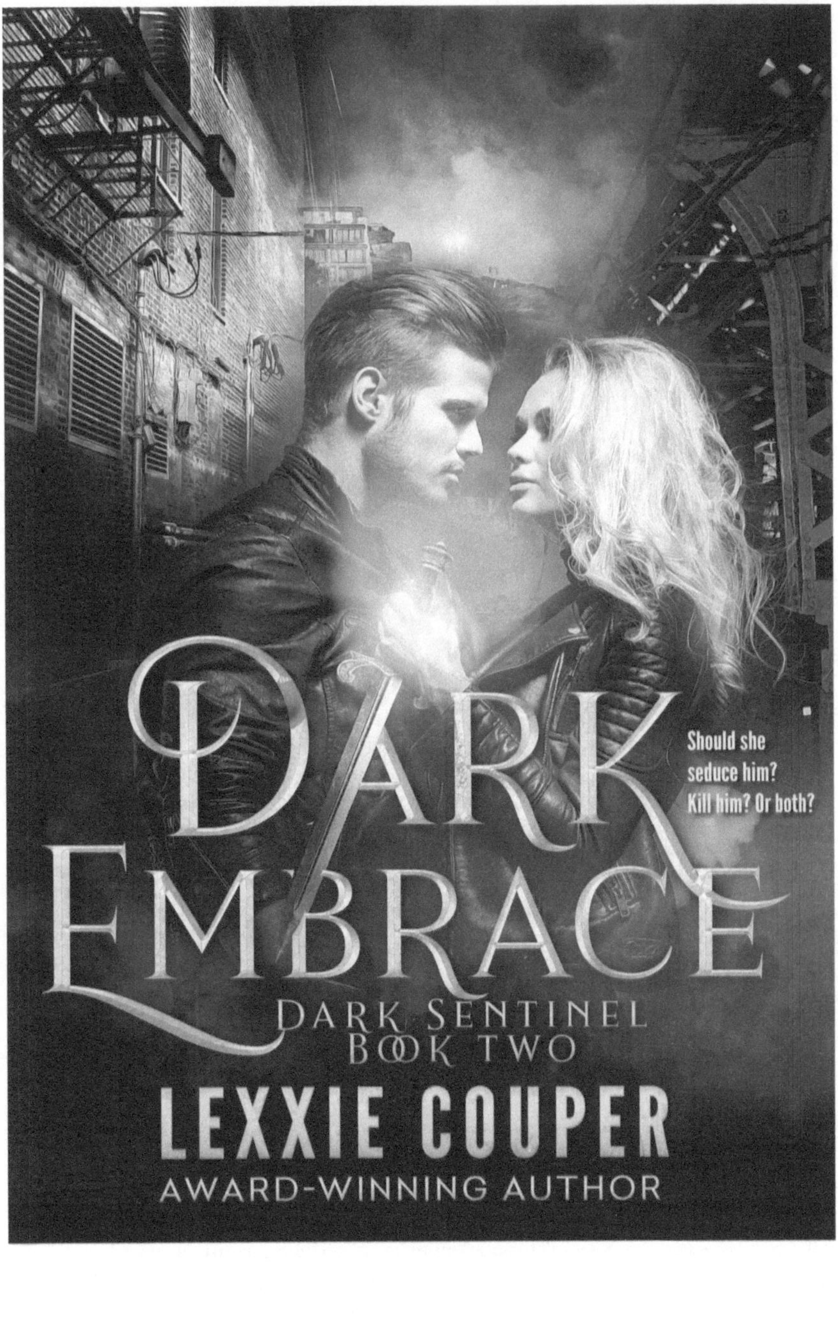

Should she seduce him? Kill him? Or both?
DARK EMBRACE
DARK SENTINEL BOOK TWO
LEXXIE COUPER
AWARD-WINNING AUTHOR

Dedication

For Tamara Yunker.
Because she is awesome.

"A Sentinel is an Agent of the Order. A hunter—of sorts—
controlled by the Deities, who gets to kick the shit out of...how
should I put this...otherworldly scum who step out of line."

—Death, aka, the Fourth Horseman of the Apocalypse.

Prologue

Sydney, Australia, twenty years ago

The succubus walked along the quiet corridor of Bondi High School, her highly tuned senses seeking her target.

"This is no place for a sex demon," she grumbled under her breath with a shake of her head. The long tumble of her golden-blonde hair tickled her neck and jaw line, making her even more nervous. She really hated her hair. It was so...so...cliched.

Goes with the whole succubus package though, doesn't it. Just like this job.

She curled her nose, her stomach knotting.

Not for the first time since the First Horseman of the Apocalypse assigned the target to her, she swallowed a lump of distaste in her throat. Three hundred years of draining humans—mostly males—of their sexual energy, fucking them within an inch of their lives, and here she was hunting down a *kid* with direct orders to drain him to death.

She didn't like it. Not at all. It was unconscionable.

Since when do you have a conscience, demon?

The little whisper in her head made the succubus scowl, and she quickened her pace. She didn't want to listen to *that* little voice. *That* little voice had no right being in her head.

A soft, tinkling, painfully familiar laugh followed, and she curled her fingers into fists. Curse it, she did not need this right now. She had a job to do.

Find. Fuck. Kill.

Simple.

But a boy, Inari? Barely eighteen? Is this what you've become? A killer of children?

This time the voice was her own, and she shook her head again, turning a corner as she tried to squelch the uncomfortable tension in her stomach. This was what she got for playing poker with the scum of the lower levels of Daemonium. Lose a freakin' hand in a high-stakes round, and she was stuck doing the dirty work for one of the Horsemen. She'd had four aces. *Four aces.* Who would have thought the bastard had a royal flush?

Four aces? How could he have a royal flush if you had four aces?

Realization smacked into her like a hot fist, forcing the breath from her in a sharp, disgusted grunt.

Pestilence had cheated. Of course he had. How could she be so stupid?

She chewed on her bottom lip, considering returning to the Realm and telling the Horseman to stick his order in his ear.

Not a wise thing to do if one wants to keep existing, is it now?

No, it wasn't. Pestilence would garrote, disembowel and decapitate anyone who offended or slighted him in anyway. All at once. While keeping them alive as he did so. And then, when he'd finished, he'd get really nasty and truly let loose. Next time she wanted to gamble, she'd do what she normally did and hit the human casinos. At least the crooks there couldn't order her about. Not if they wanted to keep their genitals intact, that was.

Hurry up. Stop procrasting.

Lifting her chin a little, she pulled in a quick breath, tasting the air for her target. The corridor hung heavy with the residue of teenagers in summer—sweat, dirt, cotton, cheap aerosol deodorant, just as cheap make-up. The odors threaded through each other, ribbons of scents and smells weaving together to become one. If she concentrated, she could distinguish each individual scent, separate the origin based on gender and narrow in on the sexually strongest in the building. From there, she would mark them as her feed and return to them that night in their dreams to take her fill. It was her typical selection process and she normally enjoyed it immensely.

Today...not so much. Today she was under different instructions —find the boy and fuck him to death.

And you're really going to do that? The annoying voice whispered in her head again. *Really? Don't you think it's wrong?*

She scowled, ignoring all the other scents as she detected a hint of the one she was after. She *did* think it was wrong. But she was just a succubus. When it came to the grand scheme of demonic hierarchy, the First Horseman of the Apocalypse pretty much had her beat. Unless she wanted to end up decaying in the bottom pits of the Realm, the unearthly network of dimensions all demons called home, she would do what Pestilence ordered: find the boy and fuck him to death.

You'll hate yourself afterwards.

Inari drove her nails into her palms and curled her lip, wishing the voice in her head would just go away already. "Shut up."

Silence answered her, and she let out a ragged sigh. She didn't like the situation she was in. Not one little bit.

Continuing along the corridor, she tuned out anybody with a double X chromosome, focusing her senses on the many teenage boys around her. All of them oozed raging sexual energy, their pubescent hormones devouring what was left of their pre-teen innocence. For a teenage boy, little else mattered except sex. It was hard-wired into their genes, and more than one succubus she knew feasted deeply and often on their rampant sexual needs. She however, was not such a demon, despite the delicious ferocity of a teenager's sexual energy. In her opinion it was wrong somehow. Of course, that rather vague argument hadn't dissuaded the First Horseman from sending her here, had it?

An itch tickled the back of her neck, urgent and hot, and she quickened her step. She was close. Her target wasn't just nearby—he'd walked this very corridor not long ago.

Following the distinctly male scent, she found herself in a doorway, staring out at a large, tree-lined oval of grass. The baking midsummer sun streamed down on her from its zenith, heating her bare limbs and face. She lifted her hand to shade her eyes and studied a group of rowdy boys dressed in blue and red chasing a round white ball around on the grass.

"Montgomery, get back in line!" a man with a paunch and receding hairline shouted from under a tree, waving a clipboard at one particularly lanky youth. "You're playing soccer, not rugby."

"Not my fault, sir," Montgomery called back with a grin, his strawberry-blond hair flopping into brilliant blue eyes. "Wato shoved me off-side."

"Bullshit, I did!" a tall, lankier boy laughed back, broad shoulders hinting at the strength of the man he would become. "Carrot can't play soccer for shit, sir."

"Cut the language, Patrick Watkins," the man with the gut and clipboard—obviously the boys' teacher—called back, "or you'll be picking the gum from under the desks in all of the science..."

The rest of what the teacher threatened faded away, unimportant.

Inari locked her stare on the young boy with the broad shoulders, her heartbeat tripling. Her mouth went dry. Patrick Watkins. She'd found her target. The one Pestilence had sent her to destroy.

No. This can't be right.

Her throat clicked as she swallowed, and she was unable to tear her stare from the teenage boy.

He is...

He can't be? How could such a being exist? And here? In Sydney?

She shook her head, every molecule in her being, every nerve ending of her existence thrumming.

She couldn't *fuck* this boy. She couldn't *kill* this boy either. Even if he were a man, even if she were on the verge of death herself, she could not take this boy. She *would* not take this boy. She'd never known of a human to be so...

He is...

The succubus shook her head again, awe and disbelief prickling the back of her neck. Whatever punishment the First Horseman meted out on her, she would not kill this boy. He was pure as the Holiest of Holies. He was as innocent, maybe more so. She gazed at him, her heartbeat wild. He defied description and made her core—that ravenous sexual center—ache. It was as if he was born of pure, concentrated power and light.

She took a step backward. She would *not* kill him. What happened to her didn't matter. She'd accept whatever punishment Pestilence brought down upon her. Willingly. She would bear it all because she would not—

A sudden heat erupted in her chest. Blistering hot, it spread into the core of her being like a tsunami of golden fire.

A shocked gasp burst from her, and she staggered back another step. By the Dark Ones, what was going on?

Unable to move, she stared out at the boys running and laughing in the bright summer sun. The fire in her body surged through her existence, rolling through her like a wave of light. What was happening?

Her pulse pounded in her neck, her skin tingled, her sex—the weapon she'd used her entire three hundred years—throbbed.

What was happening to her? What was—

She sucked in a breath, another, another, each one growing more ragged than its predecessor. The pure heat born in her chest spread farther. Consuming her, filling her, claiming her.

Changing her.

It threaded into the succubus she was, its heat growing more potent. More compelling. It threaded through her demon core. Overpowering it. Devouring it. Changing *it*.

Changing...

Changing...

She stared at the young boy with the broad shoulders, the boy almost a man. Felt his pure soul call to the world. Felt it call to her. Call to her—

A silent cry tore from her throat, and she pressed her hand to her lips, her eyes wide.

Soul?

How can I have a soul? It isn't possible. How can a demon have a soul?

She stared at the laughing boy running in the sun and gasped, hot tears stinging her eyes.

And yet, she could *feel* it. Feel its mighty pull, its undeniable purpose. Her soul.

Tears squeezed from her eyes, and she pressed her fingers harder to her mouth. She had no idea how or why, but she was no longer succubi. The hunger, the insatiable, demonic craving for sex no longer knotted in the pit of her existence. It no longer dominated her every thought. She was no longer succubi. She was...was—

Sentinel.

The word flooded her mind, her existence, in a voice of infinite time and presence, and suddenly she understood it all.

And she dropped to her knees and wept for joy.

Chapter One

T*oday*

Someone was watching her.

Or some*thing.*

Inari Chayse spun around, staring hard at the people moving over the busy Kings Cross sidewalk behind her. Tourists entranced by the gaudy beauty and bright lights of Sydney's most debauched suburb weaved in and out of impatient locals for whom the lights were nothing more than a way to illuminate the crowded sidewalk. None paid Inari any attention. Well, apart from a few appreciative glances from more than one man, but those she expected. It came with the succubus genes. But the prickling sensation currently razing the back of her neck, like a thousand fire ants nipping at her flesh, only happened when a non-human was about—an early warning system courtesy of her Sentinel soul.

She scanned the ebb and flow of pedestrians around her.

Nothing.

Facing forward again, she continued through the crowd, refocusing her senses on the vampire she'd tracked for the past fifteen minutes.

The blood-sucking bastard had been feeding on tourists for over a week now, picking off easy targets like backpackers and party-goers too drunk and unfamiliar with the suburb to realize they'd wandered from the busy main thoroughfares into the quiet, dimly lit backstreets. The trail of drained bodies he'd left in the alleys and gutters after sunset sickened her, and she'd had him on her target list long before she'd received the command to deal with him. Tonight, his feeding frenzy would come to an end.

Quickening her pace, she pushed through the crowd.

It had been too long since she'd had some action. The paranormal population in Sydney had been behaving itself of late, which meant she'd been bored. Restless.

Is that the only reason, Inari? Or does it have something to do with the fact you haven't had sex in twenty years?

Inari ground her teeth. Well, there was that. When kept busy by the Deities she didn't have time to think about her self-imposed celibacy, but now, during a relatively quiet period...

She sighed. Killing the bloodsucker tonight would, hopefully, take some of the edge off.

And then what? What do you do if you aren't given any orders for another six months? There are only so many times you can masturbate before you have to do something about the situation.

The 'situation'.

She sighed again. An ex-succubus Sentinel had no right constantly dreaming about having incredible sex with a mysterious vampire, and yet that was exactly her situation. Every night, the same dream, the same master vampire, the same insanely intense and incredible raw sex.

It was doing her head in. Making her crazier than she already was.

It was as if with every second she denied herself sex her body demanded it more, and her psyche demanded it specifically with a master vampire she'd never met. And with every night that passed without sexual release, the succubus she once was edged closer to physical control of her body and soul.

Once was? Or still am?

A dry snort sounded at the back of her nose. If she *knew* she could have sex without the risk of draining her partner she'd go for it. But she didn't. She'd queried the Deities since her rebirth, but of course they'd yet to answer her.

Shaking her head, she lengthened her stride. What she had to do was quit the self-pity party. Plenty of humans existed without sex—nuns, priests, eunuchs... She needed to get over it, tell her body to shut the fuck up, ignore the ache in the pit of her belly and concentrate on what she'd been reborn to do—kill monsters.

Zeroing her senses in on her current target once more—the tourist-snacking vampire overdue to be terminated—she smiled. He'd walked this very sidewalk only a few minutes earlier. His filth still hung on the air, his soulless rot like a slick film of decay coating every breath she drew.

She was close. Very close.

Pumping her fingers into loose fists, she turned a corner, the flashing lights and sounds of Kings Cross fading behind her. She moved quickly, almost running down the dim street, past silent houses and closed shops. Her Sentinel force stirred within, eager for release, the scent of the vampire feeding it. Her skin tingled and her muscles burned but she squashed the transformation into her Sentinel form before it took hold. The last thing she needed was some unsuspecting human stumbling upon her in her that form. It would scare the hell out of them. Besides, she'd only just bought the leather pants she currently wore and she really wasn't ready to have them stretched beyond repair, thank you very much. Nor did she want the classic *Iron Man* T-shirt hugging her torso torn as her wings burst from her—

A muffled cry sounded on the air, and Inari stiffened, her skin prickling with increasing heat. Curse it. The bastard had someone.

Hurry.

The vampire's scent flooded into her soul and she broke into a sprint. Another cry fell in the quiet night, this one not so muffled but far weaker. Whoever the bloodsucker was feeding on, they were running out of time.

Hurry. Now.

Rounding the corner, she pushed herself faster, past the sleeping terrace houses, the empty cars, her pulse pounding in her ears, her senses locked on the vamp.

She finally saw him.

He had a man pressed to the front bumper bar of an SUV, one hand gripping the squirming human's groin, the other fisted in his dreadlocked hair, holding his head back so his neck bowed in a violent curve, granting greater access to the blood-rich jugular beneath his exposed skin. Inari absorbed the sight in a heartbeat, noting the stunned disbelief on the man's face, his flailing arms, the blood trickling down his throat like a line of liquid life turned black by the darkness of the street.

She bit back a savage snarl and threw herself forward.

Her shoulder hit the vampire hard, slamming into the side of his head. Hot blood splattered Inari's arm as the impact yanked the bloodsucker's fangs from the man's throat. A gurgling scream ripped through the air, but she kept her focus on her target. Vampires never died easily. They were always too stupid to accept their fate.

This one, it seemed, was particularly dumb.

He fought against her, smashing a fist into her jaw even as they hit the asphalt in front of the car. Black stars erupted in her head, but she ignored the pain, springing to her feet before he could land another blow. He jack-knifed himself up off the road, fangs bared, chin and lips glistening with blood, demonic stare locked on her face. "Gonna fuck you—"

Inari snapped out a swift sidekick before he could finish, aiming her booted heel for his unbeating heart.

The vampire jerked to the right, blocking her kick, his arm swinging in a dark blur to strike her ankle with a crunching blow. White pain shot up her leg, but Inari didn't falter. She spun into a back kick, driving her heel high against his chest. He flailed backward, face distorting in stunned fury.

And turned and fled down the street.

"At least he's smart enough to know he should run away," she muttered, fixing his back with a level stare. She flicked the human crumpled on the sidewalk a quick look, grim relief filling her at the sight of his moving chest. She'd reached him just in time. Now to end the vampire's existence.

She took off after the escaping vamp, her own speed matching his. Which meant she'd hurt him when she'd crash-tackled him to the road. Unless she transformed into her Sentinel form, she couldn't outrun a vamp. No matter how many hours she spent working out at the gym.

Focus locked on the sprinting—albeit, sprinting with a limp—vampire, she pushed more power into her legs, letting the force of her assassin's soul seep into her muscles. Blistering heat surged through her, scalding the walls of her veins, scorching the cells of her body. And still she ran faster, holding back the Sentinel buried within her even as she leached its power, drawing closer to the fleeing vampire. Closer.

She leapt without a sound, landing on his back and driving him to the ground a second before he could cut right and disappear into a narrow, unlit alley.

He hissed, but the furious sound was cut short as she snatched a fistful of his hair and smashed his face against the sidewalk. Again and again. He flailed beneath her, scrabbling at her wrists, his fingers turning into claw-tipped talons with every swipe.

She snarled, ducking each one. Curse it, if she wasn't careful he'd rip her T-shirt.

Then stop messing around, woman.

She slammed his head to the ground once more, drove her knees between his shoulder blades and snagged his left wrist with her right hand. "This is going to hurt, fucker." She yanked his arm to the side, pulling it until his armpit was stretched taut.

"Going to kill you, bitch," he blustered, writhing under her knees. He was strong even with his injury. But Inari was stronger.

And seriously ticked off.

"Yeah, yeah." She curled her lip, jerked his arm a little straighter and ground her weight into his back. "Whatever."

She closed the fingers of her left hand around the grip of the long, silver dagger sheathed in the lining of her boot, withdrew it in a single, fluid motion and sank it to the hilt into the vampire's armpit. Straight into the side of his unbeating heart.

A screeching wail tore from the vamp's throat. He thrashed once, twice and then Inari was kneeling on the footpath, a man-shaped smudge of oily dust staining the concrete under her knees.

"Eww." She crinkled her nose, the stench of instantly decomposed vampire turning the air putrid. Climbing to her feet, she slid her dagger back into its hidden sheath and stepped away from the residue of terminated vamp. "Why are bloodsuckers always so smelly?"

She bent at the waist, casting a disgusted look at the knees of her leather trousers, and straightened immediately when the back of her neck prickled with heat.

Someone was watching her. Again.

Demon.

The word whispered through her head. She squinted into the blackness around her, seeing nothing.

But why would she? It was one in the morning on a moonless night, and she was standing on the sidewalk of a quiet side street far from the bright, flashing lights of the main strip. Not even the ten-buck hookers and crack users wandered so far into Kings Cross suburbia. She was alone on the street, surrounded by silent houses, sleeping cars and the low drone of hungry mosquitoes.

And yet...

The Sentinel force within her stirred. Agitated. Alert.

Wary.

Inari turned on the spot, scanning the darkness. The back of her neck prickled again, stronger this time. Hotter.

She narrowed her eyes, not for the first time wondering why the hell the Highest had deigned to create a demon assassin capable of incomparable physical prowess without electing to add hyper-vision.

"Shit."

Her muttered curse fell into the silence. She turned once more, her neck on fire, her gut churning. Someone was watching her, but whoever they were, they were keeping themselves hidden.

She didn't like it. Not at all.

"What are you waiting for?" She held her arms wide, her call bouncing off the houses around her.

A bird flew out of a nearby tree, the wild beating of its wings making Inari jump. She bit back another curse, shaking her head. Fuck this. If the demon wasn't going to show its face, she had other things to—

The fiery prickles on the back of her neck vanished. Just like that.

Inari frowned, far from relieved. "What the hell?"

She stood motionless, half-expecting an attack, half-convinced she'd imagined the whole thing.

Something felt off. Wrong.

The night stayed silent around her. Not even the sound of the startled bird returning to its roost destroyed the stillness.

Inari let out a sharp sigh and stared into the darkness around her one last time. Nothing. With a shake of her head, she turned and ran up the road, back to the bright lights of the sin capital of Australia.

She'd make an anonymous call to the paramedics from a payphone, tell them about the human male bleeding in the gutter, give them his exact location and then find herself an empty seat in one of the Cross' more reputable bars. It was one a.m. for Pete's sake. If she wasn't going to terminate some more demon ass, it was time for a coffee. If she was lucky, some idiot would try to pick her up before the sun rose and refuse to take no for an answer. At least then she could work out what was left of her agitation with a fistfight and go to bed more relaxed.

Hopefully.

She still needed her beauty sleep, damn it, whether she had the powers of a Sentinel or not.

* * *

Ezryn Navarro strode through the ballroom, his footfalls echoing in the cavernous space, his stare fixed on the overlord and his new bride seated on a raised dais at the far end of the room. It might be customary for master vampires to pay homage to the visiting over-lord within the hour of his arrival, but Ezryn never bothered with tradition—even less with any practice meant to appeal to the self-indulgent egomaniac currently ogling the lush breasts of the woman perched beside him.

Ezryn curled his lip. The leader of the vampire race was a disgrace to his kind—wrapped up in his own importance, courting a dangerously disrespectful and violent attitude toward humans, obsessed with the accumulation of wealth and material possessions. The moron threw his considerable weight around without thought of consequence, his only concern the fulfillment of his every whim.

It pissed Ezryn off. A lot.

"Ho, friend Ezryn," the overlord called, raising his hand and waving it a mere inch. His washed-out yellow gaze slid to his wife, and Ezryn's fangs lengthened with contempt. The royal fool actually believed he could irritate Ezryn with his blatant parading? If that was the case, he was a bigger imbecile than Ezryn suspected.

Suspected? You've known he was an imbecile for almost seven hundred years.

The overlord flashed a wide smile, his pointed fangs glinting in the muted light from the many candles littering the ballroom. "You do us a great honor with your presence, Master Navarro."

Ezryn suppressed the urge to snort, casting the room a disgusted glance. Candles? What century did the fat fool think it was?

"Although," the overlord continued, raising black eyebrows, "you are almost four hours late. We feared the Navarro master would not present himself to us before the sun rose." He shot his new bride another quick look, as if eager to see her reaction to his royal disapproval.

Ezryn gave him a flat stare. "I had better things to do."

The new bride gasped, eyes wide, the candlelight turning her extended fangs a sick yellow.

The overlord snapped to his feet, jowls wobbling. "You dare insult—"

"Give it a rest, Harry." Ezryn cut him short. "Or I'll pin you to the floor and drain you within a drop of empty like I used to."

Haral Navarro, twin son of the first family, overlord of the vampire race, turned beet red—an interesting feat for someone deprived of sunlight for close to seven centuries. His mouth flapped in silent protest, his knuckles popping as he clenched his fists.

Ezryn shook his head, a sour taste coating the back of his tongue. "Do not fret, baby brother." He ambled over to a long table overburdened with carafes of what could only be human blood, eyeing the ridiculously ostentatious ice sculpture of the overlord positioned amongst them. "I would not dream of harming the great leader of our people." He pulled an apple from his inside jacket pocket and polished it on his sleeve, turning back to the royal couple. Very few of his kind could tolerate human food, his twin brother included. That Ezryn had no difficulty consuming it caused many a vampire to clench their jaw in envy—and trepidation.

Lifting the apple to his mouth, he parted his lips, letting Haral see his fangs before biting into the fruit's flesh.

Haral narrowed his eyes, his face—so like Ezryn's if not for the signs of indulgence—still red with anger. Or was it shame? "You will not call me 'baby brother', Ezryn. I ordered you to cease doing so over half a century ago."

Ezryn bit into the apple again, enjoying the incensed impatience on his twin's face as he chewed the mouthful without hurry. "And when did I start following your orders, Harry?"

The overlord's wife gasped again, her lush breasts almost spilling over the top of her red latex corset. Ezryn gave her an indifferent glance before wiping at his lips with the back of his hand. "What are you doing here, Haral? I can't imagine Australia was your first choice for a honeymoon, especially during the summer. The sun doesn't set here until nine most nights." He finished the apple, savoring its succulent sweetness before dropping the core into the closest carafe of blood. It broke the still, red surface with a satisfying plop, the sound like a gunshot in the cavernous room. "In fact," he went on, arching an eyebrow, "I can't see any reason for you to have left your compound at all."

The overlord flared his nostrils, a pathetic attempt to look intimidating. "I wanted you to meet Chantise." He flicked his bride a quick look. "And she wanted to meet you."

Ezryn chuckled, the sound hollow. Of course she would. She would want to see for herself the fabled son groomed to be the ruler of the vampire race, destined to be the next leader of them all— before the Oracle, the vampire race's high priest, had changed everything. He gave his new sister-in-law a slow inspection and bent slightly at the waist. "Your ladyship."

The woman's gaze raked him from head to toe, her eyes aglow with the taint of a recent feed. She touched her tongue to the tip of her right fang, tracing her fingertips over the swell of her breasts. "Ezryn."

Ezryn suppressed a disgusted grunt. The woman was well-suited to his brother—he could see the covetous hunger in her blood-drunk eyes, the smug conceit in the tilt of her chin. He turned back to Haral, eager to be done with the perverse family reunion. "What do you want, Harry? I thought I made it clear the last time we spoke I never wanted to see you again. Isn't that why I moved to the other side of the world?"

Haral straightened his spine, eyes igniting with cold rage. The last time the two brothers had faced each other—over fifty years ago—the vampire lord had threatened to have Ezryn marked as a traitor to his kind. The last time they'd stood in the same room, Ezryn had come very, very close to destroying the vampire lord. Close enough for Harry to sweat blood. A lot of blood.

"I am your *lord*." The muscles in Haral's face quivered. "I can speak to you and call upon you whenever I wish."

Ezryn barked out a laugh, the sound like cracking ice. "I have no lord."

Haral stamped his foot, his human face distorting into a demonic mask. "As the supreme ruler of our people, I hereby command you to a task."

Ezryn narrowed his eyes. "Go to hell, Harry."

"Not before you, Ezryn."

With a low growl, Ezryn crossed the distance to Haral in a blurring leap. Clamping one hand around his twin brother's neck, he yanked Haral's feet off the floor. "You destroyed any right you had to command me, *brother*, when you invoked the power of the blood trial."

Haral scratched at Ezryn's hand, his eyes bulging. "And yet..." he rasped, "...the blood trial named *me* overlord. Not..." he bucked in Ezryn's hold, "...you."

Ezryn tightened his grip, the mention of the ancient ritual filling him with cold contempt.

Since birth, he'd been groomed to take over from his father as the next leader of the vampire race. For nine hundred and fifty years, he'd known little except that as the first son of the First

Family, born but a mere five minutes before his twin, he was destined to be the next overlord. He'd been educated to lead a race on the verge of imploding. Too many of their number had grown disillusioned with the old ways, the violent use of humans as a food source, an equal number disgusted with the progressive notion humans weren't just cattle. He'd been ready to restore harmony where only conflict existed. Ready to take his place as overlord. And then his father had been killed, staked by an demon-slayer wannabe with acne on his cheeks.

The day after the overlord's death, the day before Ezryn was to ascend to the position of his birthright, Haral had invoked the blood trial, an ancient and barbaric ceremony designed to reveal the *true* overlord's identity.

And on the whispered words of the human virgin sacrificed for the trial—a young woman known as the Oracle's Voice throughout the proceedings—the course of history had changed.

Ezryn stared into his brother's eyes. "Just what do you want me to do...*lord?*"

Haral flashed his fangs, his Adam's apple jerking under Ezryn's palm. "My wife's cousin was slain by a Sentinel. I want *you* to destroy her."

Ezryn clenched his jaw, a cold fist of disquiet in his chest. "A Sentinel?"

What Haral commanded was insanity. To destroy a divine assassin in self-defense was one thing—the Deities would not retaliate against such a death. If a Sentinel could not survive a fair fight with their foe, than the Deities seemed to wipe their divine, righteous hands of their failed assassin. But to destroy one in an act of revenge? That was to start a war beyond all comprehension. A war that would bring about the mass destruction of vampire and Sentinel alike.

The Sentinel were no easy kill. Once demons themselves, they were selected by the Highest for reasons unknown, granted a soul and *reborn* then and there as assassins of all things unholy and inhuman. Whether vampire, shifter or hell-spawn, if a being threatened the divine status quo, chances were the Deities would mark it for termination and send a Sentinel to carry out the kill.

A Sentinel's rebirth gave them immeasurable powers and knowledge of their target. Few of those targeted escaped to brag of the battle.

Still, the divine assassins *could* be beaten. If you were strong.

And ready to face ultimate death yourself.

Releasing his hold on Haral's throat, Ezryn took a step back. He'd never seen such a feverish light in his brother's eyes before. There was more to this than Haral would have him believe. "Why do you want me to do this? Are you not capable of the task yourself?" He flicked his gaze over his twin's soft, round body, remembering a time when it was almost a carbon copy of his own. "Are you having performance problems, Harry? *Tsk, tsk.* At your young age too."

The overlord drew himself straighter, his incensed stare fixed on Ezryn. "I charged you with a task, Master Navarro. If you do not obey your lord, you will see yourself punished by our laws."

"Punished? Laws?" Ezryn raised his eyebrows. His twin always had been a pompous pain in the ass. Now it seemed his position of power had finally gone to his empty head. "Any laws worthy of respect you perverted on ascension, Harry. As for punishment, remember who you're talking to. Every vampire on earth knows who the *true* overlord is. Do you really think your punishment would be dealt?"

His brother snarled at him, contempt and hatred etched on his face. "Yes, of course, the *true* overlord. Born first by a mere contraction of our mother's womb. And yet that simple order was proved false, wasn't it? By the blood trial itself, the chancellor who named you first born was proved a liar and executed. Thanks to ritual, the rightful son finally claimed his rightful title." He paused, his smile smug. "I always knew I was better than you, Ezryn. It just took the words of a semi-catatonic virgin to prove it to the rest of our race."

With a silent hiss, Ezryn grabbed Haral's throat again. The blood trial. Even the words made him sick.

Cold contempt laced through the anger simmering inside him and he sank his fingers into his brother's fleshy neck. The blood trial had not been invoked for over ten thousand years. Why would it? It was an ancient ritual from a superstitious, barbaric past before common sense prevailed and the position of overlord became decided by birthright. Two master vampires would feed on a human virgin selected for her purity and spiritual nature to be the "voice" of the oracle until she was almost drained of blood. They would then let her linger in the void between expiration and transformation until she was a heartbeat away from death. When her pulse began to fade, when her lips began to turn ashen and her body began to convulse, each vampire would open their own vein and let a single drop of *their* blood fall onto her tongue. The vampire whose name she uttered into the waiting Oracle's ear, seconds before he claimed her virginity, was pronounced overlord.

It disgusted Ezryn. It went against everything he believed in the vampire/human relationship.

That Haral had invoked the blood trial the day after their father's death had shocked everyone.

As had the name the dying virgin had whispered.

No one had expected the young woman to whisper Haral's name. No one except Ezryn. He knew what his brother lusted for most of all, what Haral had *always* lusted for—the position and power of overlord, supreme ruler of their kind.

A mere week after their father's end, Ezryn discovered his brother had been fucking the oracle. Unfortunately, he'd had no way of proving the forbidden relationship. Ezryn also knew his father's advisors had been unhappy with Ezryn's approaching ascension. His father, an ancient vampire less interested in ruling his people and more interested in sticking his prick into anything with pulse, had been a ruler they could manipulate and control. Ezryn, on the other hand, had proved difficult to dominate and influence in his grooming for the position of overlord. More than once he'd made it clear he would not be a puppet to their political machinations. He'd refused to destroy vampires accused of vague, unsubstantiated crimes, questioned dubious requests his father would automatically approve, and sort answers to questions few in court wanted asked.

To this day, Ezryn had to admit he'd underestimated his brother. Haral had played all the pieces to perfection. The dying virgin had allegedly whispered Haral's name in the oracle's ear, and the advisors to the position of overlord had supported and enforced that proclamation. Ezryn was denied the title a mere twenty-four hours before his ascension. But blood trial or no, Ezryn would not kowtow to his brother. Especially when he didn't believe what the virgin had proclaimed.

Anger a cold fist in his chest, he drew Haral closer. "Tell me, brother mine, supreme and oh-so-revered leader of our illustrious race, after the oracle finished raping the human virgin to her death, did he wipe his pus-weeping dick clean before sinking it into your ass?"

Haral hissed, tiny beads of saliva splattering his bottom lip. "I charge you with a task, Ezryn Navarro," he snarled. "And for every night you choose not to obey my order, I will slaughter one vampire who chose to rebel against my ascension."

Ezryn's cold blood turned to fire. "You wouldn't dare. I accepted that ridiculous proclamation to save bloodshed."

His brother sneered. "Try me, Ezzie."

The nickname stabbed into Ezryn's chest and he bit back a hiss.

From the moment Haral learned of his lower position in the family their sibling relationship turned toxic. One son born to be lord, one son born to be subservient. One groomed for the duty, the other hungering for it with every molecule in his body.

Ezryn bared his fangs, releasing his grip on Haral's throat before stepping backward. "That we come from the same blood disgusts me."

Haral smiled, the action both smug and perverted, and smoothed his hands over the crumpled collar of his shirt. "As it does me, *brother*. So tell me, will you have your loyal followers' decimation on your conscience? Will they drown in blood and burn in sunlight? Or will you do as your ruler commands?"

Ezryn's gut clenched. Hundreds of vampires had adamantly and vocally refused Haral's ascension. Vampires who had moved beyond the savagery of their race long ago. Vampires who continued to have faith in Ezryn, even when he stepped aside. Who bemoaned his move to Australia and begged him to lead a rebellion. He remembered Kristoph, his tutor and advisor in the vampiric court for close to six centuries. The ancient vampire had been one of only two to discover Haral's relationship with the oracle. Kristoph had spoken at length to the court, petitioning them not to appoint Haral, but his pleas had fallen on deaf ears. Or scared ones.

The mass slaughter of those loyal to Ezryn had begun with Kristoph. Only Ezryn's departure from Europe had halted the *cleansing*, as Haral's loyalists called it. Harry, of course, denounced his followers' actions. He spoke verbosely and grandly of peace and coexistence but did little to stop the executions. Fifty years later, and the fury in Ezryn's chest had not lessened one iota.

He stared at his brother, the disquiet in his chest growing colder. Tighter. What he was about to agree to do was insanity, but he had no choice. There was always a solution to lunacy—even if the solution was lunacy itself. "Where do I find this Sentinel you're so willing to see dead you will condemn hundreds?"

Haral grinned, fangs glistening in the candlelight, eyes shining with smug triumph. "Why, Ezzie. Here. In Australia. In the very city you now call home."

* * *

"What do you mean, kill a *Sentinel*?" Jacob Ancroft, Ezryn's closest friend and Sydney's most successful nightclub owner, frowned at

Ezryn, the glass of scotch he'd poured himself on arriving at Ezryn's home forgotten in his hand. "Is he insane?"

Ezryn grunted, took a mouthful of his own whiskey and slumped back in his armchair. "I had that very thought." He crossed his ankles on the glass coffee table before him, his smile dry. "And a few others it's probably best I don't express about our illustrious leader."

The other vampire snorted, the sound short and contemptuous. "Fat Harry isn't the leader of the vampire race, Ezryn. You are."

Ezryn shook his head and took another drink, the amber liquid burning its way down his throat like liquid fire. "No, my brother is. You know it just as well as you know *why* I'm not. And as such, I am bound to obey my lord."

"Well, your *lord* is going to start a fucking war between the assassins of the Highest of Deities and vampires the world over." Scowling, Jacob dropped into the other armchair. "Dark Ones, Ezryn. The idiot turns up here fifty years after that farce of a crowning ceremony trying to throw his weight around, and you're laughing about it? Does he even comprehend what he's ordering you to do? You destroy a Sentinel in an unprovoked attack and we may as well cry Armageddon and kiss our asses goodbye. *And* he's making you the target of both sides. Not only will the Sentinel come after you, vampires across the globe will want to tear you limb from limb for starting such a senseless, bloody war."

"I realize that." Ezryn placed his empty glass on the coffee table and leaned back, stretching his arms along the back of the armchair. "Haral has been looking for a way to get rid of me for as long as I can remember, and he's finally found one." He grinned, his fangs scraping at the inside of his bottom lip. "It's actually quite clever... for my brother. I didn't know Harry had it in him."

Jacob flashed his own fangs in contempt. "He *doesn't* have it in him. If he did, he wouldn't resort to trickery to claim *your* title. Seriously, Ezryn, don't you think this lunacy has gone on long enough? You know as well as I that you have the numbers to reclaim the position rightfully yours. The vampire race may be hobbled by tradition and ritual, but we're not imbeciles. Harry's *leadership* is sending us all on a one-way path toward mass bloodshed and revolt. For fuck's sake, only last year he ordered all bleeders swear loyalty to him or face sunrise chained to a tree. He's on a power rush, dangerously out of control, and I for one am sick of it. It's time to end the farce and put the moronic fuck in his place."

"And how many would perish in such a rebellion, Jake? How many vampires would be destroyed? How many humans would die caught in the crossfire? Haral's followers are as loyal to him as mine are to me. The difference is his zealots have no respect for life of any kind except their own. You are right, I *am* the true overlord, and as such my first duty is to the survival of my race, not the decimation of it in a blood feud."

Jacob let out a low, demonic and very disgruntled growl. "I don't know why I didn't stake the bastard fifty years ago. I was there in his compound when he gave the order to execute Kristoph. The fucker could be nothing but dust now, and none of this shit would be going down."

Ezryn cast his friend a level look, ignoring the sorrowful anger spearing into him at the mention of his one-time advisor. "You would have been dusted the second you did, my friend."

Jacob's scowl darkened. "I can take care of myself. You know that." He pushed himself to his feet, agitation clear on his timelessly handsome face. "Besides, at this point the sacrifice would have been worth it. The moment you destroy the Sentinel, Harry's signing a death note for us all. The vampire race is strong, despite our ridiculous leader, but we will not survive the wrath of the Highest. As much as it pains me to say it, we vampires would be on the losing side. Pick off an Agent of the Order for no other reason than idiotic revenge and we're all dust."

"And if I don't obey my brother's command, every vampire who opposed his ascension and stayed loyal to me will be slaughtered." Ezryn turned his gaze from the other vampire. "I cannot have their blood, *your* blood, on my hands." He rose to his feet and crossed to the bar to pour himself another whiskey, his chest tight. "I will find the Sentinel who offended my brother's new wife," he said, turning back to Jacob, "and kill her, as the overlord has ordered me to do."

And then, he finished silently, *I will offer myself to the Deities as an act of sacrifice and beg their forgiveness. Allow them to do with me what they will to appease their want for retribution. Hopefully this will halt the war before it can begin.*

He drained his glass, keeping his expression neutral. "There is no other choice."

Jacob narrowed his eyes. "I don't like it. I still say you let me dust the imbecile. I can enter his compound while he is here and have the deed done before the sun rises. He doesn't know I'm in Australia and won't expect it. Hell, Harry's followers are idiots. Those loyal to you can—"

"Follow my lead," Ezryn cut Jacob short. "I must obey the overlord's command, as must *all* vampires. It is the law of our kind." He gave his friend a hard stare. "I will not allow any of those loyal to me to be destroyed by Haral's hand. Too many have already lost their lives thanks to my brother. There can be no more. I've made up my mind, Jake. This is the way it is, and this is the way it will be. Do you understand?"

Jacob growled, threw himself out of the armchair and stormed across the room. He stopped at the floor-to-ceiling window overlooking Sydney Harbor, arms crossed, shoulders bunched.

Ezryn watched him, knowing he struggled to keep his demon sheathed. The other vampire had been his closest friend for almost six centuries, the brother he'd never had in Haral.

Ordered to the overlord's court, Jacob had been accused by a rival vampire of systematically raping and butchering the females of his territory. Ezryn's father—in a typical blood-drunk state—ordered Ezryn to execute him without further question or evidence. Ezryn had refused, unwilling to commit such a sentence before discovering all the facts. Facts that, when revealed, not only exonerated

Jacob, but proved the accusing vampire's true motives—possession of Jacob's territory and his new human wife. Jacob had stood by Ezryn ever since, swearing not just gratitude, but fealty as well to the then-future overlord.

When the oracle proclaimed Haral first born, Jacob had been ready to go to war for Ezryn—an unwavering loyalty all too horrifically proved in blood.

Ezryn had been in his family's castle witnessing his brother's controversial ascension when Harry's followers had attacked Jacob's compound in the Scottish highlands—a coward's attempt to destroy Ezryn's closest and most powerful ally. Jacob had destroyed five of them before they'd overpowered him. Five vampires decimated by a single one. The three left contained him, bound him in chains and made him watch as they butchered his entire staff, innocent people, human and vampire alike. They tortured them at length before raping his wife before his eyes. Three vampires who had all sworn fealty to Haral Navarro, the new overlord.

Three vampires who held Jacob prisoner as they slowly cut his love to pieces.

Three vampires arrogant enough, stupid enough, to think they'd bested Ezryn Navarro's general.

Three vampires who never saw the dark of night again.

Jacob never spoke of how he overcame them, but Ezryn had only had to look into his friend's eyes when he'd found him to know Haral had made himself an enemy beyond his understanding. Ezryn was old, older than Jacob, and far more powerful, but thanks to Ezryn's deranged brother, Jacob was now almost as dangerous.

Every time Ezryn found his friend staring at the small image of Cara that Jacob kept in a white-gold locket by his lifeless heart, he thanked the Dark Ones Jacob was on his side.

What will he do when he learns of your sacrifice?

Ezryn ground his teeth. He needed to circumnavigate *that* problem before he killed the Sentinel...somehow, otherwise Jacob would begin a rebellion against Harry that might prove bloodier than the war Ezryn hoped his sacrifice would prevent.

Are you really going to do this? Kill a Sentinel in an unprovoked attack? A female Sentinel, at that? Won't that single act make you as barbaric as your brother?

"I don't like any of this."

Jacob's growl snapped Ezryn's attention back to the here and now. He placed his untouched whiskey on the bar and moved to stand beside the brooding vampire at the window. Outside the yachts and motor craft anchored on Sydney Harbour bobbed up and down with the gentle swell, their small lights like dancing stars on the black water. "I must admit it's not how I saw the night progressing." He gave Jacob a wide grin, trying to assuage his friend's torment. "But think about it this way—I had nothing else planned. What better way to spend the next few hours before dawn than hunting a Sentinel?"

Jacob shot him a quick look. "If you think you're hunting alone, you're dumber than your brother."

Ezryn shook his head. "I'm not letting you come with me, Jake. Not on this one."

Jacob laughed, a short, sharp snort that made Ezryn want to grin and shake him at the same time. "And I'm not staying put."

"Don't push me, Jake."

"Don't be a moron then, Ezryn. Besides, I know something you don't."

Ezryn raised his eyebrows. Crossing his arms over his chest, he gave the Scottish vampire an expectant look. "Do you now? And what's that?"

"The Sentinel has a thing for strip clubs."

Something heavy pressed on Ezryn's chest and he narrowed his eyes. "How do you know this? According to my brother no one knows just who the Sentinel is."

Jacob grinned, the expression way too triumphant for Ezryn's tastes. "Further proof Harry is an imbecile."

"Spill the beans, Ancroft."

Jacob's grin stretched wider, his earlier irritation forgotten in the rare opportunity to rile his master. "Rumor. And terrified whispers. And you're right, as is the imbecile unfortunately, no one *does* seem to know what she actually looks like. Most of the clientele at the Pleasure Palace are petrified she's going to come in, wings spread, eyes glowing that freaky-shit white light and go biblical on their demonic asses."

Ezryn studied his smiling friend, the disquieting pressure on his chest growing heavier. "Why haven't you mentioned this before?"

"Why would I? Until Harry came you'd never indicated an interest in the insane sport of Sentinel hunting. And as I said, it's all been rumor. Who knew there really *was* a female Sentinel in town? And I thought it was bad enough having Ven Watkins in our midst." He shuddered at the name of the feared Sentinel Supreme before giving Ezryn a smirk. "A female assassin of You know who watching strip shows in one of my clubs? Hell, I'll never be able to look at my clientele the same way again."

Ezryn grunted. "I've always wondered if a Sentinel could be perverted. Seems like the answer to that is yes."

Jacob rolled his eyes. "But in one of *my* clubs? I have a reputation to uphold, you know?"

Ezryn laughed. "Well, let's go play bouncer, shall we?"

"You shouldn't be enjoying this, Ezryn."

He shouldn't. So why was the notion of one of the Highest's assassins indulging in live porn stirring something in him?

Something dark and entirely...sexual?

And what exactly did he do about it?

Chapter Two

His dark stare holds her as imprisoned as the silk ropes around her wrists. *"Do you fear me, Sentinel?"*

She draws a shaky breath in through her nose. It would be pointless to lie to him. He knows her every thought. "Yes."

With another smug laugh, he returns his mouth to her neck, his lips charting a slow path down her throat. "As it is, as it will be."

Why did he sexually torture her like this every time? Reduce her to a panting, begging creature of ravenous, unending lust?

Why did she let him?

Cool lips move over her chest to her left breast, brushing the aching tip of her nipple. "Because you want this as much as I do," he answers in a whisper. Sharp teeth scrape at her nipple, a mischievous bite that makes her gasp and buck her hips harder against his teasing hand.

"Curse you," she grounds out, writhing on the mattress. Her sex throbs, heavy and full with a desire so potent she can barely breathe. "Just fuck me. Please."

Her raw begging makes him laugh, and he bites her nipple again, punishing her for her outburst. "You know what you have to say, Sentinel."

She shakes her head, every fiber in her being straining for him. Wanting him. It's wrong, more than wrong. It's insane, lunacy, but she wants him all the same. Is lost without him. "I will not," she groans, squeezing her eyes shut. "I cannot."

"I know you want to feel my cock inside you, Inari Chayse." His voice caresses her senses like icy mist. "All it will take is one word." He slowly, slowly slides one finger into her sex, and she moans, ramming her hips upward. "One word, Sentinel and it will be my cock fucking you, not my hand." He takes her nipple into his mouth and rolls its hard form between his teeth before sucking it with bruising force. She cries out, pain and pleasure spearing through her.

"One word, Inari." He moves his lips up to her jaw, her ear. "You know what it is, don't you?"

She does. The one word she will never say.

He traces his tongue over the shell of her ear and she trembles. "One word, Inari. Say it for me, my stubborn little assassin, so we both can be as one. Say it, say it."

She grinds her teeth, riding his hand and feeling the word begin to form on her lips. Feeling it form on her tongue. Feeling it form in her soul.

One word...

Master.

She opens her eyes, that one word on her lips. And sees his fangs extend, glistening with saliva. Ready to pierce her—

Inari jolted awake, her ragged breath stripping at her throat, burning her lungs. She flicked her gaze around her dark bedroom, shame and dismay flooding through her.

"Crap," she muttered.

The same fucking dream. The same fucking vampire.

Scrubbing at her face, she let out a strangled groan, struggling to calm her rapid heart rate. Damn it, what was going on with her?

She stretched across her bed and snared her old wristwatch, a present from an enamored seventeenth-century watchmaker she'd fed on for over a decade. The tiny hands mocked her and she groaned again, slumping back to the mattress. Forty minutes. That's all the sleep she'd had. A mere forty minutes of sleep, and she'd had the same goddamn dream she'd had for what felt like forever. The same cursed vampire doing the same cursed thing to her. What in all the levels of the Realm was *wrong* with her?

Immediately, an image of the bloodsucker from her dreams filled her head, dark eyes glinting red. He smiled at her, an arrogant grin that barely curled the corners of his mouth. His light-brown hair fell over his smooth, pale forehead in a tousled mess, the thick strands brushing straight, thick eyebrows.

The pit of her stomach squirmed with instinctual interest, and she groaned.

Why did she continually dream about a *vampire* bringing her to climax after climax after climax with just his hand night after night after night? A vampire, of all things. Worse still, why did she crave more than his fingers every time she woke?

Because you're an ex-succubus who hasn't had sex in twenty years? Because since your rebirth as a Sentinel you've spent the better part of those twenty years hunting and destroying vampires and shapeshifters and all manner of demon-kind, and your previous demon existence is fucking with your already messed-up psyche?

Because deep down inside—in the dark, twisted place you fear to explore—you want to be claimed by a vampire? A master vampire?

Letting out a low growl, Inari threw herself from the bed and stormed across her room. She didn't want to think about that last question. It was too...disturbing to consider.

Leaning her flushed forehead on the cool glass window, she stared at the cityscape ten stories below. It was still dark, the sun not even close to illuminating the sinful mecca that was Kings Cross.

"Argh!" Inari threw up her hands and turned away from the window. She needed to get laid. If she weren't so sexually frustrated all the time, she wouldn't be having freaking wet dreams about a master freaking vampire.

Then go find a male, preferably human, and fuck the dream out of your system.

The suggestion sent a wet shard of heat straight into her sex, and she pressed her thighs together. Oh, if only she could. She wanted to so badly. The need for sexual release ate at her every minute of her existence, but she didn't dare risk it. As appealing as daily multiple climaxes were, she didn't *want* to be a sex demon again. She didn't want to return to that life, and she feared one moment of sexual connection with another being, no matter how soulless, would feed the succubus still inside her waiting to be nourished.

Waiting to be freed.

Which meant she currently held the all-time succubus record for abstinence.

It was safer that way.

And you'd throw that safety record right out the window if the vamp from your dreams walked through your bedroom door. You know that, don't you?

Inari ground her teeth, ignoring the little voice—*that* little voice —in her head. Crossing to the cupboard, she grabbed her vest from its hanger. She was going out again. It may be—she flicked her watch a quick look—two forty-five in the morning, but if she didn't leave her apartment right now, go to a club, or a pub, or a bowling alley or...or...shit, *something*, she'd just end up masturbating to the memory of her dream and feeling wretched the second her empty, unsatisfying orgasm faded from her body.

Tugging on the black leather garment, she snatched her skin-tight black jeans from the foot of the bed and pulled them up her legs and over her butt. It was a clichéd outfit to be sure, the kind Hollywood seemed infatuated with when it came to anything related to vampires and demons, but she wore it for a reason.

Bait.

She was tiny, barely five foot four, and the body-hugging clothes made her look even smaller. Well, except for her boobs. Like all succubi, her boobs were full and heavy and round and the corset-style vest did little to conceal their lush shape. It made her the perfect target for some absolute shitheads though, shitheads who wouldn't think twice about taking from her what they wanted, whether she said they could or not. Which made *them* the perfect target of her Sentinel rage when she couldn't find a demon to tear apart.

She yanked on knee-high stiletto boots and slid her blade into the top of the right one, beside her calf where she could get it in a hurry if she needed to. It was illegal to carry knives on your person in Australia, but with the help of a little glamour incantation she'd picked up from a love-struck warlock a century ago, anyone who saw the blade would think it a long-stem red rose.

Which came in handy. In more than one way.

Looking at herself in the full-length mirror propped against the far wall, she pulled in a long, slow breath. She looked sexy. No, more than sexy. She looked fuckable.

A bitter smile twitched at the corners of her mouth and she turned from her reflection. She hoped she got some violent, brutal action before the sun came up.

Before she really went insane.

The delicious scent of sweat, sex and human flesh threaded through Ezryn's nose as he and Jacob walked into the Pleasure Palace, Jacob's nightclub catering to Sydney's underground paranormal residents.

"I'll get us a drink," Jacob shouted over the noise, the muted lighting shrouding him in shadows.

Ezryn nodded, his stare fixed on the show currently taking place at the end of the club's main extended stage. Two females and one male, all fae, danced together around one thick, gold pole, three purple-hued spotlights capturing their every move. The females, stunning creatures with high cheekbones, large, liquid eyes and lean, sinewy bodies, wrapped their naked selves around the lone, equally naked, male, their limbs entwined with his.

Ezryn's body tightened at the sight. He'd never been one for skin-shows. He had nothing against voyeurism, nor ménages for that matter—he and Jacob had shared more than one willing female since moving to Australia. Impersonal, dirty fucking relieved their sexual hunger but didn't touch their tormented hearts. But something about this skin show piqued his interest.

No. It's the idea of hunting a Sentinel that has your juices flowing. Admit it.

The dark thought made him clench his fists. It was true. As civilized as he was, he was still a predator, still—according to the insulting definition used by all Sentinel—a demon. Hunting the very thing created by the Highest of Deities to terminate his kind gave him a rush he didn't want to think about.

"Decided we need something stronger than whiskey for the occasion." Jacob's voice rose over the din.

Ezryn turned, accepting the squat glass half-filled with an angry purple liquid Jacob offered him.

"To Harry." Jacob raised his own glass in a casual toast. "May he be dusted by a termite-infested stake." With an evil grin and a flash of fangs, he lifted his glass to his lips and drained it in a single mouthful.

"To my baby brother," Ezryn murmured, raising his drink. He pressed its cool rim to his parted lips and swallowed.

Liquid fire poured down his throat, turning his gut into an inferno. He gasped, biting back a choking cough. "Dark Ones, Jake, what *is* this?"

Jacob's grin turned demonic. "Carpathian mountain water. Trust me, you don't want to know how I get it."

Ezryn licked his lips, his gullet burning from the inside out. "I'll take your word on that." He scanned the writhing crowd, taking note of who and what enjoyed the attractions of Jacob's club. Vampires, weres, the odd warlock, a banshee or two, numerous demons and more than one human offering themselves to whichever paranormal creature pressed their buttons, taking their life into their mortal hands with every second spent in the strip joint. He turned back to his friend, the smoldering fire in his gut abating a little. "I'm going to check out the booths." He handed Jacob his empty glass. "Get me another one, will you?"

Jacob chuckled. "They're your organs."

Ezryn grinned. "My lifeless organs."

Leaving his friend, he moved into the crowd, the scent of sweat and sex pervading his senses. Detecting a Sentinel was never easy. If it were, the assassins would not be the effective killers they were. They looked human, sounded human, felt human—that was until they shifted into their *other* form. There was no mistaking them in *that* form. When they were in their human form, however, they were undetectable. But to a master vampire such as himself, one centuries old with all the power that comes with age, not to mention the supremacy of his bloodline, the Sentinel could be identified by scent. Sweet, delicate, like mist on a rose. Pure in its composition yet steely in its intensity.

If the Sentinel he hunted *was* in the Pleasure Palace, her scent would lead him to her.

And then, to use a tired phrase, the game would begin.

Weaving his way through the sweaty mass, Ezryn pulled in another breath. Sex. He smelled sex. A lot of sex. Pheromones, ejaculate, saliva. Human, demon, mage.

His cock stirred and he ground his teeth. With the level of sexual activity in the place, was it any wonder he was on edge?

He shoved past a particularly thick group of humans, clenching his fist at the overly friendly hands skimming his ass, his hips, his crotch as he did so. It seemed everyone in the Pleasure Palace was here for one thing and one thing only: to fuck. There was no way he would tolerate that kind of contact outside the club, but he ignored it now. Well, tried to.

His cock stiffened again and he growled, the cold blood in his veins running hot with carnal interest. It had been a while since he'd fed, even longer since he'd fucked. After he'd finished with the Sentinel, he'd find a willing partner or two, maybe human, maybe not, and sate his appetite. If Jake was lucky, he might even invite him to join in the—

An unknown scent slipped into Ezryn's nose, a soft tickle so subtle he almost missed it. Unknown and yet so very familiar.

He froze, eyes narrow, nose lifted.

There. To his right.

He turned, scanning the muted depths of the club. The Sentinel's scent came to him from the shadows, wafting in teasing tendrils from the back booths only those wanting to conceal their actions used.

A smile pulled at the corners of Ezryn's mouth. Perfect. He couldn't have asked for anything better.

Indifferent to the come-hither glances and stares directed his way, he began walking forward. Until tonight, he'd only known of one Sentinel living in Sydney, and the scent curling into his nostrils definitely did not belong to Ven Watkins. That could only mean unless there were more than two of the Highest's assassins in the city—a very unlikely situation—it belonged to the Sentinel he hunted.

His muscles coiled, readying for attack. Unprovoked and unexpected as it was, there was still a chance she would fight back. Ezryn's fangs extended. He needed to be quick. As ridiculous as the notion sounded, he needed to make it humane. Painless.

The shadows melted away as he drew closer, the din of the club fading to a low buzz. He zeroed his senses onto the very end booth tucked away in the corner and its sole occupant, learning everything he could as he moved toward her, everything his heightened sense of smell and sound perception could detect about her—how fast her heart beat, how clean her skin was, how she sat on the booth's seat, how her limbs moved against each other, in what position she sat, the material of her clothes she wore, what weapons she carried if any.

He drew to a halt, the sound of soft feminine moans floating from the booth stilling his feet for a moment. He recognized the emotion behind those moans all too well. Pleasure. Mounting release. He pulled in a deep breath, the musky aroma of female juices filling his body. Whatever was happening in the booth, his assassin was more than turned on by it. His cock, already half-erect, sprang to instant attention, as if the Sentinel's arousal was a beacon for his own.

Ezryn sneered. His fangs dug into his bottom lip. He was aroused for one reason only—the successful hunt of a natural enemy. That she smelled like sin and rapture combined meant nothing.

He started walking again, his pace quick, his stare locked on the darkest corner in the club. She was there. And by the sounds of it, she wasn't as alone as he'd first thought.

So who is with her? Why couldn't you detect them?

Another moan caressed his ears, a hitching whimper he knew came from her throat. An image filled his mind, unexpected but very appealing—a petite female with hair the color of dark chocolate and eyes the color of moss, her full lips parted, her neck offered to him as she slipped her fingers between the sodden folds of her pussy and rode her hand to a savage climax.

Maybe she is alone after all? Alone and needing to...

His cock jerked in straining need, rubbing against the coarse denim of his jeans. He bit back a groan.

Maybe he could sate his rising sexual hunger?

Her whimper came again. Higher, faster.

He sucked in a sharp breath, the taste of her pleasure thick on the air. She was close. Close to coming.

Concentrate, Ezryn. You are to kill her, not fuck her.

His body burned with a hunger he couldn't deny. By all the levels of hell, he wanted to be there when she came. He wanted to shove his head between her wet thighs and plunge his tongue into her sex. He wanted to taste her fully and completely. If someone was with her, he would dispose of them quickly, remove whoever had brought her to such heights of passion and take her even higher, feasting on her pleasure as she came for him over and over again. Drink of her release before puncturing her flesh with his fangs and feeding on her blood. He would feed from her in every sense of the word before ending her life. Pleasure for pleasure. Rapture for rapture. A sensual end before a senseless death.

He pushed forward, his stare locked on the booth and its shrouding darkness. Ten steps away.

Nine.

Eight.

Seven.

A choked cry shattered the Sentinel's moaning whimpers, and he leapt forward, mindless of the other club patrons as he became a blur. He crossed the distance remaining between himself and his quarry in less than a stolen heartbeat.

She lay stretched along the booth's bench seat, black denim-clad legs spread, her hand dipped below her open fly, her eyes closed, her lips parted.

The Sentinel.

Completely at his mercy.

Vulnerable.

Killable.

His mouth filled with saliva. "And so very, very alone," he murmured.

Her eyelids snapped open and green irises the color of flawless emeralds pierced his unbeating heart. Fear exploded on her face, followed by inexplicable, stunned recognition and lust. Her lips forming an O of shock, she yanked her hand from between her thighs.

"May I?" he growled.

"Yes," she gasped. "Fuck, yes."

Relief and rapture rushed through the base desire controlling him.

Permission. She'd given him permission.

And before she could say another word, he shoved the table aside, grabbed the waistline of her trousers and tore them down her hips.

He dropped to his knees and swiped his tongue up the seam of Inari's sodden folds. She arched, her raw cry bursting from her throat. By the Powers, what was he doing to her?

Exactly what you said he could.

Liquid heat rushed through her, detonating from the masterful tongue invading her sex. She threw back her head, driving her nails into the stiff leather bench on which she was pinned. Hell, she was on fire.

The vampire between her legs growled, sending a wave of vibrations through her body. She cried out again, pumping up her hips, shoving her sex harder to his greedy mouth.

Inari! This is not *a dream. Stop. Stop!*

He growled again, grabbing for her ass, holding her trapped against his lips and teeth and tongue. He nipped at her clit and fresh heat exploded in Inari's core. Stop him? Was she insane?

But you're not asleep, girl. This is real!

She didn't care. The vampire who'd haunted her dreams forever was fucking her with his mouth.

Thrusting her hips upward, she spread her legs as wide as the waistline of her jeans would let her, wanting his tongue to impale her deeper. It wasn't enough. Her bunched trousers dug into her knees, kept her thighs too close. "Fuck!"

Her guttural curse tore from her throat and she squirmed, frustration and disbelief making her burn.

The vamp chuckled, a low, purring sound that sent wicked vibrations through her sex. She arched again, driving her heels into the bench seat's padded cushion, lifting her hips higher as she fisted her hands in his thick, black hair.

He stabbed his tongue past her folds, lapped at her juices, teased her clit and then stabbed into her pussy again, each action slow and thorough and dominating. Every time she moved, every tiny little shift in her position, he sank his nails into her ass, holding her still.

His obvious control of her body, her movements, sent waves of giddy pleasure through her. Three hundred years as a succubus meant three hundred years of *her* being in control. *She* had been the taker, the catalyst for her partners' pleasure. Not once in over a million orgasms had she ever been dominated. *She* was the force.

For three centuries, she'd fed on the sexual energy of men. Coming to them in their sleep, during the fugue between waking and slumber or sometimes, when she was particularly hungry or spied a man of undeniable sexual energy, during the day. She'd drained them of their essence as she used them to sustain herself. For three hundred years, she'd milked more human males of their seed and sexual power than she could remember, drawing orgasm after orgasm after orgasm from their weak, vulnerable bodies, some —those with a particularly powerful sexual force—until their hearts could no longer cope with the exertion and stopped.

She'd been undeniable and inescapable. And here she was, the most successful succubus since the very first, more aroused than ever before and at the mercy of a nameless master vampire.

Her raw whimper slipped from her lips before she could stop it. She never wanted it to end.

The vampire raked his hands over her butt, squeezing each cheek as he inched his fingers closer to her sex. He thrust his tongue in and out, sucked on her folds and then painted them with her cream. Wetting her completely. The pit of her belly contracted and she squirmed again, her clit a molten tip of heightened sensitivity.

With just one more touch of his tongue on its swollen form, she would come. Even if she wanted to stop, she couldn't.

But you don't want to stop.

The words floated through her head, a low murmur she couldn't identify. Her thoughts? His? Or someone else's?

Does it matter?

Before she could contemplate the answer, the vampire jerked her hips higher and stabbed his tongue into the tight opening of her ass.

"Fuck!"

Inari bucked, her orgasm ripping through her, torn from her by the demon's assault. She'd never, never been penetrated there. Not by finger, tongue or cock.

Liquid electricity claimed her, radiating through her body from her invaded ass. She cried out, her knuckles popping as she tightened her fists in his hair, holding his mouth to its most exquisite placement. Her breath burst from her in shallow gasps, her toes curled in her boots. By the Powers, what was he doing to her?

Exactly what he wants.

Which is exactly what you want him to do.

The dark thought detonated another rupture of hot pleasure in her sex. She sank her teeth into her bottom lip, biting back the wild cry threatening to escape her. The reality of the situation overwhelmed her. This was no dream. This was no fantasy. This was happening. Now. Right here in a freaking Kings Cross strip-club while a fae ménage show took place on the freaking stage. The vampire of her dreams was fucking her ass with his mouth, and she never wanted him to stop.

"Then I won't."

The statement—low and smug and arrogant—whispered through her mind. She gasped, every muscle in her body stiffening. He was in her head. A demon was in her head. The very thing she hunted—

"Is going to fuck you until you can't move or cry out."

His deep growl snapped her eyes wide. She stared down her body, straight into eyes the color of midnight sin. "Who..."

He smiled, fangs glinting. "You may call me Master."

The command stabbed into her chest. She hissed, the sleeping Sentinel force buried deep within her soul surging to the surface. She whipped her legs up and wrapped them around his smoothly muscled neck, trapping the bloodsucker in the junction of her thighs.

"I call no demon filth master," she snarled.

With terrifying speed and strength, the vampire curled his fingers around her ankles and yanked her legs apart, the sound of her jeans ripping in two almost as loud as his hiss of pleasure. He shoved her back, his hips smashing to hers, his weight pinning her to the bench. "You *will* call me master," he whispered, his face so close to hers his cool flesh chilled her. Staring into her eyes, he grabbed her wrists and jerked her arms above her head. "And I plan on being very, *very* filthy with you."

Inari bucked, cold fear and hot fury flooding her very center. Her heart stilled even as her sex contracted and flooded with wet rapture. By the Powers, this was not right. This was not meant to happen.

The vampire's eyes glowed black light and he rolled his hips, his rigid shaft, contained by the coarse denim of his jeans, stroking her spread pussy.

"It is as it is," he murmured, moving both her wrists to one large hand. He gazed down at her, fangs extended, nostrils flaring. "And as it will be." He raked his free hand down her arm, her torso, his thumb brushing the side of her breast before he shifted slightly. "For as long as I deem it so...Sentinel."

The title stole Inari's breath. She glared up at him, hating him. "Go to hell."

He grinned. Indolent and smug. "Been there. Done that. Bought the T-shirt."

And, fangs extending longer, he lowered his head to hers. "Now, call me Master."

"Fuck you," she snarled, staring up at him.

And yet, she didn't move. He had the sense she could unleash the Sentinel in her and snap him in two with barely any effort, and yet, she didn't move to stop him.

"Fuck you," she said again, this time a low murmur.

He stared down into her face, into her wide green eyes. Her lips parted, her breath hitched in her throat, her breasts rose and fell in rapid succession. He dropped his gaze to their round perfection, and his mouth filled with saliva. He would drink from her there, from the main artery that ran below the under-swell of each mound.

"Y-no," she whispered, shaking her head even as her legs came up to wrap around his hips.

That she seemed to know his very thoughts didn't bother him. In fact, he found the notion entirely pleasing. He longed to see her face, her reaction to every delicious thing he planned to do to her. To see her righteous soul fight against her depraved lust.

What you plan to do to her? Kill her, right? That's what you plan to do to her, what you must do to—

He shut the thought down, uninterested in its significance.

Shifting a little, he slowly traced his fingers along the exquisite valley of her cleavage, down the flat plane of her belly, to the curve of her pussy.

She whimpered, holding his stare.

Defiance and uncertainty and hunger burned in her eyes and his cock throbbed.

"Do you want me to touch you there? With my fingers this time?" he murmured, holding himself motionless.

"N-yes," she breathed. "Yes."

Once again, relief and sweet rapture rushed through him at her permission and he rolled the pad of his thumb over her clit.

Her eyelids fluttered closed for a moment, and her teeth pulled at her bottom lip. The pulse in her neck beat like a trapped moth.

The sight made Ezryn's balls grow tight, and he pinched her clit between thumb and forefinger. "Tell me your name."

She shook her head, struggling to free her wrists from his grasp. "No."

He pinched her clit again, her hissed-in breath making his cock twitch. "Tell me your name, Sentinel, or I will keep you on the edge of your orgasm for an eternity."

Wet heat gushed from her sex, drenching his hand, and he smiled, letting her see his fangs. She was dripping with pleasure. Pleasure *he'd* milked from her. "Tell me your name," he repeated, dipping one fingertip past her folds. Two fingers.

She arched against him, her eyes blazing emerald contempt and hunger. "Fuck you."

Ezryn chuckled. "Unusual. Do you answer to 'fuck' or 'you'?" He plunged two fingers into her pussy, scissoring them inside her tight sex. She gasped, her eyes beseeching him, her pussy constricting. "Now, tell me your name."

"Inari," she cried, bucking into his hand. "I am the Sentinel Inari Chayse."

Her name scalded his senses. He could taste her power in every syllable, see the might of her force in the breath she expelled. Her pure scent curled into his being, infusing him with energy beyond his comprehension.

You're insane.

He growled, driving his fingers into her sex, feeling her pleasure coat his hand, her breath heat his face. He *wasn't* insane. He was alive. Alive.

Dark Ones, he felt *alive*.

Living energy poured through him. Consumed him. His eyes widened and his blood roared in his ears. Staring down into Inari's blazing eyes, he heard her heart thumping, a frenzied beat his body hungered for. She was close to the edge. Close to release. And he would give it to her. Master vampire to captured Sentinel. Hunter to prey.

He drove his fingers deeper into her sex, his cock so engorged he could barely think. She cried out and he captured the raw sound with his mouth, driving his tongue past her lips.

She bucked beneath him, her tongue battling his, her legs pulling him closer. He rammed his hips forward, wanting nothing more than to sink his cock into her hot wetness, incapable of withdrawing his fingers from her exquisite heat for the split second it would take to do so. His head swam. The heady scent of her desire poured into his being, the potent scent of her assassin's soul turning his prick to a pole of agonizing lust.

Dark Ones, he'd never wanted to fuck someone so badly. So desperately.

He invaded her mouth with his tongue, licked at her even teeth, nipped at her lips. He wriggled his fingers in her sex, stroked her clit, circled her anus. He would take her there. Later. Again and again. After he'd had his fill of her sweet, tight pussy, he would claim her ass and make her scream his name.

Your fill? Dark Ones, is that even possible?

The thought sent a surge of incredulous pleasure into his core and his balls turned hard, aching for release. He would *never* take his fill of her. Her taste set him on fire. Her scent made his still heart pound. She was a creature of lust and divine justice. She was his enemy, his hunter, his prey, and he would bind her to his existence and keep her as his own forever.

Is this before or after you kill her?

Ice-cold realization flooded his veins. He froze, staring down at her. She *was* his prey. She was his target. If he didn't kill her, hundreds of his kind would be slaughtered. Methodically butchered by his brother for no other reason than jealous spite.

His blood roared through his veins, at once hot with lust and icy with dawning horror. He could not let his kind be butchered, no matter how intoxicating she was. He had to kill her. He had to—

Inari whimpered, her eyes aglow with undeniable pleasure. "Please," she whispered. "Please...Master."

The title caressed his ears, raw with capitulation and surrender. Thrumming with want and desire. One word that spoke a million—she was his for the plucking. Completely and utterly his.

And he had to kill her.

No.

Cold refusal stabbed into him, sinking into his chest. His cock throbbed. His balls rose, his body hungering for her with every fiber of his being. Greedy not for her blood, but her warmth and pleasure. Craving for it. Connecting to it.

And he had to kill her. Now.

"For every night you choose not to obey my command, I will slaughter one vampire who chose to rebel against my ascension."

His brother's ultimatum hissed through Ezryn's head, and he reeled backward, disgust and dismay slamming into him with surreal force. He staggered back a step, his undead body screaming in infuriated denial. Dark Ones, what was he doing? He had to kill her.

Confusion flashing over her face, Inari pushed herself upright, her stare locked on his. "What..." A frown pulled at her dark eyebrows. "What's going on?"

Ezryn clenched his fists, driving his nails into his palms. "I can't."

"Can't?" Her eyes widened before, with a snarl Ezryn felt in the very pit of his stomach, they blazed up in furious white fire. The Sentinel rising to the surface.

The assassin finding her target.

The hunter finding its prey.

Fuck.

"Go," she growled through gritted teeth. A violent black hue rippled over her sun-bronzed skin like a shimmer of absolute death. "Now."

Ezryn's demon's soul stirred, craving not only her pleasure and the pleasure she awoke in him, but for her blood as well.

Kill her, Ezryn. Fuck her to within an inch of her life and then kill her. She is a Sentinel, the Sentinel. Kill her.

Inari bared her teeth. Another black shimmer rippled over her flesh. "Go."

Ezryn spun on his heel and fled the strip club in a blurring streak.

Away from the Sentinel and the hungry confusion twisting through him, the sound of her wanton surrender still whispering in his mind.

Master.

Chapter Three

Inari slammed the door of her apartment shut behind her and pressed her forehead to its cool wooden surface. What in all the levels of hell had just happened?

What? Do you mean showing everyone on Oxford Street your backside as you fled home in a pair of torn jeans? Or your complete and utter sexual capitulation to a master vampire?

With a sharp hiss, she banged the side of her fist against the door. "Fuck," she muttered.

Both options were bad. Even though she did have an ass a Victoria's Secret model would envy, she still didn't relish the idea of it popping up on social media after some dickhead filmed her seminaked sprint with his phone.

The latter however? Her sexual surrender to a master vampire...

"Fuck, fuck, fuck."

"Well, that was a tad childish, don't you think?" a humored voice said behind her. "And I thought *I* was the baby sister."

Inari let out a ragged sigh and squeezed her eyes shut, her already churning stomach rolling some more. "Go away."

A light chuckle followed, the sound soft and musical. "I can't."

Driving her nails into her palms, Inari turned around and glared at her sister. "Yes, Tianya, you can."

The other woman, a more petite version of Inari with blue eyes instead of green and a smattering of freckles across a small, upturned nose, grinned. "Let's not start this again." She crossed the room with ethereal grace, her fingertips almost skimming the back of the sofa as she came to linger near Inari's coffee table. "So tell me, sis, did you really call a vampire Master?"

Inari ground her teeth, slumping against the door. "Stop it."

"And you used the word *please*?" Dark eyebrows shot up in mock amazement. "What kind of succubus are you? What kind of Sentinel, for that matter?"

Inari dragged her fingers through her hair and glared at her sister. "Be quiet, Tianya. Go back where you came from."

Tianya's smile turned cheeky. A soft dimple dented the peaches-and-cream perfection of her left cheek. "Ah, if only I could." She hovered her fingers over a large vase of roses next to the sofa, eyeing the flowers with a contemplative inspection before returning her gaze to Inari. "But I'm not going anywhere until you sort yourself out, no matter how much you scowl at me."

Inari pulled a face at her sister. "You're insufferable."

"And you're in lust with a master vampire." The dimple in Tianya's cheek creased deeper. "He's quite cute, isn't he? All dark and menacing and dominating. And those shoulders. So broad and straight. I can understand the appeal."

Inari rolled her eyes, pushing herself from the door to move to the armchair opposite the sofa. She fell into it with a disgruntled huff. "Go away."

Tianya laughed again. "No."

Inari stared at the far wall, her pulse thumping in her neck. Against her will, she pictured the nameless vampire and her sex fluttered at the unsettling memory. He'd been just as handsome in the flesh as he'd been in her dreams—towering over her, at least six feet, four inches and all lean, sculpted muscle. His legs seemed to go on forever, thick and corded beneath his snug black jeans, his hips low and narrow. The perfect example of the Vitruvian Man, his body so sublimely proportioned it almost hurt to look at him. "What in all the levels of hell did I just do?" she muttered, fighting to erase his image from her mind. His jaw was square and his nose hawkish, perhaps even more so in reality. Its strength complemented the high angles of his cheekbones and the defined lines of his lips. She'd always had a weakness for a strong, noble nose, damn it, especially on a face that spoke of confidence and assured poise.

Assured poise? Don't you mean arrogance?

Arrogant men had been her favorite target while a sex demon. Their very smugness used to push her buttons, and that fact hadn't changed, even when she refused to let herself have sex again.

Would have tonight, though. If the bloodsucker hadn't—

"Why did I just let a vampire..." The words choked in her throat and she shook her head again, raking her hands through her hair. "Why didn't I stop him? Kill him?"

"Err, might it have something to do with the fact he was giving you more pleasure than you've had for twenty years? Possibly even longer?" Tianya's voice lilted to Inari's right, a soft chuckle tinkling in each word. "Or might it be because he's the very vampire you've been dreaming about now for too many nights to remember? Killing him could be a bit counterproductive, don't you think?"

Inari let out a disgusted sigh. "No, I do not *think*. I let a vampire I've never met before put his—a bloodsucking *demon,* for God's sake...make me...do stuff to..." She faltered, her cheeks growing warm. Blushing? She was blushing? Oh, that was just freaking fantastic, wasn't it? The nameless master vampire had made her do something she'd never ever done in her entire three hundred years of existence; blush.

"You know," Tianya piped up, "for a succubus, you seem to have great difficulty talking about sexual activity."

Inari shot her sister an exasperated glare. "I'm not a succubus anymore, Ti. I'm Sentinel, remember? I kill vampires, not fuck them."

Tianya smirked, dimple flashing. "Pretty certain he was the one fucking you. With his fingers *and* tongue, if I remember correctly."

"Go away!" Inari burst out, her whole face flooding with heat. She slumped back into the sofa, rubbing at her temples with trembling fingers. "How could I be dreaming about a real vampire I've never met? I thought my screwed-up psyche had created him, but he's fucking real? What the hell does it mean?"

Tianya's slim shoulders lifted in an infuriatingly delicate shrug. "Beats me," she replied, her soft voice still humored. "When it comes to this kind of thing, I have no clue. I still can't explain why *I'm* here. I'm starting to worry you're more messed up than I thought."

Inari squeezed her eyes shut again, dropping her head into her hands. "I may be messed up," she growled through clenched teeth, a heavy pressure growing on her chest, "but at least I'm not dead."

Silence greeted her declaration, and she raised her head from her hands, glaring.

The room was empty.

Thick pain coursed through Inari and she let out a ragged sigh. Her sister's ghost—if that's really what it was—was gone once again, leaving her alone. "Oh, Tianya."

Born human to sex-demon parents, Tianya Chayse had loved her family regardless of their less than humane sensibilities. A life spent growing up in Daemonium, the realm all lower-order demons called home, should have twisted her soul and unhinged her human mind. Tianya had taken it all in stride. She'd never questioned her family's actions, and like all younger sisters, had annoyed Inari to no end about every sexual conquest Inari had. Which, being a succubus, was a lot.

Rather than being shunned or killed by her parents' kind, she was viewed first as a humorous anomaly and then as a cherished member of the Realm, educated by some of demonkind's most brilliant scholars. By the time she reached puberty, Tianya had known more about the complex hierarchy of the world in which she'd been born than most upper-order demons. By the time she was a teenager, Tianya had known more about the human world as well, and set out to educate her older sister on just who deserved to be *succubussed* as she put it, and why.

Incapable of something as unfathomable, intangible and mysterious as human love, Inari had loved her sister all the same. So she was a little different. So she couldn't make a man come with a single kiss. Or drain him of his sexual energy with a roll of her hips. That didn't make her any less a Chayse. She'd had the temper of one, that was for sure. When something hadn't gone Tianya's way as a babe, all the Realm had known about it.

At the age of eighteen, and against Inari's adamant protests, Tianya had opted to move to the world of man, settling in Salzburg of all places to study under a musical virtuoso called Amadeus. Inari had visited her as often as she could, finding the males of 1775 easy prey for her particular kinds of appetites, and the music of her sister's mentor very calming. When fortune smiled on her, Inari had often combined the two. There was nothing the succubus Inari had found more satisfying than to fuck a man to death while the mellifluous sounds of good music wafted on the air in the background.

Two years after leaving the safety of their parents' home, Tianya was attacked and slaughtered by an empathic leech demon, a vile creature from the lowest levels of hell who fed on the terrified, agony-filled psyche of his victims.

A leech demon Inari herself knew well.

The same leech demon Inari had rejected a day before when he'd had the deluded audacity to suggest a sexual relationship with her.

She'd never recovered.

Nor found him. Hunting him as a succubus for almost two and

a half centuries had achieved nothing. Neither had hunting him as a Sentinel, except deeper guilt and futile rage.

She'd failed Tianya on every level imaginable.

Inari swiped at her cheeks, blinking away the tears stinging her eyes. It shouldn't wound her anymore. It shouldn't weaken her. It was over two hundred years ago, and Tianya was long dead.

But not long gone, Inari. When did you start seeing her again? Around the same time you started having the dreams of the master vampire if you recall correctly. And is it really her? Or just your messed up psyche?

Inari opened her eyes and stared at the carpet between her feet, her body aching, her chest tight. "By the Powers, I'm fucked up."

And submitting to a master vampire. Was Tianya right? Was she really that messed up? That broken?

Inari shook her head. How was it possible the very vampire from her dreams was real? How could she dream of the bloodsucker night after night after night, experience the most amazing sex of her existence with him every one of those nights only for him to walk into a strip club and find her? Masturbating, no less?

She plonked backward into the armchair, letting the piece of furniture swallow her in its deep, cushioned comfort. She'd been well on her way to a tormented climax back in the Pleasure Palace, her fingers making her body burn even as she imagined them to be his tongue, when he'd appeared at her table. The second her gaze fell on him the heat in her core erupted into an inferno.

Or so she'd thought.

A *real* inferno of pleasure, however, had claimed her the moment his skin touched hers, the very second his cool fingers plunged into her sex. She'd never felt anything like it. In all her centuries of sexual mastery, she'd never experienced anything close. It was power. It was lust. Pleasure beyond rational comprehension. What would she feel like when he took her with his cock?

A tense shudder rocked through Inari's body, clamping her sex and stealing her breath. She swiped at her lips, her mouth dry. His cock? What was she thinking? She would never let him penetrate her again with anything, let alone his cock. He was a bloodsucker. A parasitic demon.

So why is your pulse pounding now

Inari shifted in her seat, gasping when the torn crotch of her jeans rubbed against her sex. Wicked sensations shot through her body, into her core, and her eyes fluttered closed. She whimpered, her breath rapid, and pressed her legs together.

Another hot stab of pleasure shot through her, followed immediately by an image of the nameless master vampire.

"You will *call me master."* The remembered declaration quickened Inari's already rapid heart and she squirmed in the armchair *"And I plan on being very, very filthy with you."*

Her clit ached, her nipples pinched hard. Filthy. She wanted to be filthy with him. She wanted his fingers in her sex, his tongue in her ass. She wanted him to chain her to a bed and take her again and again.

No, you don't.

Yes, she did. Even if he *was* her natural enemy.

She did. So much it hurt.

Gnawing on her bottom lip, she shucked her ripped jeans from her legs and slid her hands between her thighs. Her fingers found her pussy and stroked her moistened folds with firm pressure. She pictured the vampire from her dreams, from the Pleasure Palace, raking his strong hands up her legs, pushing them apart. Warm tightness squeezed her sex and she bit back a whimper. No. She would make no sound for him, not even here, in the emptiness of her home.

That didn't stop him from grinning in her head. He touched the tip of his tongue to his fangs, rolling the pad of his thumb over her clit. Sizzling tension radiated into her core and she arched in the chair, dipping her fingers into her folds, wishing they were his— long, strong fingers that knew where to stroke her.

"You will *call me master."*

His command echoed through her head again, so like his command from her dreams. Explosive pleasure claimed her, made her skin tingle and her nipples hard. She dragged one hand up her body, over her ribcage to cup her left breast, her mind telling her this was his hand on her flesh. That is was him rolling her nipple between thumb and forefinger, pinching it, flicking it.

Ribbons of wet heat unfurled in her core, knotting in the pit of her belly. It wouldn't be long now. Not long.

She bit back another whimper, her neck bowing as she rolled her head to the side. She pictured him looming up over her, one hand buried between her spread legs, stroking the sweet spot within, one hand cupping and mauling her heavy breast, teasing her nipple until a tremble began to own her.

She was close. Close.

In her head, he smiled, fangs glinting in the muted light of her living room, black eyes burning into her, branding her. Marking her.

"You will *call me master."*

The words slipped into her ear in a nonexistent whisper, as she imagined his mouth brushing her throat, his teeth piercing her flesh.

Her orgasm detonated in her body at the dark thought, incinerating her control.

She bucked, thrusting her fingers deeper into her contracting core, even as she craved them to be his. His fingers, his tongue, his cock. She fucked her fingers and hungered for the nameless vampire. The black-eyed bastard who had taken her so easily in a strip-club booth only an hour ago. Her fantasy. Her enemy.

The scalding burn of her climax turned to ice. She withdrew from between her legs and dropped her hand from her breast. Her enemy. He *was* her enemy. And he knew it, just as much as she did.

Which meant only one thing.

"Well, that looked like fun."

Tianya's lilting voice tickled Inari's ears and, heart hammering, she opened her eyes.

Her sister stood beside the sofa, lips twitching. "Feel better?"

Self-contempt flooded through her. "No."

Tianya cocked an eyebrow. "Are you sure? I've never seen that look on your face before."

Inari turned her head to the side, gazing at the silent television. "What look?"

"Like the proverbial cat that swallowed the canary. Or should that be the succubus that swallowed the, well, you know. And blissfully happy."

"That's not funny, Ti," Inari snapped. Blissfully happy? Seriously?

Tianya shrugged. "Just telling you what I saw."

Inari slumped. She had to get the situation under control. She couldn't let this go on. There's no way she could be blissfully happy when it came to a master vampire, not even if her only connection to him was through amazing—imagined—sex.

Tianya studied her, an unreadable expression in her eyes. "So what are you going to do?"

Inari clenched her jaw and shoved herself to her feet. "Have a shower," she said, her stomach knotting as her sister's image faded to nothing. "And never sleep again."

* * *

"Are you going to tell me what's pissing you off," Jacob asked, watching Ezryn pace the master vampire's living room floor. "Or do I have to glamour you into a confession?" He leant back against the bar and crossed his ankles, flicking his attention to the floor-to-ceiling windows. "Y'know, dawn is almost breaking, and it's not healthy to go to bed with a temper. You'll get heartburn."

Ezryn shot him a dark look. "I'm not in the mood, Jake."

Jacob laughed. "Gee? Really?" Shoving himself from the bar, he scooped up Ezryn's glass—filled with lukewarm, early twenties O-positive—crossed the room and held it in front of his friend's scowling face. "Here, knock this back. It'll make you feel better. Maybe then I can get some sense out of you."

Ezryn glared at the glass. "I'm not thirsty."

Jacob laughed again. "Bullshit."

With a low growl that would have made any other vampire piss blood in fear, Ezryn snatched the glass from Jacob's hand and swallowed its contents in a single mouthful.

Jacob grinned, removing the glass from Ezryn's hand. "Now cough it up. What's got you so riled up you look like you're about to hyperventilate...a neat trick for a vampire, I might add." He turned, walked back to the bar and deposited Ezryn's empty glass on the smooth, black marble counter. "Does this have anything to do with the female I saw you sampling back in the Pleasure Palace? I gotta say she was pretty damn fine." He grinned, remembering the sight of Ezryn buried face-first between the delicious little human's thighs. If he hadn't been distracted, he would have enjoyed watching the entire act. Maybe even asked if he could join in. "What happened to you, by the way?" he asked, refilling Ezryn's glass from the decanter sitting on the bar. "I got nabbed by a vamp-groupie, and by the time I'd had my fill of her you were..." He turned back to Ezryn, the last of his sentence fading on his lips.

The master vampire stood at the window, face carved from granite, his normally black eyes burning iridescent red fire. Jacob frowned, swallowing a sudden lump in his throat. When Ezryn's eyes changed color, bad things happened. Bad things to bad vampires. The only bad vampire Ezryn had seen lately, as far as Jacob knew, was Harry. A squirming finger of hope pressed at Jacob's chest. Did that mean Ezryn was finally going to do something about his brother? Was he finally going to deal with the ridiculous situation and take back the position rightfully his?

"I had her." The flat calm in Ezryn unexpected statement made Jacob blink. "I tasted her."

Jacob's frown deepened. "Who? The woman from the club? I could see that. Who was she?"

Ezryn's molten red eyes glowed darker. "The Sentinel."

"The Sentinel?" Jacob dragged his hand over his mouth, staring at his friend. "Dark Ones, Ezryn. Did you know that before or *after* you stuck your head between her thighs?"

A tormented tension flashed over Ezryn's stony expression, and he turned to look out the window.

Jacob raised his eyebrows. "Ah, I see."

"That's good," Ezryn growled, his stare never wavering from the lightening skyline beyond the glass. "Because I don't." He folded his arms across his chest, his eyes a deep red. "I smelt her. I knew what she was. I *knew* what I was there to do. And then I saw her, I *felt* her, and all I wanted to do was sink my fangs into her flesh and make her mine."

Jacob studied his friend's brooding profile, an uneasy itch awakening in his gut. "Make her yours?" Make her his. Not fuck her, or take her or even drain her. Sink his fangs into her flesh and make her his. What did that mean? What exactly did that mean?

To a vampire, there were four reasons for fang-to-flesh penetration: to feed, to kill, to change and to bind. The first two happened frequently—although neither Jacob nor Ezryn, nor any of those loyal to Ezryn had bitten to kill for over five centuries. The third reason—to change a human into a vampire—occurred less often.

The vampire race existed in a permanent state of tenacious control—those born vampires ruled over those changed. It was a relationship born on respect and loathing. *Lifers*, those born vampires, tolerated *bleeders*, vampires created by a lifer who didn't rein in their blood lust during feeding. Occasionally, the odd bleeder rebelled against the natural order and suffered the consequences. Those consequences were not pretty. Far from it, in fact. A bleeder who forgot their place in the hierarchy soon found themselves pegged out naked and spread-eagle in a treeless field or shadowless rooftop, their flesh scored in ribbons of tiny lacerations, waiting for the sun to rise as their blood slowly oozed from their veins. A bleeder who fought to rise above their place and did so by challenging the power of a lifer soon discovered the true force of a born vampire. Unfortunately, it was the want of every bleeder to flex their new vampiric muscles, and many rarely survived beyond the first year of their new life. As a consequence, the changing bite occurred less frequently than in centuries past.

The only time a bite to change from human to vampire was condoned was when the two parties involved—vampire and human—consented to the transformation. Love or lust created bleeders, and the emotion behind the transformation tainted that new vampire's state of psyche from the second of their resurrection—a fact that led to more than one joyous joining...or bloody reprisal. Those changed for love lived long. Those born from blood lust lived until their violent birth caught up with them.

The fourth reason—to bind—was permissible only between a master vampire and their human lover. The act required monumental power and endurance on the master's behalf. Forging such a profound emotional, psychological and mental connection between a vampire and a human without the human transforming wasn't easy. It drained and exhausted them. Depleted them of their *croi*, the life essence of all paranormal beings. But the payoff—a human bound in body and soul to their vampire master—was a thing of exquisite beauty and reverence.

Rarely did a binding bite occur anymore, and Jacob didn't wonder why. In binding a soul, the master vampire created a self-weakness. If the bound lover were to be killed, the master vampire would suffer. Depending on how powerful the binding of their two existences, the suffering could range from agonizing headaches to insanity to destruction—incineration from the inside out. Never had a Sentinel been bound to a vampire. To do so...

Jacob suppressed a sharp sigh. *"Make her mine"* fell into none of those criteria, but it sounded damn near close to binding.

He rubbed his hand over his mouth again, the points of his fangs pressing against the insides of his lips. That they were even extended showed him just how unsettled he was. This was not good.

Not good? This is a fucking nightmare. A master vampire marking a Sentinel his property? Hell's pit. Killing her would be better.

"I know what you're thinking."

Ezryn's growl made Jacob jump. His master never tuned into his thoughts anymore—a privilege all master vampires held over their loyalist network—which meant Jacob's expression revealed way too much. He shook his head and bit back a curse. "Am I that transparent?"

"No," Ezryn replied. "I've just known you for a very long time."

Jacob gave his friend a level look, trying to calm the disquiet knotting in his chest. "So I don't have to tell you I think you're treading dangerous territory?"

Ezryn's jaw bunched.

"Or that you should let me take care of the situation?"

Ezryn turned his head, regarding Jacob with cold red eyes. "And how would you do that, General Ancroft? Destroy my brother?"

The ice in Ezryn's voice made Jacob swallow. "No," he answered, keeping his own voice steady. "You have strictly forbidden me to do so, and as such I will abide by your command."

Ezryn's eyes glowed a deeper red. He said nothing. He waited for Jacob to continue.

Ah, shit, Jake. You're the one treading dangerous territory now.

He swallowed again. "I would destroy the Sentinel."

Ezryn's nostrils flared. He stared at Jacob, face expressionless. "You will not." He turned back to the window, the purple glow of pre-dawn casting his pale skin in a soft light.

Jacob studied his profile. "Because?"

Ezryn didn't answer. He just watched the sky grow lighter, each second passing with oppressive silence before he turned from the window and left the room, fists clenched and jaw bunched.

Jacob let out an entirely redundant but utterly ragged sigh. Dark Ones. What the hell did he do next?

Disobey Ezryn's command not to kill the Sentinel?

He pictured the woman he'd seen stretched out on the bench back in his nightclub. She was tiny, the top of her head unlikely to reach his chin. How easy would she be to defeat?

He'd never faced a Sentinel before. By vampire standards, he was fairly formidable, but were his own strength and power enough to destroy one of the Highest's assassins?

If it means preventing a war? If it means stopping Ezryn from doing something stupid?

Jacob's gut clenched. He had no idea what his master had planned, but something told him it was more than Ezryn had revealed. He'd seen the set expression on the master vampire's face before, the night Ezryn had stepped aside for his twin's joke of an ascension. It was an expression that preceded a bleak future. Whatever Ezryn had in his mind to handle Harry's order, it didn't bode well for Ezryn. Which in Jacob's opinion *was* stupid.

Take out the Sentinel before Ezryn does. Follow her, engage her in battle and destroy her.

His stomach clenched again. Easier said than done. Now he knew what she looked like, finding her wasn't the problem, but engaging her in battle? How? Unless there was a reason for their confrontation, if he attacked her without provocation he was achieving nothing, just a senseless slaughter leading to the very bloodbath he sought to prevent.

The only way he could possibly conceive to entice the Sentinel to attack him was to go on a violent feeding frenzy of the local humans, and he really, really didn't want to do that.

To save Ezryn's life, however...

No. Not even then.

So what *did* he do now?

He didn't know.

Dragging his hands through his hair, he gave the lightening sky a frazzled scowl. Daybreak, and he was nowhere near his own penthouse.

With one last look at the fading night, he crossed to the bar, filled Ezryn's empty glass with blood and downed it in one swallow. The warm liquid hit the back of his throat, his gullet, and he closed his eyes for a moment, letting the life of the blood fill his existence. The buzz lasted but a second. He placed the empty glass in the bar's sink, walked to the other side of the room and punched in a complicated sequence of numbers on a control panel.

Instantly, the floor-to-ceiling windows turned black, plunging Ezryn's living room into pitch darkness.

With a nod of satisfaction, Jacob moved to the long, leather lounge in the middle of the room and dropped onto it, his gut churning, his throat tight. Toeing off his shoes, he raked his fingers through his hair and then stretched out along the luxurious piece of furniture.

"Looks like you're having a sleepover, General Ancroft," he muttered, crossing his ankles as he closed his eyes. "And here you are without your toothbrush."

Haral Lynwood Navarro, proclaimed first born of the First Family, overlord of the vampire race, sank his long, perfectly manicured fingernails into the young female kneeling before him. Her blood trickled from the puncture wounds in her throat, oozed over his fingers and down his wrist, dripping onto the cold marble floor beneath his feet in perfect crimson beads. He stared into her eyes, reveling in the pain and terror he saw there. The sight of her fear and the smell of her blood made his prick jerk in eager attention. When he was done with her, he would wake his new wife and fuck her until she sobbed for mercy.

At the moment he had other more pressing needs. "What do you mean, he didn't kill her?"

The female at his knees flinched, as if each word had caused her pain. Which they probably did. She knew nothing she said would save her. It was just a matter of time.

Her short, stubby fangs flashed at him from behind lips wet with both snot and spittle. "He...he didn't...he didn't..." The quivering vampire choked back a strangled sob, the pathetic action causing fresh blood to squeeze past Haral's fingers. "He didn't kill her."

Haral drove his claws deeper into her throat, bending slightly at the waist to bring his face closer to hers. "You told me you followed him. You told me he'd found her. If he didn't kill her, what did he do to her?"

The bleeder's stare flicked around the room.

"Well?" Haral snapped, giving her a sharp shake. Tiny drops of blood splattered his pajama legs, seeping into the expensive gold silk to become large, crimson blossoms. He glared at the sniveling bitch at his feet. He liked these pajamas. They were his favorite, and she'd ruined them. "What did he do to her? Fuck her?"

The vampire nodded, her blood-soaked chin slapping against his hand. "Yes. Yes, sort...sort of."

Haral narrowed his eyes, an icy shard of furious disbelief pushing into his chest. "Sort of? He fucked the Sentinel...sort of? Where?"

"In...in a strip club called the Pleasure Palace...in..." bright-red blood bubbled past the female's lips in a hiccupping gasp, "...in one of the back booths." Her wild eyes rolled, fear excreting from her pores in sickening waves. "He shoved his...head between her legs... then his hand down her pants...they kissed, she said...something I couldn't hear and then he left."

"And then he left," Haral repeated. The icy fury in his chest grew colder. His brother fucking a Sentinel? He released his grip on the whimpering excuse for a vampire and straightened, her sobs and blubbered "thank you, sire, thank you, sire, thank you" fading to silence in his head.

Ezryn Navarro, the prodigal son, fucking a Sentinel? Defying a direct command from his lord? Condemning hundreds to bloody slaughter? Haral had given Ezzie four nights to kill the bitch Sentinel before the carnage began, and this was how his holier-than-thou twin brother spent the first one? Tongue deep in the assassin's cunt?

He stared at the shuttered windows of the compound he'd commandeered for his stay in Australia, the candelabrum casting the expansive ballroom in a warm, orange glow. Outside, the sun was almost above the horizon. Sleep called him with urgent insistence, but he ignored the pull. He lifted his hand to his mouth and flicked his tongue along his fingers, the vampire's blood tingling over his taste buds.

What did it mean that his brother, the moralistic bastard, would send so many to their deaths? A vampire who'd left his home country and everything he knew behind to prevent that very thing happening? For the life of a Sentinel, no less?

And how did he, overlord of the vampire race, capitalize on it?

What did he do with this unexpected news to bring about Ezryn's utter and complete humiliation and defeat?

What did he...

A smile pulled at the corners of Haral's mouth and he laughed, the sound bouncing around the cavernous room. Of course. He knew exactly what to do.

Holding out his hand, he turned his smile on the cowering bleeder sobbing at his feet. "Hush, child." He stretched his smile wider. Softened it. Made it reach his eyes. "There is no need for tears. You have made your lord pleased."

The female hiccupped, wiping at her blood-laced snot with the back of her hand, her eyes wide. Hope flooded her face. Hope and disbelief and relief. She smiled, a toothy expression as incredulous as the light in her eyes. "Oh, thank you, sire, thank you, thank you, thank you." She took his offered hand, her trembling, snot-smeared fingers sliding over his. "Forgive me. I will do better. I will make you so pleased."

Haral bestowed her with a warm look of love. "Yes. Of course you will." And in one fluid move, he yanked the bitch from the floor and tore her head from her body.

Turning to the silent guards standing at the ballroom's main doorway, he threw the pathetic thing's remains at their feet. "Toss that into the street. Let the dogs feed on it until the sun turns it to mulch."

An image of Ezryn filled Haral's head and he grinned, his prick growing hard with cold elation. It was time to show Ezzie that *he* was the stronger brother, the *better* brother. The brother fit to rule the vampire race. Haral, not Ezryn, no matter what the fawning fools who followed the bastard believed.

It was time to show Ezzie just what his twin brother was capable of achieving. And how merciless he could be.

Chapter Four

Going without sleep wasn't working. Nor, Inari was disgusted to discover, was spending the daylight hours running on Bondi Beach. She'd spent the morning scaring off perverted men lurking near unsuspecting children before moving to her local gym to kick the shit out of a punching bag. When her clothes were so wet they clung to her body the gym owner—a gruff old retired boxer who didn't care squat for anyone—told her to go home before she collapsed. No matter what she'd tried in the last twenty hours, Inari couldn't get the master vampire out of her head.

It was driving her insane. *He* was driving her insane.

She glared at the sun sinking behind the western horizon, the towering office blocks and apartment complexes of Sydney's heart throwing shadows over her that should have chilled her warm flesh but instead made her angrier. Night was upon her, and all she wanted to do was track down the bloodsucker and pick up where they'd left off in the Pleasure Palace.

Fuck it.

Shaking her head, she turned from the sunset and shoved her

way along the crowded footpath, making her way toward home. Whether her body was telling her it wanted hard, wild sex with a vampire or not, she still had a job to do. The Deities may not have assigned her a target, but she hadn't forgotten the prickling heat razing the back of her neck last night. Somewhere in the city was a demon she needed to find and find soon. The idea of a demon watching her didn't help her current state of mind at all. As soon as she got home, she'd change into something a little more appropriate for demon killing, weapon up and go on the hunt. If she were lucky, she'd find the unknown creature making her neck feel like it was covered in fire ants within the first few hours and could then spend the rest of the night at an all-night movie marathon watching cult musicals and doing her damndest to keep the thought of the master vampire out of her head.

Yeah. Like singing "The Time Warp" is going to work. The only way you're going to get the bloodsucker out of your head is to screw him out of it, and you know damn well that's not going to happen.

She hurried her pace, the thought irritating her. She really needed to track down Ven Watkins. She needed to talk to the supreme Sentinel. Ask him the questions she should have asked when first reborn as an assassin. He was notoriously secretive, but she wouldn't take no for an answer. She'd spared his only brother's life twenty years ago, after all. He owed her. Embarrassing or not, she needed to know if she could—

The back of her neck itched. Not just a prickling heat, but a full-on, incinerating blaze that shot up the back of her head and turned her scalp to a crawling, burning skull-cap.

She spun on her heel, her stare jumping around the busy, early evening crowd. Oxford Street was its usual flamboyant self—cross-dressers, straights, gays, bis, tourists and businessman all jostling for prime footpath position as they moved together across the gray concrete past organic cafes, hydroponic shops, independent book stores and lavish restaurants overflowing with beautiful people dressed in retro fashions. Not one of them radiated any hint of demon power. Not one of them paid her any attention. Hell, not even the straight guys looked her way, their attentions firmly fixed on their phones as they weaved through the eclectic melee on their way to wherever.

The fiery prickle crawled up the back of her neck again, stronger this time.

Inari turned a perfect three-sixty, scanning the people around her. People. That's all they were.

So what's watching you? Who's watching you? And where is the bastard?

Demon. A powerful one. Close by.

She narrowed her eyes, concentrating her senses on the mass around her. The scent of sexually active males and females flowed through her, along with some ambiguously androgynous ones. The pit of her belly reacted to the stimulus, her sex contracting instinctually at the overtly potent taste of mature men on the air.

The reaction made her grind her teeth. It had been a long while since her body had been so responsive to the human Y chromosome, so...

Hungry for it?

She bit back a growl, sinking her nails into her palms. It was that cursed master vampire's fault. She'd denied her succubus nature completely before he found her in the Pleasure Palace. How was she to pinpoint the location of the demon nearby when all she could think about was fucking?

Just fucking? Tianya's voice questioned. *Or just fucking him?*

"Oh, for God's sake, shut up." Rolling her eyes, she started walking again, pushing her way through the Oxford Street crowd. The itch on her neck had not subsided. In fact, she could almost believe it had become more intense. The demon filth somewhere in her location was very powerful.

And taunting her?

Quickening her step, she headed toward Kings Cross. It would take twenty minutes, give or take a few minutes, to walk to her home via the most direct route. If the non-human was, as she suspected, tracking her, the chances of it confronting her were minimal. If she took the backstreets however, those only used by locals, those dark and shadowy and perfect for an ambush...

She felt the adrenaline turning her blood hot flow more freely through her veins. Her nipples pinched hard. She wasn't sure what aroused her so much, but she hoped to all the levels of hell it was the notion of being stalked by a soon-to-be-dead piece of demon scum. Twenty years of being in control of her libido only to have it destroyed by one nameless master vampire would really piss her—

"Hello, Sentinel."

The deep voice, smooth and yet at the same time gravelly, slipped into her right ear. She spun around and locked her stare on that very master vampire walking silently beside her. Her heart slammed up into her throat and she gasped, her eyes growing wide. "How did you—?" Her pussy fluttered, an eager throb that almost made her catch her step.

He chuckled, the sound just as low and gravelly as his voice. "Not sure, really. I thought of your delicious flesh and I knew where to go."

Heat flooded her face. Liquid heat flooded her sex. She jerked her stare from his ink-black eyes and hurried her stride. "Aren't you clever," she snarled, ignoring the licentious ache between her thighs. "Now go away."

The vampire chuckled again. The wicked sound sent a ripple up her spine. "You are an enigma, Inari Chayse. The last Sentinel I came face to face with tried to destroy me."

She shot him a sideward glance. "What? You practically rape them in a strip club too?"

His black eyes glinted red. The muscles in his jaw bunched. "We both know what occurred between us in the Pleasure Palace was mutually consensual. Do I need remind you the very title that fell from your lips?"

Master.

The shameful word whispered in Inari's head, and her feet stumbled beneath her.

Before she could right herself, the vamp curled his strong hand around her upper arm, bringing her to a halt. She turned to glare at him, the urge to smash her fist into his face almost as powerful as the urge to press her body to his. Was he the one she'd sensed? And if so, why wasn't her neck on fire now? He was touching her, for God's sake. You couldn't get much closer than that.

Yes, you can.

The soft whisper in her mind was entirely her own voice, ripe with suggestive promise.

"Why are you following me?" she demanded. "Haven't you got some emo-packed rave to be worshipped at?"

"I'm not following you."

"So, what? You just picked a random spot in Sydney to visit and it happened to be right beside me?"

He gave her a half smile. "Interestingly enough, that's exactly what happened."

She narrowed her glare.

"I told you," he went on, his fingers cool on her arm, "I thought of you...*all* of you...and knew where to go."

Her pulse thumped in her neck, the emphasis of the word *all* not wasted on her. "I can tell you where to go,"

He laughed. "Yeah, I bet you could."

"Let me go," she snapped, tugging at his grip. "And fuck off."

Refusing her request, he studied her, eyes black once again. "I find you fascinating, Inari Chayse."

Inari's already rapid pulse thumped faster. "I find you annoying."

He chuckled, his fingers curling firmer. "No, you don't."

"Fuck off."

The sides of his mouth curled. A little. "Do all assassins of the Sentinel order have such filthy mouths?"

She glared at him some more. "No. Now fuck. Off."

He laughed again and Inari bit back a groan. There wasn't a smug, snide or malevolent note to it. It was an infectious laugh, unlike any she'd heard before from a bloodsucker. Every other vampire she'd heard laugh sounded like they were auditioning for the role of arch villain in a James Bond film. His laugh, though, was completely relaxed and honest. It worried her. Not because he was laughing at her, but because it made her want to laugh too. By the Powers, what was wrong with her?

With a slight pressure on her arm, he began walking, encouraging her to walk in step beside him, and before she realized what she was doing, she was.

Maybe she'd gone insane?

She swallowed, all too aware of his hand still loosely holding her arm. All too aware of the fact she *was* walking beside him. *Walking* beside him, not struggling or fighting or trying to kill him. Walking beside him with her arm still held by his cold—

A young man of stunning beauty stepped directly in their path, his stare fixed firmly on the vampire beside her, and instantly the back of her neck prickled with heat.

Vampire. She clenched her fists.

The one that's been teasing you?

She reached out with her Sentinel power, gauging the new arrival's strength. Cold consternation rippled up her spine. The vamp standing before her, looking up at the master vampire with undeniable awe, was barely a babe by bloodsucker standards. There wasn't a hope he was the demon responsible for her earlier reaction. Hell, she was surprised her neck even itched at all.

"I am Eliah Bartowski, my master," he gushed, open reverence and worship on his seamlessly perfect face. "I came to Sydney to give you my thanks and swear my loyalty."

Inari narrowed her eyes. Swear loyalty?

The bloodsucker holding her arm shook his head, the action almost embarrassed. "You do not need to thank me, Eliah. I only stopped what was meant to be stopped."

"You faced the overlord's wrath for a bleeder you had never met. You defied his order when it would have been easier to allow his zealots to carry out his command."

"What command was that?" Inari jumped in, doing her best to ignore the master vampire on her right as he squeezed her biceps with icy fingers.

Eliah Bartowski raised his perfect eyebrows, his beautiful face marred by a horror so absolute it made her stomach roll. "To feed from my wife until she was drained. To butcher my daughter for being a half-caste."

Inari's stomach churned some more. Half-caste? The offspring of a human and vampire? She'd heard of such children being born but had never encountered one. As far as she was aware, half-castes did not survive long. She gave the obviously nervous young vamp a steady look. "Why did the overlord order such a thing?" she asked, steadfastly refusing to acknowledge the man—*the bloodsucking demon, Inari, the bloodsucking demon*—gripping her arm. "Why did my *friend* here—" she threw a sideward nod at him, "—stop it?"

Eliah's eyebrows rose again. "Because he is—"

"Very happy your wife and child are safe," the master vamp interrupted with smooth poise, his voice playing over her senses and turning her mounting curiosity to something far more irritating—sexual awareness.

"Safe and living without fear now because of you, my master," Eliah gushed, flicking her a quick look. "I cannot thank you enough."

Her vampire—*your vampire, Inari?*—placed his free hand on the young man's shoulder. "Then go home to your wife and child now and enjoy them. They must be missing you."

Eliah smiled, sharp white fangs glinting in Oxford Street's neon lights. "They are, and we are expecting our second child soon. If it is a boy, we shall call him Ezryn."

The name sent a finger of deep tight heat into Inari's core. Why was that name familiar?

The master vampire chuckled. "Can I suggest Mike instead?"

Eliah smiled, and with an awkward bow and an almost fawning, "Thank you, my master," he was gone, leaving Inari to gape at the vampire still gripping her arm.

"Mind telling me what that was about?"

"Not really."

"I know the hierarchy of your kind is weird, but anyone would think you were some almighty savior with the way that young vamp was behaving."

He shrugged, a grin playing with the corners of his mouth. "I think he had me confused with someone else."

She raised her eyebrows. "Really?"

"Yeah. I'm not *that* nice."

"You're right. You're not."

He laughed, starting to walk again, his gentle hold on her arm starting her walking as well. "So why aren't you trying to kill me then? If I'm not that nice?"

Why *wasn't* she trying to kill him? He was a master vampire. Her enemy. His extreme power and ancient prowess didn't just radiate from him—it oozed from him, infusing the air around him with something akin to electrical mist. Without testing his strength, she had little doubt he'd be a frightening force to reckon with, even for a Sentinel of her own elevated physical ability. She could feel his monumental presence in every molecule of her body. It challenged her on a raw level beyond her understanding. It was as if the very essence of the vampire race threaded through his existence. She'd executed many master vampires in her time— she'd screwed more than one in her succubus days—but all of them paled into clichéd Hollywood stereotypes compared to *this* master, *this* vampire. Every time he was near her the Sentinel within her surged for release, reacting to his undeniable existence. As did the sexual being in her. With almost as much force. Maybe more.

Disgust simmered through her. *By the Powers, Inari. Enough!*

He cocked an eyebrow, his expression somehow humored, his black eyes glinting red. "Well? What's the reason I'm still alive?"

Inari tugged at his grip on her arm. "You're not. You're dead."

He chuckled. "*Undead.*"

She ground her teeth, doing her best to ignore the delicious, cool pressure of his fingers on her upper arm. "You can read my mind. You tell me."

His lips curled a little. "Not all the time, alas."

"Oh, poor baby."

He chuckled again. "Yes. Now tell me why you aren't trying to kill me. I must admit, I'm most curious."

"I'm an assassin, not a murderer."

"Meaning?"

She let out an exasperated breath. "Meaning I have no orders to execute you." She gave him a narrowed-eyed stare. "Yet."

"So it would seem the Deities have decided I'm one of the good guys."

She snorted. "Your ego is amazing."

He grinned, obviously enjoying himself. "And is that the only reason?"

She sighed. Again. "If I answer you, will you go away?"

The vampire shrugged, his fingers still curled around her arm. "Maybe."

"An Agent of the Order, an assassin of God, a Sentinel—call us what you will—may only attack a demon marked as a target by the Deities or in direct self-defense." She paused. "Unfortunately, you fit none of those criteria at the moment."

His grin stretched wider, perfect white teeth without a hint of fang flashing. "Unfortunately?"

She clenched her jaw, tugging at his hold on her arm. "Yeah, unfortunately. I'd like nothing more than to turn you to dust."

He laughed and once again, her belly did a little flip-flop. She'd *never* heard a vamp laugh like that. They were always brooding and somber and *oh, look at me I'm a vampire,* as if there was some how-to book they read before being let loose on an unsuspecting world. Who knew, maybe there was a *Vampires for Dummies* tome out there. Either that or too many of their number watched too many bad movies. In her dreams, this bloodsucker had been the epitome of the vampire race—arrogant and smoldering and domineering. The vampire in her dreams could give lessons on demonic conceit. Here and now, however, walking beside her on a busy footpath surrounded by humans, his very food source, he seemed relaxed and almost...well, almost human.

"Something tells me, Inari Chayse," he said, slipping his hand up her arm to become less a hold and more a caress, "if you wanted to turn me to dust you would have done so by now, orders from your bosses or not."

Her pussy fluttered at the change in his grip, her pulse quickening in her throat. She closed her eyes, fighting against the pull of his presence beside her. If she didn't know any better, she'd swear he was glamoring her. What other reason was there for the irrational way her body responded to his touch? His very nearness?

Lust? Desire?

Danger?

She bit back a moan, disgusted with herself. Danger was right. This whole thing was dangerous. No matter how sexy and powerful and undeniably potent he was, he was still her enemy. In fact, those very things made him more her enemy. She had to remember that. He was a bloodsucking demon. For the love of God, she didn't even know his name.

Fresh shame and disgust rolled through her. He'd brought her to orgasm with his tongue and fingers in a public bar less than twenty-four hours ago, and she had no idea what to call him apart from—

"Master."

His low murmur stroked the side of her neck, and she flinched, jerking away from him as far as his suddenly tight grip on her arm would let her.

"Get the fuck out of my head."

He stared at her, eyes once more flickering red heat. Once more the eyes of the vampire of her dreams, the smoldering eyes of the arrogant demon who made love to her night after night after night. "Are you not the remotest bit intrigued *why* I am in your head, Sentinel?"

"No."

Liar.

He chuckled, a low, smug sound she recognized. *That* was the laugh of her dreams. Conceited superiority. Confident arrogance. She despised it. As much as she ached to hear it.

Tianya is right. You truly are messed up.

"*I* find it very intriguing," he said, his lips but an inch away from hers. "Very."

Stop him, Inari. Stop him before you can't.

His lips brushed hers, stealing her breath. Stealing her ability to run. To fight.

To think.

He dipped his tongue into her mouth, flicking at her even teeth before tugging her to his body and deepening the kiss completely.

And she let him, incapable of doing otherwise. He took charge of her body, of everything, including her senses, and she let him.

He slipped his hand up her arm, over her shoulder to bury it into the hair at her nape. He pulled her against him, scraping his fangs at her lips as he plunged his tongue into her mouth with greedy force, claiming it as his own.

And still she let him. Not just incapable of stopping him, but unwilling. Why would she stop him when it felt this good? This... this right?

"There's so much more I need to know about you, Inari," he whispered, dragging his mouth up to her ear. "And here on a crowded Oxford Street footpath isn't exactly where I had in mind for that discovery." He nibbled her earlobe. "My home is close. Very close. Come with me and we will—"

"Oi, you two!" a loud male voice filled with jovial mirth shouted from Inari's left. "Get a room!"

The pleasure-fogged heat wrapping around Inari shattered and she jerked backward, her stare locking on the vampire's face.

Run.

He shook his head, red chips of fire dancing in his black eyes. "Don't, Inari."

"Stay away from me, vampire."

He shook his head again, ignoring the surge of pedestrians pushing past them, his eyes almost entirely red. "Don't."

She clenched her fists, shutting out the throbbing ache in the pit of her belly, the pulsing dampness between her thighs. "You're right, bloodsucker," she stated, taking another step backward. An empty dismay chilled her soul when his hands slipped from her arm and hair, but she refused to acknowledge it. "I'm not the kind to wait for orders to take out a demon that needs to be destroyed."

His nostrils flared. His eyes narrowed. But he didn't move. "For future reference, we vampires hate being called demons."

She gave him a look of mock surprise, hoping to the Highest of Deities the denied want churning in her belly didn't show on her face. "Really? Gee, I didn't know that. Now, if you'll excuse me, *demon*—" She took another step back, away from the cold power emanating from his body. "I have a job to do."

She turned and began pushing her way through the gawking crowd. Searching for the man who'd yelled for them to get a room. She needed to thank him. She needed to let him know he'd saved her from making the biggest mistake of her entire three hundred years. She needed to—

Kill him for interrupting? Just when you were about to agree to the vampire's suggestion?

She lengthened her pace, shame turning her cheeks hot. A low chuckle sounded behind her. Smug and arrogant and thrumming with conceited confidence.

His laugh.

The laugh of her dreams.

And just like that, her pussy constricted with eager, wet want.

Damn him.

Damn her.

* * *

Haral watched his new bride's head bob up and down at his groin. Her fangs scraped at the sides of his cock, painful and unpleasant and annoying. He didn't stop her, as much as he wanted to. He would let her swallow his seed, let her wipe the spittle from her lower lip as she settled back on her haunches, thinking she'd pleasured him immensely, and *then* teach her never to give him head again with her fangs out.

Surprise the fuck out of her.

He ran his gaze over the glossy yellow of her hair, a silent snort sounding in the back of his throat. Married for two weeks to the pneumatic twat and already he was bored. She lay like a cold fish when he stuck his cock into her cunt and complained when he shot his load before she came.

So why did you marry her?

Because she was sex on legs to look at, tall and voluptuous with full lips and big tits. But mainly because she had come to him on her knees begging him, the overlord, to do something about the bitch Sentinel who'd executed her dumb-as-fuck cousin. Because she'd stayed on her knees for a good while after, although she'd kept her fangs retracted that time. Because as she'd sucked him off in front of his father's watching advisors—*his* advisors, the advisors of the overlord—he'd begun to formulate his plan. The very means to destroy his brother once and for all.

"Your brother is born of greatness, Haral." His mother's voice whispered through his head, the words from a lifetime ago *"He will be the leader our kind has needed for too long."*

Haral's balls rose up even as he hissed and thrust his hips

forward, driving his dick deeper into his wife's mouth. It wasn't just his mother who thought Ezryn pissed gold and shat diamonds. Whenever their father came down from his blood-drunk high, he spoke of little else. Ezryn was strong. Ezryn was intelligent. Ezryn was handsome. Fuck, Frederik Navarro had spent one whole night regaling Haral with detailed hypotheses on how virile his revered son was. Whenever Haral sought out his father's advice or counsel, Frederik was too busy with Ezryn. Whenever Haral was with his mother, her first question was always—*always*—of Ezryn. He'd never doubted the woman's love for both her sons, but once, just once, he'd longed for her to ask of him first.

She never had.

Even the last words she ever uttered were of darling, precious Ezzie. The last fucking words. The night she'd discovered Haral's clandestine relationship with the oracle, the night Haral had ended her existence, all she could think about was her first born. As Haral had sunk his nails into her neck and ripped out her throat, her very last words had been of his twin brother. *"Ezryn will..."*

There had been no more after that. He'd taken her bleeding, lifeless body outside the walls of the family mansion and left her for the sun's incinerating rays. And when her disappearance had finally registered with their father, all Frederik could say was, "Ezryn will be heartbroken."

Ezryn, Ezryn, fucking Ezryn.

Snagging a fistful of his wife's hair, Haral shoved her head downward, forcing the head of his cock against the back of her throat, controlling her every action. The right of the overlord. Supreme control. He'd hungered for it his whole life.

Now it was his, and he would do whatever it took to keep it. Including destroy his twin brother. It had nothing to do with his parents' favoritism. Truly, it didn't.

Too many vampires still spoke of Ezryn's noble strength and the reverence afforded him by the most ancient of vampires. Too many still remembered his quiet presence in court and his merciful power.

Too many still questioned the oracle's proclamation after the blood trials. And that number grew with every cursed night.

Once Ezryn was completely out of the picture, once the rest of the vampire race realized the prodigal son was not going to come in, metaphorical sword drawn, and seize back that which was rightfully his, Haral could stop worrying about rising factions, rebellions and revolt. Once that occurred, it was only a matter of time before he convinced his race it was time to treat humans exactly as they should be treated—as cattle.

And then he would be the undisputed leader of the most powerful creatures on the planet and have everything he wanted. All thanks to Ezryn's humiliating, shameful, disgraceful demise.

Which was only fitting really. Because all he'd ever wanted was everything his brother had.

Everything.

And now that included the Sentinel.

* * *

Inari weaved her way through the mass of tourists and locals crowding the main drag of Kings Cross, their faces turned into grinning masks of gaudy colors by the flickering lights of every strip club, bar, pawn shop and café lining its length.

She dodged a few groping hands, suppressing the urge to scream. Or rip the arms from those daring to touch her. Entrapment of the *Homo-sapien* kind was not on her agenda tonight. Tonight she hunted demon.

And how are you going to do that, exactly? You've spent the last four hours trying to find the fucker with no success at all. Not even your Sentinel soul can detect the creature now. It's as if it decided to stop stalking you and go on a holiday.

She sank her nails into her palms. She knew what the trouble was, and it had nothing to do with an absent demon. In fact, the trouble was the very presence of a demon. Just not the one she hunted. Ezryn, master vampire, bloodsucking demon and all-around bane of her existence was all she could think about. How the hell was she to track the unseen non-human who had made her neck raze with warning fire if she couldn't stop thinking about the arrogant vamp, his smug chuckle, talented mouth and wicked grin?

How in all the levels of Hell was she to be a demon assassin when she wanted nothing more than to fuck a demon?

The whole thing was ridiculous. As soon as she found and destroyed the unseen demon she hunted now, she'd find Ezryn and remove him from the picture as well. Surely the Deities would approve of one less vampire in the world. She'd find him, terminate him and get on with her life. Maybe then she could get some peace in her dreams.

Yeah, you keep telling yourself that. You might actually convince yourself one day. Like in about a million years.

Sliding through a particularly dense gathering of young males, Inari wrinkled her nose. Even when she wasn't in her Sentinel form, she still had a demon hunter's heightened sense of smell, and these guys smelled bad. "Excuse me," she said, trying to work her way through the group. Bachelor party. Had to be. The ritualistic indulgence of a human male about to enter a binding contract. With that much booze oozing from their pores, turning their breaths to intoxicating fumes, there was no other explanation. Inari had always found the practice bizarre. She wrinkled her nose again, pushing her way through the drunken mob. This close, she realized it wasn't just bizarre. It was stinky as well.

"Hey, sssexy!"

The slurred greeting fanned her ear. She turned and glared at the leering speaker just as he snaked a pair of hands over her hips and grabbed her ass cheeks.

"You're tha hottest thing I've seen aw night," the young man—barely in his twenties by the look of the fluff on his cheeks and the seamless skin around his eyes—murmured, his breath like a seedy hot fog on her face. "'Ow 'bout a root, then?"

Inari raised her eyebrows. "How 'bout you get your hands off my backside."

The drunken idiot grinned, stumbling slightly as he tugged her against his hips. "Wassa matter?" He swayed and his mates laughed around them. "Doncha think I'm fuckable?" His fingers dug into her butt and, an angry spark igniting in his bloodshot eyes, he slammed her harder to his groin. "I'm gettin' married t'morrow. My fiancée thinks I'm fuckable."

The group of intoxicated morons around her cheered, surging forward in a swaying, lumbering wave. They pushed her from the middle of the footpath, mindless of the pedestrians flowing around them. "Fuck him," one of them mumbled. "Suck his dick," another slurred.

More hands joined the groom-to-be's on her body, grabbing at her breasts, her hair. One of the party rammed his body to her back, sinking his fingers into her hips as he humped her backside. "You feel so fuckin' good, bitch," he grunted, his breath sour with rum. "So *good*."

The Sentinel in her existence stirred, pushing against a barrier Inari felt in her core. "I suggest you all fuck off, or I'll show you how fuckin' good I am."

"Fuck, Johno," the man behind her mumbled, his hands sliding from her hips. "I don't think she's a prostie."

"C'mon, slut," the groom growled, ignoring his friend's revelation, his words suspiciously free of any slur, his gaze clear and feverish as it drilled down into her face. "You dress like that, you're only asking for one thing." He rammed his dick against her belly. "I'm more than happy to give it to you. Me and my mates here." He grinned. "Think of it as a wedding present."

"Think of it as an execution."

The deep male voice rumbling from behind Inari's left shoulder made the groom flinch. His mates fell silent, their stares suddenly locked on the new arrival.

Hot electricity shot through Inari's body. She pulled in a swift breath, her pulse quickening.

It was *him*.

Curse it, why won't he leave me alone?

The groom drove his fingers harder into her backside. He squared his chest, jutting out his chin in a fierce show of aggression. "How 'bout you fuck off and mind your own business, mate? The little lady and I were just about to take this somewhere more private, weren't we, gorgeous?"

"I think the 'little lady' would tear your balls off," Ezryn stated. The crowd around them parted and, like the dark, malevolent creature he was, her master vampire appeared beside the groom, towering over him. "That is, if there's anything left of you after I'm finished."

He smiled, revealing a pair of pointed incisors no one in their right mind could ever mistake for fake.

"Err…" The groom's mouth opened and closed, making him look for all the world like a suffocating fish.

Inari stood motionless, her stomach churning. She should be throwing the groom off her and driving her size six pointed boot into his balls. She *should* be telling him and his friends to run away. Now. A master vampire had threatened their lives. In fact, *she* should now be doing exactly what she'd been reborn to do—destroy the bloodsucker before he uttered another word. Instead, she was frozen, the very sight of Ezryn stealing her ability to move.

The human holding her also seemed frozen, his bulging stare locked on the vampire to his right, his mouth working in soundless words.

With a slight tilt forward at the hip, Ezryn gave him a wider smile. "If you don't want to be drained like a can of beer, I suggest you run away." He touched the tip of his tongue to the tip of his left fang. "Probably now would be wise."

A hot, squirming sensation heated Inari's belly. Excited? What was she doing being excited?

No. Aroused. She was aroused. By Ezryn.

No. No no no.

"Seriously," Ezryn murmured to the human holding her, eyes glinting with devilish mirth. "Now."

With a very girly whimper, the human dropped his hands from her ass and bolted through the busy sidewalk, disappearing in the crowd.

His inebriated companions looked at each other, their faces white and slack with stunned confusion.

Ezryn flashed his fangs at them. "Boo."

They too, bolted.

"Well, I think we may have ruined their buck's night." He chuckled, turning his black gaze on her. "And probably their trousers as well."

Inari looked up at him, ignoring the curious pedestrians streaming past them, her throat tight. "Are you out of your blood-sucking mind?"

He raised his eyebrows, doing a brilliant facsimile of shocked amazement. "What?" A relaxed, all too cheeky grin curled his lips, and her pulse quickened. Damn it, why did he have this effect on her? "Surely you didn't want to go with that infant and his companions?" His gaze flicked over her body. "Although you are dressed for it. Did you go home and change? Or did you need a cold shower after we last met?"

"Oh, stick a sock in it," she snapped. Hot anger flowed through her. Damn, she needed to get her libido under control. If she was going to kill him, she had to stop thinking about sex every time she saw him.

The grin playing with the corners of his mouth faltered, and a deep red fire danced in his eyes. He took a step closer, his stare holding hers. "Now that is something I would loathe to see happen. I must admit, I rather like that you think about sex every time you see me. Not overly keen on the idea of you killing me though. Does this mean you've decided to disregard the three rules?"

A cold, numb finger pressed at her heart. How did he know what she was thinking? She gritted her teeth, her eyes narrowing. "Get out of my head, demon."

One dark, thick eyebrow cocked. "Or what?"

Without preamble, she slammed her palms against his chest and pushed.

He stumbled backward, arms flailing, the shock on his face far from fake. The pedestrians around them burst into good-humored cheers and laughter, some clapping, some smacking Ezryn on his shoulders as they halted his progress. No one seemed surprised or upset by the events—why would they? It was Kings Cross after all. This kind of thing happened on an almost hourly basis.

She fixed him with a level glare. "Stop stalking me, Ezryn."

His black stare locked on her face, but she didn't wait to see what he did next. She spun on her heel and stormed down the busy sidewalk.

She needed to get away from him.

She needed to focus.

She needed to remember what she was. Wanting to fuck a master vampire would have to be considered grounds for expulsion from the order of Sentinel. What would she do if *that* happened?

Be a succubus once more? Or better yet, spend the rest of eternity screwing the master vampire?

The mocking question flittered through her head in Ti's voice, and for a split second, Inari expected the image of her dead sister to materialize beside her.

"Shut up, sis," she ground out before the mental apparition could do any such thing.

Shove him? That's the best you could do? Shove him? What are you going to do next, call him names?

The contemptuous thought was hers this time, and she clenched her fists.

"Where are you going?"

She started, Ezryn's laughing question jerking her attention back to the here and now. He stood directly in her path, towering over her. He looked like every woman's fantasy with his tousled hair, powerful physique and designer clothes.

Before she could tell him to piss off, he grabbed her wrists and yanked her against his body, staring down into her face with that black, smoldering stare she knew all too well. She'd seen it every night in her dreams, felt its branding weight, its inescapable intent.

Her pussy flooded with wet tension. Hungry. She was hungry for him. For his tangible sexual energy. As hungry as she'd ever been when she was still a succubus. Maybe more so.

"Move." She forced the word past her lips. "Before I tear your heart out and feed it to the stray dogs."

"You're not walking away from me, Inari Chayse," he murmured. He lowered his head until she saw nothing but him. "And I think tearing my heart out is the last thing you want to do to me."

Hot shame burned her cheeks. "You conceited, arrogant bastard."

He smiled, a lazy, indolent smile that made her pulse triple. "True. But I tend to answer to Ezryn much better." He tugged her wrists farther away from her sides, jolting her closer to his hard, hard body. "Try it. Say, *Master Ezryn* and see what happens."

Volcanic heat erupted in her core. An explosive mix of raw anger and primal lust. She opened her fingers and spread them wide, flexing her wrists in his tight grip. "I have no master."

Ezryn lifted an eyebrow, pulling her arms behind her back until their bodies melded together. His knuckles grazed the curves of her ass cheeks, the feather-light contact sending sparks of wet electricity through her core. "Really? I thought all Sentinel have a master." He moved her wrists to one big hand, sliding his free hand up her ribcage. "Y'know, the big guy? Flowing white hair, blinding white light, lots of clouds?" He brushed his thumb over the side swell of her breast encased in the supple leather of her vest and she gasped, the sound escaping her before she could stop it. His eyes flickered at her response, the deep red fire in their black irises glowing brighter. "Isn't *He* your master?"

She twisted her wrists in his grasp. She had to get away. Every molecule in her body was too aware of his potent force. Too aware and too aroused. "You really have no clue about Sentinel, do you?" She flashed him a cold smile. "Keep fucking with me, and you'll see just how much leash my *Master* gives me."

The vampire's nostrils flared and he lowered his head closer still to hers, eyes unreadable. "Oh, I haven't even begun to fuck with you, Inari Chayse. When I do, you will know. Your body will be so consumed with pleasure you'll be unable to function." He moved his mouth to her ear, his lips brushing her flesh in a cool caress. "When I do, you will forget your other master in a heartbeat. All you will able to do is whimper *my* name over and over again. *Master* Ezryn, *Master* Ezryn, *Master* Ez—"

Inari smashed her knee up into his balls.

He let out a grunt. Pain ripped across his handsome face. His hands grew loose on her wrists.

With inhuman speed—whether that of succubus or Sentinel, she didn't know or care—she spun and slammed her heel into his chest in a back kick hard enough to send him arcing through the air.

"Holy shit!" someone yelped behind her. "Did you see that?" Someone else screamed, a high-pitched note of stunned disbelief. The crowd dispersed, some running, others tripping and stumbling just far enough away from Inari and Ezryn to consider themselves safe, more than one holding up their phones as they did so, recording every second of the excitement.

"Help her," a female voice screeched.

"Help *him!*" a male voice laughed.

Inari ignored them all, her stare fixed instead on Ezryn's body landing on the sidewalk in a heavy thump. The crowd scurried farther away from him, eyes wide with a feverish thrill. A blinding light flashed as one of the onlookers took a photo.

Run, the voice in her head that sometimes sounded like Tianya roared. *Run now.*

She clenched her fists, darting her tongue over her lips in a nervous swipe. Run? Or take the bloodsucker out?

In a blur of preternatural power, Ezryn was on his feet, his black gaze pinning her to the spot. "Shall we call this foreplay, Inari?"

A siren wailed above the gasping crowd, high and loud. Inari narrowed her eyes. The cops were coming.

Good. Use the distraction. Run away.

Run away? How do you kill him if you run away?

How do you fuck *him if you run away?*

She ground her teeth together. "Let's call it round one, Ezryn. Round two will see you dead."

More gasps and laughs came from the circling crowd. Another flash bleached the night. "You go, girl," the same man who'd called for help for Ezryn earlier bellowed as someone clapped. A Kings Cross crowd through and through. Too jaded, laidback or high to recognize the real danger in the situation.

Above the noise, the police siren grew louder. Closer.

Inari's skin prickled, something deep within her core knotting tight. Her muscles began to burn, her teeth to ache—her Sentinel soul stirring deep within. Rising.

A shudder wracked through her, sending new heat into her limbs and the pit of her belly. The knot there twisted tighter, a wicked, squirming sensation that made her nipples pinch. Oh no, the Sentinel in her didn't want to fight. The Sentinel wanted to *mate.*

The realization stole her breath.

No. This was not right. She was ex-succubus. Succubi did not mate. Succubi fucked and left. They took their fill and moved on. She was Sentinel. Sentinel did not mate. They killed and left. They terminated their target and hunted the next. She didn't want to mate with anyone, let alone a vampire. It was impossible, and she would not let it be so.

Ezryn—and the crowd—watched her.

She turned on her heel and, rocked by confusion and cowardice, ran, the icy burn of transformation threatening to overwhelm her. The crowd melted from her path. The screech of the approaching siren pierced her ears as she burst into an impossible sprint. Her Sentinel force—so close to release—surged through her. Or was it her succubus force? God help her, she couldn't tell.

No. It's not. It can't be.

She ran faster, the bright, blinking lights of the strip blurring into a myriad of colored streaks. Her heart hammered and her blood roared. The sounds of Kings Cross at night became an indistinct hum of white noise.

She took one corner, another, another, the hot night air cool on her flushed face, the taste of sin and sex pervading every breath she took. She fled through dark, quiet back streets, moving at an inhuman pace, her body burning not just from sexual hunger but physical exhaustion. Her feet ached, her stiletto boots less than perfect for such a marathon. She didn't care. Experiencing pain lessened the torturous longing in her core. Ten miles and ten flights of stairs later, she burst through the door to her home, charging through the small apartment until she reached her bedroom. Safe.

She threw herself down on the bed, the collection of black and red silk cushions she'd gathered over the centuries bouncing on the mattress as she rammed her face and fists into its soft surface. "Argh!" she screamed, squeezing her eyes shut. "This is not right!"

"Y'know," a familiar voice noted behind her, and she froze, her already frantic heart leaping into new life, "for a Sentinel, you've done a very bad job of keeping your home base a secret."

Chapter Five

Jacob narrowed his eyes, locking his stare on what he suspected was the window of Inari Chayse's bedroom. He'd seen her run past it in a harried sprint before she'd suddenly disappeared from view as if she'd thrown herself at something, possibly the bed.

What are the chances she's not on that bed alone now, Jake? The unsettling question made him clench his fists.

Ezryn was inside the Sentinel's apartment, and he doubted the master vampire was ending the assassin's life.

He let out a ragged sigh.

Following Inari first through Paddington in the hours just after dusk had revealed little he could use but unnerved him all the same. The Sentinel was by far the most sensual creature he'd ever seen. She oozed sex, her every move sinfully seductive. She also oozed power. A calm menace seemed to hang about her, tainting the seductive rhythm of her body, like that of a dominatrix only tenfold.

He'd found himself wondering how many of the Sentinel's male targets had sported a hard-on when destroyed.

That rather absurd but perversely arousing thought had been

crossing his mind when Ezryn had entered into his line of sight, walking up behind Inari on Oxford Street and slipping his fingers around her smooth upper arm.

The look on the Sentinel's face when she turned to his master was etched forever on Jacob's retina—shocked disbelief and unequivocal desire. And no matter how much he wished it wasn't so, that same desire burned on Ezryn's face.

Jacob ground his teeth. It was a complication he didn't need. It made what he'd planned far more...risky.

He'd lingered back in the teeming throng of pedestrians moving along Oxford Street, watching as a young vampire approached Ezryn. For a split second, he'd almost launched himself from his concealed position, ready to defend the true overlord against a possible threat. When he'd seen Ezryn laugh, Jacob had relaxed.

But only a little. A laughing Ezryn was not something he was used to. Not the completely relaxed, open laughter he'd witnessed from his master earlier tonight. It was as disconcerting as the desire Jacob had seen in his face, and all because of the Sentinel, Inari Chayse.

Does it change your plans?

He swallowed, his mouth dry. It didn't.

So what are you going to do? Go upstairs now? While Ezryn is in her home? Stop him doing...whatever he is doing to her?

"Dark Ones," he muttered. He couldn't do that.

He was brave, but not that brave.

Narrowing his stare on the Sentinel's window, he considered his next move. He could stand here until Ezryn left, but something warned him his master wasn't going to be exiting the place for some time, and as disturbing as that was, inaction disturbed him more.

With one long, final look at the open window, he slid into the shadows.

He traveled the dark, early-morning streets without a sound, his presence undetected by those he passed. He rarely used his vampire powers to move among humans anymore, but Harry's compound was on the other side of Sydney Harbor and he needed to get there fast.

Fifteen minutes later, he stood outside a mansion so overtly pretentious he couldn't stop his sneer. It was perfect for the bloated, egomaniacal idiot and so very typical.

Pulling in a slow breath, Jacob tasted the air.

The slightest tinge of decay threaded through the sweet scent of Chinese Star Jasmine hanging heavy on the night, and he curled his lip. Yes, Harry was in. There was no mistaking his vile stench.

He stepped up to the massive gates, wriggling his fingers as he studied their dagger-pointed, ten-foot iron pickets. Broaching them wouldn't be difficult. What waited on the other side was another matter.

An image surfaced in his mind, an apparition of a memory he'd long fought to suppress. He fisted his hands, the image like a stake to his lifeless heart.

Cara, his wife, in his arms...

It was her hair he always remembered first. Copper-spun silk that fell about her shoulders in a tumbled mess of curls. His wife had hated her hair, but he'd loved it. Its weight, its texture, the way it slid through his fingers like cool water, the way it turned a deep blood-red when wet. He would fall asleep every morning with its clean scent in his nose, his face pressed to the back of her neck, his arms curled around her slim body. He would drift off knowing even though she spent the daylight hours living her human life, when he woke she would be there waiting for him. And before he opened his eyes every night, that same clean scent would thread into his empty lungs and he would smile. It was always her hair he remembered first...

The silken strands clinging to his fingers, matted with blood. Her blood. She gazed up at him, her eyes, the color of the ocean on a cloudless day, glassy. Sightless. He'd shaken his head, held her to his chest. She was warm, but it was only the residue of the life once in her body. They'd ripped that life from her. Ripped it from her veins, her chest, feasting on her even as they raped her, over and over, her screams and cries met with laughs and cheers. And he'd been unable to save her. Unable to stop them. Haral's zealots, sent by the newly ascended overlord, had butchered his wife, his love, and forced him to watch it all.

They'd bound him with silver-lined manacles, holding him captive as they violated her body and drained her veins, taking turns at her until she lay limp beneath them. And the last one...the last one to sink his dick between her legs had knotted his fists in her hair and tore two handfuls from her scalp, calling loyalty to Harry as he did so. Her hair...his wife's hair...

The sound of soft footfalls to Jacob's left shattered the tortured memory. He swung his head in their clumsy direction, sensing the human female before she stepped from behind a row of densely grown evergreen poplars.

"Are you a vampire?"

Her question, spoken in a trembling whisper, took Jacob completely by surprise. As did the ridiculously tight black mini-dress barely covering a young body. She looked at him, large, round eyes ringed with smudged black makeup, her pasty-white skin marred by pockmarks and fresh acne, her lips painted black. Circling her right wrist were the words *Edward Forever,* written repeatedly in elaborate but amateurish script. Around her fleshy neck hung an ornate silver locket.

Jacob bit back a curse. Damn it, he knew exactly what this woman was.

Vamp groupie.

"A what?" he asked, making his voice sound incredulous even as the torment of Cara's memory frayed his patience bare.

"A vampire," she repeated, taking a hesitant step toward him. "I heard there was a vampire living here. A whole nest of them. I...I wanted to...to..."

She didn't finish, her black-lined eyes shimmering in the waning moon's thin light.

A dull throb thumped in Jacob's chest where his unbeating heart sat. Part anger, part grief. "Why do you want to know?"

The woman, barely in her twenties by the smell of her nervous sweat, tried to assume a haughty pose. "I want to offer myself. I want to become a...a..."

Her bravo deserted her and she stumbled back a step, her teeth catching her bottom lip.

Jacob studied her, his chest tight. The foolish child presented an opportunity he couldn't ignore. Defenseless, naïve and stupid, she was perfect. All he needed to do was rip out her heart, bathe in her hot blood and let her petrified wails rise up to the heavens as he drained her dry, and he would be the Sentinel's next target.

With the girl's death, he would have no need to initiate the confrontation. Inari Chayse would come to him.

"Are you..." The tremble was back in the woman's whisper. The air grew cloying with her fear. And her hope. "Can you..."

He thought of his wife, of what had happened to her. Of what Haral had ordered to happen. He thought of a war between Sentinel and vampires and the innocent human victims of such a war. He thought of the overlord on the other side of the iron fence beside him, sitting safe and smug in the belief he was untouchable.

He thought of Cara and her blood-matted hair...

Jacob felt his fangs lengthen in his mouth, and he fixed the ridiculously dressed young woman with a steady gaze. "You really have no idea the danger you are in, do you?"

Inari snapped to her feet, her heart smashing into her throat. Fists clenched, she glared at the vampire standing at the foot of her bed. "Don't you ever get the hint?"

He grinned, folding his arms across his chest. "You're sending mixed messages, assassin."

She folded her own arms across her chest, not wanting him to see how quickly her nipples pebbled at his words. "How can you be in here? I extended no invitation."

Ezryn cocked one of his dark eyebrows. "I opened the door and came in. I must admit, I'm as surprised as you. Perhaps it has something to do with the magic between us."

She pulled a dismissive face. "There is no magic."

He grinned, fangs glinting. "I disagree. How else would I know you were on Oxford Street earlier this evening? How else would I know you needed my rescue in Kings Cross only a few moments ago?"

"I did *not* need your rescue. You think I couldn't handle a few human males?"

"I have to wonder," he murmured, standing directly in front of her before she could register the fact he'd moved. His thighs brushed hers. His eyes held hers in a hypnotic gaze she felt all the way to her very center. "Considering your complete failure to *handle* me."

Without breaking eye contact, he placed his palms square on her chest and shoved her backward, driving her flat onto the mattress. He slammed his right knee between hers, pushing her legs apart as he bent over her, grabbing her wrists before she could strike out at him and pinning them to the bed. Hot tension knotted in Inari's belly. Damn, he was quick, even for a bloodsucker.

"See?" He grinned again. "I can shove you around too. Of course, *I* make sure you have a nice soft landing, unlike you." He slid his knee farther up her inner thigh. "The sidewalk is not the most comfortable of landings. My ass still hurts, by the way."

She gave him a melodramatic pout. "Oh, poor baby."

His eyes flickered with red heat. "Going to make you kiss it better later."

The promise made her belly knot some more—and her pussy constrict. "In your dreams," she snarled, wishing her body would behave itself.

"Tell me," he said, his grin turning smug, "have you ever had a vampire lover before, Sentinel?"

Her sex constricted again. By the Powers, what was *wrong* with her? "If you think I'm going to answer that, you're a moron."

With a sudden jerk, Ezryn yanked her arms above her head and captured both her wrists in one fist. "There are many, many answers you will give me over the course of the night, Inari Chayse." He gazed down into her face, his black eyes dancing with that same smoldering red heat she'd seen in the strip joint. "Let's start with this one." He trailed his free hand down her arm, over the upward thrust of her breasts to the top button of her vest. "Just how hard do you want me to fuck you?"

Inari narrowed her eyes, doing everything she could to ignore the molten pit of hunger her sex had become at his question. "Get your hands off me, vampire, before I rip your unbeating heart from your chest and shove it down your throat."

Ezryn cocked one very dark eyebrow. "That hard?"

She bared her teeth. "Fuck you."

"Let me ask another question then," he murmured, his finger circling the button of her vest. "Do you want me to leave?"

She stared at him. She couldn't answer.

Because the answer was no. She didn't. She wanted this. She wanted him. But to admit that aloud...

"I will leave if you want," he said, his voice lower. Husky. His eyes held hers. She saw confusion in them, as if he was as unsettled by his own actions as she was by her own lust for him. "This... magnetic force between us...it's potent. And I do not want to destroy it."

"How would you do that?" she whispered, heart racing.

His nostrils flared. "By taking what you haven't willing given."

Her breath left her in a shaky sigh of surrender. She couldn't fight her desire for him any more. She couldn't. His refusal to bow to his demonic nature with her was the final straw.

She wanted him. He wanted her.

To hell with them being natural enemies.

For now, at least.

"For tonight," she said, the words barely a breath, "I give you consent."

A low groan turned into a growl deep in the back of his throat, and he tore her vest open. Her breasts fell free and she gasped, arching her back. He traced the puckered nipple of each one with slow precision, watching his finger's path with smoldering eyes. "Let's start then, shall we?"

He dropped his head, crushing his mouth to hers with brutal force. He plunged his tongue between her lips, battling with hers before Inari realized she'd opened her mouth to his assault.

Ezryn lifted his head and stared down at her, skimming his fingers from her breasts to the waistline of her leather pants. "I don't know what turns me on the most: your own hunger for me, or your surrender to it." He dipped his fingers beneath the snug line of her trousers and stroked the smooth curve of her mons. "Both?"

Inari narrowed her eyes at him, the pulse in her neck a thumping cannon. "You're an arrogant bastard, aren't you?"

He laughed. "Of course. I'm a master vampire."

Master vampire. She was about to fuck a master vampire. What was she doing?

What you want.

Shamed heat flooded her face at the raw acceptance and she turned her head to the side, the fire in her sex blazing hotter. Tighter.

"Oh, Inari," Ezryn murmured, his voice like velvet smoke on her flushed flesh. "You should not present me with such a beautiful neck." He tightened his fist on her wrist and she felt his weight shift between her legs. "Not when you smell like heaven and look like sin."

Cool lips brushed the side of her throat, just below her ear, the contact followed immediately by the gentle flick of the tip of his tongue. Inari hissed in a breath, her sex constricting on a cock that wasn't there, every muscle in her body snapping tight. She rolled her head, pushing his mouth from her neck with a sudden blow of her chin just as she jackknifed her legs up around his hips and locked her ankles behind his back. "Bite me and I'll pull your fangs out."

He chuckled again, the action sending rumbles of duplicitous sensations through Inari. "You say the nicest things, Sentinel." In a dark blur, he returned his mouth to her neck, his lips nibbling on her flesh. "And your skin tastes so...so pure. And yet at the same time so dirty. As if the demon you once were still lingers in your new soul."

Inari sucked in a sharp breath. Ezryn's soft words ignited her fury. And her fear.

The demon she once was.

Succubus. Did he know? Was that why...

"Tell me," he rasped against her cheek. "What kind of demon *were* you before your rebirth? Because I want to know. So very, very much."

No. No, you can't *do this. You'll be lost forever if you do.*

She lashed out, smashing her fist into the side of Ezryn's head. He crashed sideways, rolling from her body. Without pause, ignoring the screams of denial in her core, she scrambled to her knees, plunged her hand under the pillow closest to her and closed her fingers around the long, silver stake she always kept there. Just in case of emergencies.

"What are you going to do with that, little girl?"

Ezryn's growl snapped her around. She locked her stare with his, the stake icy against her palm. "Turn you to dust."

Confusion flicked over his face and then his fangs glinted as he gave her a small grin. Whatever his reaction to her abrupt change of mind, he was trying to hide it. "Really?"

He chuckled, stepping back from the bed toeing off his boots.

"What are you doing?" she demanded.

"Getting ready."

She looked at him, her body screaming for his. "For what?"

He held his arms out from his sides, his grin growing wider. "I will make you a deal. You stake me with that shiny silver thing in your hand, and I will willingly turn to dust. I won't even complain when you suck me up with your vacuum cleaner." His eyes twinkled as he took a step toward her, his fangs catching her bedroom's muted light. "But if I take it from you before you can do so, you will surrender your body to me and let me do with it what I will."

Inari's sex constricted at his words, and her breath caught in her throat. "And that's it? No questions? No blood?"

Are you even considering this, Inari? Are you?

His stare locked on her face. "No blood. But I have one question first. Why are you scared of me?"

"I'm not scared of you." She met his stare, chin jutted. "I'm annoyed by you. I've had kings and slaves alike trembling in fear of me. Monsters from the sub-levels of Hell, first-order demons, semi-Powers, demi-dieties all giving me their terror." She climbed from the bed and stood straight beside it, her fist tightening on the silver stake in her grip. "Yet you don't show an inkling of respect. You piss me off."

He laughed, an infectious sound she fought to ignore with all her soul. Laughing? How could he even think about laughing? "You should know, Sentinel, that fear and respect and anger aren't interchangeable."

She clenched the stake tighter. "You are right. They aren't. The last master vampire I defeated learned *that* lesson very quickly."

That infectious laugh rumbled in his chest again. "I hate to disappoint you, Inari, but *I* have never lost to a Sentinel, especially when the outcome is so delicious."

Inari shut out the thick heat his smug drawl ignited in the junction of her thighs. "Then I look forward to kicking your ass."

He laughed again. "As do I." He cocked an eyebrow. "Although kicking isn't exactly what I have in mind with your—"

She leapt at him, face flaming.

He moved before she could strike him, streaking across her

small bedroom area in a dark blur to crouch motionless on her dressing table. Resting his elbows in his bent knees, he grinned at her. "I've never fought barefoot before." His eyebrows rose once in a suggestive expression Inari could only call cocky. "Imagine what it'd be like if I was naked."

She rolled her eyes, the pit of her belly knotting. "Don't be ridiculous," she said, wishing to hell her body would stop reacting with traitorous excitement.

"Admit it." He grinned. "You'd like to see me naked."

Yes. She very much—

He snapped straight and, in a blur, removed his clothes before the thought could finish.

Inari stared at him, her mouth dry.

Oh.

His chiseled upper body gleamed under the room's warm light, giving his pale skin a sun-kissed sheen. His chest was broad, smooth and untouched by hair. His stomach was flat and sculpted in all the right ways. A few scars marked his ribs, but rather than mar his perfection, they only heightened the sense of dangerous allure that radiated from him in waves. His cock...

Her pussy fluttered again, and she jerked her gaze back to his face, stopping herself from inspecting his lower body. The sight of his naked beauty would do evil things to her sanity.

His grin stretched wider, black eyes twinkling with mischief. "Your turn."

She arched an eyebrow. "As if."

"Ah, come on." He ran a gaze over her. "You know you want to."

Yes. You do.

She shoved the wanton thought of getting naked with him aside, as she did the irrational, ludicrous urge to grin back at him.

Don't you dare smile at him, Inari. He's the enemy.

She ground her teeth. She'd never had an enemy look so damn gorgeous. This definitely wasn't fighting fair.

Ezryn's gaze roamed her face, his grin turning contemplative. "It eats you up. Doesn't it?"

She tightened her grip on her stake and forced herself to glare at him. "What does?"

"The unexpected feeling of happiness you experience when we're together."

"How do you—" Inari snapped her mouth shut, her heart leaping up into her throat. "You are the most conceited individual I've ever known, vampire," she said instead.

He gave her an accepting nod. "Probably."

Before she could roll her eyes again—*roll your eyes? Aren't you meant to be turning him to dust?*—he threw himself off the table in a graceful flip and landed directly in front of her. "But I bet I'm also the most impressive."

He grabbed her wrist and yanked her against his body. His cool chest crushed her breasts. His mouth silenced her indignant shout, his kiss quick and cheeky.

Inari froze, her breath catching in her throat seconds before she drove her right knee up into his balls.

Or would have, if the bastard hadn't leapt away in a backward arc so fast she felt the very air suck past her.

He grinned at her again, this time sitting atop her low chest of drawers on the other side of the room. "Now, did you try to do that so you'd have an excuse to kiss them better later?"

The laugh bubbled up her throat and she pressed her hand to her mouth, her stake cold against her lips. No, she couldn't let him know she was having fun. With him.

"Sod off," she said instead, forcing a surly glare at him.

"At this point," he murmured, stepping down from the piece of furniture with fluid ease, "a true gentleman would say something pithy like 'It's okay, sweetheart, I don't bite'." He was in front of her again in a split second, so close his thighs brushed hers. "But as we both know, I do."

She looked up at him, her pulse thumping in her neck. *Do something. Don't let him win. Don't let him...*

His stare slid to the base of her throat, and she saw his Adam's apple jerk up and down. "I *do* bite, Inari." He lifted his hand and feathered the back of one knuckle over the fine muscle above her collarbone, a brilliant red shimmer filling his eyes. "But only when you give me permission."

Her blood roared in her ears. "I won't."

His gaze returned to her face and he smiled, a languid, crooked smile she felt all the way to the center of her soul. "Yes, you will. Trust me."

"Trust a bloodsucker?" She snorted, trying to force the constricting heat in her core away. This was too surreal. She was turned on more than ever, and despite all her internal lectures she was enjoying every second of their conversation. "Step out in the sun and I'll trust you to turn to ash."

He chuckled, brushing the back of his knuckles along her jaw line. "Where are you from?" he asked unexpectedly, that crooked smile still playing with his lips. "You don't have an Australian accent, and I know of only one Sentinel here in Sydney."

Her stomach knotted. She never talked about her demonic heritage. Nor her past, and that included her connection to the supreme Sentinel residing in the city. She gave Ezryn a pointed stare. "You don't exactly sound like Hugh Jackman yourself, vampire."

He laughed again as the tips of his fingers skimmed the length of her throat. "I was born in Denmark over seven centuries ago, but have been in Australia for almost fifty years now. I thought I'd mastered the art of the Aussie vernacular quite well." His grin widened. "G'day, mate."

She laughed. "That was atrocious."

He shrugged. "Perhaps I need to work on it more. I'm usually much better with my tongue."

"I bet you are," she muttered.

He grinned.

Damn it, why was she enjoying herself so much with him?

"What are you doing in Australia?" she asked. "It's a long way from Denmark, and much more sunny."

A flash of fangs followed her statement, and he took a slight step closer, brushing her hips with his. "Hunting," he murmured.

She looked up into his dark eyes, her pulse thumping in her neck. "Hunting what?"

Stake him! Stop flirting with him for Pete's sake and stake him!

He lowered his head. "At this very moment?"

George Thorogood started singing "Bad To The Bone" from the floor behind him.

With a growl, he turned his head and glared at his discarded jeans. "Perfect timing, Jake," he muttered.

Inari raised her eyebrows, an unsettled relief fluttering through her. Why did it feel like she'd just been saved? And why was a part of her so angry about it? "Shouldn't you get that?"

He returned his gaze to hers, his phone falling silent. "My general can wait."

"Your general?" What kind of master vampire had a general?

The kind who has vampires called Eliah Bartowski swearing loyalty to him in the street?

"My general. You however, cannot."

She gave him a barbed frown, even as her pulse quickened. "And what am I so impatient for, bloodsucker?"

He lowered his head closer to hers once more, smug mirth in his eyes. "Being caught by me."

Stake him! Now!

She slammed the heel of her palm into the center of his chest, driving him backward. "God, what am I doing?" she ground out, watching him stagger backward, her confusion growing to churning disbelief.

His lips pulled away from his fangs in an ambiguous grin. "Playing hard to get?"

"Fuck you."

"Isn't that what we've been trying to do?"

He leapt at her, hitting her in a dark streak of solid speed. She tumbled back onto the mattress, his weight pinning her to her bed as he snatched the stake from her hand.

"See?" His eyes glowed red heat. "Told you I would win."

She jackknifed her legs up, twisting as she did so, and wrapped them around his neck, flinging him off her body.

He crashed against the vermeil mirror leaning in the corner, and shards of glass showered down on him as he hit the floor with a solid thud.

Inari propelled herself off the bed and leapt at him, a part of her mind screaming at her to stop. She didn't listen. She couldn't. She was a Sentinel, not some bloodsucker groupie.

She slammed her foot against his chest just as he was rising to his feet, driving him backward into the wall again. He let out a choked *oof*, his arms slapping the wall as his face contorted in pain.

Or was it shock?

She didn't wait to see. She whipped out her leg, smacking her instep into his jaw. The turning kick sent him spinning, his feet stumbling beneath him. He fell forward, but before he could hit the floor, he flipped himself into a roll.

Eyes blazing red, fangs glinting in her bedroom's muted light, he spun to face her, waggling the point of her stake at her. "That hurt."

"It was meant to."

She charged at him, throwing herself into a flying roundhouse kick.

This was it. Take him down. Take back her stake. Take him out. Game over.

Her heel smashed into the wall half a second before he snaked his arms around her waist and thighs. "Gotcha."

Her stare snapped to his. Just as he kissed her, a quick, cheeky kiss like his previous one. And just as it had before, her pussy flooded with tight heat. It didn't matter he held her captive. It didn't matter she was trying to kill him.

No, you're not. Admit it.

"Let me go."

He cocked an eyebrow. "Okay."

Without even a grunt, he threw her across her room.

She landed on her bed, her breath bursting from her in a violent gush. By the Powers, how had he—

He slammed into her, driving her flat onto the mattress, his hands snaring her wrists. "Can I say gotcha again?"

A wave of insidious lust surged through her, and she sucked in a sharp hiss. "Get off me."

In a blurring move, he straddled her, his thighs hugging her hips, his groin resting on the curve of her sex. His cock jutted up between them, long, thick and rigid. "Why would I do that, Inari?" He placed one hand beside her head and bent closer to her, sliding the tip of her stake over her chest to the swell of her left breast. "When we both remember what happens now; *you will surrender your body to me...let me do with it what I will...*"

Her heart leapt into her throat as he repeated his earlier words. Words she'd foolishly agreed to.

No. She couldn't. She couldn't let him.

Yes, you can.

"You will, Sentinel," he murmured, finishing her duplicitous thought. "And you will beg me to never stop."

With pointed arrogance, he tossed her stake aside, the sound of its silver length striking the wall turning her mouth dry. He'd beaten her, he'd unarmed her and now he was going to use her any way he wanted.

Her pussy fluttered at the terrifying reality.

His eyes glowed red again. The hand with which he'd held her stake only seconds earlier came to rest on the column of her neck. "I will not hurt you, Inari." He traced the pad of his thumb up her throat to the wildly beating pulse beneath her ear. "But I will make you moan."

She shook her head, desperate to stem the mounting rush of base pleasure surging through her, to regain some semblance of control. "I won't."

He chuckled, the laugh of her dreams, and her heart quickened at the smug power in the sound. "Yes, you will."

He smoothed his hand lower, over the upward thrust of her breasts, first one then the other, exploring their heavy form through the thin leather of her vest. Her nipples puckered into hard peaks, pushing at his palm.

"Your body can't lie to me, Inari," he whispered, watching his hand as he moved it over her right breast to cup its swollen weight. "No matter what your lips say, your body tells me the truth."

She closed her eyes, rolling her head to the side in a woeful attempt to hide her telltale blush. He was correct. So very correct. He'd turned her into a being of lust and wanton hunger.

So what does that make you now? And what does that make him? Your master? Or your source of nourishment?

"Touch me," the words tumbled from her in a husky plea before the ominous questions could chill the desire consuming her. "Touch me."

With a low growl, he moved his hand lower, over her stomach and under the waistline of her pants. "Dark Ones, your skin is so soft." His voice sounded strangled. Tormented. "How can you feel so soft, so beautifully warm? How am I to—"

He cut the question short and plunged his hand between her legs, dipping two fingers into her pussy at the same time that he claimed her neck with his mouth. He closed his lips over the exact spot where her pulse beat wildly beneath her skin and sucked hard.

Wicked pleasure tore through her—a traitorous response she could not control nor deny. She arched beneath him, grabbing at the duvet. *Oh, God, yes.* The pit of her stomach knotted and her nipples pinched hard.

A whimper escaped her and she caught her bottom lip with her teeth, pushing her hips higher to Ezryn's body, driving her sodden sex farther onto his fingers. Her clit ached, swollen with blood and desire. The master vampire sucked harder on her neck and ground his hand against the tiny nub in her folds, sending tight ribbons of pleasure into her core. She whimpered again, the sound echoed by a low moan in his throat. He dragged his mouth down the column of her throat to her collarbone, his lips hotter than a vampire's should be. They branded her flesh. Made her giddy. She thrust higher, wanting him to fill her. Wanting him to take her. Use her.

Inari closed her eyes, arching into his penetrations.

He lifted his mouth from her neck, and blew a fine stream of cool air over her freshly kissed flesh, stroking his fingers inside her pussy with wicked attention. "You are very tight, Inari."

Appreciation thrummed in his voice, any sign of his earlier torment gone. Her body reacted to his words in ways she couldn't fathom. How could he almost make her come with just his voice? With just a few simple words? Surely it was just the twenty years of abstinence. What other explanation was there?

"Your heat grips my fingers with such exquisite pressure," he continued, lips brushing the base of her neck, tongue dipping into the shallow hollow in her throat. "So tight, so wet. As if you were made for me and me alone. What will it feel like to sink my cock into this hot, wet sheath?" He traced a line up to her ear with the tip of his tongue, all the while slowly moving his fingers deeper into her. "To penetrate you completely?" He nipped her earlobe and flicked at the inner shell of her ear with his tongue. Twisting jolts of pleasure shot into her core, and a silent cry burst past her lips. A low chuckle vibrated in his chest and he pressed his mouth to her cheek. "Tell me how you think that will feel, Inari. Tell me what it will feel like to have my cock sink into your sweet, sweet pussy."

A gush of wet electricity erupted in her center. She threw back her head, the brutal orgasm taking her by force. Surprising her with its savagery.

Ezryn moved so quickly he was nothing but a blur. He loomed above her to tear her trousers from her legs and shove her thighs apart. He plunged his tongue into her dripping folds and lapped at her cream, curled his hands around her inner thighs to hold her open to his mouth.

She bucked, ramming her hips upward, the sudden feel of his teeth on her clit jolting another harsh orgasm from her. She snatched at the duvet again, anchoring herself to the bed for fear she would be lost to the raw pleasure consuming her. This wasn't right. This wasn't what was meant to happen. She was once succubus. *She* took the pleasure. She controlled it. Not her partner.

And yet, here she was.

She came again.

"Fuck!" Her cry shattered the silence of the room. She rammed her feet to his shoulders, her body on fire. Fire. Fire. She was on fire. Her very center was an inferno of sensations she'd never experienced before.

With a low moan, Ezryn lifted his head. "Dark Ones, I want to taste you." He dug his blunt nails into her inner thighs. A small smile, hesitant and wretched at once, played with his lips, revealing the whiteness of his teeth. Teeth, not fangs. "I shouldn't, but I do. I want to taste all of you."

She stared down her body into his midnight-ink eyes. Her two violent orgasms still echoed in her center, even as the thought of his fangs piercing her flesh rapidly built a third. She clenched her jaw, denying the insane want. "You will not bite me."

A red shimmer flashed in his stare. His nostrils flared. He slowly rose from between her legs. Sliding his hard body up hers, he pressed her back to the bed, pinning her to the mattress with his hips, his erection digging into the spread folds of her sex. "I *will* bite you, Inari. But only when you beg me to do so."

"Then you'll be waiting for a long time."

An ambiguous tension crossed his face. It was there and gone in less than a heartbeat. His eyes shimmered again. "I'm a vampire. I have all the time in the world."

Her pulse quickened, the thought of an eternity being pleasured by the master vampire almost undoing her. She shook her head again, forcing the intoxicating idea away. "Not if someone stakes you."

He chuckled, a low, arrogant rumble that made his cock nudge harder against her pussy. "Trust me, Sentinel, I will taste your blood before I am dusted. On that I give you my word."

She parted her lips, knowing she should tell him to go to hell, but he leaned back onto his knees before she could make a sound and gazed down at her with that same unreadable intensity. "I am cold to touch, Inari, but curse it, you make me burn inside."

Her gaze fell on his chest, on the sublime muscles coiled beneath his pale skin. A damp beat shuddered between her legs and she licked her lips, her fingers itching to touch his smooth perfection.

Your fingers? Don't you mean your lips? Your tongue?

Her blood roared in her ears. Her stomach knotted. She pushed herself upward from the bed, slid her arms around his butt and pressed her mouth to his chest.

His skin *was* cold. She knew it would be, but she wasn't prepared for the hot shard of excitement the icy temperature sent into her core. She sucked in a quick breath, and the subtle scent of still mist curled into her nose. She'd smelled many vampires before —their lifeless scent made them easy to track—but Ezryn's was different. It spoke of death and timelessness, and yet at the same time it spoke of unending energy and power.

The contradiction terrified and excited her.

She touched her tongue to his skin and he moaned, his hands fisting in her hair to hold her still. "I want you to suck my nipples," he stated, the waver in his voice making her pulse quicken.

She moved her mouth to his right one and flicked its hard point with her tongue. He hissed in a sharp breath, gripping her hair tighter. "I said suck."

His growled order should have made her angry. Instead, it aroused her more. God, what was it about Ezryn that made her so damn horny? So damn lustful?

She sucked.

"Yes." The word slipped from him in a ragged groan.

She sucked on his nipple harder, wanting to hear the word again. Wanting to hear the pleasure she gave him in his deep, growling voice.

"Fuck, yes," he moaned, the fists in her hair balling tighter still. "Your mouth feels so fucking good."

She moved her mouth to his left nipple and took it into her mouth.

He trembled. "Dark Ones, Inari. That feels so fucking good. How am I to..."

His words turned into a strangled groan and Inari's head swam. There was nothing stopping her destroying him now. He was at her complete mercy, and all she needed to do was rip his throat out. In the time it took him to press his hands to his severed neck, she could retrieve her stake from the floor and drive it into his chest. Piercing the exact spot on which she now pressed her lips.

"I can't," Ezryn moaned. "Dark Ones, I can't. Curse me, but I can't."

She pulled away from him, the tortured contempt in his voice stirring something in her soul. "Can't what?"

He closed his eyes and lifted his face to the ceiling. His jaw bunched. He loosened his fists in her hair. A little.

"What can't you do, Ezryn?" she asked, her breath shallow, her hands resting on his chest. She was so close to coming, and yet she had to know what he couldn't do. Her soul demanded it. As did her heart.

He stared at the ceiling, a low growl rumbling under her palms before he returned his gaze to her face, his eyes burning with an emotion she couldn't comprehend. As if he was haunted by something. Torn apart.

"I can't deny who I am, Sentinel. I can't deny *what* I am." He tightened his fists in her hair again. His eyes smoldered red heat. "What I want."

For a moment, he didn't move, his face etched with that strange, unreadable tension. And then, with a guttural snarl, he snatched her wrists in his fists and yanked her hands away from his body. "And what I want right now—" he shifted slightly, moving her empty hand to the junction of her thighs, "—is for you to touch yourself."

She stared at him, her gut telling her the words of his growled claim were not the words he'd intended to say. There was something else, something he kept from her.

Something dark and foreboding. Something that explained the haunted look in his eyes. Something that made her heart beat faster.

What have you got yourself into, Inari? What does he truly want?

"I told you," he murmured, pressing her fingers to the smooth mound of her sex. "I want you to touch yourself. Now."

Her body's aching want took over. Who was she to question him now when the need to touch herself ripped through her muscles? Her own body was powerless to deny his request.

Stare still locked on his, her wrists still gripped by his strong hands, Inari stroked her folds with her fingers. Another whimper vibrated low in her throat, and this one she could not hold back.

Ezryn's nostrils flared. "Fuck yourself with your fingers."

She did as he ordered, spearing one finger, two, three into her pussy. Tight muscles gripped them with greedy lust. She thrust deeper, Ezryn's inescapable hold on her wrist guiding her action, feeding the lascivious hunger consuming her.

"Harder," he growled.

She plunged her fingers into her sex. Ground her knuckle against her clit. Spears of exquisite pleasure shot through her body, and she whimpered. She was going to come. By her own hand.

He watched, his jaw bunched. "A depraved vampire would find other far more enjoyable uses for the silver stake you threatened me with, Sentinel."

A dark shiver rippled through her at the insinuation in his growled statement. Fear laced through her. Fear and something more powerful still. *God, Inari, could you refuse him if he told you to...*

"I am not depraved," he whispered, eyes flickering red desire. "Just..." His grip on her wrists lessened and he slid his hands up her arms, over her shoulders. "Keep fucking your hand until I tell you to stop."

She wriggled her fingers, pushing them deeper and higher into her sex, staring into his face as she did so. She was going to come again. Again, and he hadn't even penetrated her.

"Do not move," he murmured, lowering his head to the curve of her shoulder. Teeth scraped her flesh, just below her ear.

"Until I tell you to, you are not to do anything but fuck your hand." He brushed his lips against her throat, their cool softness like a brand on her flushed skin. "Fuck your hand and imagine it is my cock."

The command pushed her over the edge. She came, her sex slamming tight around her fingers, pulses of wet tension rocking her to the core. She cried out, arching her back, unable to control the shudders of carnal pleasure claiming her.

"Yes," he murmured, seconds before he hooked one arm around her waist and crushed his mouth to the base of her throat. He sucked on her neck, savage pressure sending shards of glorious pain into her body. Joining the spasms of her climax.

She cried out once more, engulfed by a pleasure so elemental she could not bear it. And still, she fucked her hand. Still, she worked her own sex with her fingers, Ezryn's lips on her neck, so close to her jugular it only heightened the wanton lust scorching through her.

Yes, yes, yes.

She closed her eyes, threw back her head. If he bit her now she could not stop him. Control had left her. Deserted her. Replaced instead with a need she could not understand.

Fangs scored her throat and she cried out again, bucking into her fingers, wanting them to be the master vampire's cock. She wanted him inside her. Stretching her. Filling her. Fuck, she wanted—

"Everything," Ezryn whispered into her ear. "You want everything I can give you." He shoved her back onto the bed, grabbed her wrists and pulled her hands from her sex. His cock jutted upward from his pubic hair, long, thick and rigid, its distended head bulbous and blood-purple. Inari gasped and her heart hammered against her breastbone. "Everything I am going to give you."

He moved above her, a dizzying blur of color. He grabbed one of her legs and jerked it upward, ramming his shoulder beneath her knee. She bit back her cry, fisting the sheets beneath her instead, unable to look anywhere else but his eyes. His burning, black eyes.

He grew motionless. Watched her.

Waited.

For her permission.

"Fuck me, Ezryn," she said, holding his stare.

With a curl of his lips, fangs flashing at her in the muted light, he slammed his hands beside her head and plunged his cock into her sex.

Searing heat claimed her. She arched her back, the action taking him deeper into her. His balls slapped her ass, and she heard him growl. The sound vibrated through his body and into hers seconds before he closed one hand over her right breast, palmed it, squeezed it. He pinched her nipple, hard, echoing the savage caress with his cock, thrusting into her with a rhythm both powerful and forceful. She rolled her head from side to side, every nerve ending in her body on fire.

"Dark Ones, you are so tight," he growled. "So fucking tight."

His nostrils flared and, with the same blurring speed that should have alarmed her, he dropped his head to her other breast and claimed its nipple with his mouth.

Wicked pleasure shot through her, straight into her core. She arched beneath him, scraped at his shoulders and his arms with her nails. A whimper sounded in her throat, raw and desperate. It had *never* been like this. Three hundred years of being a creature whose very existence demanded sex, and not once had it felt like this. Twenty years of denying herself that which her first three hundred years had solely required, and not once had she ever believed it would *feel* like this.

Rapture and completion and potent life. Unlike anything she'd experienced or remembered.

Teeth nipped at her nipple, sending exquisite pain into the pit of her belly, and she cried out. God, how did he make her feel so on fire?

Ezryn lifted his dark head and stared straight into her eyes. "Because I am your master."

"Fuck you," Inari gasped, angry tension knotting in her gut at his arrogance. Her body didn't care. A sizzling tension gripped her spine and her ass clenched.

"I can make you come by sucking your breasts, Sentinel," he murmured, his penetrations slowing. "I can stay embedded in your sweet pussy without moving, without letting *you* move, and make you climax just by sucking your nipples." His eyes flared red again, his shaft filling her with motionless possession. "Sucking them, pinching them, biting them." He curled his lips into a smug smile as she groaned. His fangs caught the room's light. "Would you like that? Would you like me to make you come that way?"

She glared at him, hating him even as her sex squeezed his unmoving cock buried deep in her drenched center. "You're an arrogant prick. You know that?"

He chuckled, the motion making his intimate occupation of her body jerk a little. The barely felt vibrations ricocheted through her body and, before she could bite her lips, a moan escaped her and her pussy pulsed.

Ezryn's nostrils flared again. "Yes. I do. And yet, we are still here. And you still want me. Want this."

His arrogance flayed her fraying control. She bared her teeth at him, willing his sexual enslavement of her body to hell. "Yes, I do. But that doesn't change anything. You may be the master of my body, you may be able to make me wet with just a single word, make me come with a single touch, but you are not the master of my mind. And my mind tells me everything about this is wrong."

"I don't believe you." His stare drilled into her, holding her imprisoned. "I can hear your thoughts, Inari. Remember? They whisper to me with such wanton hunger. Your mind wants the exact same thing your body wants—for me to make you mine."

"Screw you." The words burst from her in a strangled moan. She had to fight him. She *was* the master of her body, not him. He could not do this to her. "You don't hear all of them."

He chuckled again as if he found her futile rebellion humorous. "Your climax is close, Inari." He slipped his cock ever so slightly from her pussy. "I can feel it building." He withdrew a little more. "Mounting." His eyes shimmered red and a low growl rumbled deep in his chest. "Tell me you are scared of what you feel between us and I will let you come."

She hitched a ragged breath. Was this what it was like to be a prisoner to lust? To desire? Was this what her victims had felt when she was succubus?

Ezryn's cock penetrated back into her folds with slow force. "Tell me, Inari."

"Why?" She panted, every molecule in her body tuned to the connection of their sex. Straining, aching.

"Because I want to know."

She tried to move, tried to slide her pussy deeper down his cock. "So you can use it against me?"

"No."

The single word sounded...confused. She stared at him, hungering the feel of his penetration and hating herself for it.

Dark eyes looked back at her, an emotion she couldn't decipher flickering in their black depths. "Tell me," he whispered, "please."

"I am scared of this." The confession slipped from her before she could stop it.

His nostrils flared. "Don't be." He lowered his head, pressed his lips to her throat and thrust back into her sex with slow ease. "There is nothing to fear but denial." He withdrew again, an inch, another, another, before sinking up to his balls in a long stroke. His tongue touched her skin and she trembled, unable to do anything else. "Denying what this is, denying what it will become." His lips charted a line up to her ear, exploring the dip at her jaw with languid worship. "Tell me to bite you, Inari. With two little words from you, I can not only make you wet, I can make you mine."

Make you mine.

His statement flooded her with complete and utter happiness. And *that* petrified her. She could never be happy with a vampire. She couldn't let herself think otherwise.

Make you mine.

She had to stop this lunacy. Now.

She swung her fist into a tight curve, a mere heartbeat before he grabbed her wrist and pinned it to the mattress.

"Why did you do that?" he whispered, grinding her wrists to the bed beside her head.

"You know why," she snarled, her pulse pounding. She had to get away. She had to clear her head and gather her defenses. She had to—

"Because I scare you?" he whispered, fangs glinting. He shoved her legs wide with one knee, and she choked back a cry as the undeniable musk of her juices threaded through her breath. "Or because what I awake in you scares you?"

She glared at him. "Get off me, vampire."

Black eyes flickered red fire. "Is that what you truly want me to do?"

He smoothed his hand down her body, over her waist, skimming his fingers over the curve of her hip with teasing purpose. She shifted beneath him, trying to escape his touch, trying harder to make his cock sink deeper into her folds. Nothing made sense anymore. One moment she wanted to kill him, the next she was laughing with him, and now here she was wishing him to hell even as she wished he'd take her to heaven. "This is not right," she moaned.

His stare shimmered red heat again. "I know, but I don't want to stop."

"I..." She closed her eyes, a whimper catching in her throat. "I don't want you to either."

"Look at me."

His murmured command caressed her control. She opened her eyes and gazed up into his face.

He rolled his hips, sliding his cock farther into her heat with steady force until he was buried completely inside her. She pulled in a slow breath, arching into his thrust until she felt his balls against her ass cheeks, the feel of him stretching her to the limit already an addictive drug. "This can't be wrong," she moaned. "Not when you feel so right inside me. If we are meant to be enemies, why do you feel so right? How can fate treat us so cruelly?"

An unreadable tension pulled at his face. He grew still, his muscles tensing. For a split second, his expression contorted with wretched confusion and his eyes were haunted once more. Then a dark glint filled his eyes. "So, does this mean I've won, Sentinel?"

Inari frowned. "Won?"

His lips curled into a slow, cold smile. "I'm not dust, Inari, and in case you've forgotten, I pulled that silver stake of yours from your fingers and have been using your body for my own gratification since."

Cold shame punched into her stomach. Sickening and chilling. She glared at the man still buried in her sex. "You bastard."

His smile faded, his expression growing ambiguous. "It would seem so, wouldn't it?"

He snarled, punching his cock deeper still into her center, thrusting hard, fast. She cried out, a sound part human, part Sentinel. She arched her back, bucking her hips into his. Waves of pleasure crashed through her, swept her away. With every thrust, he took possession of her body. With every brutal stoke, he drove her closer to the precipice. She sank her teeth into her bottom lip, curled her fingers into fists, drove her nails into her palms. Fuck, she was drowning.

And still he continued to take her. There was no other way to describe it. He mauled one breast with his hand as he ravished the other with his mouth, sucking on her nipple so hard black blossoms of pleasurable pain erupted in her vision. A throb beat in her pussy. She moaned, overwhelmed by the savage aggression of his thrusts, by the raw pleasure each one created in her core.

She should be fighting him. She should be fighting what he was doing to her, what he'd awakened in her. Yet all she could do was stay alive. Stay alive and drown in the sensations claiming her. Marking her.

"Oh, God!" she called out, her body ablaze, her orgasm about to break. To consume her. "*Yes!*"

"*Yes!*" Ezryn growled, the hand on her breast closing harder, his fangs scraping her throat before, with a roar that made her stomach twist and her pussy contract, he threw back his head and lost all rhythm in his thrusts.

She felt his climax flood her sex. She cried out, her own detonating in perfect sync with his. "Damn you, you fucking vampire!" she screamed, bucking her hips into his frenzied thrusts. "Damn you, damn you, damn you!"

Liquid fire consumed her, stole her breath, devoured her. She cried out once more, a keening call of release echoed by Ezryn's deep, ragged groans.

"Damn us both, Inari," he rasped in her ear, the savage brutality of his possession fading, fading. His strokes grew slower, longer. Gentle. His hands slipped from her body to cup her face with tender care. "Damn us both, for I have no idea how I am to go on from here."

The proclamation sent a shiver up Inari's spine. She closed her eyes, his tortured voice and the reverent caress almost undoing her completely. Where *did* they go from here? What came next?

"Open your eyes, Inari."

She did as he asked.

He studied her face, wordless, brushing a loose strand of her hair from her forehead. She waited for him to say something, anything. Instead, he touched his lips to hers in a kiss so soft she caught her breath. She'd never been kissed so.

"Ezryn..." she began, but he shook his head, snuggling in beside her and pulling her to his body.

"Don't," he murmured. "Let's at least pretend for a while we're not what we are."

Tight pressure knotted around her heart, and she closed her eyes again, breathing in his scent. Yes, let them pretend for a while they were not what they were—demon and demon assassin. Let them have the moment.

And when the moment is over? What do you do then, Inari? What do you do if those random thoughts of yours Ezryn reads reveal what kind of demon you used to be? What do you do if you receive your next orders from the Deities and the bloodsucker still buried in your sex is to be destroyed? What will you do then?

She let out a slow breath and pressed herself closer to Ezryn's cool body. When that time came—*if* that time came—she would do what had to be done.

As she always had. Since her rebirth as an assassin of the order of Sentinel.

Until then...

"I will pretend," she whispered, sleep reaching for her with surprising strength. She surrendered to its embrace. Willingly.

Chapter Six

Ezryn felt Inari fall asleep before the muscles of her body told him she'd done so. Her breathing grew steady, even and deep, the fingers threaded through his grew relaxed, less fraught and tense. He lay motionless, his arm resting over her chest, enjoying the steady rhythm of her heart pumping her blood through her veins.

Dark Ones, he was confused.

Confused is an understatement. How about totally fucked in the head?

He let out a silent sigh. He'd fought his desire for her every second since he'd crossed her threshold. He'd followed her to her home to... Hell, he didn't know *why* he'd followed her. He just knew he'd been unable to let her run from him. He'd followed her to her home and found her on her bed, her hair a tousled mess, her face flushed, her breasts heaving with rage, and any thought of killing her had deserted him. Nothing mattered. Not that he'd entered her home without invitation, not that he had less than twenty-four hours to kill her, not that hundreds of vampires would be butchered if he didn't.

Nothing mattered but tasting her again, taking her again, filling her body with pleasure as he took his pleasure from her.

The moment he touched her, he knew. Knew he was in trouble. He'd lashed out, been cruel, spiteful, hating himself, hating where his desire for her had taken him. He'd fought himself and ultimately lost. And now he lay beside the very woman he was to kill while she slept in his arms.

She was warm to lie beside, soft where she should be, firm where she needed to be. Her ass, pressed so distractingly against his groin, was both smooth and hard. The muscles of her ass cheeks were sculpted from what he guessed was a lifetime of hard work.

All paranormal beings were born close to physically perfect for their genus, but that didn't mean they stayed that way. Too much hard living, careless health practices or indulgent decadence impacted a being's body just as it did a human's. His twin brother was a perfect example of that fact. Ezryn and Haral had been identical in every way until Haral stopped caring about anything else except indulging his most decadent appetites. The last fifty years of overindulgence had turned what was once a lean, muscled physique into something found in the medical journals under *obese*. The overlord's ass alone was wider than Ezryn had believed could ever be possible for a vampire.

Inari's ass spoke of dedication, determination and sweat. So did the rest of her, in fact. Her sinewy, womanly muscles were toned and trim and firm with latent strength. Whatever demon she had been before her rebirth as a Sentinel, he had little doubt she'd kept her body in sublime form. The power and force of her assassin's existence could not be solely responsible for such...perfection.

Aren't you still the slightest bit interested about what type of demon she was before her rebirth? Maybe you should ask her.

Ezryn shifted slightly on the mattress, pulling her closer to his body. He was still interested, although it made little difference to his already messed-up situation, and he would ask her. Just not now.

You could bite her. Taste her blood. You'd know exactly what kind of demon she was once her blood flows over your tongue.

His cock jerked a little at the idea, the base creature he was more than eager to do just that. She would kick his ass if he tried. She'd come very close earlier on. He'd been taken by surprise by her sheer strength and speed. He had little doubt the second his teeth touched her skin, she'd not only wake, but transform into her Sentinel form. He didn't want that. Truth be known, he was enjoying himself too much now watching her sleep in his arms.

A thought occurred to him and he chuckled softly. He was spooning. Who'd have thought he'd ever be spooning with a Sentinel? Not just spooning, but reveling in the position, in the closeness. Holding her like this as sleep rendered her calm and still, her neck exposed to him in a beautiful column of creamy skin...

His mouth filled with saliva, and he lifted his arm from across her chest to trace the tip of his index finger down the line of her neck, following the path he knew her carotid artery took hidden beneath her flesh. Waiting to be punctured by his fangs.

But you don't want to bite her, do you?

Ezryn let his gaze roam over her profile, the throb of her pulse a delicious beat under his fingertip. No, he didn't want to bite her. Well, yes, he did—his body hungered for the sensation of piercing her flesh with his teeth—but it was a purely physical response. He wanted to bite her but he didn't. Not until she wanted him to. And he knew she didn't. Not yet.

Dark Ones, he was making no sense.

Nothing makes sense about this. Nothing.

So why was he still here? Holding her? Why wasn't he biting her? Feeding from her?

Killing her? Just as he had been ordered to do by the overlord?

Dark guilt twisted through him and he closed his eyes. His time was running out. If he didn't end her existence by sunup tomorrow, Harry would begin the methodical slaughter of hundreds of innocent vampires.

And if he *did* kill her, he would never be able to hold her like this again. Was that what he wanted?

He bit back a silent growl, shutting the confusing jumble of questions out of his mind. At this very point in time, he didn't want to face the answers.

But you will have to. And very soon. You can't escape that, no matter how much you want to close your eyes, hold Inari close and stay this way until the sun sets again.

She sighed in her sleep, as if she too thought the idea agreeable, and wriggled her backside closer to his groin. Ezryn's cock twitched, and this time he couldn't stop his growl. He'd never been so fucked up. Nor so wanted to make love to a woman again.

Then wake her and do just that.

The suggestion, as dangerous as it was, was too appealing to ignore. He smoothed his palm over her ribcage, down her belly to her—

Inari jerked awake and slammed her elbow into his rib.

"Hey, hey, hey," he soothed, catching her wrist in his hand. Damn, she could hit hard. His side felt like it was on fire.

She snapped her stare to his face, her confused expression still glazed by sleep. "What..." she began, twisting on the mattress until her hip pressed against his stomach. "Did I doze off?"

He smiled, brushing a strand of her hair from her eyes. "You could say that."

She pulled a face, her nose wrinkling. "Damn it, I can't let that happen again."

Ezryn raised his eyebrows. "What?"

"Fall asleep with a vampire in my home."

He laughed, returning his hand to the flat plane of her belly just below her navel. "I'm not going to rob you, y'know."

She pulled another face. "That's not what I'm worried about."

"Ah," he said, nodding his head in mock seriousness. "I see. I won't bite you either."

"Ha!"

He gave her a level look. "Trust me."

A slight frown dipped her eyebrows as she studied him. He didn't say a word, and neither did she, but if his heart had been capable of beating, Ezryn knew it would have been thumping like a sledgehammer. He waited for her to say something. Instead, she rolled back onto her side and wriggled her body into the curve of his. "So, master vampire," she said, her voice the definition of deliberate off-handedness, "what do you do when you're not doing... whatever it is you do?"

He laughed, curled his arm around her waist and snuggled her closer to him. "I enjoy long, moonlit walks on the beach, Piña Coladas and getting caught in the rain. I'm not much into health-food junkies—their blood always tastes of kale—and I'm pretty certain I like making love at midnight." He laughed again, tightening his arm around her when she began to pull away from him. "Kidding. I'm kidding. Sorry." She relaxed, but not before she gave him a mocking, sideways look. He smiled and ran his hand over her hip. Dark Ones, it was so smooth, so warm. "I spend most of my nights observing," he said in all seriousness. "Listening."

"To what?"

He shrugged, for the first time conscious of the real lack of obvious purpose to his existence. "The world."

Unsettled discontent stirred in the pit of his gut. *Born to lead the vampire race, and you do nothing but protect it from afar.*

She didn't respond, and Ezryn found himself wishing for one of those inexplicable moments when he could hear what was going through her mind. When she stayed silent, he gave her a slight squeeze. "What about you? What are you doing when you're not watching skin shows at the Pleasure Palace?"

Another stretch of silence followed his question before she said, "Movie marathons. Specifically, cult musicals."

The answer, completely not what he'd expected, made him laugh. For the third time. When had he laughed so often so quickly? "Cult musicals? As in—"

"*Rocky Horror Picture Show, Little Shop of Horrors, This Is Spinal Tap, Mamma Mia,*" she finished for him, and he could hear the self-deprecating mirth in her voice.

"So you go to these movie marathons by yourself?"

She made a noncommittal sound. "Sometimes."

A wave of jealousy crashed over him at the idea of Inari sitting in a dark movie theatre with someone else, their arms sharing a seat armrest, their knees close to touching. Tight, hot and undeniable jealousy. "Sometimes?"

It was her turn to shrug. The action made her breasts move against his arm in such a way his head spun. "Sometimes."

The urge to press her to her back, pin her to the mattress and make her tell him who she went to the cinema with and where he could find them surged through him. He almost did. Until he felt her laughing. Silent shakes vibrated through her body into his. Tiny quakes that not only made his head spin but his cock twitch. "What so funny?" he growled, the turmoil of unprecedented emotions churning in his gut irritating him.

"I just had an image of you sitting in a movie theatre dressed in a black corset, suspenders and fishnets singing 'The Time Warp' at the top of your voice and throwing popcorn at the screen."

"Right," he muttered. "That's it." And he yanked her onto her back, slid atop her body and kissed her.

She kissed him back without hesitation or delay. She snaked her arms up around his neck, and her lips parted to his tongue.

The candor of her response sent him reeling. He'd kissed her many times since finding her in the Pleasure Palace, but never once had she been so straightforward, so immediate in kissing him back. She slanted her lips over his and her tongue mated with his, purposeful and confident. Gone was the battle he knew had waged within her from the second he'd touched her flesh. Gone was the fierce determination to fight the chemistry between them. She kissed him, wholly and totally, fisting her hands in his hair in a grip far from tender, wrapping her legs around his.

He groaned, more than a little stunned, a lot more than a little turned on. The woman in his arms, the woman who enjoyed cult musicals and could decimate a demon with her bare hands, wasn't just a woman of sublime sensuality. She was a sexual force to be reckoned with.

Dark Ones, he loved it.

And still I have to kill her.

He refused the thought, deepening the kiss instead. She arched beneath him, sliding her foot up the back of his leg to his ass, down to his calf and back up again. The simple sensation of her ankle rubbing over his cool flesh sent wicked pulses of lust into his belly, and he tore his mouth from hers, hungry to taste more of her. Before he could capture her breasts in his hands however, before he could claim one rock-hard nipple with his mouth, she growled and flipped him onto his back.

She straddled his hips, staring down at him through heavy-lidded eyes, her thick, black lashes hiding all but the tiny glint of her emerald-green irises. "Touch me," she ordered, a very small, very cheeky smile curling the edges of her mouth. "I so want to feel dirty right now."

Ezryn recognized a lyric from one of the musicals she'd confessed to enjoying in her command, but the waves of pleasure rolling over him at her sudden assertive turn destroyed any hope of remembering the next line. Or maybe it was the way she looked.

He gazed up at her. She was beautiful. So beautiful. "Fuck, you are gorgeous."

Her smile stretched wider. "Thank you." She leaned closer to his body and curled her fingers around his wrists, raising his hands to her breasts. "Now, touch me."

He did as she told him, for the first time in his seven hundred years taking orders from a sexual partner. He flattened his palms over each heavy swell of flesh, massaging them, kneading them with growing pressure. She moaned and her eyes fluttered closed for a brief moment. "Oh..."

He bent upward, determined to capture one of her nipples with his mouth, but she pushed him back to the mattress, curling her lips in an entirely too sexy grin. "Not yet," she stated with a quick shake of her head. She rolled her hips, stroking her sex up the length of his erection. Her wet sex. "Touch me."

He returned his hands to her body, sliding them up her ribcage, over her breasts and back down to her hips. He closed his fingers around them, tugging her a little forward, desperate to align her pussy with his cock. She relinquished control—for exactly half a second, the folds of her sex parting to the domed head of his dick— before squeezing her thighs together and shaking her head once again. "Not yet."

Ezryn laughed, even as his body began to ache with undeniable want. He flashed his fangs at her, smoothing his palms down the length of her thighs, following her calves to her ankles. Circling each one in a loose grip, he levered his body upward again, feathering his lips over the base of her throat. The throb of her pulse beneath her fine, delicate skin made his mouth fill with saliva, and he felt his fangs lengthen. Dark Ones, he could bite her now. He could—

Kill her. Or Harry will destroy your—

She pushed him back to the bed, a glint in her green eyes. She raised herself slightly from his hips and he groaned, the loss of her damp heat pressed to his cock beyond painful. Without a word, she extended her body, hovering just above him on all fours, her gaze holding his as her nipples brushed two tormenting lines up his chest. He groaned again, cock jerking, balls aching.

"Touch me," she whispered, her lips level with his.

He did as she ordered, skimming his hands from her legs up to her ass cheeks. He explored each one, reveling in the toned muscles bunched under her flawless skin. *Not just hours of hard work and dedication,* he thought, running his fingers over her butt. *Centuries. An ass this perfect comes from a lifetime of hard work. A lifetime of sweat and...*

He dipped his fingers in the cleft between each cheek, finding the puckered hole of her anus, and he lost the train of thought. Oh, what would it be like to penetrate her there?

"Not yet." Inari's whisper, barely audible in her trembling moan, filled his cock with new desire and agonizing anticipation.

Nostrils flaring, jaw clenched, he moved his hands from her ass and slid them up the line of her spine to the defined angles of her shoulder blades. He gazed up at her, the featherlike caress of her nipples on his chest driving him insane. If he wanted to, he could yank her to his body and thrust his cock into her pussy. His arms already circled her, and she was in such a tenuous position, suspended as she was above him by only the strength of her hands and knees. He could yank her to his body and drive his length into her sex, burying himself in her tightness in one swift move.

And then sink your fangs into her neck and drain her until she is an empty, lifeless shell.

He ground his teeth, anguished conflict drilling into his chest. No.

Are you really going to sacrifice hundreds of vampires, those who declared their loyalty to you in the face of Haral's wrath, for a Sentinel? An assassin of the Highest of Powers? The born enemy of your kind?

Yes.

No.

Dark Ones, all he wanted to do was forget who they both were, what they both were and make love to her until they were too weak to move.

He ran his hands over her back and then to the side swell of her hanging breasts. For the moment, she was in charge, and he loved every minute of her control. Admired it. Was turned on by it.

He brushed the back of his knuckles over the outer curve of each breast, watching her face. She gazed back at him, her breath ragged. Shallow. Still, she didn't move, the heat of her body, so close to his and yet a world away, stimulating the ancient vampire he truly was. He'd never released that side of himself during sex. Not once in his seven hundred years, but at this very second, he wondered how much longer he could contain it. For as long as he could remember, the demonic creature he truly was hungered for only one thing—blood. Tonight, it hungered for something more. And she rested above him on all fours, the musk of her juices a heady perfume on the air as she watched his face with unreadable eyes.

Not much longer. I can't last much longer.

He moved his hands to capture her breasts completely, squeezing each one with a force he knew was not gentle. She sucked in a sharp breath, her eyelids fluttering closed, her pulse quickening. The potent power of her blood surged through her veins. He could feel it. Dark Ones, it was beautiful.

"Touch me," she whispered once more.

A spasm of base need claimed his cock at the raw urgency in her voice. He understood it all too well. He'd never been so strung out, like a bleeder junkie craving a blood hit. Except it wasn't blood he craved. It was Inari's body, her sex, her pleasure. Her desire.

Curse it, Ezryn Navarro. What are you thinking?

He wasn't. He was existing purely on instinct. A state he'd never allowed himself to be in.

Studying her face, her eyes still closed, her lips parted, he smoothed his palms up the column of her throat, wanting to feel her pulse beat against his hand. Wanting to feel her life against his flesh.

Her life in his hands.

She opened her eyes and gazed down at him. The white fire burning in their once green depths should have petrified him. They were the eyes of a Sentinel, ablaze with righteous, divine power. It should have petrified him. But it didn't. Not at all.

"Fuck me," she said. "Now."

He rolled her to her side, raking one hand down to the back of her knee and tugging on it. She complied, her pussy lips spreading with the extension of her leg as her musk filled the air.

Giddy, he skimmed her rib cage and flat belly with his hands, followed the edge of her hipbone and then traveled the delicious line where her thigh met her lower belly. He brushed his fingers over the velvet junction and his head swam, his mouth filling with fresh saliva. She gasped softly at the contact and he moaned.

Don't rush. Don't—

But it seemed she was impatient. Reaching up, she curled her fingers around his wrist and guided his hand deeper toward her very center, her eyes holding his.

"We've got forever to take it slow, Ezryn." Her voice was husky. Strained.

Her creamy heat wrapped around his delving, seeking fingers, driving him to the very edge of madness. She pulled in a deep breath, her chest swelling, her breasts rising upwards as she received his fingers' gentle attention. Her hand left his wrist, and she skimmed her own fingers along his arms, splaying over his unbeating heart before trailing down to the jutting pole of his cock.

He moved his hand, twisting and probing, brushing the pad of his thumb over the tiny button of flesh hidden in the folds of her sex. She gasped again, arching her back and pushing her hips harder into his hand. "Don't stop," she ordered in a whisper. He curled his fingers, aiming for the sweetest spot deep in her tight, slick channel. "Oh, Ezryn!" She thrust her hips forward. The musky scent of her passion filled each breath he drew. Scalding heat licked through him, charging his body into life beyond the physical.

Nothing but Inari existed.

His eyes fell to the pulse in her neck, fluttering with frenzied life. Lowering his head, he placed his lips lightly against that wicked beat, touching the tip of his tongue to it.

She tasted so good. And it was his undoing.

Control deserted him.

His mouth crushed hers, plundering and demanding. She tangled her fingers in his hair, balling them into painful fists that made his blood sing with need. With each stab of his tongue into her mouth, he thrust his fingers deeper into her wet pussy, her creamy passion slicking his skin. Driving him wild. She moved against him, hips writhing under his hand, rotating against his palm.

Dark Ones. Yes. Her heat and smell and taste invaded his mind. *Yes.*

Flattening her to her back, he rested on his palms above her, reversing the very position they'd held but a moment ago.

"There's no going back from this, Inari. No matter what is demanded of us, there's no going back. No matter what we want, or what must be, there'll be *this* forever." The statement left him on a growl, each word and syllable cut with conflicted certainty. He had to kill her, he knew that. But he couldn't, and he knew that too. Which left him nowhere but wracked with tortured suffering and consumed with pure pleasure.

"Forever," she repeated on a breath, her eyes smoldering white fire.

Liquid heat shot straight into his groin. His balls.

He gazed down at her, wanting the unobtainable. Wanting her. Just her. "As it is," he whispered. "And as it will be."

He lowered himself to her body. His hipbones brushed hers, their heat mingling as his stomach slid over the flat plane of hers. She shifted, raising her right leg to wrap it around his hip as she curled her fingers around his neck. There was a mutual thrust, and he felt her sweet heat wrap around him, folding around his rigid length with tight, wet pressure.

"By the cursed ones, Inari, I can't..." he ground out.

"Oh God, Ezryn!"

The gasp left her lips in a sharp breath and, before she could draw another, he thrust inside her again, his head filling with colors so intense he felt blinded.

She was everywhere. She surrounded him.

Their bodies moved together, a rhythm that was natural and elemental, driving Ezryn toward a precipice that was both terrifying and sheer ecstasy. He would never recover from this. Ever.

Explosive heat erupted in his body, its epicenter the very point where Inari's heat engulfed him. Tight and wet. Just as her name burst from his lips, he heard her call his in a voice that shook with released power. He felt his seed pump into her. He felt her sex contract, squeezing his shaft in pulsing pressure.

Kissing her shoulder, her neck and her jaw, he returned his gaze to her face. He'd wanted for it to last so much longer. He'd wanted to show her just how much he could pleasure her, to fill her with the same powerful, passionate rapture that engulfed him, but when he'd felt her sliding around him so completely...

He opened his mouth, not sure what he was going to say, but she placed a soft kiss on his lips, stopping him.

"If you apologize for that I think I will hit you," she whispered. A lazy smile curled her lips, swollen from his kisses. "Or turn you to dust."

"I won't apologize," he replied, not withdrawing from her body's intimate hold. "But I promise it'll be slower next time."

She chuckled. "Sure sure."

He raised an eyebrow. "You don't believe me?"

Her lips twitched. "Prove it."

He moved his hips, dragging his hands down her back to cup her ass. "Prove it?" he growled, moving against her as his desire flooded strength back into his rapidly growing length. "Now?"

Her fingernails drew lazy lines along his spine. "Now."

She gripped his shoulders and pulled his head to hers, her lips capturing his in a kiss that sent liquid fire through his cold body. Without words, they rolled, moving as one until he lay on his back and she straddled him. He looked up at her, finding her face flushed in heady passion and her eyes burning green fire. Marveling at the satiny smoothness of her golden skin, the finely toned strength of her body, he brushed his hands over the firm flatness of her stomach.

He'd never known anyone like her, had never wanted to know anyone the way he knew her. He traced the delicate line of her stomach muscles with a slow fingertip. "You're gorgeous." It was the absolute truth.

"So are you," she replied, her fingers making their own wicked way over his torso. When they found their way to his nipples and circled each with tantalizing pressure, his head spun, a single sharp breath catching in his throat. Such a simple touch, and yet it was like being branded by an angel.

Not an angel. A Sentinel. One you are meant to kill.

He bit back a curse. He was her property, her possession, and he wouldn't have it any other way. Come hell or high water or holy battle.

Ever so softly, she drew her fingertips across the tightening tip of his nipple, a small smile pulling at her lips as she watched and felt his response. Her eyes flicked to his, that iridescent fire still blazing in their depths and, with deliberate slowness, she lowered her head, capturing one of his rock-hard nipples with her teeth as she slowly rolled her hips against his. Ezryn gasped, a spasm of concentrated pleasure ripping through him. He curled his fingers around her hips, holding her against him as he rose to meet her body's demands. "Dark Ones, Inari," he groaned, his throat tight and raw.

She lifted her head—slightly—a thin stream of cool breath playing over his skin as she gently blew against the nipple her tongue had only just tasted. The effect was instantaneous and all consuming, and Ezryn could control himself no more.

Growling, he flipped her onto her back and thrust deeper into her. Deeper. Deeper.

"Ezryn," she breathed, her hips undulating in perfect rhythm with his, taking him completely and utterly.

His mouth found the perfect, tight peak of her breast and he flicked his tongue against it, her throaty cries of pleasure filling the room, exciting him even more. She arched her back, pressing her nipple harder against his lips. "Don't stop," she begged, voice husky. "By the Powers, please don't stop."

So he didn't.

Pulling the puckered tip of her breast farther into his mouth, he nipped at it with his teeth, the sound of Inari's resulting gasp and the taste of her sweet flesh almost driving him insane.

He dragged his lips across her flesh, replacing his mouth on her abandoned breast with his hand. The heavy swell of flesh under his fingers was soft, pliable to the touch. He squeezed it in rhythm with his suckling mouth, enjoying the way Inari writhed and moaned under his touch.

"Ezryn."

She raked her hands down his back, scoring lines of painful pleasure over his skin. She shoved her hips up harder, meeting his penetration, her fingernails sinking into his flesh as she locked her legs around his body. Holding him close.

The silent demand was too much. Exquisite heat began to tear through his lifeless veins. His balls tightened. Lifting his head, he stared down into her face, seeing her pleasure in her eyes, on her lips. "I can't hold on much longer, Inari." His breath was short. Shallow. "Dark Ones, I don't know what you've done to me, but I can't hold on much longer."

White eyes flashed. "Then don't." She dragged her nails up his back, digging into his shoulders, her breath hot and moist against his neck. When her teeth found his flesh, nipping with superb pressure, a hot tidal wave crashed through him, scorching him like a river of molten lava.

He thrust into her, and she took it all.

Her back bowed and her hips drove hard. When he thought he could survive no more, that he was going to be totally consumed by the searing heat rolling through him, she gasped, her body gripping him in pulsating spasms as she cried his name.

His own release surged from him like an eruption of molten fire. Draining him utterly. Filling him completely.

They lay in silence for a long moment, Ezryn staring at the ceiling, his undead heart heavy. As if the organ thrummed full with energy and life. Letting his head drop to the side, he ran his gaze over Inari's face, smiling at the completely sated expression softening her features. Her eyes were closed, but a small smile played on her lips, and Ezryn felt his own smile stretching his mouth.

"Ezryn?" Her voice was soft, almost a whisper.

"Yes?"

"Thank you."

"For what?"

She gently rolled onto her side, tucking her hands under her head as she studied him. "Y'know." A delicate blush began to color her cheeks and she closed her eyes again.

He chuckled quietly. "Any time."

"Hmm. I'll keep you to that."

"Okay."

She smiled at him, and Ezryn could not miss the utter contentment that softened her features. He smiled back, slipping his arm around her waist and pulling her closer to his body. He didn't want her even that far from him.

She wriggled around a bit before turning onto her other side, pressing her butt to his groin. He bit back a groan, the contact stirring forces deep within him. His demon, his lust, his desire. He closed his eyes, cupping her breast with gentle care as he pressed his face to the back of her hair. Contented. He'd never felt more contented. Or relaxed, and while that notion should have worried him, it didn't.

He smiled against the soft, cool strands of Inari's hair, her heart beating against his palm, her bottom pressed to his groin.

And fell asleep.

* * *

The demon moved his hands up her arms, a lame attempt to tug her closer to his repulsive body. Disgust rolled in her belly, and she pushed him away. "Don't be absurd."

"You're saying no?"

Inari pulled a face, rubbing at her flesh where his clammy hands touched her. "Of course I'm saying no."

Watery-blue eyes narrowed, and the empathic leech demon stepped closer to her again. Invading her personal space. "Why?"

The putrid stench of his excreting body oil turned the air to a cloying mist, making her almost gag. Dark Ones, he was repugnant.

She cocked an eyebrow, letting her revulsion and distaste show on her face. "Why? Does 'you're not my type' mean anything?"

He lifted his own eyebrows, genuine surprise filling his face. "But you're a succubus. Anything with a dick is your type, and my dick is fucking huge."

The disgust in her belly rolled again and she ground her teeth, resisting the urge to slam her fist into the leech's ugly face. "I am a succubus. Which means I can fuck whomever I want." She flicked her gaze to his crotch and curled her lip. "Besides, something tells me I've had human males with bigger dicks than yours."

The leech stared at her, eyes wide. Angry. "I am a second-order demon. My power grows exponentially with the fear I create in these men you speak of. I can turn a human man to a blubbering baby with a single image in his mind. I am more powerful than you—a mere sex demon—could ever hope to be." He leaned forward, and she curled her nose at the sickly sweet stench seeping from his body. "Are you saying you'd rather fuck a human for simple pleasure than me? One of your own kind?"

She laughed, the sound dismissive. "We may both be second-order demons but that does not make us the same kind. You're a para-site. I'm an artist. You feed on your victims using fear and torture and infantile mind tricks. I feed on mine using sheer rapture and bliss and sexual ecstasy. You give them terror, I give them lust."

"I can give you lust." He reached for her again. "One little subliminal image in your mind, and you will soon be moaning for more."

Her stomach rolled. She took a step back, shaking her head. "You even think about planting something in my mind, and I'll rip your dick off and shove it down your throat."

The leech blanched, his eyes narrowing to slits. "So you're saying no?"

"I'm saying get-the-hell-away-from-me no. If you want to experience the ultimate in sexual pleasure, leechy-boy, you're going to have to find a succubus with really low standards. Or a really expensive human whore, 'cause frankly, I'm just not that hungry."

With one last shake of her head and a repulsed snort, she turned and walked away from him, amazed he'd even approach her. Her. The most successful succubus the Realm had known since Lilith. What was he thinking? It seemed the Dark Ones were letting any old freak monster be elevated to the second order these days. Sheesh, before she knew it, the upper levels of the Realm would be overrun with freaking demons suffering delusions of grandeur, and she'd have to move to the freaking world of man just to get some—

Inari's eyes snapped open, her blood roaring in her ears as she jerked herself awake. The empathic leech demon? Had she just dreamed about the empathic leech demon?

She lay motionless on her side, her heart hammering. The ghost of the dream still reverberated through her soul, making her stomach roll. Why in all the levels of hell was she dreaming of the leech demon she'd rejected centuries ago?

Because you're feeling guilty?

She closed her eyes and pulled a deep breath, trying to calm her frantic pulse. She'd refused to think of the leech demon who'd killed Tianya. She'd banished the memory of the despicable bastard to the darkest depths of her mind where it couldn't send her insane with guilt. She had to. If she hadn't, she would have lost her mind by now. She was more than half convinced Tianya's constant presence in her life was that very insanity fighting to claim her. Was her subconscious trying to tell her something now?

Or *was* it her guilt?

Her chest tightened. What did it mean?

You just fucked a vampire, Inari. After twenty years of abstinence for fear of awakening your succubus force, you fucked a demon more powerful than any you've met before. Not just fucked him, but surrendered to him. And then fell asleep in his arms. What do you think it means?

Succubus.

The word whispered through her mind and her mouth went dry.

Oh, no. Please...no...

A cool arm like solid marble slid over her hip and she started, flinching at Ezryn's touch.

Calm down. Calm.

Keeping her body motionless, she twisted her head to the side, casting him a quick look. He was asleep, eyes closed, face relaxed. Calm.

What kind of vampire sleeps like that, Inari? There's nothing corpse-like about him. What kind of vampire sleeps like a human?

She didn't know, but then nothing about Ezryn made any sense to her.

Breath held, she slipped from his loose embrace, sliding from her bed with silent movements. She had to get away from him. Until she could work out what the hell was going on, she had to get as far away from him as she could. Now.

Crossing her room, she snatched up her discarded clothes and hurried to the door, her pulse a thumping hammer in her neck. She'd get dressed and go find Ven Watkins. She needed help. As much as she hated to admit it, she needed help, and the supreme Sentinel was the closest thing she had to family. If it weren't for her, his brother would be dead now and his soul most likely the plaything of Satan. Why the First Horseman of the Apocalypse had sent her to kill the boy all those years ago, she didn't know, nor care, but that didn't change a thing. He *had* sent her, she *hadn't* killed the boy and now Watkins owed her. Big time. And she'd start with demanding some answers.

What answers are those, exactly? Are you still Sentinel now you've slept with the enemy? Are you succubus again? Can you keep fucking a vampire?

The rustle of cotton behind Inari killed the unnerving thought and she turned, expecting to see Ezryn's black gaze locked on her. Instead, he was stretched out on his stomach, eyes closed, just as still as he'd been before. Just as relaxed.

By the Deities, he's gorgeous.

Inari turned away from the far too confusing sight and exited her bedroom. She pulled on her clothes in record time, for the first time squeezing into her skin-tight black leather pants and zippered bustier with little effort. She bit back a snort. Fate was an ambiguous bitch sometimes. If she didn't know any better she'd swear she was meant to get out of her apartment in a hurry.

Now you're just being melodramatic, Inari. Get out, find Ven and get some answers.

Who knew, she might be getting worked into an emotional state over nothing. Ven Watkins might shrug those impossibly broad shoulders of his, flash her one of his ambiguous half smiles and tell her she could sleep with whomever she wanted as long as it didn't interfere with her work.

Her belly flip-flopped a little at the notion. It would make her life far less complicated. Or even more so.

Slipping her house key into her back pocket, she crossed the threshold and closed the door behind her. Locking it. None of her neighbors were stupid enough to try and enter her apartment without her permission—they'd worked *that* situation out the night she put the obnoxious jerk on the fifth floor in hospital for trying to catch her in the shower the week she'd moved in—but better to be safe than sorry. It was almost sundown. Until the sun dropped below the horizon, Ezryn was vulnerable.

Vulnerable? What, now you're worried about his wellbeing? Looking out for his safety? For the love of God, woman, you are messed up.

"Oh, just shut up, will you," she muttered, descending the stairs two at a time.

Forty seconds later, she was outside her apartment complex, the swarm of tourists and locals flowing around her over the footpath. She pulled in a slow breath, all too aware of the nervous knot forming in her chest. She'd never approached Ven on such a personal mission. In fact, with the exception of a very short conversation a few years ago, she hadn't swapped words with him at all. He'd approached her where she'd sat on the steps of the Sydney Art Gallery trying to come to terms with the target she'd just been assigned by the Deities, a succubus who was draining adolescent boys on the outskirts of Sydney. Inari had yet to kill the succubus despite having the order for over an hour.

Ven had ascended each step with a steady stride until he'd stopped directly before her. His green eyes had shimmered an almost blinding white before he'd sat down beside her without greeting

"Feels weird, doesn't it?" he'd said, his voice a deep rumble she'd felt in the pit of her stomach.

"What does?" she'd whispered, still in shock from the surreal events of only an hour earlier.

"Killing one of your own," he'd answered. "Or at least, killing what you used to be."

His statement had snapped her spine straight. "What are you talking about?"

He'd chuckled. "I'm an Agent of the Order, Inari Chayse. A Sentinel. A pretty important one, in fact. Let's call me a supreme Sentinel. It means I know everything."

His statement had made her stomach clench. "A *supreme* Sentinel?"

He'd nodded. "Family connections. Now tell me, why do you question your target?"

She'd shaken her head in reply. "Not question. Just..." She'd floundered for words, her belly a knot of conflict. "How am I to destroy a succubus? What makes me better than her?"

Ven's smile had been warm. "Your soul makes you better. And the choices you have made since the day you earned it."

He'd studied her, waiting for something. Whatever it was, she hadn't given it to him. With a sigh, he'd shaken his head. "You know what you are, Inari. You know what you have. Don't fight your soul. Don't doubt it, either. The big guy would not have bestowed it upon you if He didn't believe you were worthy of it. Trust me, I know." He'd grinned at her. "Being a Sentinel isn't easy, but it does have its perks. Don't worry. You're meant for this life. Your soul is strong."

She'd let out a ragged breath, his words stirring the sleeping force within her. She *was* Sentinel. She was the Highest's assassin. She hunted and destroyed any demon or non-human malevolent being whenever commanded. From the moment she'd gained her soul, she'd been tapped in to the Deities and followed their commands. She hadn't questioned who They were—somehow she'd known. They were the counterpoint divine immortal beings to the Dark Ones. She'd spent her entire succubus existence obeying the commands of the Dark Ones and the second she'd gained her soul, she obeyed the Deities instead. She'd known all those things and more without question.

Destroying a succubus like she had once been wasn't just her job now. It was righteous.

She could do it. She would gladly do it.

With a silent nod, Ven had straightened to his feet, his eyes green once again. "You'll do fine," he'd said.

He'd walked away from her then, the crowd of tourists on the art gallery steps parting before him.

"Wait!" she'd shouted, jumping to her own feet. "What's your name?"

"Ven Watkins," he'd called back over his shoulder.

It had taken but a second for the relevance of the name to sink into Inari's shocked stupor, but when it did, she'd blinked.

And in that split moment of blindness, Ven had vanished. She'd never seen him again in Sydney, though she knew he was still around. She'd tried to contact him a few times, to no avail, but after three years or so she'd just accepted the fact he was out there, somewhere, and she was on her own.

She'd never needed him until now. She'd never questioned her new existence. Until now.

What would she do if Ven told her she had to kill Ezryn? What would she do if—

A familiar prickling sensation razed the back of her neck and she froze.

Demon.

The same demon.

Again.

Inari spun around, scanning the crowd around her, beyond her. The sinking sun cast the area in reaching shadows, only a few of the store fronts and souvenir shops illuminated by their neon lights and flashing displays. Outside the strip clubs, the hawkers had started to do their thing, calling out to the passing pedestrians, regaling anyone who cared to listen—and most who didn't—of the erotic joys that waiting within. A few cast her an interested inspection, no doubt in part due to her far-from-chaste attire, one even offering her a sly wink. As before, no one stood out as the reason for the prickling heat on her neck. No one waved their arms and shouted, "You-hoo! Demon right here!"

But even in hidden obscurity, the demon was definitely here. Watching her. Just outside her home.

Cold anger flowed through her. Her home. The bastard knew where she lived. Deep within her Sentinel soul, the assassin inside her stirred. Waiting at her home changed the situation completely. She wasn't searching for him anymore, waiting for him to come to her. Now she was hunting him. In earnest.

Incinerating black heat shimmered over her, turning her pale flesh as pitch as midnight for the briefest of moments. She suppressed the sudden urge to transform, instead forcing her muscles to relax. Apart from the hawker who'd given her a wink, no one around her seemed to have noticed the weird blackness that had rippled over her body. The hawker stared at her, his mouth hanging open, his eyes wide. She ignored his reaction. With luck, he'd pass it off as a surreal hallucination brought on by bad crack or too much pot.

With a quick shake of her head, as if dismissing something inconsequential, she began walking through the crowd, heading northeast. She needed to draw the stalking demon away from humans. The Royal Botanic Gardens were thirty minutes north of where she was, the one hundred and thirty hectares of display gardens hugging the harbor's edge behind the Sydney Opera House. By the time she got there the sun would be completely behind the horizon, turning the massive parkland with its minimal lighting, ambling walking tracks and ancient trees and bushes into the perfect place for an ambush. Locals never ventured into the gardens after dark, and the tourists would be too busy with the beauty of the Opera House at night to wander into the shadow-heavy, unknown park.

She'd lure the demon to the gardens, allow him to confront her there and deal with the situation once and for all.

Keeping her pace steady but purposeful, she weaved through Kings Cross, sticking to the busiest streets. Keeping to the populated areas meant the demon would be less likely to attack.

If that indeed was what he'd intended to do.

What else would it be, Inari? You think he wants to discuss global warming?

She ignored the question.

The lights and thrum of Kings Cross gave way to the opulence of Woolloomooloo. It was just as busy, but with an entirely different class of pedestrian moving over the footpaths. The cafes here all exuded a pretentious air, those sitting in the designer chairs sipping their soy lattes and espressos wrapped in a conceited attitude of superiority. There were no strip clubs to be seen in Wool-loomooloo, rather subdued restaurants, boutique galleries and heritage-listed pubs lined the streets, all so trendy as to defy good taste in Inari's opinion. Rows of BMWs, Audis and Jags sat in silent luxury by the kerbs, waiting on their owners to sink themselves into their leather interiors and zoom off into the night. More than one Australian celebrity called Woolloomooloo home, but the only malevolent beings Inari had ever encountered in the suburb were bored trophy wives sharpening their perfectly manicured nails on gossip.

She didn't slow her stride as she made her way through the designer-dressed crowd. The briny tang of Sydney Harbor had begun to filter into every breath she took, tickling her sinuses and making her mouth a tad salty, which could only mean the Botanic Gardens were close. Very close.

Inari lengthened her stride, trying to not look like she was in a hurry.

As soon as the shadows engulfed them she had no doubt the fun would begin, and to be honest, she was sick of the burning itch on the back of her neck.

Just out of interest, have you noticed your neck doesn't prickle when Ezryn is near? Or looks at you? What does that mean, hmm?

Inari rolled her eyes and walked faster. Could she not go a whole fifteen minutes without thinking of the damn bloodsucker?

Obviously not. Still, why doesn't your neck burn when he is—

She shut the thought down, grinding her teeth as she rounded a corner. The last corner before her destination spread out before her —the Royal Botanic Gardens, an area perfect for an ambush. Dark, bushy. Full of hidden nooks and crannies, massive overhanging branches.

And unpopulated.

Without slowing down, she entered the parkland, leaving the revealing lights and bustling activity of the city streets behind her. The sun had sunk far enough below the horizon to shroud everything in ash-gray shadows and gloomy light, making it difficult to see beyond a few feet.

Adrenaline coursed through Inari's veins, its force heightened by her Sentinel soul and power. Every muscle in her body drew tight, ready to fight. Every fiber in her body welcomed it. She needed this diversion. She really did. She needed to bring pain to something bad, something evil. So much more than she wanted to acknowledge.

The night air turned moist, sweet with the scents of an entire world of different flora all growing in one area. English roses, native lilies, exotic cherry blossoms, hardy desert blooms and pungent herbs all mingled together, turning each breath she took into a smorgasbord of sensory stimulation that would have made her smile if not for her rather insidious purpose for being here. Beneath her feet, the smooth concrete path gave way to gravel. The sound of her boots crunched against the rough stones shattering the peaceful silence. A bird burst from a nearby callistemon, screeching its protest at being disturbed as it flew away.

Inari continued deeper into the gardens, keeping her shoulders loose and her stride casual. The hulking building of the New South Wales Art Gallery sat to her far left, aglow with warm orange light. She veered right, putting more distance between herself and the building. At this time of night the gallery was closed, but that didn't mean she wanted to risk some foolish tourist admiring the building or a late-night worker stumbling upon her as she fought with the—

Something slammed into her back, hard, smashing her to the ground at the exact second the back of her neck erupted in a raging inferno.

"Finally got you alone, cunt."

The guttural snarl sank into her ear, familiar and repulsive at once, the putrescent stench of cloying decay flaying the side of her face with each word. Her stomach lurched.

The empathic leech demon. The one she'd rejected over a century ago.

The one who'd killed Tianya.

Inari's heart stopped. For a split second. *Oh, fuck.*

Thick fingers wrapped around her throat, driving into her flesh. Choking her. Heart leaping into furious flight, she flattened her palms to the ground and shoved her body upward, a violent jolt that threw the leech off balance. He tumbled to the ground and she lashed out with her foot, driving the toe of her boot into his flabby belly. A squishy sound punctuated the blow, and she gritted her teeth in a feral grin.

"Bitch!" the leech spat, scrambling at her on all fours.

She leapt to her feet and smashed her pointed heel into his face, driving him back in a screaming arc. "You have no idea how painful I'm going to make this for you," she growled, stalking toward him, hate flooding her veins. "I'm going to make you suffer so much for what you did to my sister."

The leech leered up at her, blood oozing from his mashed nose and punctured cheek. "You know, of course, when I couldn't have you I took the next best thing, just like you told me to. Your sister. Sweet little thing she was too. So tasty and innocent."

Inari hissed, throwing herself at him. Her fingers hooked in his lank, greasy hair before he could dodge her, and she yanked his head downward, slamming his face into the upward trajectory of her knee. The sound of splintering bone filled her with cold rapture and, deep within, her Sentinel force roared.

She smashed her knee to his face once more, the blow flinging him backward. She leapt at him again, her blood on fire, hate and rage engulfing her.

She staggered back as he snapped his leg out in a wild sidekick and punched his foot into her belly, followed by another to her ribs. "I'm not that easy to kill, bitch." He sprung upright and smashed his fist into the side of her face.

Hot pain erupted in her jaw, shooting up into her temple. Black stars exploded in her vision, and for a sickening second, the whole world swam.

Fucker.

He circled her, his gray flesh glistening with snot-green blood, watery blue eyes bulging from his chinless face. "I will tear the limbs from your body and fuck your legless corpse, bitch. I will ram my thick, hard cock down your throat and pump your gut full of my cum." He bared his teeth. "Just like I wanted to all those centuries ago."

"I am *so* sick of your voice," Inari snapped, swiping at her jaw. He'd landed a punch. How the hell had he landed a punch?

Does it matter? For God's sake, once you've kicked his butt and he is nothing but a trail of dust in the gardens, then you can lament the fact he landed a punch, okay? For now just cut the crap, swallow your pride, control your emotions and destroy this piece of murdering filth.

An angry snarl rumbled at the back of her throat, deep and primeval. She drove her nails into her palms, suppressing the urge to assume her Sentinel form. She didn't need to transform to gut the leech staring her square in the face. She didn't *want* to transform. She wanted to destroy the sick fucking thing in the form her sister knew and loved. In the body Tianya knew.

Then do it. Now!

She ground her teeth, glaring at the demon standing before her. He wouldn't be for much longer. She would turn the grass of the Royal Botanic Gardens green with the leech's blood. For Tianya. For what he did to her.

So why is the leech still breathing, Inari?

She narrowed her eyes, keeping her stare locked on his face. "What kind of dumb Euro-trash demon stalks a Sentinel?"

He flashed pointed yellow teeth at her, orbiting her in slow steps. "One with unfinished business."

Inari snarled, her flesh beginning to singe. Her Sentinel soul smoldered, burning for release. For control. "You really can't take no for an answer, can you?"

"No doesn't mean no coming from a succubus. Every demon in

the Realm knows that." The leech inched closer, leering grin stretching wider as he ran an insolent gaze over her body. "Like your outfit, by the way. You've nailed the slutty look to perfection."

Icy hate and contempt rippled through the fire in her soul. "Got some news for you, leechy-boy. I haven't been in the Realm for over twenty years. And I'm not a succubus any more. In case you missed the memo."

The leech demon snorted, the throaty sound wholly offensive. "I can still taste the slut you once were in your sweat, traitor." He inched a step closer, still circling her, still crouched ready to pounce. Blood trickled down his face, thin congealing lines of green blood that made him look like he was covered in slime. His shirt, a filthy orange plaid number, hung from his narrow shoulders, two missing buttons allowing his gut to protrude like a grotesque growth. On the whole, he was the vilest thing she'd ever seen.

He smirked. "Tell me, who'd you fuck to be reborn a Sentinel? God Himself?"

"Didn't I tell you I'm sick of your voice?" Inari cut him off, driving her nails into her palms.

"Too bad, bitch." He took another step closer. Saliva dribbled off his bottom lip. "It's going to be the last thing you hear as I fuck you to death."

She curled her nose, letting the force of her power flow through her being. "Sorry, you're not my type. Remember?" She lunged, the ribs the leech had cracked earlier screeching with blinding pain. She ignored it, sinking her nails into the demon's spongy neck, the feel of his hot blood gushing over her hotter flesh wonderful. "I prefer my lovers to bathe once in a while."

She jerked him off the ground and threw him against the thick trunk of a nearby ancient fig tree. Leaves and twigs and dried bat shit showered down upon them, the flurried flapping of disturbed fruit bats echoing through the silent park.

The leech snapped upright, his wide-eyed stare fixed on her

with baleful intent. "You want me to bathe? I'll bathe in your blood. After I split you in two with my dick and—"

Inari didn't let him finish. Rage engulfed her, flaying her control. She threw herself at him, transforming into her Sentinel form mid lunge. Her wings tore through her flesh as they burst from between her shoulder blades, skimming the edge of her corset until they spread to their full span. Her skin turned to a smooth, leathery hide almost impossible to puncture.

The demon squealed, thrashing beneath her against the splintery bark of the tree trunk, blood and piss pouring from his body, his arms flailing wildly as he struggled against her might.

But she was a Sentinel, reborn from a demonic existence to become the ultimate demon assassin. And now she had transformed, a mere empathic leech could not survive her punishment, no matter how strong or nourished he was. Especially one responsible for her sister's death. This one never stood a chance.

"Time for you to die, fucker." She drove her knees into his flabby gut, dug her left fingers deeper into his neck and stared him straight in the eyes, feeling his demented power scramble in vain for her psyche. It wouldn't work, of course. An empathic leech demon needed saliva-to-saliva contact, and there was no way in hell she was letting him kiss her. "By the power of the Sentinel, I hereby declare you punished."

Cocking her right arm, she hooked her hand into a claw, ready to rip out his heart.

At the exact second he spat at her.

A thick wad of bloody saliva struck the side of her mouth, burning her flesh like boiling acid. She slapped at her face, her heart slamming into her throat. God, no! Her knees buckled and she stumbled sideways, wiping at the spittle in frantic swipes of pain and horror. No, she had to get it off her face. If it dribbled past her lips...

"Sis?"

Inari blinked and gazed at Tianya. Her sister hung in her grip, her throat soft and bruised under Inari's fingers.

"What are you doing, In?" Tianya's soft voice tumbled from her cracked, bleeding lips. Her blue eyes grew wide, filling with horror and confusion. Tears streamed down cheeks smooth and soft and streaked with blood. "You promised to protect me."

Inari recoiled, her heart slamming into her throat. She stared at her sister, her gut knotting. "Ti?"

Fresh tears squeezed from Tianya's eyes and her bottom lip wobbled. Her long, delicate fingers fluttered against Inari's tense arm. "Please don't hurt me, sis. Please."

"Ti?" Her sister's sobs tore at her heart. "How...what?"

Tianya stared at her with terror in her eyes. "Why are you trying to kill me, Inari? What did I do wrong?"

Inari frowned, her grip on her sister's throat slipping.

No! Tianya is dead, Inari. It's the leech demon, not your sister. It's the fucking leech demon. You know that. The leech demon who raped and butchered her before you could save her. He's fucking with your head. Don't let him do it. Don't let him—

"Please let me go, Inari," Tianya begged, her fingers scraping at Inari's arm. "Please. I don't understand. Why are you—"

Inari sucked in a ragged breath, the air sickly sweet with her sister's fear.

No, not her fear. His stench. Oh, Inari, it's the leech's—

"Ti?"

A hot ball of guilt slammed into her. Ripe and putrid. Tianya's face seemed to distort, her eyes burning a baleful hate. The fingers on Inari's arms dug at her flesh, a punishing contact she couldn't break. "Yes, Inari, it's me."

Inari shook her head, the guilt in her gut wriggling into her soul. She stared at her sister's twisted expression, her head screaming. "No. You're dead."

Tianya's eyes filled with tears and she let out a broken sob, gripping Inari's arm harder. "It is *me*, Inari. You saved me. You saved me in time."

Inari shook her head again, her pulse screaming. No, it *wasn't* her sister. It was the leech. The very one who killed Ti over a century ago. She had to destroy the vile thing now. She had to—

"I love you, sis," Tianya whispered, nails scraping at Inari's flesh. She stumbled to her feet, blue eyes wild and hateful. "You saved me." Blood streaming down her face, iridescent green blood oozing from the puncture wounds in her throat, she gazed up at Inari through welling tears. "I knew you would. Kiss me, sis. Kiss away my pain."

Inari squeezed her eyes shut, her head swimming. Her stomach rolled. Why was this wrong? Why did this feel so wrong?

"Kiss me, Inari. I so want to kiss you now."

Kiss...

Kiss...

She opened her eyes and stared at the crying young woman she grasped by the throat. What was she doing? She couldn't kill her sister. She loved her. So much. All she wanted to do was kiss her. A simple kiss. "Oh, Ti," she whispered, tears stinging her eyes as she drew her head closer to Tianya's. "Oh, baby."

Tianya flashed teeth glistening in green blood and saliva. "Love you so much, sis," she whispered, the words becoming a guttural growl.

The stench of rotting meat poured through Inari's nose, down her throat, and she froze, every muscle in her body stiffening. "What?"

A shimmer rippled over Tianya's form, and Inari's cry of dismay choked her as her sister vanished, the leech snarling at her instead. "*So* much."

Inari's heart smashed into her throat. "*No!*"

She threw the leech against the fig tree again, fury and stunned disbelief tearing through her. The demon hit the ancient trunk with a bone-crunching thud. Blood gushed from his nose.

She fixed the leech in a furious glare, her wings cocked, her fingers clawed. "Gonna make you pay for—" Her knees buckled and excruciating pain ripped over her face.

Oh, by the Dieties...what...

She took a lunging step for the leech, shutting out the agony as she forced herself to stay on her feet. She had to kill him. She had to. She couldn't let him—

He spat at her again.

The burning wad hit her chest. She let out a roar and threw herself forward. Wrapping her hands around his throat, she slammed him against the tree, again, again. Bright green blood ruptured from his nose, his eyes. He flopped in her grip, his fingers scrambling at her wrists, his claws gouging deep furrows into her flesh.

And still she didn't stop.

Not even when he thrashed and wailed, blood gushing from his mouth.

Not even when his hands found her face and clawed at her eyes. Not even when he—

Fresh pain ripped through her, a shearing wall of excruciating agony. She stumbled backward, her grip slipping from the leech's throat, her knees collapsing. Her muscles raged with cramping fire, her mind screaming in such pain she could barely breathe.

Oh, God, she was...

Get up. Get up.

She lurched to her feet, her stare locking onto the demon.

"Later, cunt," he rasped before, with a gurgling hiss, he turned and screeched away into the blackness of the night, the shadows of the park swallowing him whole. Gone from sight in less than a heartbeat.

Inari watched him, her body engulfed in pain, her legs refusing to move.

She shook her head, a crushing pressure building in her chest. No. He'd gotten away. He'd gotten...

Her cry rent the air, high and tearing. She collapsed to the ground, her cheeks burning with tears of disgust and shame, her body returning to human form. She punched the ground, the wet grass icy on her burning skin, blood oozing from wounds deeper than flesh. What had she done? How could she be so stupid? So weak?

Undone.

The word reverberated through her head, a single word spoken in a choir of voices. The voice of the Dieties.

She gasped and as soon as the sticky night air surged into her lungs, she knew what the word meant. She'd failed.

Her sister. The Dieties. Herself.

She'd failed. And she had no one to blame but herself and her own stupid—

"Inari?"

She froze, her breath trapped in her throat.

Ezryn. Ezryn was behind her.

"Inari?" the sound of his voice behind her, unexpected, low and somehow hesitant, struck her like a physical blow, turning the grief inside her to rage. Pure rage. She spun around and threw herself at him, releasing all control over her Sentinel soul, unleashing its power. Ready to strike out. To maim. To hurt.

To kill.

Nothing happened.

She crashed into him, pain ripping through her body. Her human body.

Oh, no.

Strong hands grabbed her upper arms, his fingers curling around her *human* upper arms, holding her still. "Inari, what—?"

Oh, no. No.

She stumbled back a step, the blood draining from her face. She stared at the vampire before her, her soul still and hollow. And powerless. "Oh, my God, no."

Ezryn's fingers closed tightly around her arms, halting at her backward stagger. He gazed into her eyes, his eyebrows knitted. "What's wrong, Inari."

She shook her head, an unseen pressure crushing her chest. *No, this can't be. It can't...* Wild trembles wracked her body and she shook her head again, struggling to stop them. *No, please...no... Why didn't I transform? Why didn't I change?*

Ezryn tugged at her arms, trying to pull her closer to him. "Inari, tell me what's going on?"

Another jarring shudder claimed her. She glared at him and jerked free of his hold. "Stay away from me."

His eyebrows pulled into a deeper frown, and he closed the minute distance she'd put between them. "Why?"

She threw him a hateful snarl, her heart constricting. "Because I'm a Sentinel." The title sheared into her undone soul, mocking her failure. "And you're a vampire."

Red flames flickered in Ezryn's eyes. "So?"

The rage scalding through Inari's veins faltered, suddenly etched with empty agony. Could he tell? Could Ezryn feel the emptiness inside her? God, what happened now? What *was* she now if not a... She choked back a tearing breath, turning from him. "So we're enemies. We can't..." The words caught in her throat, too painful to speak aloud, and she turned away from him, unwilling to let him see her grief.

This is what she got for being weak. For allowing a vampire to touch her. For allowing a leech demon to fool her.

"Can't what, Inari? Be together? Enjoy each other's company? Exist in the same world?"

She clenched her jaw, squeezing her eyes shut. "Please, just stay away from me."

"I don't want to."

His blunt statement made her already thick throat thicker. "I don't care."

Cool fingers closed around her elbow in a firm grip, holding her still as he stepped in front of her. "What happened just now, Inari? Tell me. Why did you let the leech demon go?"

Inari's stomach rolled at his question. He'd seen. He'd seen her failure. She ground her teeth, opening her eyes to glare at him. "Let me go before I rip your heart out."

His eyes flared red, his jaw bunching. "Why did you stop fighting him? You had him beat. I saw it. Why did you let him go?"

She turned away, refusing to let him see her face. Refusing to let him see her shame, her grief. She'd never felt so torn apart. How did she survive this? How did she recover?

"What did he say to you?" he continued, his voice low, gentle. "Why did he do to make you look so sad? So broken?"

She bit back a sob, hating him. "Go away," she whispered through her teeth. "Just leave me the fuck alone."

He didn't say anything, his fingers still curled around her arm.

"Leave me alone," she whispered again, turning more away from him. By God, what was she to do now?

"Who is Tianya?"

Her sister's name, spoken with such gentle inquiry by the master vampire, ripped her heart apart. "None of your business." Grief, as raw and overwhelming as the night she'd learnt of Tianya's murder, consumed her. "Just leave me alone. Please, for the love of the Dieties, leave me alone."

She fought against Ezryn's hold, only to feel him close his fingers more firmly on her elbow. Only to feel him press the fingers of his other hand under her chin to turn her face back to his. She glared at him, her eyes burning with unshed tears. She would not cry. Not in front of him. Not ever.

He studied her, a silent inspection she neither wanted nor asked for. "You're wrong, Inari," he stated, his stare holding hers. "Everything about you is my business."

She jerked up her chin. She had to get away from him. More than ever. Before she did something she'd never forgive herself. "Why?" she snapped. "Because we fucked? Because I allowed you to stick your dick between my legs? Call it a moment of stupidity. Call me a slut if you want to. It's not like we need to pick out curtains together."

Ezryn's lips curled again, that same soft, small smile she'd grown to love in far too short a time. It unnerved her. Scared her. Made her heart quicken and her pulse pound. "I can't stop thinking about you, Sentinel. Even if we are enemies, you're always in my mind. For whatever reason, I can't stop. Is that so bad?"

A chill, like the icy breath of Death herself, stabbed into Inari's empty soul, and she stiffened.

Can't stop. The confession flayed at her pain. Can't stop. Like the chosen victim of a succubus—always wanting more, always craving more. Constantly thinking of the sex demon feeding on their existence, incapable of functioning or living a normal life. Aching for the succubus's presence even when sex was not occurring. Aching for it, craving it, needing it. Wasting away as they longed for every new touch, every new orgasm. Obsessed and enslaved by their own sexual need and the demon in control of it.

Ezryn's words whispered through her mind like the screaming cries of a dying man. *Can't stop.*

She bared her teeth at him, emptiness threatening to devour her. "Try."

His eyebrows knotted in a puzzled frown, his gaze searching her face. "What scares you so much about us, Inari?"

"There is no 'us', bloodsucker."

"Yes, there is. Admit it."

"Leave me alone. You've had your fun. You can gloat over your triumph. A master vampire fucking a Sentinel. I bet all your undead friends can't wait to hear all the details. Or are you friendless as well as soulless?"

He didn't react to the barbed insult. "Fine, you want me gone that badly, tell me who Tianya is and I will leave you alone."

She dragged in a shaking breath, the pain in her chest, her soul, undoing her completely. Or was it the worry, the open concern in

Ezryn's eyes? "My sister. Tianya was my sister. The leech demon I was fighting raped and murdered her over two hundred and fifty years ago."

An unreadable expression fell over Ezryn's face. His stare held her gaze. Seeking, searching for something she could not let him find. Her heart.

"Oh, Inari," he finally murmured, and her breath caught at the undeniable regret in his voice, "you know there's not a hope in hell of me leaving you now, don't you?"

He lowered his head and brushed his lips over hers. A gentle kiss. As if Inari herself was something delicate and fragile that needed to be cherished.

And she let him.

For the briefest of moments.

Head spinning, stomach knotting, she placed her palms on his chest and pushed him away, stepping back a step as she did. "Don't."

He followed her, reaching for her hands. "Let me take you home. I want to take you home. Take you somewhere safe and—"

She shook her head, taking another backward retreat from him.

"Please," she said, her voice barely more than a scratching whisper. "Just leave me alone. Nothing good can come of this."

He shook his head. He was stubborn and arrogant and used to getting what he wanted, a master vampire through and through. Her master vampire, her enemy, who was studying her with such open concern she felt her chest constrict.

Can't stop.

His confession slipped through her head, taunting and foreboding. Terrifying her. Making her sick. The words of a male entranced by a succubus who would do anything to have her use his body.

With one last look at his face—a face she'd seen forever in her dreams, a face she knew would haunt her forever—she turned and ran into the pitch-black park.

Her chest squeezed with relief when he didn't follow her.

Her heart broke with pain.

* * *

Jacob watched the woman wander away from him, his mouth coated in sour disgust. He raised his right hand and swiped at his lips, his stomach roiling.

She'd begged him to bite her. Begged and pleaded, clung to his arms and offered him her body as well as her blood, anything to have him bite her.

He hadn't. He couldn't bring himself to.

Which made him what? Weak?

He suppressed a low growl, tracking the young woman as she ambled along the grass strip running parallel to the overlord's compound, her skin-tight miniskirt riding up her black-stockinged thighs. She would have no memory of their encounter. He'd removed any trace of him from her mind with a gentle glamour. He couldn't afford for her to divulge his presence at Harry's gate if she was stopped by any of the overlord's guard, nor could he stand the idea of her broken, wretched grief at being rejected.

Under the influence of his glamour, she'd openly spoken of her heart, her voice soft and trembling. So fragile. So human. She was sad and lonely and ached for someone to make her feel something apart from dejected contempt. She'd come looking for escape from her miserable life in the arms of the vampires she'd hoped resided in the mansion. She'd read all the books, you see. She'd read them and fallen in love with the vampires depicted on the pages. She wanted that existence, the eternal beauty the words of the book promised her. She wanted the romance so powerful it was beyond life, beyond definition. She wanted a vampire to save her. To turn her. To give her what she longed for with every fiber in her body that no one living would love.

He wasn't that vampire.

He'd sent her on her way, sending a prayer to the Dark Ones she would find herself safe in her home before the sun rose.

He shouldn't care—who was she to him, after all?—but he cared all the same.

With a lumbering, somehow sweet little skip, the woman—Alicia Whitehead of Parramatta—disappeared around the corner, gone from his sight.

Which left him no farther ahead in his plan.

Because you're weak?

Jacob shook his head, turning back to the iron gates of the overlord's compound. What did he do now?

Haral had given Ezryn four nights to kill the Sentinel before Haral began to slaughter Ezryn's followers. Two of those nights had already passed; another was but a few hours from doing so. If he didn't do something soon, Jacob knew his master would.

But you've seen him with the Sentinel. You've seen him touch her. You've seen the way he looks at her. He's never looked at another being with such undeniable desire. Do you really think he will kill her?

Narrowing his stare on the hulking mansion on the other side of the gates, its windows flooded with warm light, its garden shrouded in shadows, Jacob clenched his fists. Did Ezryn really have a choice?

Since the moment he'd met Haral, Jacob had always considered Ezryn's brother an idiot. It was obvious the second born of the Navarro line lusted for power, but as far as Jacob—and many of the vampire race—had been concerned, it was fortunate it wasn't his to wield. But then the bastard had fooled everyone and claimed the position of overlord, and now, fifty years later, he was to claim his brother's life as well.

No matter which way he looked at it, Jacob could see no solution. He had given Ezryn his word he would not destroy the fucker, and regardless how much he wanted to end Haral's pathetic existence, he could not break that word nor disobey his friend's command.

He could not kill the overlord.

But the Sentinel can.

The thought whispered through Jacob's mind, soft and unexpected and very, very true.

A squirming knot of something close to hope filled Jacob's chest. If the Sentinel killed Haral, all their problems would be solved. If the Sentinel killed Haral, Ezryn would be returned to the position rightfully his, and order could be restored to the vampire race. If the Sentinel killed Haral...

The tight tension in Jacob's chest squeezed tighter, and he turned away from the overlord's compound.

He knew what to do now.

It was time to seek out Inari Chayse.

Chapter Seven

Ezryn slammed the door shut behind him, its solid thud offering no satisfaction as he stormed across the floor of his living room. He snatched a heavy crystal glass from the bar and splashed it full of one-hundred-year-old scotch, downing the liquid in a single mouthful. Curse it! What the hell was that woman doing to him?

He tossed the glass onto the bar and prowled the room, ignoring the deep-purple tinge on the dark eastern horizon outside. He'd never been so affected by a female, human or vampire, as he was by Inari Chayse. It was as though her very existence brought out the primitive, carnal demon he was, making him a creature of base lust and appetites. Yet at the same time it awoke in him the human he'd never been. It wasn't just sexual pleasure either. She brought out the side of him he'd never let anyone see, not even Jake—the side that knew how important it was to laugh, to joke. A side his mother had tried to nurture in him even as his father had tried to beat it out of him. When he was with Inari, all he wanted to do was see her smile, see her laugh. See her move with pleasure on every level— intellectual, physical, emotional...

Emotional? Dark Ones, when was the last time he cared what anyone *felt*, let alone one of the Highest's assassins? And yet, when he'd tracked her into the Royal Botanic Gardens and found her mid-battle with an empathic leech demon all he'd instantly wanted to do was save her, protect her from the hideous thing. Rip it to dismembered pieces for hurting her. Witnessing her transformation into her Sentinel form, all he'd wanted to do was cheer her sheer power and terrifying beauty. Seeing the pain and confusion on her face as the leech spoke to her, all he'd wanted to do was take away her pain.

Watching the leech flee her, he knew all he wanted to do was wrap her in his arms and make her safe from the world.

Dark Ones, he'd never been so conflicted.

If he wasn't thinking about making love to her, he was thinking about making her laugh, seeing her smile. If he wasn't remembering the sweetness of her pleasure, he was remembering the beauty of her voice. What was wrong with him? What had she done to him?

And why hadn't he gone after her when she'd run away from him? Why hadn't he pursued her and made her tell him what was going on in her heart? Her soul?

Snarling, he dragged his fingers through his hair. He didn't know. Every fiber in his cold body had wanted to. Not just wanted to, but demanded it. Demanded he go after her as she ran deeper into the park. Demanded he hold her, make love to her. Bite her. Not just make her his, but bind her to him. And him to her.

He let out a sharp hiss, his fangs extended at the idea of her blood flowing down his throat. Not the blood of a Sentinel—*her* blood. Inari's blood. Inari the woman.

So why did you let her go?

He poured another shot of whiskey, his grip on the squat crystal glass growing tight. He knew the answer to that question, but he didn't want to ponder it. Nor its significance.

You let her go because she asked. Because you knew she couldn't take any more hurt tonight, and as much as you wish it weren't so, for whatever reason, being with you hurts her.

"So much for the big, bad vampire." He pushed the glass aside without drinking a single drop. "You're pussy whipped by a Sentinel."

The mocking jibe didn't have the effect he'd wanted. Instead of igniting his ire, images of Inari filled his head. Inari in the park, shaking with grief. Inari glaring at him, telling him to fuck off. Inari beneath him on her bed, her body shuddering as orgasm after orgasm claimed her. Inari, Inari, Inari. Her touch, her taste, the way her lips parted to his soft kiss, the way her sweet pussy constricted around his shaft, the way she trembled at his arrogant domination...

His body tensed with fresh hunger and indecipherable need, and he growled. Damn, he wanted to take her again. Now. Hard. Slow. Savage and gentle. If it wasn't sixty minutes until dawn broke he'd go straight back to that shoebox of an apartment she called home, throw her on the bed and make love to her again and again and again until she begged him to never leave her. Until she poured out the secrets of her soul and heart and pleaded with him to make her his forever. Until she screamed her feelings for him on the cries of her release, feelings he too—

"Dark Ones, Ezryn!" he burst out, killing the thought. He dragged his hands through his disheveled hair once more. "What the fuck are you thinking?"

He wasn't. It was that simple. Centuries of priding himself on being above the base, sadistic behavior of his ancient family line and here he was, acting just as depraved and heinous and selfish as his baby brother.

The brother who has commanded you to kill her. Have you forgotten that? Three nights have passed already. If you don't kill her by sunrise tomorrow, Haral will begin the slaughter of those vampires who stood up and proclaimed their loyalty to you.

The bleak thought brought his furious pacing to a halt, and he closed his eyes. His gut knotted. He'd been lost in her, lost in the happiness he felt when with her, and he'd denied what he was meant to do—murder her.

He'd never been bested in battle. Demon hunters, vampire slayers, his brother's zealots—all had attacked him at one time or another and not once had he come close to being defeated. He was the first born of the First Family, regardless of what the oracle had proclaimed. He was the ultimate vampire, and yet if faced with fighting Inari, he doubted he would win. He'd seen the power of a Sentinel in her. Not just when she was angry at him, but in the last few moments he'd witnessed of her fight with the empathic leech demon. In all his centuries, he'd never seen anything so terrifying and powerful. He'd faced Sentinel before. Had been the target of more than one in his youth, during the decades before he denied his father's deranged demands and refused to feed on innocent humans. He'd killed those Sentinel regardless of their demonic heritage, but Inari Chayse was unlike any he'd seen before.

Why?

"I have no idea." His muttered growl burst past his clenched teeth, harsh with frustration.

Killing a female hell-bent on destroying him was no different from killing a male. If they had a stake or blade in their hands and swung it at him with intent, it didn't matter whether they had a penis or not—they were dead.

So why then, when Inari had threatened him with that silver stake of hers earlier tonight, had he let her live? Why was she different?

The memory of her pleasured screams of release echoed through his head. He wanted to hear those screams of undeniable pleasure again. Hear them and have his own join them.

Why? Because she was an amazing fuck? A conquest?

No. It was more than that. Something he couldn't fathom.

Ezryn opened his eyes and studied the pre-dawn activity through his window. Water taxis skipped across the harbor like glowing dragonflies, rushing to pick up passengers or drop them off. Early sailors navigated their crafts through the dark waters, heading for the mouth of the harbor and the freedom of the open sea beyond it. A few windows radiated warm light in the luxury houses hugging the harbor's edge, their occupants rising for a new workday or morning gym session. Fruit bats glided through the still-black sky, crisscrossing his line of sight, their sonar cries to one another a soft note in Ezryn's ears. It was a sight he'd enjoyed often, a still calm he took in most mornings before retiring for the day. It normally relaxed him—the city he now called home coming awake, alive—but this morning it made no difference to his mood.

Why did Inari Chayse affect him the way she did? There had to be an answer. How could a Sentinel reduce him to a creature of base lust and inexplicable emotion?

And why could he not kill her, no matter the consequences?

Haral's ultimatum came back to him, and he bit back a curse. Four nights to destroy the Sentinel or the slaughter began. Three nights had already passed. Three nights with the assassin in his hands. Three nights where he could have easily ripped her throat open and gorged himself on her blood, and he'd gorged himself on her sweet, delectable body instead.

A tight spasm claimed his cock and he ground his teeth. No, he hadn't gorged himself on Inari's body. The word gorged implied he was satiated, satisfied, but he wasn't. Not even close. He wanted her again. And again. Right now, right this very instant, even with the memory of the tortured contempt in her eyes as she'd told him to leave her alone. He wanted her again with such hungering force his balls ached and his chest felt tight. The honey between her legs, the elixir in her veins, her softness, her strength. Her laughter, her anger. All of her. When it came to the feisty Sentinel, he doubted he would ever be sated.

Why?

Ezryn pressed his palms against the window and stared blankly at the view below, the heat of the approaching summer dawn beyond the glass warming his cold flesh.

He had to know. Was it just because his brother wanted her

dead? Or was it something else? Something far too abstract to consider?

Turning from the window, he crossed his living room. He had to know.

Even if it meant tempting the sun's burning rays.

Exactly twelve minutes and thirty-four seconds later, he stood on an empty and dark Bondi Beach, a row of powerful arc-sodium streetlights meters behind him stretching his shadow into a distorted shape along the famous stretch of sand. The night sky hung overhead, its reassuring black expanse marred by a bruised-purple smudge on the Eastern horizon. He studied the cool color, the salty tang of the Pacific slipping into his nose and stinging his sinuses. By Ezryn's reckoning—and his internal vampire awareness of the sun's global position—he had just short of ten minutes before dawn broke and he ran out of time.

He slid his stare from the worryingly lighter sky to the tall man with broad shoulders and shaggy blond hair strolling casually from the surf. He noted the dripping surfboard tucked under one muscled arm, the long, lean legs covered in a skin-tight black wetsuit, the water streaming down his wide, hairless chest in glistening rivulets.

An uncomfortable foreboding fluttered in Ezryn's chest, and he swallowed, keeping his gaze on the approaching surfer despite the want to look away. The very nature of the man's activities was like a threatening challenge, one he was in no mood to deal with.

"Haven't you heard the sun's not altogether favorable to your kind?" the man commented, the vowels almost a low purr, the harsh consonants close to a growl. He walked passed Ezryn, not even remotely flicking him an interested look, nor an indifferent one. "I'd recommend getting your arse back indoors unless you've got some serious shit sunblock tucked away in the pockets of those designer jeans."

Ezryn turned, fixing a hard stare at the other man's back as he continued walking farther up the beach. "I need to know about a Sentinel."

A casual snort of mirth followed Ezryn's statement. The man neither slowed down nor changed direction, his graceful footfalls barely indenting the soft sand with each step he took. "And why would I tell you anything like that, Ezryn Navarro?"

Ezryn bit back a frustrated hiss. "Because if you don't there will be war between the vampire nation and the Agents of the Order."

The muscles in the man's back tightened and he stopped. The fingers gripping the surfboard grew tense, the knuckles white. He turned, his eyes catching the streetlights' glow for a split second, their sharp green depths flaring with iridescent light. His lips stretched in a cold smile, the action revealing fangs, long and pointed. "Now, you know better than to make threats like that, blood-sucker."

Ezryn bared his own fangs, every nerve ending on edge. It wasn't just adrenaline surging through him at that moment. It was borderline fear. Even with the power and strength of his ancient bloodline, what he was doing would be considered suicide by most of his kind. "And you know me well enough to know I don't make threats, Watkins." He cocked an eyebrow, refusing to be intimidated. He was Ezryn Navarro, after all. He wasn't just some bleeder flexing his muscles. "And by the way, who are you calling a blood-sucker?"

Ven Watkins, supreme Sentinel and ex-vampire, gave him a steady look, his eyes green chips of ice. The knuckles on the hand gripping his surfboard grew whiter. His jaw muscles bunched. "Be careful, Navarro." His voice was low, his accent thicker. "I believe you may be close to pushing our friendship somewhat."

Ezryn nodded, his own gaze unwavering. "True. But then we've never really been close, have we, Ven? Even before your 'rebirth'? We may both have been vampires, but you kept to yourself, too concerned with looking out for your brother. In fact, I think I recall you telling me to 'piss off' out of the country at one stage. Wasn't that the night I met your girlfriend?"

A shimmer of black rippled over Watkins's face, and Ezryn had to stop himself taking a hurried step backward. This wasn't going the way he'd hoped. Not at all.

How did you think it would go? Did you think the guy would offer to buy you coffee? Maybe invite you to share breakfast? You do know who you're talking to here, don't you?

Ezryn squared his shoulders a little, refusing to break eye contact.

Ven Watkins had once been a vampire, a *good* vampire, in Ezryn's opinion, but something about the Australian had always troubled him. An aura of immense power and untold force. The first time Ezryn had met the young vamp, he'd been surprised to discover he was a bleeder. The man radiated not just the strength of a born vampire, but the icy potency of a master. It came as no surprise to Ezryn when he'd learnt Ven had become a Sentinel, although what happened to elevate the vamp to an assassin of God, Ezryn didn't know. There were whispers amongst Sydney's paranormal world of deals with the Fourth Horseman of the Apocalypse, Death herself. Ezryn could only consider himself fortunate he and Ven had never been forced to square off.

It was rumored Watkins could kill a demon of any genus with a simple thought—if he was inclined to do so. Ezryn didn't doubt it. He'd seen what Ven Watkins the Sentinel could do, the assassin dealing with a blood-frenzied horde of *cambion* who'd decided to assault a busload of tourists during the last Sydney Mardi Gras. It had not been pretty, and if Ezryn was capable of having nightmares, he believed what he'd witnessed that night would have left him sleepless for some time.

They had an uneasy truce, he and Watkins, and tolerated each other's existence in Sydney with what came close to studied indifference. But Ezryn had little doubt that truce would dissolve with just the wrong word or action. And then Ven would render his existence null and void.

A chill rippled up Ezryn's already icy spine.

It was an unnerving thought, especially given his current mission.

He needed to be careful, no matter how much he wanted answers. When it came to the decimation of demons, Watkins was close to God-like—his power was unfathomable and no one escaped him. Ever. Which meant Ezryn couldn't afford to antagonize him now.

Can't afford to have your unbeating demon heart ripped from your chest, either.

"I know there is no reason to trust what I say, Steven." He kept his voice calm and composed, the use of the supreme Sentinel's first name deliberate. And risky. "But this is important. For both our kinds."

A mocking expression fell over Watkins' face. "Both our kinds?"

Ezryn didn't say a word, all too aware he walked a dangerous tightrope.

Watkins regarded him, nothing about his stance or body language hinting at what went on behind his piercing green eyes. For all Ezryn knew, the Sentinel could have been thinking about what he was going to have for breakfast.

Me?

He flicked a quick look over his shoulder at the sky behind him. The cold, purple smudge had spread to a golden-pink hue, the disconcerting coloring rising higher from the horizon. He forced his muscles to relax. Dawn was almost upon him. If he didn't get the answers he needed soon, he'd be toast. Literally.

As if hearing his thoughts—*maybe he does, Ezryn. You don't know everything about him*—Watkins moved his gaze passed Ezryn, taking in the hint of sunlight low in the night sky behind Ezryn's back. "Looks like it's going to be a beautiful day, doesn't it?" He returned his steady gaze to Ezryn, his face expressionless.

Ezryn bit back a growl, his control close to snapping. He'd had enough of being played with. Watkins wasn't a cat, and he sure as hell wasn't a defenseless mouse. "Curse it, assassin! Either agree to tell me what I need to know or try and rip my heart out." He took a step forward, his fists clenched, his fangs growing longer, readying to be attacked. "Either way, get it over and done with."

Watkins raised his eyebrows, what almost looked like a grin playing with his mouth. He slid the surfboard from under his arm and stabbed its tail into the sand beside his bare feet before loosely draping an arm around its edge. "War, you say?"

Ezryn nodded, jaw clenched. War would mean little to Ven Watkins—the vampire-cum-supreme Sentinel was likely to survive any battle between vamps and the Agents of the Order. But despite the mystery surrounding him, one thing was known—whatever brought about the transformation from vampire to Sentinel, Ven Watkins now had a certain distaste for mindless slaughter and destruction, regardless of the species of corpse. Since his transformation, he'd dealt with more than one demon and hell spawn with such icy, sardonic calm few dared enter Sydney anymore, but of late he was, for the want of a better word, retired.

Like everything else surrounding Watkins, no one knew why and no one dared ask, but the Sentinel spent most of his days on the end of a wax-coated surfboard riding the waves at Bondi and most of his nights sliding between the sheets as he moved over and into whatever gorgeous female he desired.

"Please," Ezryn said, the word like bitter essence on his tongue. "I have to know."

Watkins narrowed his eyes, and Ezryn couldn't escape the feeling he was being weighed and measured. "Name?"

He swallowed. "Inari Chayse."

Even the sound of her name passing his lips made Ezryn's blood heat, despite the dangerous position he was in. He stared at the Sentinel, unable to miss the lightening shadows stretching over the beach behind him.

A gentle heat teased his back, the rays of the rising sun beginning to warm the cool night air around him. He resisted the urge to fidget. Damn it, he was running out of time. Quickly.

"Inari Chayse," Watkins repeated. His green eyes flickered with an enigmatic light, and an icy finger of nervous apprehension stabbed into Ezryn's gut.

Fuck, what is going on? Why is he being so obtuse? So—

"What do you want to know about her?"

Ezryn swallowed again, the pit of his gut tightening. *Why I can't stop thinking about her? Why all I want to do is claim her? Why I want nothing more than to bind her to me? Make her mine and lose myself forever in her—*

A cold grin pulled at Watkins's mouth, a glimpse of wickedly sharp fangs peeking from behind his lips. "Ah," he said. "I see."

And with that, he chuckled once, pulled his surfboard from the sand, tucked it under his arm again and walked up the beach toward the street with long, comfortable strides.

Ezryn blinked. What in all the levels of hell?

Knowing he was pushing his luck, he blocked Watkins's path. "What in the name of the Dark Ones does *Ah, I see* mean?"

Watkins gave him a level look, his pale eyes shimmering white for a split second. White. A Sentinel's eyes. But Ezryn didn't budge. He couldn't. He needed to know.

"Inari Chayse," Watkins said, his voice as controlled as his gaze. "Ex-succubus. Over three hundred years old. And one of the most lethal Sentinel I know. You'd do best to stay away from her if you want to continue existing."

He began walking again and Ezryn stepped out of his way, a strange pressure wrapping around his chest. Did he just hear...?

"Oh, and by the way," Watkins threw over his shoulder without slowing his pace, "my family is greatly indebted to her, so I'd be a touch miffed if something were to happen to her, if you understand my meaning."

He didn't wait for Ezryn's response, turning away from him as if he no longer mattered and moving across the sand.

Ezryn stood motionless, watching him go, one word replaying over in his head. One word echoing in his mind. Repeating it in a low whisper louder than a scream.

One word. Only one.

Succubus.

He squeezed his eyes shut, rubbing his hands over his face.

Succubus.

A hot beat thumped in his temple, his throat. He dragged his nails through his hair.

Succubus.

He drove his nails into his scalp, piercing his flesh. Damn. He'd been made a fool. A fucking fool.

Succubus. A female sex demon who feeds on the sexual energy of her victims, seducing them until they are enslaved to her by their lust and fucking them until they were drained of their life force. Mating with them over and over and over and over again.

Succubus.

"One more thing." Watkins's distant call jerked Ezryn out of his dark stupor and he stared after the Sentinel, black rage snaking through his very veins. "Tell your brother if I so much as even see him on my streets while he's here, I'll come out of retirement."

Ezryn sucked in a sharp hiss, his black rage turning to a darker, dense fury. He was right. The bastard Sentinel *could* read his thoughts.

There came a low chuckle from Watkins's direction, the man moving over the loose sand with graceful ease, his arm hugging his now-dry surfboard with casual comfort. "*You* should probably *think* about getting out of the sun soon." He tossed Ezryn a quick, smug grin over his shoulder, never slowing his stride. "Just a friendly safety tip from me to you. Agent to bloodsucking demon."

Ezryn spun around, his attention snapping immediately to the east, his throat growing thick at the sight of the horizon awash in brilliant golden light.

Fuck.

He turned from the beach, looking west. Ven Watkins was nowhere to be seen, swallowed up by the waning night shadows. Or gone by other less natural means.

A strange beat throbbed in Ezryn's temple. A charged tingle heated his flesh. He scanned the buildings stretching before him, the scattered lights glowing in their windows reflecting a populace about to start the new day. Already he could see the cafes and restaurants preparing for their morning customers. It wouldn't be long before joggers appeared on the beach. Life had come to Bondi Beach, and he was standing alone on the sand with no close refuge from the sun. Even at his fastest, it would take him too long to get back to his home before the sun's rays found his vulnerable flesh.

He had to move. Now.

Curling his fingers into fists, he launched himself forward, defying natural law as he propelled himself away from the lightening horizon. Jacob's Woolloomooloo penthouse was five miles away. If he hurried—and he planned on doing just that—he might just make it.

It's only four miles to Kings Cross...

The insidious suggestion flittered through Ezryn's head. Four miles to Inari Chayse's apartment.

A growl rumbled up his throat, the sound low and completely demonic. Four miles.

Go there, Ezryn. Take her. Claim her. Fuck the lying, deceiving sex demon until she screams and begs for mercy and then gorge yourself on her blood and body.

He moved through the rapidly filling streets, the houses and buildings nothing but streaks of shadows and light around him.

Three miles.

Two.

One.

The gaudy neon lights of Kings Cross flared in his sights, the distinctive stench of the suburb of sex and sin filling his nose.

Fuck her, Ezryn. Bite her.

Bind her.

He could almost believe her scent wafted on the still dawn air. Taunting him. Teasing him.

He moved in a dark blur through the waking streets. Past drunken tourists who had little memory of the night just gone and the harried beat cops trying to decipher from their slurs and mumbles where their accommodation was. Past early morning dog walkers and businessmen running late for their buses.

Faster. Closer. Closer to his destination.

And, in three effortless leaps, he landed on Jacob's fourteenth story balcony, smashing the glass sliding door's lock as he flung it open and stormed into his friend's living room.

Jacob looked up from the newspaper on his lap, not a hint of shock at Ezryn's appearance evident on his seamless face. "Well," he said, a grin twitching on his lips, "this is a surprise. I didn't know you'd taken up extreme *parkour*. Or is it extreme freerunning? I can never tell with the fads today."

Ezryn didn't respond. He couldn't. All he could think about was seven short words. Seven short words that said it all.

Succubus. Sex demon. Fuck her. Bite her.

"I take it by your foul mood you've been visiting with the Sentinel again." The grin on Jacob's lips stretched wide, although there was a tension around his eyes that seemed to mock the smile. "Is that why you didn't answer my earlier phone call?" He paused, and for the briefest of moments that same tension pinched the skin on either side of his nose. "I wanted to tell you Eliah Bartowski was in Australia."

Ignoring the unusual strain on Jacob's face, Ezryn gave his friend a slow, cold smile. "Are you ready for hell on earth, General Ancroft?"

Jacob's grin vanished, his body becoming still. "What have you done, Ezryn?" he asked, putting his paper aside and rising to his feet.

Ezryn turned away from his long-time friend and most loyal ally. Standing in the room's cool shadows, he studied the soft line of the sun's heat creep across the plushly carpeted living room floor. If he stood here long enough—a few minutes, if that—the golden light would find his feet and he would begin to burn.

Yet even that heat would pale to insignificance compared to the black rage Ven Watkins's revelation had awoken in him.

His mouth filled with saliva and his nostrils flared, his mind turning to Inari Chayse. No, not turning to it. Turning to it would imply he'd stopped thinking about her. He hadn't. Not at all. She'd been at the center of his every thought since he'd found her in the Pleasure Palace. Every deluded, irrational, feverish thought. And now he knew why.

The anger boiling in his gut, his chest, twisted into a writhing snake of icy resolve. Ruthless purpose.

"Ezryn?" Jacob spoke behind him, his tone urgent. "What have you done? Tell me you haven't killed the Sentinel? Tell me you haven't taken her life?"

Ezryn ignored him. He watched the weak morning sunlight inch toward him and smiled again, the feel of his fangs pressing inside his lips a clear reminder of who—*what*—he was. What he was and what he could do. What he was *going* to do.

"Ezryn?"

Jacob's voice was a distant buzz lost in the roar of his blood in his ears. He lifted his stare to the window, studying the pale, golden-tinged blackness beyond and seeing only the Sentinel. He looked forward to the coming night. Dark Ones, did he look forward to it.

Succubus.

Sex demon.

Fuck her.

Bite her.

"Kill her."

Chapter Eight

"So what's your plan now?"

Inari didn't lift her head from her hands. She kept her stare fixed on the spot between her feet even as her sister's voice played over her back like a cool breeze.

"You know you can't keep running away forever, don't you?"

She frowned at the floor, her teeth catching her bottom lip to gnaw on its fleshy fullness. She needed to shampoo the carpet. Or maybe rip it up and have new carpet laid. Or better yet, polish the floorboards beneath back to their original life, restoring them to what they'd once been. Or maybe—

"I'm not going anywhere, sis," Tianya pointed out, each word growing colder. "I can stand here and watch you sulk all night if I must, and you know it. You've been at it for most of the day already, by the way. Just in case you didn't notice."

Tianya's mocking statement made the skin on the back of Inari's neck prickle, the sensation so like the warning she'd get when a demon was about.

When you were a Sentinel, you mean?

The thought was a dagger of dark pain burying deep into her

chest, and she stared harder at the spot of carpet between her feet. Maybe she should by some rugs? A shag one?

"You have to do something, In." Tianya's voice danced on the air behind Inari's bowed back and she gritted her teeth. "You've submitted to a master vampire so many times now I've lost count." Tianya paused. "The *same* master vampire."

Damp heat blossomed in the junction of Inari's thighs at her dead sister's words, and she snarled silently.

"It's like your body's trying to tell you something," Tianya went on.

"My body has shit for brains," Inari mumbled, stubbornly refusing to take her eyes off the floor. "And do you really think I'm worrying about a vampire? After what just happened?"

"Contrary to what you think, I'm not always hanging around with you. Did something bad happen? Did you kick your toe on the table? Or drop mustard on your—"

"I let the demon that killed you escape," Inari snapped, cutting her sister's humored questions short. "I let him fuck with my head and get away."

"Oh, that?" Tianya said, the question making Inari's stomach roll. "And now you seem to have lost any ability to transform into your Sentinel form, yes?" she continued, as if she knew exactly where Inari's tormented train of thought was going.

"And now I seem to have lost any ability to transform into my Sentinel form," Inari repeated, the words a low murmur.

She let her gaze move over the floor, studying it with an unblinking stare. Maybe red plush pile carpet? The kind Hollywood was fond of laying on the floor of almost every brothel depicted on film. A fitting floor covering given her past existence, to be sure.

"Could this be a self-imposed punishment?" Tianya piped up, a judicious tone in her voice no eighteen-year-old should have, even one dead for over two and a half centuries. "Could you be crippling yourself with guilt?"

Inari closed her eyes for a quick moment, her throat thick. Guilt. Her sister's murder, the leech demon's escape...all her fault. And as much as she'd like to think her wretched grief came from nothing else but guilt, her mind kept coming back to one thing, one moment in the evening's nightmare of events—Ezryn uttering six damning words.

I can't stop thinking about you.

She swallowed at the tight lump in her throat. Succubus. She was succubus once more. Surely that was the only answer for a vampire wanting her, wasn't it? She was a demon assassin and Ezryn was a demon. By that indisputable fact, there could be no other reason he would desire her.

He'd had hunted her down, seduced her, fucked her and now the succubus force she'd once wielded over men had ensnared him and he kept coming back for more.

She bared her teeth in a grim smile, her gaze flicking over the space between her feet.

Yes, definitely red plush pile. The color of blood. That way, when I kill the bloodsucking bastard no one will notice the stain on the carpet.

Tianya laughed. The sound made Inari's nerves fray further. "When you kill him?" The air swirled behind Inari, a cool caress on her tense back, and she closed her eyes, refusing to shiver. "Seriously, sis, we both know you're not going to *kill* the vampire. Lick him, maybe. Kiss him, definitely, but kill?"

"Shut up, Ti."

"No."

The single word struck Inari in the back of the head with a violent smack, hard enough to make her teeth click together. She flinched, and a surprised gasp caught in her throat. Tianya's legendary patience, it seemed, had snapped.

"Why do you see me, Inari Chayse?" Tianya's voice scraped at Inari's right ear, her dead sister sounding more demonic than the ghost of a human should. "You've done so for a long time now, weeks before the master vampire came into your life, so we know I'm not just the product of sex with the bloodsucker. There must be a reason. Am I a ghost? The product of your loneliness? Your guilt? Am I your voice of reason or a curse you've inflicted upon yourself?"

Inari didn't answer. Hot tears welled behind her eyelids, and she blinked them back. She wouldn't cry. She wouldn't.

"Well?"

"I see you because I love you," she ground out, her eyes stinging. "Because I didn't save you when I could have."

"Bullshit," Tianya snapped. The air above Inari's crackled, as if each microscopic particle there had suddenly turned to ice. Very cold, very angry ice. "You were a sex demon doing what you were born to do when I died. I never expected you to save me, and I never blamed you for my death."

"But the demon...the leech..." Inari swallowed again. "Because I refused him, he came after you."

"Did you want to have sex with him?"

A repulsed shudder rolled through Inari and she shook her head. "No."

Icy air trickled over Inari's neck, down her shoulders, her back. She shivered, her skin breaking out in ripples of gooseflesh. "Did you tell him to find me in Salzburg? Did you give him my location?"

Inari ground her teeth. "Of course not."

"Then stop it." The air crackled with icy temper again. "I've had enough. I never expected you to save me, Inari, but I sure as hell expected you to save yourself."

Inari jerked her head up, glaring at the image of her sister standing before her. "What does that mean?"

Tianya raised her shoulders in a little shrug. "It seems to me the Deities have had enough of your pathetic dithering and decided to send someone who *will* save you, whether you want him to or not."

"And the vampire is that someone? Ezryn? A master vampire sent to save an ex-sex demon?" She let her expression turn overtly curious, crossing her arms over her chest and cocking her head to the side. "Tell me, little sister, what do I even need saving from?"

"Yourself. You've spent so long denying what you were, what you *are*, letting it scare you and control you, that until the master vampire came along sex had become nothing but a ghost more haunting than me, and I gotta tell you, I'm pretty damn haunting."

With a snort, Inari dropped her head again, returning her stare to the floor. "You have no idea what you're talking about. Shit, you're not even here. I may as well be talking to the wall."

"Interestingly enough," Tianya said, "I find myself thinking the same thing."

"Ha," Inari barked. "When did you become a comedian?"

"When *you* became a stubborn pain in the ass."

Inari snarled at Tianya through her fingers. "Go away," she muttered.

Tianya responded with a short laugh. "Not until you tell me why you are denying so furiously—and irrationally, in my opinion—what you feel for the vampire."

"Hate?"

Tianya cocked an eyebrow and didn't say a word.

Inari let out a violent breath. "Because I don't know if what I'm feeling for Ezryn is real or the force of the monster I once was. How can something so...so...powerful be real? And if it's not, if I *am* succubus again, will I lose more of my soul every time I let him touch me? Every time I draw pleasure from his body, will I become less what I am and more what I was born?"

She slumped, the ache in her chest all-consuming. Succubus. How was it the thought of being a sex demon again made her sick to her already sick stomach? Made her want to cry and scream with furious rage?

"I don't want to be a sex demon, Ti," she whispered at the floor, angry tears stinging the back of her eyes. "But I want the vampire more. So much more. Every fiber in my body wants him in every way imaginable and then some." She blinked, her vision turning into a watery blur.

"When I should be wondering why I can't transform any more, why I can't 'feel' my connection to the Powers, I'm thinking of the blood-sucker. When I should be wracked with disgust over the empathic leech demon's escape, I'm wondering what Ezryn is doing now. When I should be eaten alive with guilt over your death, I'm longing for the arms of a master vampire to comfort me. What do I do, Ti? Tell me?"

Silence answered her.

She closed her eyes, knowing Tianya's ghost—or whatever she really was—had once again left her. "Christ, Chayse," she muttered under her breath, "you're fucked up."

And still no farther ahead with what you are going to do about Ezryn.

The heat between her legs pulsed again, and she bit back a curse. Two hundred and eighty years of being a succubus should have left her immune to sexual lust, and yet the mere thought of Ezryn had her wet. As always. Was it a glamour?

She shook her head, frustration eating at her. Couldn't be. A vampire's glamour did not work on a succubus *or* a Sentinel.

But are *you still Sentinel?*

Cold unease curled in the pit of her belly. What if the way Ezryn reacted to her, the explosive sexual energy between them, had nothing to do with natural desire and everything to do with what she was? What she'd always been?

She pushed herself to her feet, killing the terrible notion as she tugged at her clean clothes. She needed another shower. She still felt like the empathic leech demon's vile, green blood was caked in her hair, like his spittle dribbled down her face. Another shower followed by some food and then some sleep.

It's not the leech you need to wash from your psyche, is it?

She let out a contemptuous sigh. It wasn't. No matter how cold the shower she'd thrown herself into the second she'd arrived home, no matter how vigorously she'd cleaned her teeth, her body still remembered his touch. She needed to wash Ezryn's scent from her flesh. Remove the taste of his kisses from her mouth. If she had to use a whole tube of toothpaste, she'd clean away any hint of his kisses before climbing into bed. If she didn't, she'd only fall asleep and into his arms in her dreams. If that happened...

No, she needed to close her eyes and escape the memory of his touch, not relive it.

Inari's gut churned and she stormed to her tiny bathroom, flicking on the cold water and only the cold water. She needed to do all those things, but most of all she needed to forget her sister's hideous death.

And her own complete failure to avenge it.

She stepped under the icy needles of the shower, welcoming the cold shock on her flushed skin. She *was* fucked up. And it was nothing more than she deserved.

Undone.

The word whispered through her head. One word with so much meaning.

The last word she'd heard from the Powers.

Can't stop.

Ezryn's confession followed, more harrowing than even the Dieties proclamation.

Inari slammed shut the water regulator. She stepped from the shower cubicle, a heavy beat thumping in her chest as the memory of the arrogant vampire's words rolled through her. "Damn it." Standing under cold water wasn't going to fix her problem. She could stand under the shower spray until she grew gills and she'd still have no solution to the situation. She had to *do* something. She'd always been a proactive person, going after what she wanted rather than waiting for it to come to her. Regardless of what she was now—sex demon or Sentinel—hiding in her home whining and carrying on stupidly about the carpet wasn't helping.

She snatching a towel from the rack and rubbed herself dry, the course cotton abrasive on her skin. Knotting it between her breasts, she prowled through the tiny living area of her apartment, throwing angry glances at the night sky outside her window.

What should she do? Tianya was right about one thing, the idea of killing Ezryn left the pit of her belly empty. Whatever was going on between them—and she had to be honest, *something* was going on, something smoldering and inexplicable and way too intense—Inari knew she could not drive a stake into Ezryn's unbeating heart. If the Highest of Highest materialized here in her apartment and commanded her to do so, she couldn't. If she'd been serious about turning him to dust, she would have done so yesterday. Instead, she'd fallen asleep in his arms.

So what's your plan now?

The thought echoed Tianya's earlier question and Inari let out a ragged, frustrated sigh. *Forget him.*

Her chest constricted. Cold pain wrapped around her. The idea was wrenching but it was for the best. Forget him and find the empathic leech demon. Go after Tianya's killer and make him suffer. Make him wail and plead and grovel for her forgiveness as she ended his vile existence. And after that...track down Ven Watkins. Ask him what she feared to know—was she still Sentinel and could she have sex without destroying her soul? Or was it already too late? Was she succubus once more?

Crossing to her bedroom, she unknotted her damp towel and tossed it onto the foot of her bed. She was going hunting. Sentinel or no, she was going hunting and she needed to dress accordingly. Who knew, if she really was succubus once more, perhaps she could kill the leech with sex.

A snort of disgust sounded at the back of her throat, and her stomach rolled. She would rather rip out her own heart than fuck the leech to death. End of story.

She flung open her cupboard doors and yanked out the tightest black satin shorts she owned, her favorite black satin, boned corset and her most comfortable and practical knee-high Doc Martins. She was channeling English punk rocker to be sure, but it fit her state of mind—rebellious. The ironic fact she was partly rebelling against herself wasn't lost on her.

Five minutes later, she shoved her knife into a hidden holster at the small of her back, tied her hair into a knot at the back of her head and fastened two thick, solid silver slave bracelets around each wrist. As striking as they were with their ancient glyphs worked into the silver, they weren't just for show. If needed, both could crack a man or demon's skull open quite nicely.

With God's luck, she'd get to use them tonight. She had to admit, the thought of splintering the leech's skull made her very happy. Very happy indeed.

She turned on her heel and faced the broken full-length mirror in the corner of her bedroom, the one she'd thrown Ezryn into only last night. Refusing to linger on the memory of that moment, she studied her splintered image reflected back in the cracked glass. She looked good. She looked sexy. She looked...tormented.

She drew in a long breath. *Okay, Chayse, are you ready for this?*

Her pulse quickened. Her stomach churned. She pulled in another breath, ready to face what the night held for her. And froze when someone knocked on her apartment door.

He's here.

Inari stared into her reflected wide eyes.

He's here.

Her pulse leapt into violent life, thumping in her neck like a trapped moth.

Who? Ezryn? Or the leech?

Keeping her movements calm, steady, she turned and walked from her bedroom. She felt numb, and at the same time destroyed by fire. Her heart smashed against her breastbone, a painful tattoo that grew faster the closer she drew to her apartment door.

She reached out her hand and wrapped her fingers around the doorknob, its solid metal form cold against her skin. Its chill radiated through her palm and up her arm. Pinched her nipples tight.

He's here. To kill you.

Her pulse thumped in her neck at the ominous thought, quick and breath-stealing. She clenched her jaw, placed her left hand on her knife's hilt and opened the door at the exact second the back of her neck erupted with prickling heat.

A tall, blond and stunningly handsome man stood at her threshold, light blue eyes focused on her face, broad shoulders almost as wide as her doorway.

Vampire.

The word roared through Inari's head. The itch on the nape of her neck grew fierce. She yanked her blade from its sheath, every molecule in her body instantly charged with potent force, ready to attack. To fight.

"Inari Chayse," the vampire said, a strong Scottish accent roughening her name to almost a snarl. "If you want to survive the night, you need to come with me."

Chapter Nine

Jacob studied the petite little thing standing before him and thought, *Curse it.*

This close, he could see just how petite she was. Barely coming up to his chest, she looked as fragile as a china doll with features just as delicate, but that didn't lessen the impact of her presence or the power of her sexuality. Damn it all, if he didn't know Ezryn would rip out his throat, he'd sink his teeth into her flesh right this very moment and feed on her sweet Sentinel blood.

Dangerous, General Ancroft. Keep your fangs sheathed and your mind on the task at hand. Tasting Inari Chayse is not why you are here.

He clenched his teeth. The aggressive hunger simmering through his veins was unexpected and worrying, but he welcomed it. His reaction to the Sentinel was a sharp blow of harsh reality. He had to remember what she was, what Ven Watkins had told Ezryn she was—a succubus. A sex demon assassin of the order of Sentinel.

Vampires were not easily influenced by a sex demon's force, but they weren't immune either. That he was overcome with the instant urge to tear the clothes from her delicious body, bend her over the closest bench, chair, bed, stair rail and sink his fangs into her flesh and his dick into her sex told him she was a *very* powerful succubus. It reminded him he was walking a treacherous path.

But it's the only path you have available, Jacob. You're going to have to walk it carefully.

"I'm sorry, there is no time for me to explain," he said, keeping his stare locked on the woman's exquisitely beautiful face. It was safer that way. Just. "But you need to understand, if you don't come with me now there will be a war between our two species mankind will have little hope of surviving."

Inari Chayse's dark eyebrows pulled into a scowl and her grip on the wicked knife in her left hand tightened. "Understand this, vampire. I don't know how you know who I am, or found your way to my door, but you have two seconds to leave before I turn you to dust."

Her husky voice played with Jacob's senses, and despite her threat his dick jerked with lust. It was like listening to a siren's call—every syllable she spoke threaded into his being and set him on sexual fire. Was it because she was succubus or Sentinel? He'd never faced a Sentinel before, let alone a female one. Was it the assassin's very gender that aroused him? The idea of a creature born to be his mortal enemy in such a sexy, desirable form? He curled his hands into balls at his side. Fuck, he wanted to bite her. Now. And not just bite her. He wanted to bury his dick in her sex and let her ride his body until he came.

All he had to do was grab her, throw her against the wall and—

No. You won't. You could not betray Ezryn any more than you could betray yourself. Besides, you can't enter her home. She hasn't given you permission.

He bit back a curse, staying his right hand before it could test the invisible barrier separating them. If it wasn't there, or it wasn't strong, he doubted he had the strength to stop himself doing exactly what his body wanted him to do. If he did that, his plan would be shot. He hadn't counted on the overwhelming hunger the woman evoked in him, but if he was to prevent Ezryn's destruction, he had to control it. Inari Chayse was off-limits. For more reason than one.

He clenched his teeth, the gnawing urgency in the pit of his belly unnerving him. "I am General Jacob Ancroft, and it doesn't matter *how* I came to your door, Sentinel. What *does* matter is I am here to save your life."

The intoxicating scent of her flesh seeped into his being with each word he spoke. The delicate perfume of her sex slipping over his tongue. There was no need to draw breath, but he found himself doing so just to experience her on even the most removed level. His mouth filled with saliva, his cock grew heavy and his balls began to throb. Dark Ones, he actually felt giddy.

Inari Chayse's ice-green eyes narrowed. Her stare grew more contemptuous. "And just why do you think my life is in jeopardy, General Ancroft?"

Jacob felt his ancient vampire force rise at the angry heat radiating from her body, reacting not just to a possible threat but a possible feed. His lineage was old and noble, one of the original vampire families of the Isles, but he was still a creature of horrific myth, and the Sentinel's anger provoked that creature like a child stirring an ant's nest with a stick. He shoved the unhelpful response deep down into the pit of his gut and held her stare. "My master, the vampire Ezryn, is coming for you."

The contempt left Inari's face in a split second. Her eyes grew wide. Her full lips parted in a soft gasp. The potent aroma of her feminine juices flooded the air and her heartbeat doubled, the frantic sound almost a deafening thump for Jacob's hypersensitive hearing. "Ezryn?" she whispered on a breath.

Something scalding hot and acrid punched into Jacob's chest, making his nostrils flare. Jealousy?

He sank his nails into his palms, the unmistakable emotions catching him by surprise. Jealousy? Hell's Pit. What the fuck was he doing experiencing jealousy?

Determined to deny his ridiculous reaction, he took a step closer to her only to be stopped by the invisible wall he knew would be there, a wall of no substance and no tactile composition but still capable of halting him cold in his tracks.

A low growl rumbled in his throat, and he punched his fist against the doorjamb. He let his stare turn hard, desperate for the Sentinel to—*invite you in?*—to understand the situation. "Please, Ms. Chayse, we are running out of time." He struggled to keep his voice calm and modulated. "When I left Ezryn he was—how shall I put this? Less than happy."

She started a little, her cheeks flushing, her breath growing rapid. His gaze strayed to the tiny pulse beating at the base of her neck, the whisper-loud roar of her blood journeying through her veins mocking him. Saliva filled his mouth again. He felt his fangs stab at the inside of his lower lip, needle-point sharp and long, and his inner vampire growled for release.

He jerked his stare back up to her face, disgust surging through his lifeless veins. Dark Ones. Where was his control? His loyalty?

"If you do *anything* I don't like, I *will* destroy you. Regardless of who your master is."

Inari's blunt statement, plus the deadly promise in her eyes, filled Jacob with perverse relief. She was coming with him. He gave her a sharp nod. "I understand."

Inari studied him with an unwavering gaze before she too nodded. "Good. Now tell me why you would risk saving my life when others of your kind would want me dead?"

Jacob let out a sharp breath. "I need you to help me stop a senseless slaughter." He shifted his feet, the passing minutes pressing down on him. On them both. Ezryn would not be far away. He couldn't be. Curse it, he had to hurry up and get her out of her home. "There is a vampire here in Australia who needs to be destroyed," he said, the struggle to keep his voice calm growing more damn near impossible, by the second. "I have sworn to my master I will not be the one to do so." He stopped. Fixed her with a level stare. "I need you to do it for me."

Inari's eyebrows rose, her face effecting an incredulous expression of pointed surprise. "Oh, do you now? Who is this vampire?"

Jacob bit back a growl. "Dark Ones, I will tell you on the way, I promise. Please, Ms. Chayse, we must go now."

She shook her head. "Tell me."

"The overlord of the vampire race," Jacob snarled, his nerves at snapping point. "And Ezryn's brother."

A soft intake of breath slipped through Inari's lips, and for a split, irrational second, Jacob longed to feel their fullness pressed to his. "Ezryn is Ezryn *Navarro*?" she said, her voice as soft as her breath. "The twin son of the First Family? The *true* overlord of the vampire race?"

Jacob stiffened. "How do you know...?"

"Every Sentinel knows of the unjust, moronic events that took place fifty years ago. It becomes part of our psyche the moment we are reborn."

Jacob drove his nails into his palms. Anger coursed through his still veins, thick and hot. Of course a Sentinel would know of Harry's lies. It was a given, wasn't it? But if that was the case, why hadn't the Deities ordered the treacherous, dangerous bastard disposed? "And yet," he snapped, his tenuous composure fracturing, "nothing was done to stop it? Even when it was clear Haral was a power-drunk imbecile? "

She flashed him an ambiguous smile. "We are assassins, *demon*, not political activists. What better way to weaken your enemy than to allow the rot to spread from within?"

Jacob studied her, unsure what to say. If she was shocked at discovering her lover was the true overlord of every vampire on the planet, she did not show it. Nor did she show any sign of how the information affected her. Did it change anything? Knowing who Ezryn was? Knowing he was, essentially, the ultimate vampire? How had she not already put the pieces together?

"And this is why he is coming for me?" she asked suddenly, her voice composed. "To save his twin brother's undead life? The brother who sits in his position through fallacy and deceit?"

"No." He forced his voice to be as level as hers. "He comes for you because he now knows what you are."

Inari cocked one dark eyebrow. "Sentinel? Come now, bloodsucker, I think he already knows I'm an assassin of God, don't—"

"Not Sentinel, Inari Chayse," Jacob cut her off, dread feeding his impatience. "Succubus."

Inari's face went pale. The word hung on the air between them, its meaning not lost on Jacob. She stared at him, but whatever thoughts went through her mind did not form as words on her tongue.

"Ezryn is coming for you, assassin," he said, the statement blunt and spoken with desperate haste, "and I don't know what he plans to do when he gets here, but I need you to come with me to destroy his brother before we are all condemned to a bloody war by that fucker's egomaniacal actions."

She still didn't say a word, her face a pale mask of perfect beauty.

"The overlord has commanded Ezryn to kill you," Jacob continued, deciding now was not the time to pull punches. "If he doesn't, as of tomorrow night the overlord will begin systematically butchering every vampire who opposed his ascension. I don't need to tell you what will happen if he does."

Inari's expression didn't change, but Jacob could feel the tension rolling from her in heady waves. She knew, all right. How could she not? She was a Sentinel, after all.

"So he is on his way to kill me then."

It wasn't a question.

He swallowed, not just his throat thick, but his blood as well. His response to her nearness was stirring the base creature he was with such alacrity he could barely think. "Until Ezryn discovered what you are," he said, holding her gaze, "I genuinely believed my master was not going to do it. Now...” He let the threat hang on his unfinished sentence.

“But now he knows what kind of demon I was before my rebirth...” An expression of lost torment etched her face and she closed her eyes, her straight eyebrows pulling into a slight frown. “Now he knows why he can’t stop fucking me...and thinking about me...” She let out a soft sigh, her shoulders slumping.

Jacob suppressed a low groan, his chest heavy. Damn Haral for the nightmare he’d thrown them all into. Damn the bastard prick to the lowest pit in Hell.

He stood motionless, watching her, waiting, willing her to move. To open her eyes and see his desperation. The situation was beyond any he could fear, but if he could just see Harry destroyed, everything else would right itself, including whatever was going on between Ezryn and the woman standing before him. Of that, he was certain. “Please, Ms. Chayse. Time is our enemy.”

She didn’t respond, nor open her eyes to look at him.

“Do you understand, Ms. Chayse?”

“Understand what, General Ancroft?”

The deep male voice behind him turned Jacob’s cold blood to ice. He froze, his stare locked on Inari’s face, his throat squeezing tight as her eyes snapped open and flooded with fear.

“Ezryn,” she whispered, taking a step backward.

“I have told you repeatedly, Inari Chayse,” Ezryn said, “to call me Master.” There was a dark blur of mass, a surge of displaced air, and suddenly Jacob was staring at Ezryn’s back, his master towering over Inari in the middle of her apartment, his right hand cupping her throat. “And you are wearing far too many clothes.”

With barely a flex of his shoulders, Ezryn threw her against the sofa. Her ass hit the cushioned armrest. The knife in her hand clattered to the floor. Before she could regain balance, he crossed to her in another blur, curling the fingers of his left hand around her upper arm and hauling her against his body. She slammed into him, and Jacob could only watch from the threshold, stunned and painfully aroused as she smashed her knee upward, aiming for his master's groin.

Yet Ezryn seemed to predict her move. He snatched at her leg, grabbing her high on the thigh and yanking her knee beside his body. "Now, now." Ezryn's guttural murmur reached Jacob across Inari's living room, and Jacob felt his stomach knot at the molten fury in each word. "Anyone would think you don't like me...succubus."

He spun her about, his arms and hands encircling her, imprisoning her with impossible speed to jerk her back against his body. He flattened one hand over the plane of her belly, skimmed his fingertips across the curve between her thighs while snaking the other hand up her ribcage to capture one satin-covered breast. Two pairs of eyes stared at Jacob from within the small room—Ezryn's black and smoldering cold fire and Inari's green and wide with...with...

Fear? Expectation? Excitement?

"Tell him to leave, Inari."

Jacob's body flooded with grim foreboding at Ezryn's murmured command. If he left the Sentinel alone with his master and friend it was unlikely she'd survive the night. He'd never seen Ezryn so furious. Ever. He couldn't let Inari Chayse be killed, however, no matter how angry Ezryn was. How would he rid the world of Fat Harry if she was—

"Tell General Ancroft he's not needed here, Inari," Ezryn repeated. He slid his hand lower down her belly, dipping his fingers between her tightly pressed thighs. "Now."

Inari shook her head. "No."

The fingers between her thighs moved, a slow, short, stroking motion that made Jacob's groin throb and his fangs extend. Ezryn lowered his head to Inari's, brushing his lips over her cheek as the hand on her breast began to inch higher on her chest. "Tell my general to leave, Inari, or I will deny you what the wet heat between your legs tells me you so desperately want."

She whimpered, the sound sending a surge of hot hunger through Jacob.

Hunger for what? The Sentinel's blood or the succubus's sex?

Ezryn's black eyes glinted red power and he cupped her chin with firm fingers, holding her head motionless as he feathered a row of kisses down the column of her neck. "Tell him to leave, Sentinel, so I can make you scream."

Jacob held Inari's stare, his body on fire, his chest constricting. This was bad. Very bad.

"Tell him to leave us," Ezryn ordered against her neck, his fangs scraping her flesh. "Now."

"Leave us, General Ancroft." The command fell from Inari in a whispered breath.

Jacob's nostrils flared. He pressed his fist to the doorjamb, gazing hard into Inari's eyes. "Ms. Chayse," he said, ignoring Ezryn's heavy stare. "Please. I need—"

"Go home, Jacob," Ezryn's low voice silenced him, and he stiffened as a faint pressure brushed at his mind. "You are not needed here."

* * *

The overlord moved through his commandeered compound, grinding his molars together. Fucking Sydney. The level of loyalty for his brother in the shit-hole of a city pissed him off. Finding a vampire willing to act against the *venerated* Ezryn Navarro in this backwater dump was harder than finding a bleeder willing to step into the sun.

He stormed along the corridor, heading for the ballroom. The only thing he'd found remotely pleasurable about his sojourn *down under* was the feeding. Something about the summer sun in the southern hemisphere seemed to permeate the females from which he'd fed. Their warm flesh tasted fresh and crisp under his tongue, their blood different in an indefinable way from the humans in the northern hemisphere, as if the very essence of the place infused the elixir flowing through their delicate veins.

A dry snort escaped him and he shook his head. It was both delicious and jarring, and he wanted no more of it. He wanted to go home. He'd had enough of Sydney and Australia. There was too much sun, too much heat. He liked the bitter cold of Denmark. He liked the subservient minions of his home as well, groveling vampires who dared not make mention of his brother. Lifers who knew better than to balk at his commands, who accepted his position of authority without question or doubt. Bleeders who wanted nothing more than to please the overlord, the supreme ruler of the vampiré race.

During his time in Sydney so far, he'd had to slaughter five of his own kind. Five lifers he'd thought his own loyalists who were more willing to face his wrath to follow the great and reverent Ezryn. *Lifers.*

Five *born* vampires who should have known better.

You know there are more. You know Ezryn's followers are beginning to outnumber your own. Not just here in the ass of the world, but everywhere. It's why you came to Sydney in the first place. Your rule is being questioned more every night, and not just by lifers but by bleeders as well. The doubt of your position is spreading like a pathetic human disease, and if you don't do something soon, Ezryn's loyalists will see you overthrown.

Haral curled his hands into fists and bared his teeth in a hiss. The moment he ascended to overlord, the vampire world should have bowed to his authority. The position allowed no dissension and came with immediate deference. It was the way it was and the way it would always fucking be. But it *wasn't* the fucking way, was it? Instead of respect and grateful servitude, he'd spent every night dealing with uprisings, dissidents and revolts. Instead, he'd destroyed more than one doubter of the oracle's proclamation. Instead, he'd killed one after another after another of his brother's loyalists. And still Ezryn's devotees grew stronger. Louder.

Worrisome.

Threatening.

Haral needed to destroy the hero worship held for his brother. He needed to make Ezryn's loyalists desist in questioning why the blood trials had named him overlord. He needed to make them hate his brother, not long for Ezryn's inevitable ascension.

He needed to turn devoted love to vile contempt.

What better way than to have Ezryn responsible for a bloody, senseless war between vampires and Sentinel? What better way to cement his own right to the supreme position than to be the voice of reason, the voice that brought peace between the Realm and the assassins of the Highest?

What better way than to disgrace his brother in the eyes of his own deluded kind?

He threw open the doors to the ballroom and stormed into the massive room, its opulence soothing his wounds. The candles lining the walls and adorning the gilt antique furniture flickered and spluttered in his wake, their warm yellow life fighting for survival. He understood their struggle. They were, indeed, the perfect metaphor for his very existence.

A faint scuffing noise tickled Haral's senses, and he turned his attention from the room's candles to stare at the six human females chained naked in the far corner. Fear oozed from their sun-kissed flesh, mingling with their sweat. Six Australian women who never in their wildest nightmares dreamed vampires existed until they were plucked from the streets by his loyal host, the human owner of the mansion, and delivered to him as a welcoming gift.

In a silent blur, he crossed to them, enjoying the frightened gasps his unnatural speed elicited from them. Letting his expression become contemplative, he studied them, noting the absolute terror in their eyes. As scared as they were, they knew better than to scream. The last woman who screamed in his presence had had her head ripped from her body before the screeching note could finish leaving her throat.

Their fear, silent it was, brought a smile to his face. He was Haral Navarro, and he was born to be feared. This was the way it was meant to be. This was power. Strength.

"The way it is," he whispered, his gaze roaming from one terrified cow to another, "and the way it will fucking be."

His mind mulled over the course of events to come, his dick growing fat with eager anticipation. One more night before Ezryn was forced to comply with his orders. One more night before big brother's reputation and existence were decimated.

Which gave Haral one more night and one more day to locate the Sentinel slut. With the Sentinel in *his* hands, his plans for his brother rose to a whole new level.

He chuckled. On learning Ezzie was tongue-deep in the assassin's cunt, his plan had begun to formulate. A plan that would not just see his big brother dead, but vilified beyond all measure. A simple plan really, but a very effective one—capture the Sentinel, chain her naked and spread-eagle in the ballroom, fuck her and feed from her until she was almost an empty shell before ordering Ezryn to kill her there and then. Simple.

Unless he truly wanted the blood of his followers on his hands, Ezzie would have no choice but to do as commanded. The second he did, Haral would release footage of the heinous deed to the world. With a little bit of creative editing, the vampire race would see their hero, the prodigal son of the First Family, butcher a naked, chained and obviously raped female Sentinel while she was defenseless in her human form. They would see Ezryn rip her throat out as she no doubt begged him not to. They would see Ezzie murder her in cold blood. Undeniable, irrefutable proof Ezryn was not the fucking vampire messiah.

Haral chuckled again. Not just a simple plan but also a sweet plan. The absolute destruction of his brother with a delicious added bonus. The blood of a Sentinel was, from what Haral had heard, quite a rush. He looked forward to discovering how much.

You still have to find her. And bring Ezryn to heel. How many of your own guards do you think he will slaughter trying to save her?

He sneered at the thought. It didn't matter. The end justified the means. A lesson taught long ago by his blood-drunkard idiot father.

Turning his mind from his troublesome brother for a moment, he let his attention linger on one particular female cowering in the corner before him. Her thighs were plump and dimpled with cellulite, her belly round and fleshy, her breasts full and tipped with pale pink nipples pinched hard with fear. Her sweat leached from her pores, salty sweet and tinged with the metallic tang of her body's female blood. He smiled, his mouth growing wet. She was menstruating. Even better. The perfect feed. He would sate his lust and then sate his hunger.

"My Lord?"

Fury flooded through Haral and he hissed, spinning on his heel. How dare he be intruded upon in the ballroom? He locked his stare on one of his many servants scurrying toward him from the far door, the whimpering cries of the women behind him enflaming his rage even more.

The bleeder came to a halt before him, half-bowing, half-cringing. "You wished to be advised on any news of Ezryn Navarro?" he gushed, eyes downcast. "He was spotted moving through the city's streets less than an hour ago."

Haral narrowed his eyes. "Spotted by whom?"

"A human pet," the servant blurted, head lowered, hands knotted. "The source is to be trusted. He is one of our most loyal donors, eager to be granted the transforming bite."

Haral looked at the vamp before him, trying to ignore the familiar unease stirring in his gut. "Is there anything else?"

The vampire nodded, his expression wary. "General Jacob Ancroft has been seen moving through the streets as well. Heading for—"

Haral snapped his hand up, silencing the servant. Ancroft was in Australia as well? Why had he not known this? His throat grew tight and he ground his molars again. He should have known his brother's lackey wouldn't be far away from Ezzie's side.

A heavy pressure squeezed his chest. General Ancroft presented a problem he hadn't counted on. The Scottish vampire was a threat. Ancroft despised him. Ancroft wanted him a pile of smoldering ash. Ancroft wanted to *make* him that pile of ash and was quite capable of doing so. Only Ezryn held him in check.

Haral let out a guttural growl. He would need to eradicate the general as well as his brother. He stamped his foot, the sound like a shot in the ballroom's silence, and the women behind him squealed. "Fuck. Why isn't anything ever easy?"

Use this information. Use their weaknesses against them and destroy all three at once.

The thought slid through Haral's head, soft and absolute. He narrowed his eyes, considering the possibility. Ezryn's weakness had always been his compassion, but Jacob Ancroft's weakness was his heart. He was ruled by it. Friendship? Love? Ancroft believed in both.

Use those weaknesses then. Use them to destroy them all.

He turned away from the bowing servant and slid his gaze back to the silent females staring at him. Back to the plump woman with the full breasts and oh, so delicious fear.

Ezryn, Ancroft and the Sentinel. Destroy all three at once.

He smiled, letting them see his fangs.

And to think his father had accused him of never amounting to anything, of never being as great as the prodigal son. If only Fredrik Navarro were alive to witness his son's triumph…if only he could see what Haral was about to achieve. Maybe then he'd give his son the attention he deserved. Maybe then he would look at him the same way he looked at Ezzie.

His smile stretched wider as he stepped toward the woman with the dimpled, blood-smeared thighs.

All three at once.

Dark Ones, he couldn't have planned it better.

Chapter Ten

Ezryn felt his general's resistance surge through his mind, a thick sludge of demonic force tainting his normally calm subconscious. Jacob did not want to leave, did not want to walk away from Inari. The very notion filled him with such intense unease his vampire's core was taking over.

"Jacob." Ezryn fixed his stare on Jacob's face, noting with detached interest how pointed his general's fangs had become. How elongated. The vampire coming to the surface. "Jacob, go home."

A shudder wracked Jacob's body. He bared his teeth, jaw clenched. "I can't do that, Ezryn. I need Inari—"

Cold jealousy rolled through Ezryn, irrational and pressing. Jealousy that his general dare believe he had reason to be near Inari. Jealousy that Inari had been speaking of something secret with Jacob—even through the doorway.

Jealousy that Jacob looked at Inari as if seeing her for what she was. What she *truly* was.

He snarled, yanking Inari harder to his body. "Go home, Jacob." He pushed the command deeper into Jacob's resistant mind. "Now."

"Let me go, Ezryn." Inari struggled in his hold.

He ignored her, his focus narrowed on Jacob's face. Dismay twisted in his gut at the turbulent uncertainty etched there. His friend fought his true self just as much as he fought Ezryn's command to leave.

Jealousy rippled through him again, building into a crashing wave of rage. "Jake." He narrowed his thoughts into a single, pushing suggestion. "You need to go home."

His dismay drilled deeper into his gut, his rage mounting. He'd never had the need to influence Jacob's will before. That he did so now tormented him. And infuriated him.

Succubus.

The word slipped through his head like an oiled serpent, and his anger turned hotter.

Inari. Succubus.

A low growl rumbled in his chest and he tightened his arms around her body. Curse it, he wanted to fuck her. Even knowing what she was, what she was doing to Jacob, he wanted to bury himself in her wet heat.

Succubus.

Gut heavy, chest tight, he sent out another concentrated push to his friend. "Jake, go home." He kept his voice calm but forceful. "Now."

Jacob blinked once. His gaze slipped to Inari, his nostrils flared and he turned on his heel and left, moving away from the door and along the corridor in a blur of cold flight.

"What in all the levels of hell—" Inari began, but Ezryn didn't let her finish.

He shoved her away from him, pinning her against the wall of her living room with his body before she could regain control. His cock pressed against the junction of her thighs, his chest crushed her breasts. He could smell her musk, taste it on the very air. Dark Ones, he wanted her. "What did you do to him?"

Her eyes widened. "What do you mean? I didn't do anything to him."

"I beg to differ." He snaked his hands up her arms. Snaring the silver bracelets circling her wrists, he grit his teeth against the pain searing into his flesh and yanked them off, throwing them aside with a sneer. Fixing his stare on hers, he curled the fingers of his right hand around her throat. Her pulse beat against his palm, wild and erratic. "I've never had to influence my general like I had to just now."

Inari's eyes narrowed. "Influence?" She squirmed beneath him. "No wonder you were born to be overlord. Could you be any more of a control freak?"

Ezryn chuckled, dragging his thumb over her bottom lip. "Most definitely, succubus."

"Fuck off, vampire."

He lowered his head closer to her face. "Not until I've finished what I came here to do." He closed his fingers tighter around her throat, stared into her eyes, drew her sweet scent into his body and took possession of her lips with his.

His kiss was savage.

His tongue delved into her mouth, battled with hers. Explosive heat erupted in the pit of her belly, a heat further stoked by the head of Ezryn's erection massaging the tiny button of her clit through her pants. She whimpered, and the wretched sound was captured by Ezryn's brutal mouth. The heat in the junction of her thighs grew wet and she rolled her hips, hating herself even as she grew desperate for Ezryn to enter her.

Instead, he dragged his lips from hers and chuckled in her ear, a low, husky laugh of pure malice. "Tonight, *I* am the master of your sexual slavery, Inari. I *am* the one in control. You have no power. No say. *I* decide when you are pleasured and when you will come."

"Fuck off," she growled again.

Ezryn laughed, brushing his lips against her cheek, a cold caress that made her pussy weep. "Tell me to remove your clothing."

Inari's mouth went dry. "Go to hell."

He pushed his hips to hers and ground his erection against the curve of her pussy. "We've had this conversation before, succubus." He slid his left hand down her ribcage, over her hip to her ass. "And we both know where it ended. With me between your thighs, feasting on your cream. Now tell me to remove your clothing."

Anger ripped through the black desire consuming her. "Just who the hell do you think you are?"

"I know who I am," Ezryn squeezed her ass cheek with brutal pressure before sliding his hands back to her hip. "And now I know who you are, *what* you are too. Now tell me to remove your clothing."

"Fuck you."

The red shards in his eyes glowed brighter. "Very well."

He lifted his hands to the deep V of her corset and popped the top clasp.

The slight release of pressure on her breasts sent a jolt of wicked excitement through her, and she gasped. She kept her stare locked on his eyes, the lust she saw in their clear depths making her pulse pound, keeping her motionless. Rooted to the spot. Or was it his thick, restrained cock nudging between her legs? Or both?

Whatever the reason, she didn't shove him away. She didn't want to. By the Dieties, she was...

Without a word, Ezryn released another clasp on her corset, and a liquid charge of pleasure shot through her.

"Tell me how it feels to not be in control, Inari," His low order sent another jolt deep into her very center. "To be defenseless against a force greater than yours."

She couldn't reply. Her throat felt thick. She stood frozen, held prisoner by his arms and smoldering eyes. He wasn't just a vampire. He was *the* vampire, the first born of the first family. The vampire born to be the leader of them all, denied that role by a corrupt, meaningless ritual. Was that the reason for his power? Was that the reason he could reduce her to a slave of her own pleasure with just a simple word, a single look? Did it all make sense now? Or was she grasping for truths that weren't there?

"Tell me how it feels to be the slave to your own pleasure," he murmured, pressing the thick steel of his erection harder to her sex. "*Succubus.*"

At the hissed title, he grabbed the front of her corset with both hands and tore it open.

Inari cried out, her breasts tumbling free, her sex flooding with traitorous cream.

He scooped each revealed curve of flesh into his palms and dragged his thumbnail over her rock-hard nipples. The fire in his eyes flared to a scalding blaze and he dropped his head, his mouth claiming her right nipple with fierce greed.

She arched her back, her ass slamming into the wall behind her as he sucked hard on her nipple. Wet electricity shot through her body, sinking into her core with alarming speed. Her pussy gushed damp heat and she whimpered, Ezryn's teeth nipping at her flesh.

"Yes, Inari." His growl vibrated through her breast, into her body. "I can smell your arousal." He slipped his hand between their bodies and rolled his fingers over her crotch, stroking her clit through the drenched satin of her pants. "I can feel how hot you are. How wet." He slid his hand from between her legs and, unable to stop the shameful sound, Inari whimpered.

He chuckled, smoothing his hand over the flatness of her belly. "Tell me how much you like the feel of my mouth on your breast." He dipped his hand back to her sodden groin and slapped it lightly with the tips of his fingers. "How much you like the feel of my hand on your sweet, wet pussy."

His cruel order made her moan and she shook her head. No. She wouldn't. She wouldn't.

He chuckled again, his low laughter setting her nerve endings alight. She squirmed in his hold, pressing her thighs together, her clit a tiny ball of swollen need, her womb heavy with urgent want.

He returned his mouth to her breast, suckling, biting before sliding his lips up her chest to her neck. She felt his fangs score a lazy line over the base of her throat and another whimper slipped from her. By the Dieties, she was going to come.

"Not until I say so, Sentinel." His whisper tickled her ear and he took a step backward, his nostrils flaring as he gazed at her with blatant hunger. "Tell me to remove your pants."

Inari's breath caught in her throat. She thought of Ezryn between her legs, of his hands pushing her thighs wide as his tongue delved into her folds. She thought of his cock, thick and hard and oh, so long, pressed at her sex, its bulbous head teasing the tight cleft. Her pussy throbbed, squeezing with base lust and primitive desire.

"Tell me, Inari," Ezryn commanded, the tips of his fingers playing with the waistline of her shorts. "Or I will tie you to the bed and leave you untouched."

"Remove my pants, Ezryn."

The words came from her in a wavering whisper. Her surrender clear. Undeniable.

Slowly, his stare never leaving her face, he lowered himself to his knees and popped the button of her fly. He pulled down her zipper.

Inari's pulse quickened. She could barely breathe. *Oh, Dark Ones, yes...*

Her cry to the dark, demonic gods should have terrified her. It didn't. She was once their most faithful servant. A succubus who delivered more than their fill of human souls. The memory of that former life, her former self sliced into her with horrifying, seductive pain.

Fight it, Inari. Don't lose yourself. Don't...

"Tell me, Inari Chayse." Ezryn's cool lips brushed the flatness of her belly and she bit back another whimper. "Would you like me to touch your breasts while I fuck you with my tongue?" He placed a soft kiss at the base of her navel and let the tip of one fang touch her flesh before pulling his head away. "Or would you like me to cup and squeeze your ass with my hands while I suck on your clit?"

Inari closed her eyes, her knees weak. How did she survive this? How did she survive Ezryn's cruelty?

How did she beg him to never end it?

Cool fingers skimmed over the tip of her right nipple, sending a shard of concentrated pleasure into the pit of her belly. One touch. One barely felt touch. "Answer me, Inari."

"Yes, Ezryn," she whispered, pressing her hips forward, wanting him to pull her shorts down her legs and sink his tongue between her thighs.

"Yes, what, Inari?"

She felt Ezryn studying her, his eyes like a molten caress. Smelled her own musk on the air as his stare roamed her face. "Yes, I want you to touch my breasts while..." She faltered, her cheeks filling with shamed warmth even as her sex filled with wet heat.

He feathered his fingertips over her nipple again. "While what?"

"While you fuck me with your mouth."

"How much, Sentinel?"

Inari ground her teeth, squirming against the wall. "Curse you, bloodsucker."

"How much?"

Bastard.

She glared at him, pressing her hips forward, wanting to feel his mouth on her sex.

Ezryn chuckled. "Will you tell me if I do this?" He slid his lips over her belly, explored the curve of her waist and slid back down to her navel. "Or when I do this?" He blew a fine stream of cold air on the path his lips had just traveled, and Inari's flesh rippled with an elemental response. "Or this?"

He touched his lips to the curve of her sex exposed by her open fly, tracing his tongue in a small circle on her sensitive skin before he lifted his head to stare at her again.

Inari bit back a cry. He was a bastard. An absolute bastard, and she was going to kill him.

"Tell me you are mine, Inari, and your first orgasm of the evening will be but a flick of my tongue away." He skimmed his fingers up the underswell of her breasts and circled each nipple with languid arrogance. "And your second but a twist of my fingers."

She was burning. On fire. She was going to come. All it would take was one more touch. One more... "Go to hell."

He hooked his fingers into the waistline of her shorts and tore them apart.

"Aren't we already there, my sweet little demon?"

He slid hard hands up her partly exposed thighs, played long fingers over her cleft for a tantalizing second before he pushed her legs wide. "You smell like honeyed wine, Inari," he murmured, blowing a thin stream of cold air on the damp folds of her pussy. "I am going to drink of you so deeply. Now—" he flicked his tongue at her slit, a teasing stab that made her hiss, "—tell me you belong to me."

The word *no* formed in her mind.

The words, "I'm yours, damn you, I'm yours," fell from her lips in a raw, choked moan.

Without preamble, he grabbed the back of her knees, jerked her feet off the floor and hooked her legs over his shoulders. She gasped, his abrupt action ramming her back harder to the wall. She grabbed at his hair and held him in a death grip as his mouth took possession of her sex.

"Oh, God!" Inari cried out, her body erupting in explosive pleasure. He stabbed his tongue into her folds, rolled it over her clit. She bucked, her spread pussy slamming harder to his open mouth, her shoulders pushing harder to the wall. She reached for him and buried her hands in his hair, holding on as he sucked savagely on her clit, his hands mauling her ass with increasing frenzy. "God!"

"*He* has no say in your pleasure either, Inari." Ezryn lifted his head from her sex. His black stare pinned her to the wall as surely as his hands and body did. "Only I do." He gripped her thighs. "And that is the way I intend to keep it. Succubus or no, you are my slave, my food source now." His face was so close to her sex she could feel the chill of his body seep into her flushed folds. A shiver rippled up her spine, its menacing bliss intensified by the cool moisture of his saliva on her spread thighs and pussy. By the Powers, how had this happened? How had she become a prisoner of not only a master vampire but also her own licentious pleasure?

Who cares?

"To think," Ezryn whispered, "all this time I believed it was some ridiculous notion of desire drawing me to you."

Her breath caught in her throat and Ezryn chuckled, the sound soulless, callous and wickedly carnal. "Time to scream, Sentinel."

His eyes shimmered red fire and his mouth reclaimed her pussy, his teeth capturing her clit.

Her orgasm claimed her, sharp and savage. She arched, bucking into his mouth, her cries growing louder with each abrupt wave of tension crashing through her. Ezryn lapped at her cream, his tongue penetrating her folds, stroking her heat.

"Fuck!" Inari burst out, both at his invading tongue and masterful hands. He massaged her butt cheeks in tightening squeezes, the pressure echoing the building eruption in her sex. It was as though he could feel her climax through her wanton body and gave it back to her, his fingers detonating pulses of pleasurable pain that seemed to feed her orgasm until it consumed her. Owned her. "Oh, God, yes, yes!"

His tongue lashed faster at her clit. He sucked the aching tip into his mouth, flicking his tongue over it again as he sank one finger, two, three into her pussy.

Stars of dizzying color filled Inari's vision. She slammed her head back into the wall, eyes squeezed shut, incapable of thought. Without warning, Ezryn removed her legs from his shoulders and snapped upright, charting a path with his lips up her neck to her ear and back to her neck again. "Dark Ones, you smell so delicious." His growl caressed her senses, and in a distant part of her mind, the coolly rational part on which she'd survived since becoming a Sentinel, she heard a tremble in his voice. "So cursedly delicious." He scraped his fangs along her throat and she shuddered, her juices slicking her thighs.

He captured her chin with a punishing grip and jerked her face to his, crushed his mouth to her lips with a growl so demonic and primitive she felt her skin prickle.

Fire. God. She was on fire.

He plunged his tongue into her mouth, possessing it with total domination, and the woman she was, the female being drowning in sensual bliss, surrendered. A willing servant to the vampire's ownership of her pleasure.

No!

Her shout of terrified dismay shattered the heady lust fogging her mind. She clamped her fist tighter in Ezryn's hair, shutting out the rapture of his kiss as she yanked his head backward.

He tore his mouth from hers, and for a split second, she swore his face contorted with confused regret. And then he chuckled again, that low, throaty laugh that made her pussy throb and her throat thick. "So the succubus still fights for control? Or is it the Sentinel?"

Mindless hunger blazed in his eyes. The same mindless hunger Inari had seen before in the eyes of so many of her victims from a lifetime ago. Her breath caught. She *was* succubus again. She could feel it in her very core, in the very center of what made her female.

Is that so bad?

Fangs glinting, he smiled at her. "Either way," he murmured. "I will enjoy the battle."

Ezryn skimmed his fingertips over her breasts, her arm, and

curled his fingers around her wrist in a grip she knew she would never be able to break.

Then don't try.

The silent command whispered through her head and, as in the Pleasure Palace, she could not tell if it was her voice or his.

She looked up at him, her heart racing. For a still moment—barely a heartbeat in time—she thought he was going to say something else. And then it was gone, replaced by an unreadable expression, a *human* expression that made her pulse leap into fierce flight.

No, Inari. Don't do that. Don't humanize him. Don't try to make excuses for the pleasure you're feeling. Don't lose yourself to the lust or you will—

But her body wasn't listening to her head. Why would it when Ezryn smoothed his free hand over her hips, her belly, down to the wet folds of her sex on which he'd only recently been sucking and nibbling? Why would it when he stroked his other hand confidently up the length of her arms, over her shoulders to tangle in her hair? To hold her head motionless as his lips brushed hers. Caressed them with a feathery kiss so light, so unexpected she moaned.

"Oh, Inari," she heard him whisper, the words choked and hoarse. "What are you doing to me? Why can't this be real?"

Torment quavered through his questions, sending a tight shiver into her core. *Was* she doing it? If she was, why did she not feel stronger? If she *was* succubus, why did the demon force in the core of her existence not bloat with gorging hunger? She stood in the hold of a master vampire who was doing everything in his power to bring her to sexual rapture, and yet she felt nothing of the elated, smug glee a succubus feeding on her prey experienced. She felt only weak and vulnerable, made so by the raw pleasure Ezryn wrought on her body. She hated him, hated his debasing treatment of her, and yet the pleasure he wrought on her body overruled it all. If she didn't know better, she'd believe Ezryn an incubus and she his victim.

But she did know better. He was a master vampire and hate was the furthest thing from her heart, even if she wished it so.

Hate had nothing to do with the confusion tearing at her soul. Hate had nothing to do with the ache in her heart.

If she was succubus, why did she want him to pierce her flesh with his fangs and fill her with exquisite bliss?

She had no answer, and her stomach knotted even as her body ached for more.

Unable to stop herself, she lifted her arms and slid them around Ezryn's neck to pull his head down into her kiss.

He kissed her in return, a slow, gentle kiss unlike any he'd given her before. It made her knees weak and her head spin. It frightened her. Truly frightened her. But before she could pull away, a growl rumbled in his chest and his mouth turned wild. His tongue assaulted hers, as if the very kiss would decide the victor of their battle.

He drove one hand between her thighs, plunged his fingers into her pussy, driving them deeper, deeper until he stroked the inside of her sex, on the sweetest spot of all with relentless torture. She wanted to cry out, but his mouth still claimed hers. All she could do was cling to his shoulders as he fucked her with his hand, bringing her higher and higher toward the summit. Higher toward release.

She wanted to fall over the edge. By the Powers, she wanted to fall and smash against the rocks beneath and have the vampire feed on her spent body. She wanted Ezryn to—

Bite her. Claim her. Bind her.

The disconnected thought held no meaning to Inari, but it brought with it a powerful surge of raw hunger. Of pure pleasure. She shifted against him, sliding one hand from his shoulder and dragging it down his torso until her fingers found the waistline of his trousers. She wanted him inside her. She *needed* his cock in her sex. Like she needed breath to survive, she needed the master vampire's sex in her own. Filling her. Possessing her.

She tugged at his belt and the hard head of his cock nudged at her hand through the tented material of his jeans. The contact almost drove her over the edge, and she whimpered again. By the Dieties, she could not hold on much longer.

Dark Ones, neither can I.

Ezryn's groan echoed through her head, made her belly knot. His kiss holding her prisoner, he grabbed at his fly and tore it open.

His erection sprung free, jutting from the bunched denim of his jeans before he could shove them down his hips. Hot electricity shot through Inari and she closed her fingers around Ezryn's engorged shaft, the power of its rigid length stealing her breath.

He moaned into her mouth, a low, raw sound that vibrated right into her core.

Yes. Oh, God and the Dark Ones and all the Dieties, yes.

Her heartbeat doubled. Her skin prickled. An immense, elemental force stirred in her core, but whether that of succubus or Sentinel, she could not tell.

Ezryn dragged his mouth from her lips, scored a burning path up to her ear as his hands joined hers on his thick, turgid cock. "I do not care," he said.

Inari gasped, preparing for his bite. Wanting it. Craving it.

And then he dipped his fingers into her sodden sex and painted the folds of her pussy with her cream. "I want you to come for me."

Her breath burst from her and she rolled her hips forward, desperate for his finger.

"I want to make you come." He slid his fingers past the folds of her sex, over the swollen button of her clitoris. "Many times tonight."

Inari's breath came quicker. Shallow. Exquisite pleasure shot through her and she moaned, the sound hoarse and stripped raw.

He dipped his index finger deeper between her thighs, the tight muscles of her vagina gripping its delving length. "Come for me, Inari."

She stood motionless, Ezryn's command coursing over her body, his massive erection in her hand. Every fiber of her being thrummed with an energy she'd long denied. She felt like she was stepping out of a shadow, the mastery of Ezryn's touch fueling the heat of her repressed need. Why had she been scared of this? Why had she been terrified of what he awoke in her? It made no sense.

His cock twitched in her grip, its length growing thicker. "See what you do to me, Inari?" He moved his lips up to her temple. "I can't hold on much longer, but I will not come until you do."

A soft whimper sounded in her throat and she squirmed, squeezing her muscles tighter around the finger penetrating her sex. She rolled her hips forward, pressing her clit to his knuckle. Another jolt of wet tension shot through her and she bit down on her lip, capturing the cry wanting to escape her throat.

"Come for me," Ezryn whispered against her throat, slipping another finger into her pussy. "Come on my hand so I can lick your cream from my fingers." He scissored the two together, stroking the inside walls of her sex until she hissed in a sharp breath. Glorious shards of exquisite tension speared through her at his invasion and she closed her eyes. "Oh, God..." she panted, rocking on his hand. Her orgasm rushed at her, an unstoppable force greater than the Deities themselves. "God..."

He closed his fingers harder on hers, making her hand squeeze his swollen shaft with punishing pressure. "Come for me before I erupt."

He thrust his fingers deeper, deeper, all the while holding her hand to his dick, letting her feel it pulse and grow inside her fist.

"Come for me, Inari," he ordered again, the words a ragged groan. "Please."

She did. Just like that, her climax detonated with such power a cry tore from her throat. Shudder after shudder claimed her. Took her. Consumed her until she slumped against him, drained of anything but the constricting pleasure in her core.

"Thank you, my sweet," Ezryn rasped against her shoulder. He pulled away from her a little, withdrawing his hand from between her thighs. "Thank you."

He raised his fingers to his lips and touched the tip of his tongue to their glistening length. "It scares me how addicted I have become to your taste."

His confession sent a ripple through Inari. Addicted. A word of absolute foreboding, and yet she reveled in its meaning. *She* was addicted to him as well. In such a short space of time, she was addicted. "And it scares me I will never taste you enough," she replied.

He groaned, his cock jerking in her grip. She pumped it with slow, even strokes, the squirming beginning of her next climax building in the pit of her belly at the feel of its impressive length. Pre-come oozed from the tiny slit at its point, trickled down the domed head to wet her fingers. Her mouth filled with saliva. She wanted to taste him. She wanted to lick the glistening beads from his flesh.

Without needing her to utter a word, Ezryn took a step backward, his jaw bunched, his eyes red fire, and she lowered to her knees and took his cock into her mouth.

He tasted of salt and timeless pleasure. She licked at the clear moisture anointing his cock and his low moan of appreciation made her belly flutter and her pussy constrict. He ran his hands over her shoulders and her throat in a feverish, wicked exploration that made her suck his daunting member deeper into her mouth.

"Dark Ones, that feels so good," he groaned. "So fucking good." His rhythm in her mouth grew faster. Wilder. "So fucking good I want to..." He groaned again, the sound animalistic, aggressive, and Inari felt a sudden shift in his body. A coiling of muscles. An awakening of something more primal and potent than she'd ever believed existed.

With frightening, unnatural speed, he tore his length from her mouth. She straightened, gasping for breath, watching him stare at her. What was he going to do?

Fangs bared, eyes burning black fire, he flattened her to the wall, slid his hands over her ribcage, her hips and down her thighs to the backs of her knees. He jerked her feet from the floor, driving her shoulders harder to the wall behind her and wrapped her legs around his hips, impaling her on his cock in one fluid move.

"Oh my God!" Inari cried. Ezryn filled her, stretched her beyond her limits. He pumped into her, his penetrations stroking her within. He took her, possessed her, his hands on her breasts, his mouth on her neck, her shoulders, her throat. He filled her and worshiped her and drove her higher, higher. He drove her past the summit of her pleasure, past the peak of known rapture until she could take no more and cried out again.

Ezryn's rhythm turned wild. His cock grew thicker, longer in her sex. She heard him roar, and the Sentinel she'd thought was silent roared back. Surged to the fore.

She threw back her head and stared up into Ezryn's eyes. Saw something there she couldn't understand. Something that made her heart squeeze tight and her mouth turn dry. Something right and deep that made her soul ache for that which she couldn't fathom but wanted with every fiber of her body. Something that petrified her. Something that electrified her.

Something like true, pure desire. Something like...

"Bite me, Master," she begged on a silent breath. "Bite me. Please. Make me yours and mark me as such."

Ezryn growled low and long. His eyes ignited, his nostrils flared and he tightened his fists in her hair, thrust his length deeper into her sex and sank his fangs into her neck.

Inari came again, her sex gushing with pure pleasure, her neck gushing with blood, and Ezryn fed on both.

Inari's sweet blood flowed down Ezryn's throat. Like liquid fire and life. He drank of her, his fists in her hair, his cock in her sex. She cried out. Her moans fed the lust driving him. Her body fed his hunger. Dark Ones, she was like ambrosia. No, she *was* ambrosia. He'd feasted on Sentinel blood before, but none had tasted like Inari

—so potent and intoxicating and addictive. So sensually alive. Hell, he felt on fire.

He sucked hard, and with every mouthful, he felt his still heart grow hot. Felt his blood surge. Felt his soulless core reach out, seeking the golden heat of her life. Felt his soul thread through hers, twisting into intricate knots, melding into thick, beautiful bands of dual existence until she was irrevocably entwined in his existence and he in hers.

A silent roar filled him as the binding bite connected them. This was not his plan. Not his intent, and yet he could not stop. He didn't want to stop. Now it had begun, now he could feel her within his being he never wanted to be without her. He'd intended to punish her. Punish the succubus for the way she'd manipulated him. Kill her and drain her of her deceiving assassin's blood. And yet that very plan had gone to hell in a handbasket the second he'd entered her.

No, before that. The very moment he'd seen Jacob at her door, the very moment he'd been almost undone by jealousy at the sight of his most trusted friend at her home, he knew he could never kill her. Just as he knew he would never let her go. She was his and he was hers. And then she'd begged for him to bite her, as he'd promised her a lifetime ago she would. And he'd known before his fangs even punctured her flesh what he was doing.

The binding bite.

Bound forever together.

He thrust harder into her sex. She was his. She would never be anyone else's. Inari Chayse was bound to him until the end of time.

And you to her.

The thought should have chilled him—bound to a succubus Sentinel, his very existence tied to hers. It exposed him to vulnerability. Weakness. Instead, it made his chest heavy with a warm pressure he couldn't identify. He thrust harder, drank harder, mindless of everything except the woman in his arms.

She was his. As he'd wanted her to be the second he'd laid eyes on her.

Yes, oh, yes, yes, yes.

Inari's voice whispered through his head and he let out a raw groan, his balls rising. Their connection was utter, total, and it made his heart—that lifeless, cold organ that had never once beaten—burn hotter still. He pulled her into his penetrations, felt the muscles of her sex constrict around his cock. The tight, wet sheath pushed him closer to the edge and he groaned again, the taste of Inari's blood pouring down his throat rushing him closer still.

Oh, oh, I'm going to come, I'm coming, I'm coming.

Her rapturous thought cried through his pleasure just as her pussy constricted on his thrusting cock, and it was too much. Too much to fight against, too much to comprehend. His own orgasm detonated, exquisite release surging through him, powerful and incinerating, as if exploding from his very soulless core. He tore his fangs from her neck, threw back his head and roared.

My demon...my master vampire.

Inari's voice whispered through his mind, the fevered words of a woman claimed by utter release and pleasure.

My overlord...give it to me...yes, that's it, that's it.

The whisper grew louder. Fiercer. She dug her short nails into his shoulders. Her hot, tight pussy squeezed his cock. Milked his seed.

Give it to me. Give it all to me...all of it...all of you.

An icy fist slammed into Ezryn's chest and he reeled backward, breaking their most intimate of connections, her words—thrumming with rapturous bliss—shearing into his sanity. Words of possession, of ravenous hunger.

"Ezryn?"

Inari's husky moan jerked his stare to her face. She stood slumped against the wall, her features softened with obvious bliss, a sated smile on her lips even as a small frown began to pull at her eyebrows.

Sated.

He forced his fangs to retract.

Sated. Well fed.

She'd fed from him. She'd—

"What's going on, Ezryn?" She took a step forward, her frown growing darker, her hands going to her bare hips. She looked delicious and sublime, her eyes shining, her breasts heaving, a tiny line of blood trickling down the smooth column of her neck. Dark Ones, if he didn't know better, he'd slam her to the wall and sink his cock and fangs into her once more. He was ready. Fuck, more than ready. His balls ached with a swollen weight he could barely believe possible given the force of his orgasm but a moment ago.

Sated. Succubus. My master vampire.

Give it to me.

All of it.

All of you.

All.

His gut churned at the possessive nature of the word and he glared at her, hands curling into fists. "Dark Ones, how could I let you do this to me again?"

An uncertain expression flickered over her face. "Do what?"

He snarled and closed the distance his backward step had created between them. "Don't play the innocent here, Inari." He flashed her a cold smirk, raking his stare over her naked form. "It doesn't suit you."

Waves of stunned shock rolled through him, followed by searing contempt—Inari's contempt—and he bit back a sharp hiss. The bonding. Curse it, he could feel her every emotion.

She was pissed off. Royally pissed off. She bared her teeth at him. Her perfectly even, white teeth. "Fuck off, vampire."

He took another step closer to her, fisting his hands into balls to stop himself grabbing her. If he did, if he touched her, he had no idea what he would do. "What did you do to me?"

Her eyes sparked icy hate. "Nothing you didn't want me to."

"What the fuck does that mean?"

She glared at him, her face set in indignant anger. But underneath the rage he felt radiating from her, underneath her absolute fury he sensed not just in his core but in his blood, something else simmered. Something cold. Something fragile. Something that made him pause, made him hesitate. Something like...

Fear?

"It means you got everything you deserve."

Her venomous statement killed Ezryn's wavering conflict. He straightened, towering over her. Forcing her to tilt her head back to meet his glare. "And I should have known better."

An unreadable light shimmered in her eyes and she curled her lip. "That's right. A master vampire should know better than to fuck with a succubus."

His balls rose up, her words like a shard of garlic-dipped silver spearing into his chest. "So you are admitting it?"

She narrowed her eyes and bunched her jaw. "I'm admitting nothing. I'm stating you are an idiot."

It was too much. The hate in her voice, the contempt in her eyes, the indefinable *something* that threaded through each smoldering emotion. He snatched her wrists, yanked her arms behind her back and jerked her against his body with brutal force. She gasped, the sound altogether too surprised, too frightened for his peace of mind, her body altogether too warm and soft and crushable. He bit back a harsh growl. She was driving him insane. "So, *succubus*," he hissed. "What are your plans for this idiot now?"

She stared at him, motionless in his cruel hold, her heat seeping into his cold body. "Nothing." She turned her head away, the bowed column of her neck exposed to him in vulnerable perfection. "I've had my fill of you, and you've left a bad taste in my mouth."

Again, that ambiguous *something* threaded through everything he sensed in her, a disturbing undercurrent of restless fear that pushed his anger to an emotion he could not fathom. He lowered his head and brushed his parted lips over her cheek, down to her jaw and up to her ear. "Funny," he whispered, closing his grip harder on her wrists, drawing her closer to his body. "Your willingly offered blood has had the opposite effect on me. I feel rejuvenated. Invigorated. Like I've fed on pure energy." He scraped the tip of his right incisor down the velvet curve of her ear and nipped once on her earlobe. She sucked in a hitching breath and he chuckled, using her own imprisoned wrists to push her hips harder to his. "I feel powerful enough to pull the wings from—" he nipped her earlobe again, "—a Sentinel."

Her low, throaty laugh took him by surprise. He raised his head from her neck and studied her with a cocked eyebrow.

She gave him a wide grin, her eyes green chips of ice. "You think you're a match for me, master vampire?" She laughed again, the sound husky and full of smug conceit. "I've been destroying your kind for decades. It's like swatting a mosquito." Her smile vanished, and she stared at him with even colder eyes. "Go. Before I kill you where you stand."

He ran his gaze over her face, knowing the mounting pressure in the pit of his loins had little to do with rage. "Kill me, Inari, and you will be killing yourself."

She stiffened against him, every muscle in her body coiling. "What does that mean?"

He touched the tip of his tongue to his right fang. "Oh, Inari. I'm sure you can *feel* what that means."

She stared at him, her eyes searching his. She shifted slightly, her shoulder muscles flexing as she tried to move her left arm. He relaxed his hold a fraction, enough to let her wrist slip from his imprisoning grip, and watched her raise her hand to her neck.

Her fingertips hovered over the still-weeping wound in her neck where his fangs had punctured her skin, as if she were afraid to touch the blood seeping from each hole. A slight frown pulled at her eyebrows, her breath quickened and, with barely any contact at all between her fingers and her neck, he saw realization flood through her. He felt it flow through their bond. A wall of blistering heat and sinking cold.

Her eyes widened and she shook her head. "You bastard."

For a split second, the urge to fold his arms around her with gentle care and beg her forgiveness for his cruel treatment consumed him. To hold her and stroke her hair and murmur soothing sounds against her temple that meant nothing and said everything. And then she slapped her palm against the side of his face so hard his head snapped to the side and the vampire he was took back control. He captured her wrist again, jerked her arm back behind her body and smiled down at her. "That may be, Inari, but it doesn't change the fact you are bound to me for the rest of eternity. Mine and mine alone. Mine to feed from whenever I choose." He touched his tongue to the tip of his fang again, holding her eyes with his gaze. "Mine to use however I want, when I want."

Their bond surged through him, and even as he felt her hate and anger, he tasted the potent force of her arousal. She hated him, of that he had no doubt, but she wanted him. And he wanted her. Fuck, did he want her.

He crushed her lips with his, plunged his tongue into her mouth, yanked her harder against his stiff, straining cock. She fought him, writhing in his arms, struggling against his invading tongue, his assaulting mouth. He didn't care. He knew what she wanted—her desire heated her blood and turned the ice in his to lava. She would never be able to deny him her want now. He knew it. He felt it. He lived it.

He growled into her mouth and hauled her closer still, biting her lip, sucking her tongue. Heat pooled in his groin, his heart, and suddenly she was kissing him back, as he'd known she would, her groans as wild as his, her hips rolling up and down as she ground the curve of her sex against his engorged shaft. He tore his mouth from her lips, dragging them to her jaw, her neck. "I am a lucky vampire," he murmured against the small puncture wounds just below her ear, the taste of her skin and sweat and blood a heady mix that filled his mouth with saliva and his balls with swollen hunger. "A succubus pet and a Sentinel blood source all rolled into one delicious little package."

Inari became still in his arms. "Get out."

The words fell from her lips in a guttural snarl. He lifted his head and stared down at her. His body seemed to be on fire, a scalding heat that burned away all possibility of rational thought and fed the demonic beast he was at the same time. "Make me."

A look of absolute grief flashed across Inari's face, followed by a shudder that wracked her body with such force he felt it in the pit of his stomach. She looked up at him, another shudder claiming her body, her eyes shining.

Ezryn's throat slammed shut and his fingers slipped from her wrists. Tears. Dark Ones, he'd made her cry.

"Get out, Ezryn," Inari growled through gritted teeth, her eyes erupting in an inferno of green fury. Another tremble rocked her. Another. Another. "Go. Or I swear we both shall perish."

He stumbled back from her, his sanity slipping, his desire and hunger for her taking over his mind. It pushed him to fever point until he wavered on his feet, unable to tear his gaze from her.

"Go."

The cry burst from her in a voice he didn't recognize, a voice, resonating with endless fury, tortured grief and indescribable power.

He staggered back another step, raw confusion fisting in his gut. He stared at the woman bound to him forever.

"*Go!*" she cried.

He turned, leaving her apartment in a sprint that sheared time and space, Inari's tortured cry piercing his ears as he did so.

He did not stop nor slow until he arrived at his home, the hot night air scouring him as he tore through its humid density, a physical touch he'd never once paid heed to until tonight. Now its sultry, inescapable heat reminded him of the very woman whose tortured cry had sent him from her home.

He stood at his front door, fangs digging into his bottom lip, nails digging into his palms. Dark Ones, what the fuck was going on?

An image of Inari ripped through his head and he closed his eyes. His throat squeezed tight, his chest tighter. Bound to a Sentinel succubus? Had he gone mad?

Mad with lust, Ezryn? Or is it something else? Something you won't let yourself consider?

He *couldn't* consider it. It served no purpose here. What was relevant, at least to him, was her sexual control of his actions and mind. Curse it, he was bound to a succubus.

Cold anger flooded him. He shoved open the front door to his home and stormed through the foyer. Inari was right about one thing—he *was* an idiot. But for all his seething rage, he could not undo his idiocy. The binding bite was irreversible. Inari was bound to him just as he was bound to her. Master vampire to succubus. Succubus to master vampire.

Are you sure she is a succubus? Remember exactly how Ven Watkins described her. Ex-succubus. No one truly knows if a Sentinel retains their original force and power. It's all conjecture and speculation. Perhaps how you feel about her, how undeniably you are drawn to her has nothing to do with demon magic and everything to do with—

He refused to let the thought finish. It was not important. He was Ezryn Navarro, first born of the First Family. He would bend her to his will and make her his on every level imaginable. Succubus or Sentinel or lowly human, he was stronger than she and he would own her and possess her and control her. She was now his sex slave, his food source, his pleasure, his entertainment, his...

He froze, staring at the night sky beyond the windows of his living room. A sinking sensation of contempt settled in his stomach. Dark Ones, what was he thinking? He *was* insane. And as callous and ruthless as his egomaniacal brother. As unhinged as his long-dead father.

Releasing a sharp sigh, he moved to the bar and splashed some single malt into a squat glass. He wasn't thirsty—not for alcohol anyway—but he needed something to burn away the lingering taste of Inari on his tongue.

Ha. And you really think whiskey is going to do that?

With a disgusted grunt, he threw back the liquor and slammed the empty glass onto the bar counter. Before he even swallowed, he knew the woman would still haunt him. Not just her taste, but everything. Her scent was in his nose, her warmth on his flesh, her image in his head, the sound of her voice, her moans and her laughter still caressed his ears.

"Fuck." The curse burst from him like a guttural bark. He turned from the vista of Sydney Harbor at night and crossed the room to the wide, glass table he used as his desk. He didn't need an office, but despite his removal from the position of overlord and being on the other side of the world, he still kept a close watch on the vampire race. To the rest of his kind, he was disconnected from the politics of the court, but he knew everything that needed to be known.

Except what the hell Inari Chayse had done to him.

He lowered himself into the high-back chair and opened his laptop, the brushed steel casing warm under his fingers.

The screen illuminated into instant life, the familiar home page of the *Lamia Cruor Libri*—The Blood Books—open before him. He keyed in his brother's password, shaking his head as he always did at how easy it was to access the overlord's personal database. Haral's password—oracle—was a joke. However, Ezryn was not in the mood to be humored by his twin's predictable ineptness. While it may be risky hacking *The Blood Books*, he needed more information than what he had, and unless he felt like having another conversation with Ven Watkins, which he didn't, he knew no other way. The *Lamia Cruor Libri* contained the sum total knowledge of the vampire race and all known paranormal elements impacting on it, including all information gathered on active Sentinel. If anything had been noted about Inari Chayse, it would be in here.

Keying her name into the search field, he hit *enter*, impatient irritation spearing into him when the colorful pinwheel replaced his cursor on the screen. He didn't want to wait, curse it. Not even a few seconds. He needed information now. Surely he wasn't being unreasonable, was—

The screen changed before he could finish the thought, flashing to a white page with five lines of text.

Teeth clenched, muscles tense, Ezryn read each line.

Inari Chayse: Sentinel rebirth date unknown. Possibly mid to late twentieth century.

Demon species before rebirth: Unknown. Likely second-order. Rumor linked her to the First Horseman of the Apocalypse before rebirth. This is unconfirmed.

No known associates or affiliations.

Last known vampire termination: Aldus Hichstette. Brussels.

Current location: Sydney, Australia

That was it. Nothing else, not even an image.

Ezryn bit back a disgusted grunt. Nothing. It was as if the Dark Ones plotted with the Deities to frustrate him.

Well, almost nothing. The name Hichstette was the maiden name of Haral's new wife. Obviously the cousin Haral had mentioned and was so readily eager to avenge.

Sitting back in his chair, he raked his fingers through his hair, staring at those five annoying lines.

What did you expect to find, Ezryn? Detailed files? An essay about Inari filling in all the blanks?

He curled his hand into a fist on his keyboard. He should have known he was grasping at straws. Why would the *Lamia Cruor Libri* contain any information of any use to him anyway? What was he looking for? Something to prove Ven Watkins a liar? Noted evidence telling him Inari was a water demon before her rebirth? A dark elf? A sprite?

You were hoping to find something, anything *that would prove you weren't controlled by your dick, weren't you? Something to convince you she didn't use her succubus force on you. Something to convince you not to carry out Haral's command.*

He scrubbed at his face, teeth clenched. That's exactly what he was doing. And just as he had failed his brother's order to kill her, he'd failed to find anything tonight to keep her alive.

Except his own lust.

The memory of the first moment he'd heard her moans in the Pleasure Palace tickled at his senses, and he let out a low growl. Moans of wanton release and raw hunger. He should have known what she was then—a creature of sex and power. Why hadn't he killed her there and then?

Because your dick was in control.

No, it wasn't his dick. Lust had been in control. The succubus had been in control. What better food source for a sex demon than a master vampire, and not just any master vampire but the first born of the First Family, the twin son born to be overlord.

So who was playing whom here? Were the Dark Ones so bored they must use him as a toy now? Why would fate place him in Inari's sexual control when he'd sacrificed so much for his cursed bloodline? When he'd already committed himself to the ultimate sacrifice? The ultimate end to his existence?

Closing his eyes, he let the memory of the night he'd found her in the Pleasure Palace roll through him. He'd felt drawn to her. Powerfully. Inexplicably. He wanted her, needed her on a level he couldn't fathom and didn't question. Not then, at least. He'd smelled her, felt her and wanted her. Period.

"Fuck." He opened his eyes and stared at the words on his laptop's screen, seeing Inari instead. "Fuck."

There was one simple answer from this revelation. The sexual connection he could not deny between him and Inari Chaysc had nothing to do with real desire, real attraction. What he felt for her was nothing but the direct result of her succubus magic.

"Fuck."

Cold anger surged through him, and he shoved his laptop away. This was getting him nowhere. He was wasting time when he had a decision to make. He either carried out his brother's command to kill her, thereby destroying himself, or he didn't kill her and bore the blood of those loyal to him as Haral began slaughtering them.

Why not let Jacob take care of Harry?

The dark thought slithered through his anger and he straightened, cold guilt stabbing into his gut. Jacob.

He leapt to his feet. Damn it, he needed to find his general. Not to turn Jacob loose on his brother—he would never do that, no matter how much his friend wished he would—but to touch base with him. After the unexpected events in Inari's apartment, he wanted to make sure Jake was okay.

And apologize for slipping into his head.

He cast a quick look outside, noting the position of the stars in the sky. On a balmy mid-summer Saturday night like this, he would make it to Jacob's apartment quicker by foot than he would by car. Sydney's tourists and partygoers were undoubtedly congesting the traffic to a standstill through the heart of the city. If he stuck to the side streets and alleys he'd be at Woolloomooloo in a heart's beat.

Three minutes later, he swung open Jacob's penthouse door, the eight kilometers between their two residences having passed in a blur. He moved through the minimally luxurious apartment, ignoring a persistent itch in his gut. He knew what it was from—the bond between them grew more agitated with every second away from Inari. If he didn't slake his thirst on her blood again soon, or at least breathe in her scent and feel her warmth, that agitation would begin to pervert into aggression.

Halfway across Jacob's living room floor, he stopped, his silent surroundings finally catching his attention.

He turned slowly, taking in the still room, the blackened windows, the dark lights and lamps. "Jake?"

His voice fell in the silence like a soft echo.

"Jake?"

Silence.

A thin ribbon of something close to panic snaked through him, and he frowned.

"General Ancroft?"

Still, there was silence. He moved through the apartment, heading for his friend's bedroom.

The king-size bed sat in the middle of the massive room, its bedding inarguably masculine and immaculately pristine and un-rumpled.

Ezryn frowned, the ribbon of panic becoming a knot. Where the hell was Jacob?

He walked back to the large windows in the living room and deactivated the opaque tint to study the black waters of Wool-loomooloo Bay and the hive of activity skirting it. There wasn't a sign of Jacob in the crowd but Ezryn hadn't expected there to be. Jacob had no need for restaurants and cafes, not unless he was cruising for a feed of an entirely different variety, one not catered to on the trendy iPad menus.

His frown deepened. He reached into his back pocket, pulled out his phone and punched in Jacob's number.

It didn't ring. Just went straight to the message service. Ezryn hung up on the pre-recorded sound of Jacob's voice telling him he was, "definitely unable to take your call. I'm probably in the middle of a tasty snack". His panic knotted tighter. "Damn it, Jake," he growled under his breath, shoving his phone back into his pocket. "Where are you?"

He glared out the window, eyes narrow. He'd told Jacob to go home. Not just as a friend, but as his master. He'd not only told him to go home, he'd *suggested* he go home. Jacob should be here.

But he's not, Ezryn. Which means...

Anxious unease reached into his gut at the ominous thought, competing with the bond's itch and his growing apprehension.

If Jacob wasn't here, something had stopped him from being so. Something or someone.

Closing his eyes, Ezryn forced his muscles to relax. He stood motionless, letting the foreboding silence of the empty penthouse slide over him as he focused his mind on nothing but his friend. He drew his friend's existence into his subconscious. Tuned everything out—including the itch of Inari's absence—until the only thing in his psyche was Jacob Ancroft. He was a master vampire probing for his underling's presence. Searching for him. Seeking...seeking...

Nothing.

Not a hint of his *croi*. It was as if Jacob didn't exist anymore.

Ezryn opened his eyes and stared out the window at the life beyond its impenetrable glass, cold disquiet stirring the demon deep within. What the fuck was going on?

Jacob opened his eyes and squinted at the dense shadows surrounding him, an odd numbness making him feel heavy. Where was he?

Flashes of sights and sounds came at him, memories, senses—the Sentinel, the ravenous hunger she awoke in him, his worry, his frustration, Ezryn arriving, Ezryn entering Inari's apartment, grabbing her, holding her, ordering him away...

He frowned.

He couldn't remember leaving her apartment. Dark Ones, he couldn't even remember turning from her door. Had Ezryn done that? Exerted his will over Jacob's own? And why?

He peered into the darkness, its inky shadows seeming to writhe and move around him. Where was he now? How did he get here?

The frustrating memories blurred, grew distorted, tainted by something else. Something like...

Numb heaviness seemed to wrap around his extremities, a hot blanket that made his stomach churn. He tried to move, tried to lift his hand to his face.

Excruciating agony ripped through him, tore into his body like jagged teeth. He let out a sharp shout. Something imprisoned his arms.

He snapped his stare to his left wrist, his right, pain fogging his vision. Thick, silver manacles encircled each one, attached to two taut chains that stretched his arms wide from his body. The two chains were attached to two thick beams of wood on either side of his head.

Jacob froze, studying each one.

Cold fury crashed through him and he yanked against his bindings, shutting the unbearable agony from his mind. He was chained to a whipping post. *Chained.* Some fucking prick had chained him to a fucking whipping post.

"I must admit, General Ancroft," a smug voice sounded in the darkness, and Jacob became completely still, his fury turning to something much, much darker. "I have thought of this moment for a long time."

The room exploded in stark white light. It sliced into Jacob's eyes like shattered glass, but he didn't flinch. He didn't move.

Because standing in front of him, dressed in grotesque purple velvet and black leather, was a fleshy version of Ezryn, a wide smile splitting his pale face, thick fangs extended, eyes blazing vile yellow triumph. The idiot overlord himself.

Haral smirked at him, rubbing his hands together. "A very long time."

Letting every second of hate he'd felt for the man shine in his eyes, Jacob fixed the overlord with a level look. "Hello, Harry," he snarled. "Welcome to Australia."

Chapter Eleven

"He bit me."

"You asked him to."

Inari lifted her head from her hands and glared up from the floor at her hovering sister. Tianya returned her glare with an altogether too composed expression, the corners of her mouth twitching slightly.

Inari shook her head, the hardwood floorboards biting into her bare knees and shins. "I didn't ask him to bind me to him, Ti. The rightful freaking overlord of the freaking vampire race has bound me to him. Forever. The Deities are never going to communicate with me again."

Tianya tilted her head to the side, lips curling into an ambiguous smile. "Is that really what's bothering you, sister?"

Prickling heat rolled through Inari, an unsettling wave that set her cheeks on fire. "Of course that's what's bothering me." She shifted on the floor, trying her best to look indignant. "The bastard bit me."

Her sister cocked an eyebrow. "Ah, but what you're really

worried about is why he bit you, isn't it?" She moved closer to Inari, not so much a step, but a glide. "Or more to the point, *who* he bit."

A cold finger traced a lazy line up Inari's spine at Tianya's observation. She suppressed the want to shiver, opting instead to glare some more at her annoyingly dead and all-too-knowing sister. "I know who he bit, Ti," she grumbled. "He bit me."

Tianya lowered herself onto the armchair before Inari and gave her a level look. "You the woman, or you the succubus?"

Inari stared at her, motionless, angry and aching. In the very center of her existence, the core of who she was, a pulling sensation itched. A yearning she'd never experienced before but recognized all the same. The bond between her and Ezryn. Even now, tortured by confusion and contempt—both for herself and the arrogant vampire—she wanted to go to him. Wanted to be with him, not just sexually but completely. Wanted to see him, feel him, hear him. Every sense she possessed ached for him, an inescapable itch growing inside her. And despite the distance between them, she *knew* he felt the very same.

The bonding bite. Why else would Ezryn have bitten her so if not because of what she was? God, what a fucked-up situation.

She let out a bitter sigh. "So, I *am* succubus once more."

Tianya shrugged. "Maybe? Maybe not. My long-dead soul says no, but what do I know? I'm a ghost." She paused, giving Inari a mischievous grin. "But consider this—when you were succubus, you consciously and deliberately fed on the sexual energy of your prey. Have you done that to Ezryn Navarro?"

Inari stared at her sister, her blood roaring in her ears. There had been no conscious decision to drain the vampire. In fact, she'd fought her desire for Ezryn every time he touched her. And if she *had* fed on his lust, why did she feel so drained? So exhausted?

But what other explanation is there, Inari? The moment Ezryn first saw you in the Pleasure Palace he sank his tongue into your sex. The next time he all but ravished you on a footpath. The time after that he threw you on the bed and fucked you until you both screamed. Why would he do that if not under the influence of succubus force?

She dragged her hands through her hair and looked at her sister. "I know what a binding bite does to a vampire. Why would he willingly expose himself to such weakness?"

Tianya gave her another entirely too ambiguous smile. "Love?"

"Love?" Inari let out another sharp snort. "He's a vampire, Tianya. He has no soul. He is incapable of love."

"There are many creatures in this world with souls who do not love, Inari. You do not need a soul to feel." Tianya's smile softened. "A soul does not give you the ability to love, nor the ability to know what is right and what is wrong." She paused, her eyes clear and direct and intense. "I was loved more deeply, more strongly by my soulless succubus sister than any human I knew."

Inari's throat squeezed tight. Tianya had her there. Her love for her kid sister knew no bound or limits. Never had, never would. Not even death could make it otherwise. She blinked back tears, hating every second of this conversation. Hating that her sister was dead, that she could never hold her or hug her again. Hating that every word Tianya said only made her ache with ridiculous hope. Dangerous, insane hope for a future she'd never dreamed possible.

Tianya studied her with unreadable eyes. "Does the master vampire make you feel good?"

Exasperation shot through her. She threw up her hands, her pulse thumping in her neck like a trip hammer. "He makes me *feel*, period. Happy, sad, furious, insane, scared. Christ, the bastard makes me feel emotions I never knew *existed*, let alone ones I didn't think I could experience again. I want to kill him. I want to hold him. By the Dieties, I want to spend the rest of eternity just looking at him." She stopped as prickling heat razed her flesh and the itch in her core erupted. What was she saying?

She shook her head, fixing her sister with a flat stare. "I hate him."

Tianya burst out laughing. "No, you don't."

Inari ground her teeth. "Yes, I do."

Her sister raised her eyebrows, a pointed action so similar to her own Inari felt a little chill ripple up her spine. "Because he makes you feel? Are you sure it's hate in your heart, Inari Chayse?"

Tianya's question sank into Inari's confusion and she stared at her sister, mouth turning dry. *Oh, no. Not that. Not...*

"You know what, sis?" Tianya said, her laughter abruptly absent from her voice. "I'm sick of the angst. You're a three-hundred-year-old demon assassin, not a moping teenage girl with a crush on a vampire. Despite the fact you've done nothing but try to kill each other or fuck like rabbits since the second you met, the master vampire makes you happy. Accept it, deal with it and move on."

Inari snorted. "Easy words for a ghost, Ti, or whatever the hell you are. I don't see *you* moving on."

"Ah, but I'm not the Sentinel of the family. Nor the succubus."

"Were you this annoying alive?"

"Yes." A puzzled frown pulled at Tianya's straight eyebrows. "Have you ever wondered why you were chosen to be reborn a Sentinel?"

Something intangible stirred in Inari's chest. "Because I chose not to kill an innocent boy barely old enough to be a man when ordered to do so by the First Horseman of the Apocalypse."

Tianya tilted her head to the side. "There are many demons out there who, by their own choice, decide not to kill or torture or maim an innocent, and they do not become Sentinel. So why you? Haven't you once wondered why, of all the monsters preying on mankind, you were one to be elevated? Reborn? Don't you think there must be a reason for that?"

"The boy was special. I'd never felt a soul more pure. More... divine. Like the soul of the Highest."

"He was special. And he became more so. But Inari, were you chosen just because of who you saved? Or because of what *you* became when reborn as well? A Sentinel capable of using fear and lust as a weapon? The two most elemental emotions of them all?"

An indefinable sensation stirred in Inari's chest. It spread through her, making her skin prickle and her breath short.

"I think you still command the power of a sex demon," Tianya went on, voice completely matter-of-fact. "I don't think you ever lost it. If you really wanted to, Inari, I believe you could drive a man—or demon—insane with lust without even touching him. Just as you did when you were a succubus." She paused, a pointed expression on her sweet, innocent face. "What a powerful weapon for an assassin of the Highest to have."

Inari blinked.

Was that possible? Wouldn't she know?

Why would you? It's not like you had lessons on how to be a Sentinel. One moment you were a succubus, the next, an assassin of God. One second your head is full of every way possible to make a male or female orgasm, the next you're a walking killing machine with a single-minded drive to hunt and destroy all demon kind and a direct download of targets from the Dieties. Ven's the only other Sentinel you've had any contact with, and you can count the number of words he's spoken to you on two hands.

She blinked again and a roaring noise throbbed in her ears.

Tianya smiled, the expression so warm Inari's heart ached. "It's time to let go of your guilt, sis. Time to let go of the fear of who you are, *what* you are, and face what must be."

"What does that mean, Tianya? What exactly 'must be'? A happy-ever-after with a bloodsucking demon? And not just any bloodsucking demon, but the born leader of them all?"

"Why not?" Tianya grinned. "I've heard of stranger things happening. Like a human child being born to demon parents, for one."

"That's different."

"Why?"

Frustrated, exasperated, *scared* of what her sister suggested, Inari dropped her head into her hands and scrubbed at her face. "Damn, I hate being confused."

"Don't be confused, In." Tianya's soft whisper tickled the back of her neck and a shiver rippled over her skin. "What you want is in your soul. You can feel it, I know you can. It's like a little itch pulling you where you know you want to be." There was a brief pause, barely a second, and then Tianya said, "I love you, sis. Forever."

Her sister's words jerked Inari's head up from her hands and she stared at Tianya. Or would have if she'd still been there.

"Damn you, Ti," Inari growled, glaring at the empty space where her sister had just stood. She grabbed at her bottom lip with her teeth, replaying every word Tianya had spoken.

Succubus. Assassin. Lust. Love. Everything she had said, Inari knew—*knew*—to be true. Everything.

"So what does that mean?"

Pulling a deep, slow breath, she closed her eyes and an image of Ezryn instantly filled her head, his dark eyes ablaze with undeniable desire, burning with irrefutable anger.

The itch in her belly flared, powerful and demanding. It pulled her, owning her.

She let out a ragged sigh. From the very second she'd laid eyes upon Ezryn her world had turned upside down. From the very moment his hands had touched hers, she'd become an emotional, physical and psychological mess. And now here she was, bound to him eternally.

What do you plan to do about that, Inari? What do you want to do?

A slow smile curled her lips at the unexpected swell of warmth and acceptance rolling through her. She opened her eyes. "A happy-ever-after with a blood sucker." She snorted a soft chuckle. "Who would have thought?"

Now all she had to do was convince said bloodsucker she hadn't succubussed his ass.

Before he chanced his own existence and killed her.

* * *

The Pleasure Palace writhed and pulsed and thrummed around him, a living, breathing testament to the power of sex, lust and desire. Fae strippers copulated on the runway stage, their sublime, ethereal beauty feeding the sexual appetites of the strip club's patrons. Bodies moved against each other, feeding, fucking, watching. The air hung heavy with the wet products of their pleasure. Sweat, musk and blood.

Ezryn ignored all of it.

He stormed through the club, searching the crowd for a hint, a *hint*, curse it, of his general.

Nothing. He couldn't see him, couldn't smell him, couldn't sense him.

He raked his hands through his hair, guilt and apprehension gnawing at his fraying calm. A feral growl rumbled in his chest. "Where the fuck are you, Jake?"

"What part of 'I'd be a touched miffed if something were to happen to her' didn't you understand?"

Ven Watkins's deep, smooth voice made Ezryn start, and he snapped his head to his right, finding the supreme Sentinel beside him. The assassin stood calm and still, his tall, lean frame covered in an immaculate black suit, the black shirt he wore beneath the jacket open at the neck, a black tie knotted loosely at the open collar. His lips curled in an almost sardonic smile as he watched the skin show taking place on the stage. To a casual observer, he would appear the perfect package of a sexual being. Until you looked into his eyes. His eyes burned infinite, icy displeasure. He was not happy.

Ezryn met those eyes with deliberate defiance, every nerve ending in his body sizzling with rising agitation. *He* was not happy either. "What do you mean?"

"I mean, you bit Inari Chayse." Watkins gave Ezryn a long look. "With a binding bite." He raised a squat glass filled with blue liquid to his lips and a detached part of Ezryn's brain recognized it as

Carpathian mountain water just before the Sentinel drank the entire contents in a single swallow.

A sudden thump smashed into life in Ezryn's temple. He narrowed his eyes and stepped directly in front of Watkins, forcing the assassin to follow his movement not just with his eyes, but his head. "How do you know that?"

Watkins's eyes flared colder. "For a master vampire, you don't know much about your enemy, do you?"

A low snarl vibrated deep in Ezryn's throat. Anger sawed into his control, but he kept his expression composed. Just... Now was not the time to pick a fight with the supreme Sentinel. "Inari is not hurt, nor is she harmed." He cocked an eyebrow, meeting Watkins's contemptuous gaze. "Trust me, I would know."

"And yet you are here, in a strip club dedicated to the pleasures of the flesh." Watkins cocked his own eyebrow. "Without her."

Ezryn's anger grew hotter. "Why I am here has nothing to do with you or Inari."

"No, it has to do with your general. And your brother."

Ezryn stared at Watkins, unnerved shock and irritated frustration a balled fist pounding in his stomach. "What do you know about Jacob?" he snarled, taking a step closer to the Sentinel. "And what does my brother have to do with it?"

Ven's eyes flared green ice. "Your brother is an idiot who has no concept of how to lead his people. He believes torture will get him what he wants."

The ball in Ezryn's gut punched harder. "Are you telling me Haral has Jacob?"

The Sentinel said nothing.

A tsunami of incinerating rage flooded through Ezryn. He growled, the urge to shift completely into his true vampire form turning the blood in his veins thick and hot. If Harry had Jacob...

Struggling for control, he glared at the assassin standing before him. "You know why my brother is here, don't you?"

Watkins barely inclined his head.

Ezryn's anger burned hotter still. "Then why don't you do something about it? You're the Dieties' fucking golden boy. Help me end my brother's tyranny and save my general."

Watkins's indifferent expression didn't falter. "This is a blood feud, Ezryn. It does not affect me or those I protect."

"Those you protect?" Incredulous fury crashed through him. "Dark Ones! You were once vampire, Ven. Surely that means something to you? Surely the future of your ancestral kind deserves your protection as well?"

Watkins curled his lip, a slight action that revealed fangs long and pointed. "This is not my fight, vampire, but I will make it mine if something were to happen to Inari Chayse because of it." His fangs glinted in the club's muted light, his eyes almost an iridescent white. "You do not want that to happen, *Ezzie*."

Ezryn ground his teeth and glared at him. "Inari is bound to me, Sentinel. She is my concern now."

Watkins's face became stone. "Do not be mistaken, vampire. Inari will always be my concern, no matter how deep and strong your bond with her is."

"Why?" Ezryn demanded. "What makes her so special to you?"

The supreme Sentinel's expression didn't change. His eyes however, grew...flinty. "She chose not kill my brother when ordered to do so."

The unexpected answer took Ezryn by surprise. When had someone from the Realm tried to kill Ven's brother? Why? There was nothing special about Patrick Watkins, was there? He was just a—

"And in doing so," Watkins continued bluntly, as though he knew the questions in Ezryn's mind and wanted no part of them, "she became a Sentinel."

Ezryn narrowed his eyes. There was more. He could tell from the guarded tone in Watkins's voice. But what? "What is going on? Tell me."

Ven Watkins said nothing for a long moment, his eyes haunted.

"Inari's human sister was raped and butchered by an empathic leech demon in the eighteenth century."

"I know that," Ezryn growled. "I held her last night when the disgusting thing got away from her."

"Inari doubts who she is now. Doubts her Sentinel existence."

A cold finger of disquiet pressed at Ezryn's still heart. "How do you know this, Ven?"

The man watched the strippers, face expressionless.

"*They* told you, didn't They?" Ezryn snapped. "The Deities told you what was going on. What did They do, tell Inari she was fired?"

The Sentinel gave him a cold stare. "The Deities are not known for Their tact, bloodsucker. Nor Their communication skills."

Cold anger replaced the disquiet in Ezryn's heart and he clenched his fists. "So your *Lord* takes the only life Inari knows away from her when she saves your brother, gives her something else entirely foreign and then takes *that* away when she is at her most vulnerable?"

Watkins's face became stone again. "The *Lord* has not taken anything away. The Dieties, however, have spoken in haste and too rashly."

Ezryn snarled with disgust. "Then I thank the Dark Ones she is now mine."

Watkins lowered his head, cold menace turning his eyes to ice. "You bound yourself to her for a reason, Ezryn. For your sake I pray it wasn't just your dick making the decisions."

Ezryn hissed and bared his fangs.

Before he could strike, before he could slam Ven to the floor and tear out his throat for such a contemptuous, disrespectful slur, the Sentinel pressed his hand to Ezryn's chest, directly above his dead heart, and stared hard into his face. "*Primoris prognatus ut primoris prognatus. Navarro vadum attero Navarro.* Make it happen, Ezryn. For Inari and the entire vampire race."

A scalding pressure squeezed Ezryn's heart.

Primoris prognatus ut primoris prognatus. First born to first born. *Navarro vadum attero Navarro.* Navarro shall destroy Navarro.

He sucked in a sharp breath, eyes wild, blood surging, and realized he stood alone. Ven Watkins was no longer to be seen.

"What the hell?"

He squinted, searching the crowd around him for any sight of the supreme Sentinel.

Not a sign.

It doesn't matter, Ezryn. Haral has Jacob. You know what that means.

The ominous thought cut into his incredulous disbelief. He turned and moved through the club in an unseeable blur.

Haral's compound was on the other side of the harbor, nestled amongst the opulent mansions of Mosman. No matter how quickly he moved, it would take him close to ten minutes to get there. Ten minutes of Jacob in his brother's sadistic hands.

His gut rolled.

* * *

The itch in Inari's belly ignited into an explosive flutter. She gasped, stumbling to a halt in the middle of the busy Kings Cross footpath. The bond between her and Ezryn was growing...agitated? She didn't know how else to explain it. It was as if the very distance she'd forced him to put between them for his own safety now served as a punishment for her stubborn stupidity to accept what was happening.

And that is what, exactly, Inari?

Desire. True desire. Maybe even...

She chewed on her bottom lip. Was she really ready to go that far? To admit to that emotion? Was she?

Yes. You are.

She closed her eyes, the sights and sounds surrounding her

fading to white noise as she focused on the drawing itch and the connection she now shared with her master vampire.

Instantly and without delay, she felt him in her core, in her soul, a potent, arrogant strength that made her breath catch and her heart race. Whatever future she and Ezryn faced together would be fiery, she knew that. By the Dieties, he was the true overlord of the vampire race. He was born to be arrogant and domineering. And she was a succubus. She was born to make men her slaves. They would argue, fight and annoy the shit out of each other every day, but damn, she had little doubt their sex life would make their heated arguments seem like glaciers of ancient ice.

She smiled, the thought of any future with the pain-in-the-ass bloodsucker setting the throb in her pussy off once more. A vampire who chose to relinquish everything he knew to save hundreds and a messed-up sex demon who may or may not still be a demon assassin. What a couple they made.

The fluttering itch in her soul erupted again, impatient and furious. Inari frowned, ignoring the shoves and jostling bumps from the pedestrians passing by her. There was something about the connection between her and Ezryn...something...

Drawing her concentration onto the bond, she pictured Ezryn in her mind.

A wave of fury rolled through her, dark and red with disgust. Cold and wrought with...with...

Dread.

Inari snapped open her eyes. Ezryn was furious. Wherever he was, he was enraged. And scared. She needed to go to him. Now.

But how could she help him if she was no longer Sentinel? What could she possibly do against something so fierce it scared the true overlord of the vampire race?

"Who cares?" she growled. "I'm still going."

The itch fluttered again, and this time its impatient demand was echoed by something stronger. Something deep within her existence.

Sentinel, a voice whispered through her head in a pure note. The same voice that had granted her her soul twenty years ago. *That* voice. A ripple of infinite elation slipped through Inari, and she closed her eyes, welcoming the pure force of the proclamation. She *was* Sentinel.

Of course.

She frowned, staring at the jostling people around her without really seeing them.

"Then why couldn't I...?"

"Because you need to listen to your sister more," a deep voice replied at her right. She flinched and jerked around to find Ven Watkins standing at her elbow. He gave her a smile, the expression both serene and somehow wan at the same time. "A Sentinel cannot exist, cannot retain their soul if they don't have the strength to believe in themselves first."

"How..." She stared up at him, her mouth open. "How do you know..."

His smile pulled a little wider, a little more lopsided. "I've got connections."

She raised her eyebrows, her heart thumping. "Connections? Can you hear *That* voice in my head?"

Ven gave a small shrug. "I hear a lot of things."

If Inari thought her eyebrows couldn't go any higher on her forehead, she was wrong. "What else have you heard? Do you know about..." She stopped. Swallowed. "Are you—"

"Here to help you? Yeah. I think you need a kick up the arse." He slid his hands into the pockets of his black trousers and leveled an unwavering expression at her. "As someone you know very well recently pointed out, you need to let go of your guilt and fear of what you are and face what must be."

The words echoed Tianya's so closely a chill raced up Inari's spine and sent a wave of gooseflesh over her limbs. She closed her eyes, her thoughts turning to the empathic leech demon and the crippling doubt he'd awakened in her. The guilt. The leech had defeated her by playing on her vulnerability—her sister's murder, her guilt for the crime she could not prevent.

"She's pretty smart, your sister, especially for a ghost," Ven went on, his voice calm. Almost off-hand. "They usually just hang around moaning."

Inari swallowed, her mouth dry. Her world was spinning on a skewed axis. "So she *is* a ghost?" She caught her bottom lip with her teeth. "Not a…a…"

"Figment of your imagination?" Ven shook his head. "No."

A relieved breath escaped Inari and she pressed her hands to her face. "She always was smarter than me," she murmured, picturing her sister.

Ven chuckled. "Tianya knows it's about acceptance as much as it is about strength."

Inari's chest grew tight. She'd been so guilty about failing Tianya she'd let it weaken her. Let it almost destroy her. It wasn't the leech who'd defeated her, it was her guilt. And her doubt.

"Acceptance of self," she whispered, her pulse throbbing so hard her lips tingled.

"Acceptance of self," Ven repeated.

Inari let out a ragged sigh and caught her tingling bottom lip with her teeth. She understood it now. What Tianya had been trying to tell her. What her own heart had been trying to tell her. She was what she was. She'd spent so many years hating herself, longing to be something unobtainable, something perfect. She couldn't do that anymore. She hadn't failed Tianya when she was a succubus, and she hadn't failed herself when she was a Sentinel. "Acceptance of self," she whispered again.

"Well," Ven chuckled, "that and the fact you are willing to fight for the one you love. Even if it means certain death."

She jerked her stare up to his face. Her heart slammed against her breastbone. "You *do* know?"

"About Ezryn Navarro?" He nodded.

"And you're not telling me I have to kill him?"

Ven burst out laughing. "I'm telling you, *He's* telling you—" he pointed skyward, "—to stop thinking you have to keep *everyone* happy and think about the one you love."

"But the Dieties..."

"Have been told to mind Their own business." He smiled. "And your heart, Inari Chayse, is none of Their business."

She looked at him, gnawing at her bottom lip.

"You know what's in your heart," he said. "I know what's in your heart." He flicked a quick look to the heavens. "*He* knows what's in your heart, but does Ezryn?"

And with another of those lopsided grins, he turned and walked away from her, weaving his way along the busy sidewalk.

"That's it?" she called, uncaring of the smirks and curious looks her raised voice earned her from the crowd. "What do I do, Ven?"

She saw him shrug once, a casual lift of his broad, straight shoulders, and then he was gone.

"Damn it," she muttered, watching the swell of people walk around her. "That's the second time he's—"

Something cold and angry knotted in her belly, and she sucked in a quick breath. The bond between her and Ezryn. Her blood roaring in her ears, her whole body awash in tingling energy, she closed her eyes again and took a slower, deeper breath. The very essence of the bond flowed through her, its intangible force like the pull on a compass arrow toward magnetic north.

It was blistering cold with fury and dread. It snared her core like a tight fist and tugged. Hard. Undeniable.

Wherever Ezryn was, he was still enraged. And still fearful.

"I'm coming, my master vampire" she whispered, every fiber in her body burning with righteous force and protective love. "I'm coming, and I'm bringing certain death with me."

She turned, knowing exactly where her lover was, and stared straight into the leering faces of five vampires standing silently before her. "A little birdie told us you'd be here, sweeting," the tallest said, the words almost lost in a thick Irish accent. "We've been looking for you all night. The overlord demands an audience with you, and we've got the job of making you come." He flashed long, pointed fangs at her, his gaze raking her body. "Lucky us, eh?"

* * *

Sydney became indefinable. Ezryn sped through the streets, the humid night air lashing at him, the smells and sounds a thick mist he sliced through effortlessly. The closer he drew to Haral's compound the faster he moved. The dread in his chest twisted, knotted, folded over on itself until the demon deep within his existence controlled him. Ruled him.

He leapt the compound's ten-foot perimeter fence without slowing down, his feet barely touching the night-wet grass as he moved toward the mansion. Fangs bared, he flung the first vamp that came at him away. The guard's body smashed against the mansion's granite wall. He tore the throat from the second vamp before the first's body slid to the ground, uncaring of the blood and oily dust he left in his wake.

A wild howl came from the far corner of the compound and he narrowed his eyes, disgust curdling in his mouth. His gutless baby brother had bleeders guarding him, vampires who had no ties to tradition or reason for loyalty.

He moved quicker, cold fury fueling his actions, his stare already locked on the third guard coming at him, fangs extended, eyes petrified.

Petrified.

The word spat through Ezryn's head, and icy guilt sheared into his rage.

These guards were still his people. Bleeders they may be, but they were still vampires. Protectors of the overlord doing nothing more than an honorable job—guarding their leader. That their *leader* was a sadistic megalomaniac was not their fault, nor reason for them to be butchered by their true leader.

He stumbled. And the slight decrease in his speed was enough for four other vamps to slam into him and take him down.

They hauled him off his feet, fangs bared, eyes wild and demonic. The overwhelming need to throw them from his body and rip out their throats surged through him, but he fought it. Just.

"You're going to die, fucker," one of them snarled in his left ear, sinking claw-like nails into his arm.

He turned his head and gave the guard a level stare. "I am Ezryn Navarro, bleeder. The *true* overlord, first born of the First Family, and you will die before I do."

Four choked gasps punctured the air. The guard's already white face bleached whiter, his yellow eyes bulging. Ezryn snarled. It seemed even bleeders knew who Ezryn Navarro was. The claws in his arm were retracted, somewhat, leaving behind a dull ache Ezryn pushed from his mind. He swung his gaze back to the looming mansion before him. "I am here to see my brother."

The guard to his left swallowed, and the grip on Ezryn's arm tightened again. "The...overlord cannot be disturbed."

Ezryn flashed his fangs at the vampire. "Harry already is *disturbed*."

The guard flicked his stare to his three companions, and Ezryn could practically taste their nervous uncertainty. He bit back a snarl. He didn't have time for this.

With a silent hiss, he threw them off. "I do not wish to harm you," he stated, "but I will if you force me to do so." He fixed them all with a stare full of flat promise. "I need to see my brother."

He stalked toward the mansion's double-door entryway, a distant part of his mind noting the guards did not follow. Good. He did not want to shed more vampire blood tonight than he must.

A dull, cold pain skimmed his consciousness—Jacob's pain—but he ignored it. Retracting his fangs, he forced calm through his body. He needed to be at his most composed and focused. He needed to keep control or his general would suffer the consequences of his brother's vengeful ire. Pushing the doors open, he stormed through the opulent interior, knowing exactly where his brother was. Family blood called family blood. He could feel Harry as well as he could feel Jacob, his twin's presence like an oil slick tainted with decay. It sickened him.

Vampire after vampire scurried aside as he headed for the ballroom—Harry's groveling cronies, their baleful glares drilling into him even as their awe-struck fear leached from them in stinking waves. He put them out of his mind. They were of no consequence.

One thing mattered. Getting Jacob out of his brother's hands.

The heavy doors to the ballroom loomed before him. He pushed them open with one hand and strode over the threshold into the massive room. The stench of wax and smoke curled into his nose, and he flicked a contemptuous snarl at the hundreds of lit candles lining the hall. His brother and his dramatics. It was time to end this whole fucking charade.

He scanned the room, stomach churning. In the far corner, six naked, chained human females cowered against one another, their bodily excrements turning the air rancid. He studied them, disgust coating the back of his throat. How had he let it come to this? How had he let his brother's depravity debase the vampire kind for so long?

He bit back a growl. Jake was nowhere to be seen, but he was close. The Scottish vampire's blood stung his senses. Nostrils flaring, he fixed a flat glare on his brother perched upon the ridiculous throne domineering the end wall of the hall. "Where is he, Harry?"

His low voice echoed in the silence, and it was only the complete lack of noise following his snarled question that told him he and his brother were alone in the room.

His stomach tightened. It was unlike Haral not to surround himself with fawning underlings and guards. That he did so now spoke of an arrogance even greater than Haral's usual conceit.

Haral gave him a smug smile. "Ho, Ezryn."

Ezryn brought himself to a standstill five paces from the overlord. He took a deep breath, never taking his eyes off him. The stench of blood both stale and fresh flooded his nostrils, poured over his olfactory nerve. Anger crashed through him.

Jacob's blood drenched the air.

Fucker.

Haral's smile faded, replaced with a condescending pout. "No friendly words for your twin brother, Ezzie?" He pulled a contemplative expression. "Actually, now that I come to think of it, probably not, given the situation."

Ezryn kept himself motionless. "Bring General Ancroft to me now, Harry, or—"

"Or?" Haral cut him short. "Surely you remember our agreement? Four nights to kill the Sentinel or I begin slaughtering those who opposed my ascension?" He raised his eyebrows in another melodramatic show. "What better vampire to begin with than the one who opposed me most ardently?"

Ezryn's anger turned to blistering ice. He narrowed his eyes, barely keeping his fangs in check. "I will tear your head from your body, Haral, if you truly have been so stupid."

Haral studied him, eyes revealing nothing. "Yes," he murmured, fingers stroking the armrest of his throne. "You would do just that, wouldn't you?" He ran his tongue over his fangs. "If given half the chance."

"Enough," Ezryn snarled. "Bring Jacob to me now."

With a flourish of purple-velvet-swathed arms, Haral stood, smug smile firmly in place. "Come, brother mine. Let us walk."

He descended the raised dais, smiling at Ezryn as he strode with a casual pace toward an unassuming door almost hidden by the wax-laden candelabra to the left of the throne.

Ezryn watched him cross the floor, nerves strung beyond taut. Fury threatened to unravel his control. The urge to leap on his brother, slam him to the black granite and tear his dead heart from his chest almost undid him. His fangs extended. He curled his fingers into fists, knuckles popping.

Control, Ezryn.

Blood roaring in his ears, he crossed to Haral, his full attention on his brother's eyes.

Until Haral pushed the door open.

The smell of Jacob's blood crashed over Ezryn. Suffocating and overpowering. Without hesitation, he shot into the darkness, his gut rolling as his stare locked on the silent, blood-soaked body hanging limply from a whipping post in the center of the room.

Dark Ones... Jake.

He spun to Haral, glaring at his twin where he stood in the open doorway. "You've crossed the line, brother."

Haral raised an eyebrow. "I gave you an order, Ezzie, and you failed to follow through. Unless you intend on killing the Sentinel in the next two hours, General Ancroft will be, I'm afraid to say, the first of your loyalists to be destroyed." A contemplative expression crossed his fleshy features, melodramatic and mocking. "Wait, that's not right. Unless you intend on killing the cunt in the next two hours, General Ancroft will be, I'm *delighted* to say, the first of your loyalists to be destroyed."

Ezryn's throat slammed shut. Murderous rage pumped through his veins. "You cannot do this, Haral."

Haral gave him a smug smirk. "What did you think I was going to do? Twiddle my thumbs until you decided to stop fucking the very Sentinel I commanded you to kill?"

The urge to leap at his brother and rip his tongue from his mouth overwhelmed Ezryn. But he held it in check. Barely. Instead, he gave Haral a bored snort. Haral *wanted* him off-kilter. Angry. For that very reason, he couldn't be. "Perhaps you should be taking notes, Harry. I've heard your performance in bed is just as woeful as your performance as overlord."

Haral's answering sneer was contemptuous. "Still, it is I who fucks whomever I want in our father's bed." He flashed his fangs in a sneering smile. "Not you."

Ezryn cocked an eyebrow, keeping his face calm. "You really

need to address this sibling rivalry problem you have. It's getting a bit old."

"Sibling rivalry or not, the more resourceful brother won on the day it mattered, didn't he?" Haral snorted. "You may have had our father's undivided attention, you may have had the loyalty of the numbers, but it meant nothing when the oracle spoke, did it? Tell me, how did it feel, hearing the Oracle's Voice moan my name in complete rapture fifty years ago? You never told me and I've been most curious."

"I heard the *oracle* wheeze your name, Haral, the way I'm sure he did most nights. What the human virgin being sacrificed for your power lust said to him is another matter altogether."

"It doesn't matter what the virgin said, Ezzie. It was what the oracle proclaimed she said that was important. And *that* was what *I* wanted her to say. I know how to play the game, Ezzie. Our father might not have been bothered to teach me, so preoccupied with the prodigal son, but I watched. And I learned."

Ezryn let his lips part in a cold grin. "Which explains the power-drunk ego and utter lack of humility, I guess."

Haral's face flooded with fury at Ezryn's obvious slur. "We can't all be noble bastards, brother."

"We can't all be moronic imbeciles either."

Haral hissed. "You have always thought you were better than me, but I still outmaneuvered you. When it really mattered, I was the victor. Fuck a Sentinel all you like, but I am the one who rules our race, not you. I am the one who will be written about in the *Lamia Cruor Libri* while you will be just a footnote, the cast-aside son who fled to the bottom of the world to escape his shame. I've always wondered why Australia?" His lips twisted in gleeful pleasure. "Did that old fart Kristoph tell you which country to sulk in? Oh, wait. No, he couldn't have. Your most cherished mentor and advisor was already dusted before you left, wasn't he?"

Incredulous rage punched through Ezryn's chest. When had his twin become so vile?

Haral smirked. "He wasn't much of a court mentor, was he, ol' Kristoph? The overlord's advisors hardly paid him any mind when he petitioned them to deny the oracle's proclamation." He chuckled, the sound smug and cruel. "You know, I never understood the human saying 'squealed like a stuck pig' until Kristoph and I had a little chat. Very verbose he was, for such a decrepit vampire. Filled me in on all sorts of little secrets he knew about our reverent family. With the right...encouragement of course." He snickered. "How does it feel, brother, knowing if it wasn't for one simple piece of evidentiary proof, you would be sitting where I am now?"

He narrowed his stare onto his brother's face, forcing his voice to stay even. "Sitting where you are now?" He raised his eyebrows, his rage a cold fist in his head. "In crushed velvet with a bloated gut and an even more bloated ego?" He snorted a dry laugh. "Perhaps I should be *thanking* the Dark Ones your affair with the oracle was so clandestine after all."

"Oh, you are the funny one, Ezryn, and yet you're also the one sticking your dick in the cunt of a Sentinel. Fucking the mortal enemy of vampires everywhere. Often, from what I hear. Whatever will your loyalists think of that little piece of information?"

Ezryn bared his fangs. "What I do with my dick is my business, Harry, not yours."

"Tell that to General Ancroft, Ezzie. He's the one about to have his heart ripped out and skewered on a silver spike for your *business.*"

"Christ, Harry," a low, almost inaudible mumble sounded on the air, "can you...shut the fuck...up?"

Ezryn spun to the whipping post, a loathing so deep he almost buckled under its concentrated force surging through his conscious-ness. Jacob Ancroft's loathing. For the overlord.

Jacob glared at Haral through a veil of blood-matted hair, his eyes burning fathomless icy hate. "You always...*were* a...fuck-knuckle. You just got...fatter."

"Fuck-knuckle I may be," Haral snarled, his eyes flashing

incensed rage and yellow unease, "but I am not the one about to be sacrificed by my master and friend for a Sentinel cunt."

Jacob's lips pulled into a slow grin, his own blood seeping down his face making the action all the more menacing. "No," he growled, incisors extending to wicked points. "Neither am I."

Chapter Twelve

Jacob threw himself forward, tugging against the silver chains binding him to the whipping post. The creature he truly was, the malevolent being feared the world over surged through him, fed by fathomless hate and unending loyalty. He roared, no longer human, completely vampire, every muscle in his body coiled steel. Searing pain sliced into his wrists, up his arms, into his chest. Searing pain incinerated by the full force of his revulsion and hatred for his master's brother.

He threw himself into the agony, welcoming it. Cherishing it. Feeding on it. And the chains snapped.

"No!" Haral squealed, scurrying backward through the door.

"Jake! No!" Ezryn's shout scraped at his fury, a compelling voice he could not ignore, but could not obey either. Not at the moment. All that mattered was what had to be done—and what had to be done was the utter and complete decimation of Haral Navarro.

Jacob flung himself at the gibbering vampire, a clear and rational part of his mind noting the horde of guards charging into the ballroom at the overlord's screech. Their presence meant little.

He landed on Haral with fluid speed. Hands fisting in the fucker's velvet collar, feet planting against his flabby gut, Jacob slammed him to the ground.

Haral squealed again, eyes bulging. "Get him! *Get him!*"

The overlord's wails filled the air, almost drowned out by Ezryn's roar, "Jake! Get off him! You're leaving yourself—"

Jacob smashed his fist into Haral's face, mashing his knuckles against the vampire's cheek. He felt the bone shatter, and cold satisfaction speared into his incensed hate. "For my wife," he snarled, smashing his fist into the vampire's jaw. "For my friend." He slammed his forehead into Haral's nose. "For my kind." He grabbed two handfuls of Haral's hair to pound his head into the floor.

Haral flailed and bucked beneath him, squealing and screeching like a gutted pig. *"Get him! Get him!"*

"Jake!" Ezryn roared. "You need to—"

The wet sound of flesh being torn apart slapped against Jake's consciousness, and he jerked his stare from Haral just in time to see Ezryn rip a guard's throat out beside him. Two more vampires launched themselves at his master, their eyes wild with fear. In the corner of the room, the chained women squealed. Human women. Defenseless against a vampire's true power.

Just like Jacob's wife.

"Get him!" Haral screeched, thrashing beneath Jacob, hot spittle spewing from his mouth in thick tendrils, blood pissing from his nose in ropey snot. *"Kill him!"*

Jacob hissed and smashed his forehead into Haral's shattered nose again. "I should have done this fifty fucking years ago," he snarled, smacking the wailing vampire's head to the tiles over and over again. "But better late—" he slammed his fist into Haral's jaw, his cheek, his temple, "—than never." He grabbed two fistfuls of Haral's hair and sank his teeth into the side of the overlord's face, biting deeply into the cold flesh before yanking his head away and tearing half of Haral's cheek off.

Stare locked on Haral's mashed, oozing face, he spat out the chunk of cheek muscle. "For my Cara," he whispered, an icy calm falling over him. He pulled back his arm and opened his fingers, his nails growing into long, hooked claws. Perfect for tearing a deranged, sadistic, walking corpse's dead heart from his chest. Perfect for killing the overlord.

"N...no...no..." Blood bubbled past Haral's split lips. "D...don't." His head lolled, eyes rolling.

"Jake!" Ezryn yelled. "Stop! You can't kill the overlord, no matter how much he deserves it. You have to stop. Now."

Jacob bared his fangs in a silent snarl. "Good riddance, Harry."

Haral's head dropped to the side, bleeding eyes focusing on something behind Jacob. "Kill...him."

"Stop!" Ezryn roared. "Don't shoot!"

A sharp sound splintered into Jacob's fury, and he jerked his stare up from Haral's face. To find three vampires surrounding him, aiming stake-cocked crossbows straight at his chest.

"I am Ezryn Navarro." Ezryn's growl ripped at the silence, powerful with command and menace. "*First* born of the First Family, true and rightful overlord, and I order you to lower your weapons and stand down."

Jacob glared hard at the vampires standing over him. They flicked each other silent glances, their pale faces draining white.

"Stand *down!*"

Faces whiter still, they staggered away from Jacob, eyes uncertain, crossbows wavering.

"What are you doing?" Harry thrashed beneath him, spittle showering Jacob's face. "What the fuck are you—"

"Stand *down!*" Ezryn roared. "Stand *down n—*"

Ezryn's command stopped dead. Jacob swung his head toward his master, cold fear destroying his fury in an instant.

Ezryn's eyes were wide, his stare fixed on the hall's closed door. A look of absolute dismay etched his face. "May the Dark Ones have mercy on us all," he whispered. "She's here. God's assassin."

. . .

Ezryn stood motionless, even as the itch in his gut—the bond between him and Inari—burst into a wild inferno. She was here. And she was furious.

A scream rose from the other side of the dark room. Another. Another. Someone screamed something he couldn't understand, a wailing cry full of abject terror.

A solid thump shook the room, as if something had hit the wall on the other side.

"Kill him," Haral croaked again from beneath Jacob, but no one was listening to him. All eyes were locked on the gaping door. Waiting...waiting...

"My lover." The whisper fell from Ezryn's lips at the exact second the itch in his gut exploded afresh into rabid life. The exact moment Inari Chayse stepped through the doorway into the ballroom, as petite and sexy as always, looking for all the world like a goth Daisy Duke in knee-high boots and a black leather corset.

Her gaze found him instantly, the corners of her lips curling even as her eyes blazed with seismic rage.

Ezryn's tight throat squeezed tighter. The itch in the pit of his core vanished, replaced by a joy so pure, so elemental he blinked.

Dark Ones, he loved her.

Who? The Sentinel or the succubus?

"The Sentinel!" Haral cried, thrashing under Jacob's pinning weight.

The guards' eyes widened. A collective hiss filled the room, and a warped sense of pride slashed through Ezryn as he watched each one stumble back a step from the unassuming woman standing in the doorway. They were petrified of her. A cold grin pulled at his mouth. Good. So they should be.

"Get her!" Haral screeched. "She is mine!"

Ezryn roared, his vampire *croi* surging through him. Every deadly, demonic instinct took over. He threw back his arms, flinging the guards holding him across the room. *"No!"*

He leapt the distance between him and Inari, icy alarm

devouring him. Haral would not take her. He would die before he let his brother even touch her.

He planted his feet on the floor and reached for her, his stare locking on her eyes. *I will—*

"Ezryn!" She screamed, lunging at him, horror distorting her face at the exact second a crossbow bolt speared into his back high on his left shoulder. Excruciating agony ripped through him. He screamed, twisting his body to snatch at the pointed length of wood. He tore the stake free of his flesh, spinning away from Inari's distraught face to glare at the guard staggering backward, crossbow wavering in his hands. "Not a wise move."

"Ow, you fucking bastard!"

Jacob's furious shout punched into Ezryn's rage. He turned to his general just in time to see Haral shove him away from his body. Blood gushed from Jacob's side, and it took Ezryn a split second to see the stake buried into his friend's armpit.

Fuck.

Haral leapt to his feet, human façade gone. "I'm going to rip your gods-cursed head off, Ancroft."

"Try it," Jacob spat, his face contorted in pain even as his eyes flashed cold hate.

Two guards threw themselves at Jacob just as three threw themselves at Ezryn.

They slammed into him, smashing the butts of their crossbows against his face, his chest, his ribs.

Why aren't they staking you?

The incredulous question shot through the pain erupting in his body a second before the chilling answer destroyed that pain. His twin wanted him alive.

"Get me the Sentinel!"

The triumph in Haral's shouted command made Ezryn's gut churn. He reeled backwards, spreading his arms to protect Inari, and the guards struck him again and again with their crossbows. Dark Ones, how was he going to keep her safe?

From the corner of his eye, he saw the two guards raining blow after blow down on Jacob, each struggling to avoid the vampire's savage counterattack. Blood poured from the stake wound in Jake's side, the thick length of sharpened wood jutting from his flesh like a surreal growth.

Fuck. How was he going to get them *all* out of here alive?

"I want the Sentinel!" Haral screamed, and Ezryn felt a solid wall of something cold and contemptuous hit him from behind. It was coming from Inari. If the situation hadn't been so dire, he would have laughed. It seemed his lover didn't like his brother either.

"Get me the Sentinel!" Haral screeched again. "Get her, get her, get her!"

"Inari Chayse is not just a Sentinel, Harry," Ezryn heard Jacob snarl, pain distorting his voice to a strangled breath. "She is a succubus."

"And a damn good one." Inari's calm, matter-of-fact voice sounded behind Ezryn. "Watch."

A sudden wave of concentrated pleasure crashed over him, through him. His balls rose up, tight and hot with instant lust. His cock surged with hot, eager blood. He spun around, his body on fire with molten desire, and stared at Inari.

Have her have her fuck must have her

Scalding lust ripped through him. His cock strained against the inside of his trousers, rigid and throbbing with want. His mouth filled with saliva, his fangs extended farther.

Want her, want her, want her

He craved the taste of her flesh on his tongue, hungered for the feel of her nipples in his mouth. Lusted for the tight, wet heat of her sex, her ass around his cock. Lusted for it. Needed it. Had to have it. Had to have her. Now.

Want her, want her, oh fuck, want her now

And then the uncontrollable, consuming lust was gone. As if it hadn't been there at all.

He gaped at her, the ghost of his overwhelming desire still

throbbing through his dick in a fading, empty heat. Dark Ones, was *that* the power of a succubus? Had he really thought she'd turned that power on him before?

Real. What you've felt for her all this time has been real.

A wild moan rose on the air above him, killing the joyous realization. A raw gasp, a hitching groan. He spun back to the guards behind him, stunned disbelief robbing him of his ability to speak. Each one was on their knees, crossbows hanging limply from their fingers or dropped to the floor altogether. Each one gazed at Inari with open, unadulterated, ravenous rapture.

"I will fuck you all," she murmured, her eyes smoldering with green fire. A chill shot up Ezryn's spine. Her body, her face said she was a being of sexual appetites, willing and waiting to bring absolute pleasure, but he was bound to her, he *knew* her, and what he felt folded through the sensual purr made his balls shrink.

Rage. Powerful, icy, righteous rage. The rage of a Sentinel.

"I will let you possess my body," she went on, her eyes glowing hotter, greener. She lifted her hands to her breasts, skimming her knuckles over the taut tips of her nipples pushing against her top. The action elicited another groan from the vampires staring at her, their lips growing wet with drool. "I will let you use my body, abuse it, devour it. All of you." She shuttered her eyes with a coy downward glance, stroking the sides of her breasts, her ribs, her hips with her fingertips. "If you all do something for me."

"What the fuck is going on?" Haral's shout cut the moans, but not one guard moved or tore their hungry gaze from Inari. "Get her!"

"Anything!" the guard to Ezryn's right burst out, swaying toward Inari. "Anything for you, my goddess."

A husky giggle slipped past Inari's lips, and she touched the tip of her tongue to her top teeth. "Anything? Then so be it. Tear your dicks from your bodies and stuff them down your throats."

The brutal, shocking order came from her on a breathless whisper. Ezryn's throat squeezed tight and he stared at her, Jacob's stunned gasp barely registering.

"What? *What?*" Haral yelped.

Ezryn turned back to the guards, shocked to see each and every one ripping at their flies, their crotches bulging, their eyes feverish.

Dark Ones, they're going to do it. They're really going to do it.

"Stop!" Haral bellowed, glaring with shocked fury at his guards. "What are you doing?"

A sharp bark of mirthless humor sounded to Ezryn's right, barely audible over the hideous noises of pleasure, tearing flesh and muffled gagging. "It's pretty fucking obvious, isn't it, Harry?" Jacob said, his voice a jarring mix of revulsion and impressed awe. "They're yanking their cocks off and choking on them."

"No!" The overlord shook his head, disbelief twisting his face into a contorted mask. "No!" His stare jerked to Inari and a shard of acrid unease stabbed into Ezryn's chest. "How...how?"

"I believe you wanted me, Haral Navarro?"

Inari's question stroked the room like velvet. Ezryn tensed, his gut knotting. He could feel her anger pulsing through her. A terrifying force matched only by the inescapable, undeniable force of her demon sexuality.

He shot his brother a quick look, gut knotting tighter.

"Then have me," Inari whispered.

Haral's eyes grew wide. His lips parted in a silent gasp Ezryn heard all the same before he fell to his knees, blood flowing from the gaping bite wound in his cheek, his enrapt gaze ablaze with hungry, mindless lust. "Oh, oh, oh." His groan ripped from his throat, a sound so carnal, so ripe with licentious pleasure Ezryn's gut rolled.

He knew what was happening to his brother. Haral hungered for Inari Chayse. Completely and utterly. He was consumed by desire for her. Mindless with it.

"Have me," Inari whispered again, stepping forward. She didn't look at Ezryn as she brushed past him. She didn't have to. He felt everything she felt. Her rage, her contempt, her revulsion...

Haral groaned again, reaching for her from his subservient position, his hands trembling, his nostrils flaring. "Want you, want you."

"Have me."

The command caressed the room. Haral roared, grabbing at his trousers. "Want you, want you, want, want, *want*."

Sour bile rose in Ezryn's throat at the sight of his brother tearing at his clothes, desperate to get his hands on his erection. Ezryn bared his fangs, the urge to smash his fists into Haral's gut, to obliterate his twin's lascivious cravings for Inari almost overwhelming him.

He took a step forward.

Wait.

The word slipped through his head like a silent breeze. He stopped and shot Inari a quick look.

"Do you want to fuck me, Haral Navarro?" She ran her fingertips up her belly, over her breasts, up her throat.

Haral nodded his head with such violent agreement Ezryn swore he heard the bones in his twin's neck grind together. "Yes, my goddess. Yes."

"Then tell me, how did you become overlord?"

Ezryn froze, his stare snapping to Inari's face.

"No, my goddess. I can't..."

Harry's tortured whimper jerked his attention back to his brother, and he bunched his fists. Harry was shaking, eyes bulging wider, face a sickly white. "Please, not that," Haral blubbered, wringing his hands together.

"Do you want to fuck me, Haral?" Inari asked again, her voice lower, huskier. "Do you want to sink your fangs into my neck and feed from me?"

Harry's mouth fell open and he scurried forward on his knees, arms held out to her. "Oh, yes, yes, yes, yes."

"Then tell me, how did you become the overlord?"

"The oracle wanted Ezryn," Haral burst out, the words running over each other, his stare never leaving Inari's face. "The oracle wanted Ezryn for his bed, but our father refused him. Our father always cherished Ezryn more. So I went to the oracle and offered myself. Wasn't that clever, my goddess?"

"Very clever, Haral." Inari's tone grew calm. "Tell me more."

"I knew, you see, what the oracle could do," Haral gushed, scurrying closer toward her, spittle shining on his lips. "I knew if I let him fuck me whenever he wanted, if I let him pretend I was my brother, one day he'd let me have what I wanted. Would do what I wanted him to do."

"And what was that, Haral?"

The overlord hesitated, terror flicking across his pudgy face. "My goddess, please, no..."

A wave of rapture radiated from Inari and Haral whimpered, reaching for her again. "I wanted him to declare the human virgin whispered *my* name after the blood trials, not Ezryn's," he cried, tears of blood leaking from his eyes. "*I* wanted to be overlord. Not my brother."

Ezryn stared at his twin, disgust churning in his gut, and relief—cold and empty and somehow hollow—igniting in his chest. The truth was revealed. He ran an unwavering stare over the vampires around them watching the spectacle. Their faces registered shock and disbelief. Followed by contempt.

"So you lied?" Inari whispered, husky voice all but inaudible. "You aren't the true overlord? You aren't the first born of the First Family?"

"I lied," Haral moaned. "I'm not the first born. I am not the true overlord. I killed my mother when she discovered the truth of my relationship with the oracle, and I arranged for my father's murder." He wrung his hands again, gazing at her. "Will you fuck me now, my goddess? Will you let me feed on your blood as I fuck your beauty?"

Cold shock slammed into Ezryn. He narrowed his stare, his brother's confession chilling him to his very core. Their mother's death? Their father's... How had he never known the true depths of Haral's lust for power? How had he not felt his twin's true hatred?

He took a step forward, the blood in his veins like ice. It was time to end it. Time to finish the woeful situation once and for all.

"Goddess?" Haral wailed, staring at Inari with beseeching, pathetic hunger. "I want you. I want you."

"Then have me," Inari stated, and she spread her arms out to the side. "Have *all* of me."

The air shimmered. A pulse of raw lust blasted through Ezryn. Jacob groaned, the sound strangled.

And Haral threw back his head, a wail of absolute rapture bursting from his throat, his hands grabbing at his cock, his balls, pulling at them, mauling them as bright red blood began to ooze from his ears, his nose. "Want, want, want, want, want..." He thrashed on his knees, eyes wild and glazed, body shuddering. "Want, want, want..."

Something intangible wrapped around Ezryn's chest. He let out a choked growl, his brother's wails and cries piercing his unbeating heart. Haral *was* his twin brother. Second born of the First Family. His twin brother who was never meant for the power, the responsibility of the overlord.

He squeezed his fists harder, watching Haral gouge at his groin, eyes rolling, saliva drooling from his mouth.

Brother.

Disgusted pity twisted in Ezryn's core and he shot Inari a quick look. "Enough, my love. The truth has been revealed. There is no need for any further proof."

Without hesitation, she lowered her arms and Haral collapsed forward, as if the power to control his body had suddenly been cut. She looked at Ezryn over her shoulder, an uncertain, almost shy frown playing with her eyebrows. He gave her a small smile and she nodded once. She understood. He could sense her acceptance of his decision and the reasoning behind it. *"He is your brother, Ezryn. Your twin brother."*

He turned back to Haral, studying his brother's slumped, trembling form. "It is over, Haral. You have no influence, hold no sway over the fate of the vampire race anymore. I accept my birthright as the true overlord and am commanding you to abdicate."

Haral lifted his head, staring at him with eyes still wild, still empty. "No... Want..."

Ezryn clenched his jaw, a numb ache settling in his gut. "What you want you can no longer have, Haral. I will let you live—you are my brother. But know this, you are no longer the overlord, and any attempt to challenge my ruling will be severely punished. This is the way it is, and this is the way it will be."

A low groan rumbled deep in Haral's chest. A shudder rocked him and he glared up at Ezryn, hate etched on his face, his eyes suddenly clear. Baleful. "The way it will fucking be," he sneered.

"Master!" Jacob yelled, "Look out!"

Ezryn reeled backward, a split second before Haral launched himself from the floor, a purple streak of hissing speed, and slammed into Inari.

"*No!*" Ezryn spun toward them, dread smashing into his heart.

Haral staggered away from him, crushing Inari against his body, hiding behind her. One hand hooked into her breast, his pudgy fingers sinking into its full curve, the other rammed her head to her shoulder, straining her neck into a shocking curve even as she struggled in his hold. "You can have the position of overlord, *brother*," he snarled, fangs glistening with saliva. His glare locked on Ezryn's face. "I claim the Sentinel."

"*No!*" Ezryn roared again, just as Haral sank his fangs into Inari's throat.

Piercing pain detonated in her neck, up into her head, down into her chest. Ezryn felt it as surely as if his brother had punctured his own neck. Her spine snapped into a violent arch and she bucked in Haral's hideous embrace, her neck and shoulder on fire, Haral's teeth sinking deeper into her flesh.

"*Bastard!*"

The word shot through Ezryn's head, Inari's thought both incredulous and furious. His gut rolled. His chest squeezed tight. She bucked again, her stare locked on his face. Her blood gushed past Haral's lips, a drowning flood streaming down her neck, over her shoulder, her chest. Painting her flesh red.

"Ezryn."

His name was whispered in his head, and with it came a wisp of something delicate and powerful at once—love—before he felt nothing but an icy ripple and a surging force.

The Sentinel was emerging.

God's assassin rising. Ready, eager to destroy.

Inari flung her arms wide, throwing Haral off her back with little effort, his fangs gouging her flesh, his nails raking over her breast. Ezryn experienced her pain, her repulsed disgust, and it unleashed his own. Completely.

He smashed into his twin, pinned him to the floor by the neck and glared down into his face. "After everything you've done to everyone I've loved, after what you did to Jacob...to Inari..." Cold resolution flowed through him. "I have to kill you."

He slammed his fist into his brother's face, shattering his teeth. His knuckles stung, ripped open by Haral's fangs, but he didn't stop. He hit his brother again, his vampire's soulless *croi* taking control, the years of betrayal, hate and denial pushing him beyond rational thought. It turned him into the monster he so despised—the bloodthirsty, soulless killing machine.

He hit Haral again, each punch shattering the face so like his own, each blow showering him in his twin's blood.

Until something vise-like grabbed his wrist.

He snapped his stare over his shoulder, fangs bared, the blood rage boiling in his veins.

Jacob stood beside him, his fingers curled around his wrist, his face bruised, broken but already beginning to mend. He gave Ezryn a silent shake of the head, the stake buried in his armpit dripping blood. "You will hate yourself, Ezryn," he stated, pushing Ezryn's arm down, lowering his killing strike.

Ezryn swung his gaze back to his brother, the savage damage to Haral's nose and teeth a mirror to the damage Haral had wrought on Jake.

"What are you going to do, Ezzie?" Haral rasped, glaring up at him through bleeding eyes. "You're too noble to kill me?"

"He may be, Harry," Jacob said, his voice full of menacing promise. He stepped forward, placed his hand on Ezryn's shoulder and moved him away from Haral with gentle but inarguable force. "But I'm not." He reached up, wrapped his fingers around the stake buried in his armpit and withdrew it in one slow, steady pull. His blood ran down its pointed length, dripping on the floor beside his foot, an unspeakable message to all. "Ready?"

Ezryn studied him, on the verge of telling Jake to stand down. And then he thought of Jacob's wife, of what Haral had ordered done to her, what Haral's zealots had forced Jacob to watch. He thought of what Haral had done to Kristoph, what he'd tried to do to Inari, and he gave his best friend a single nod.

Haral may be his twin brother, but that would not save him. Not from the Scottish vampire. Not from a just punishment long overdue.

He cast his gaze over the vampires still mingling around them, some still writhing in the pain of Inari's earlier control, most standing silent, struck dumb with shock. "I am Ezryn Navarro." His voice carried throughout the hall, each syllable resonating with the ancient power of his bloodline, each note reverberating with half a century of denied leadership. "*First* born of the First Family. Let it be known, by right of birth and confession, I *am* the overlord of the vampire race and reclaim the position denied me for fifty years."

Every vampire still standing dropped to their knees, their stares locked on Ezryn.

"The tyranny of Haral Navarro's rule is over," he spoke, his blood roaring in his ears, Haral's whimpering pleas echoing around the room. "The vampire race has a new leader. The *true* overlord has returned."

He swung his gaze to the far corner of the ballroom, his mouth filling with disgust at the six naked, chained females staring at him. Six petrified, degraded women. "The humans are to be released. Now. We do not feed on the unwilling, nor treat them as cattle."

With a nod, three of Haral's guards hurried over to the women and the solid chink of metal falling to marble ricocheted through the charged silence. Sobs of relief and gratitude came from the corner, the completely human sound filling Ezryn with a heavy sensation.

He turned to Inari, to the Sentinel he'd once sought to kill, the succubus he'd once planned to punish, the woman he knew he loved beyond measure and who loved him in return. A wave of warmth rolled through him, an emotion he recognized as pride.

She was proud of him. He gave her a small smile. It felt good. Very good.

Swinging his attention back to the waiting vampires, he fixed them with a long, steady stare. "Change is coming, and you should prepare for it." He thought of the overlord's advisors back in Denmark, he thought of the oracle. He thought of their reaction to the situation, to his reclaimed leadership. He thought of their faces when he walked into the overlord's compound in Copenhagan and told them they were no longer required, and couldn't stop his smile stretching wider. "*All* our kind should prepare for it."

He turned back to his sniveling twin brother. "*Primoris prognatus ut primoris prognatus,*" he stated, his heart heavy, his earlier resolution as cold as it was before. He knew what he had to do to begin to heal the wounds his brother had rent on the vampire race. Knew it without doubt or hesitation. "*Navarro vadum attero Navarro.*"

"No," Haral wailed. "No, you fucking piece of piss-soaked shit. You can't kill me. I am your brother. You can't kill your only brother. You can't!"

"Navarro shall destroy Navarro," Ezryn murmured.

He moved his gaze to his best friend, noting the congealed blood down Jacob's side. The puncture in Jacob's armpit had healed, but it was the hurt and loss and grief swimming in his clear, blue eyes that made Ezryn clench his fists. Emotional wounds Haral had wrought upon Jacob's heart that would quite possibly never heal. For the Scottish vampire, the torture and rape of his human wife would never be forgotten. "He is yours to do with what you will, Jake."

"No!' Haral screeched. "No!"

With one final look at Jacob, Ezryn returned his attention to the waiting guards around him. "Leave now. And send word of what happened here tonight to all our kind."

They nodded, their expressions shocked as they ran from the room. It had begun.

"Brother?" Haral whimpered from the floor, his voice cracking. "Please, brother, have mercy."

Ezryn closed his eyes, drawing an image of Haral into his mind —Haral as a young vampire child. Laughing, playing. The Haral he'd known before their fates took over their lives. He would remember his twin that way. The Haral he'd once loved.

"Ezryn?"

At Inari's soft voice, he opened his eyes and found her standing beside him, her face composed. He felt her worry thread through their bond, a cool ribbon of concerned love he felt all the way to his very center. Without another glance at his brother on the floor, he placed his hand on the small of her back and began to walk. Away from his twin. Away from his best friend and most trusted general.

And as he did, Haral began to shriek.

And shriek.

Her heart wouldn't stop beating. Not that Inari *wanted* her heart to stop beating, but she sure as hell wanted it to stop beating as fast as it currently was. She moved through the compound, marveling in wary amazement at the vampires falling to their knees and pressing their foreheads to the floor, their eyes wide with fear and reverence.

Their subservient actions had nothing to do with her, of course.

She shot the silent vampire striding across the black granite floor beside her a surreptitious look, and her heart thumped out a rapid rhythm.

He hadn't said a word to her since his calm, "Enough, my love" when she'd released the full force of her succubus power on his brother. She frowned, a squirming tension making itself at home in her belly. There were many things she could sense in the overlord of the vampire race, yet none of them told her what was going on in his head.

The only thing she could do was focus on the cool pressure of his hand at the small of her back, draw comfort—of a sort—from its physical contact until they were clear of his brother's compound. Then, if he hadn't said something to her, she'd kick his ass for being a prick. After she threw him against the wall and kissed him stupid.

"Now that is the most sane thought you've had since we left Haral to Jacob's devices."

Inari startled at Ezryn's deep voice. She gave him another look, this one less clandestine and more infuriated. "What?" she snipped. "The thought of kicking your ass for being a prick? Glad you agree with me."

The corners of Ezryn's mouth curled and he slipped his hand a touch farther down her back, his fingertips skimming the curve of her butt cheeks with a teasing caress. He didn't say anything, nor did he have to. For the first time since she'd opened up and let her succubus powers flow, she could truly feel what was in his head.

Her nipples pinched tight.

Ezryn chuckled and kept walking, his pace even and arrogant.

Inari clenched her fists and shook her head. Of all master vampires to be bound to, she had to go and get herself bitten by the supreme lord and commander of the bloodsuckers. She'd be dealing with his conceit for decades.

Ezryn chuckled again and stroked little circles on the tops of her ass cheeks. "As I will be dealing with your righteous calling."

She opened her mouth to tell him to fuck off and closed it without uttering a sound. What could she say? He was right.

The massive double doors of Haral Navarro's compound loomed before her, and a tight tingle rippled through Inari's body. She didn't need the bond between them both to know what awaited her on the other side. They might spend the rest of eternity arguing like cats and dogs, or vamps and werewolves, but one thing was very, very clear—the make-up sex was going to be—

"Going to fucking kill you!"

A high-screeching female voice shattered the silence of the mansion and Inari gasped, spinning around to see a voluptuous blonde poured into blood-red leather running at them both, fangs bared, fingers hooked into claws, eyes venomous with insane hate.

"Chantise!" Ezryn snapped. "Enough!"

The female vampire hissed, running at them faster. "I'm going to fucking kill you both. Starting with the cunt."

Ezryn moved like a blur. But not before Inari.

She transformed. In the space of a heartbeat.

Her flesh razed with a million pinpricks of blistering heat. The bones in her body tore apart and reformed until she was taller, leaner and roped with steely muscles. Two wings of epic proportions tore through her flesh, unfurling from between her shoulder blades, their membrane-taut width launching her from the floor with infinite speed and grace. Her mouth filled with needle-sharp teeth, her nails hooked into talons.

Sentinel. Assassin of the Highest. In her most terrifying form.

The female vampire screeched again, eyes bulging. She scrambled backward, shaking her head, stare glued on Inari. "I want you dead! *Dead!*"

The acrid stench of urine and terror sliced into Inari's heightened sense of smell. Lips curling, she landed on the shrieking woman and sank her talons into the female's neck. Pinned her to the cold black floor. "And I want you to shut up."

"You killed my cousin!" The vampire bucked beneath her, spittle spraying from her mouth.

Inari cocked an eyebrow. "If he was a soulless bloodsucker who preyed on the innocent, it's quite likely."

The female hissed, thrashing against the floor. "Kill you! Fucking kill you! And the traitorous fuck who's been fucking you."

"Now, now, Chantise." Ezryn stepped up beside Inari to shake his head at the writhing blonde in Inari's inescapable grip. "You really need to expand your vocabulary. Three fucks in one threat?"

Chantise hissed again, glaring at Ezryn. "You let that... that...*Scottish* filth kill my husband! I will kill you all. I will—"

"Enough," Ezryn growled. A dark expression fell over his face, and Inari felt the icy force of his demon roll from him. "I think you need to go back to Denmark, Chantise," he said, voice low and even, stare locked on the female's eyes. "Australia isn't the right place for you." He straightened and turned away, giving Inari an unreadable look as he did so.

Her stomach knotted, all the more so because the only emotion she could feel emanating from him through their bond was cold distaste.

"Release her, Sentinel," she heard him say, his voice as ambivalent as his earlier stare.

Sentinel. The title sent an uneasy shiver up her spine and her wings flexed. Once, Ezryn had seen her in her assassin form. He'd seen—and felt—what she could do with her succubus soul, and now she couldn't tell a thing about what he was thinking or feeling. She ground her teeth. Her stomach knotted tighter.

Chantise whimpered, a scared, child-like sound that vibrated against Inari's palm.

With a silent sigh, she removed her hand from the female vampire's throat.

Why? Is Ezryn your master now as well as your lover?

She rose to her feet and looked at his retreating back, noting the coiled muscles, tense shoulders and clenched fists.

Is he even that now?

"I am the overlord's wife!" Chantise sobbed from the floor, voice weak, defeated.

"Not anymore," Ezryn threw over his shoulder.

He kept walking, the silent vampire guards surrounding them scurrying farther away as he strode past them, their eyes down-turned, their expressions reverent. Inari narrowed her eyes. They knew who their new master was. Knew and accepted it.

She closed her eyes and swallowed. Acceptance. What a bitch of a word.

So where do you stand now, Inari?

A shimmer of prickling heat razed her flesh and, with a slight shake of her shoulders, she stood in her human form again, her torn clothes hanging from her body.

Opening her eyes, she glared at Ezryn's back.

Acceptance. She'd finally accepted who she was, what she was, and she'd never been more bloody confused.

Releasing a low growl, Inari stalked after the overlord. Confused she may be, but one thing was certain, Ezryn Navarro was about to get the biggest ass kicking of his life. And there would be no kissing afterwards.

The humid night air from outside slid over her as she approached the open mansion doors, the soft *scree scree* of cicadas doing nothing to calm her agitation. What lay ahead of Ezryn was not just intimidating, but monumental. He stood on the cusp of a revolution that could change the status quo between man and vampire forever. She wanted to be there for him through it all, help him, but even with their bond, she had no idea if he wanted her to. And how could the born leader of the vampire race take a Sentinel as his partner? How could the Dark Ones and the Deities allow it?

Where did that leave her?

She crossed the compound's threshold, the stares of the vampire guards drilling into her back, the hitching sobs of the once-overlord's wife scraping at her nerves. Bloody vampires. She couldn't wait to be—

A hand snared her wrist—hard—and before she could do anything but gasp in shock, Ezryn yanked her from her feet and slammed her against the mansion wall.

He grabbed her other wrist and pinned it beside her head, his gaze a black inferno roaming her face. "I can tell you where it leaves you, Inari Chayse," he murmured, ramming his hips to hers, his long, thick erection grinding against the junction of her thighs. "Exactly where I want you to be. With me. Mine. Forever." His fangs glinted at her in a smile Inari felt all the way to her core. "And I don't care what the Dark Ones and Deities think."

His mouth crushed hers.

"Forever."

The word echoed in her head, an entirely enthralling notion. She rolled her hips and lifted one leg to wrap it around the back of Ezryn's thigh, holding him to her.

The symbiotic existence of her succubus and Sentinel forces purred with anticipation, and her nipples puckered into pinched tips. Oh, fuck, forever.

"Yes," he growled against her lips, sliding her hands up the stone wall of the mansion until her arms were stretched above her head. "Forever." He pulled back, barely a fraction, his cool breath caressing her face even as he pressed his body closer to hers. "If you think one little pair of wings is going to scare me off, you have another thing coming."

He dragged his hands down her arms, over her breasts, to her hips and back up to her arms again, pinning her to the wall with his lower body. "I am the overlord of the vampire race. My wife needs to be just as tough as I am."

Inari's heart thumped into her throat. "Wife?" The word left her on a breath.

He nodded. Once. "My wife." His gaze roamed her face, as if

charting it, devouring it. Branding it in his mind. "My lover. My Sentinel."

The absolute hunger in his thought flowed into Inari, through her, and she arched her spine, pressing her hips closer to his, letting him feel the heat of her own hunger. The potent desire in his eyes made her sex constrict, and she let out a small, hitching sigh. "My lover," she murmured in reply, wrapping her arms around his neck. "My master vampire. My husband." She let her lips into a small smile. "You just better buy me a really, really big diamond ring."

"A really big one," he murmured back, and claimed her mouth as his.

Epilogue

elbourne, Australia. Six months later

The constant *thump-thump-thump* of the loud, monotonous music pounded against Ezryn's head. He suppressed a scowl, scanning the club's writhing patrons mashed against each other on the tiny dance floor with feigned disinterest. The *Sang Frais* might be Melbourne's premium nightclub catering to the city's paranormal world, but it was a far cry from the Pleasure Palace. For starters, there were no fae strippers copulating on the stage. For another, they didn't serve Carpathian mountain water.

Ignoring a particularly determined human female's efforts to gain his attention, he took a sip from the sweating glass in his hand.

The single-malt scotch whiskey slid down the back of his throat with ease but did little to calm his thirst. Only one thing did that now, and Inari was currently nowhere to be seen.

He didn't like that. Not one little bit.

His mouth filled with saliva at the mere thought of his bound mate, the sweet taste of her blood, the heady scent of her sex, and he growled, the sound rumbling deep in his chest like thunder. Where was she?

"Here, lover."

Her soft voice tickled his left ear. He turned, snaked his arm around her slim waist and yanked her against his body with preternatural speed and strength, letting his agitation and instant desire throb through their bond. "Dark Ones, you've had me worried, Sentinel," he murmured, gazing down into her face. "And angry. Where have you been?"

She slid her fingers up his chest, pressing herself closer to his body. "You were worried?"

He smoothed his hand down her back and cupped her ass in a firm hold. "Yes." The exquisite muscles of her butt flexed under his touch, and for a split second, he wanted nothing more than to rip the skin-tight leather pants she wore from her body and sink his fangs into one of her ass cheeks. Slake his thirst. Feed his hunger. But neither he nor Inari was here for fun, at least not *that* kind of fun. Inari had work to do. A task long overdue and weighing heavily on her soul.

He held her close, wanting her to feel every second of careful warning he would not express in words. He knew her well, and telling her to be careful would only irritate her. Instead, he let his thoughts open to her. She released a soft sigh, the coiled tension in her body relaxing for a brief moment before she stiffened and pulled slightly away.

"He's leaving," she murmured, skimming her fingers down his chest in an act he knew was designed to appear casual and fitting to their current location. Her stare, unwavering and icy cold, tracked someone moving behind him. With a silent snarl, Ezryn narrowed his senses onto Inari's prey, and a vile stench filtered into his nose like poisoned fog.

He straightened, shooting a quick look over his shoulder at the creature responsible for such a foul odor.

Without a word, Inari turned and walked away from him, weaving her way through the packed club, disengaging herself from more than one overenthusiastic grope as she did so.

Ezryn clenched his jaw and followed her, keeping his control firmly in check. He'd seen her do this many times. He knew she was more than capable of handling it, but *this* target, *this* job, was different. Personal. And in Ezryn's mind, that made it dangerous.

Icy cold air wrapped around him as he stepped from the Sang Frais, the Melbourne winter attacking with savage gusto anyone foolish enough to be outside at four a.m.. He ignored it, his attention focused solely on Inari.

She stood on the footpath, the glossy waves of her black hair whipping around her face, her lithe body coiled and honed to a perfection he could not describe, her eyes green fire. Yet beneath her sensual beauty, the power of her *croi* thrummed, growing closer to release, stronger with every second. His spine tingled at its nearness and his fangs extended.

She turned her head and nodded to him. *"This won't take long."*

Unnerving unease churned through him, but he hid it, cocking an eyebrow in return. "Show-off."

She stepped off the footpath onto the deserted road, following her target as he made his way down King Street. She moved like fluid steel, and Ezryn's chest constricted. She was powerful, deadly and sensual in every way he could imagine. And she was his. How had that happened?

"Stop it. You're distracting me."

He snorted at her silent reprimand and took his own step off the footpath, the icy wind lashing at him as he followed her path. *"Be careful."*

She didn't respond, and he saw why. Her prey was about to turn the corner into a narrow alley sandwiched between two dark office blocks. Perfect.

A wave of prickling heat blasted at him and his spine tingled again, seconds before Inari quickened her pace to a blurring sprint. Heading for the nameless alley.

He burst into a run.

The alley's shadows folded over him as he entered the narrow mouth, the stench of piss, vomit and sex assaulting his nostrils. He scowled, scanning the darkness for Inari.

She stood but a few meters away, her legs spread, her booted feet planted firmly on the ground. The winter wind did not reach them here, and her hair fell down her back in a mass of tousled waves, looking for all the world like she'd just spent an hour or more in bed. He narrowed his eyes, moving closer to her on silent feet, his stare sliding to the creature pissing against the brick wall of the south office block.

His spine tingled again, his balls grew heavy, his chest tight.

"You really are a disgusting creature, aren't you?"

Inari's casual comment shattered the thick silence of the alley. The urinating empathic leech demon jumped and spun around to gape at her, a pungent stream of piss arcing from his jutting dick. "You?" he gasped, eyes widening. His stare snapped to Ezryn and he hissed, shoving his dick back into the folds of his flesh. "What? You need a vampire to help you now, slut?"

Before Inari could respond, Ezryn burst out laughing, raising one hand in a dismissive wave. "Dark Ones, no." He chortled, shaking his head, his spine tingling hotter, hotter. "I'm just here for the show."

And he took a step back as Inari leapt at the repulsive leech, watching her transform mid-air into her Sentinel form, her talons sinking into the demon's neck, slamming him against the brick wall. "My sister sends her condolences, fucker," she whispered, the words full of deadly promise as she hooked her fingers into a deadly weapon. "And her goodbyes."

She struck out, the first blow of many to come. The punishment of a Sentinel, the vengeance of a sister. And this time Ezryn knew Inari would not let the leech escape.

Ezryn felt a wide smile pull at his lips as he watched his lover at work. He crossed his arms over his chest, leaned his shoulder against the brick wall beside him and let out a contented sigh. Dark Ones, she was magnificent. And he loved her. By the Deities and God, he loved her.

"The way it is," he murmured, the blazing heat of Inari's deadly, righteous power surging though their bond to make his heart burn. "And the way it will *always* be.

Even the Apocalypse can't stop desire like this.

DARK DESTINY

DARK SENTINEL
BOOK ONE

LEXXIE COUPER

AWARD-WINNING AUTHOR

Dark Destiny

Dark Sentinel Book One

Available Now

Is love enough to save the world?

The First Horseman of the Apocalypse, Pestilence is tired of waiting. Mankind is his to destroy. But first he has to defeat one of his own, the Fourth Horseman, Death, along with the lowly human she's so fond of. The one prophesised to save the world.

Patrick Watkins wasn't prepared for the way his body—and soul—respond to Death when she suddenly appears in his bedroom. He's just a normal guy, saving lives at Australia's busiest beach. But a lifetime of feeling he's meant for something bigger haunts him, and it only intensifies at Death's touch and crystalises with her kiss.

Death isn't interested in bringing about the end of humanity. She's focused on claiming the souls of the departed, thank you very much. And then she encounters Patrick Watkins. There's an enigmatic significance to the sexy Australian that pulls on her very existence. And makes her question her very purpose.

Falling in lust with a human isn't a problem, but falling in *love* with one? The one who stands in Pestilence's way. That's dangerous.

Apocalypse-level dangerous.

When it comes to love or duty, for Death and Patrick, picking a side might just lead to the end. Of everything.

First Chapter Preview: Dark Destiny

Dark Sentinel, Book One

"Ven, you're being an idiot."

Seriously, if his brother wasn't *already* dead, he'd kill him.

Turning from the sea-spray-crusted window, Patrick Watkins ground his teeth, mobile phone clenched in his right hand, blood boiling with frustration. "I'm not coming home. I have a job to do and I'm not leaving the beach just because you've got a freaking bee in your bonnet."

"When are you going to listen to me, brother?" Ven's normally deep voice growled unnaturally deeper. Whether from anger, worry, or the high position of the sun, Patrick didn't know. Ven was usually asleep at midday. Being awake and in an argument with his younger brother probably brought the demon lurking in Ven's blood closer to the surface than usual.

Patrick didn't care. Not with the way Ven was carrying on. Anyone would think Patrick was walking around with a *Kill Me* sign taped to his back.

"It feels wrong," Ven grumbled. "Let the other guards babysit the tourists. You're the boss. Delegate."

"Yes, Ven. I *am* the boss." Patrick turned back to the window, studying the thousands of swimmers—tourists and locals alike—enjoy the gorgeous summer's day at Bondi Beach. "Which means I can't just bugger off."

Danger lurked out there in the famous beach's crystal blue waves. Sharks. Rips. Undertows. Blue-bottles...all waiting to catch a swimmer unaware. To bring pain, suffering, maybe even death. He'd be damned if he was leaving those swimmers' fates to chance. His team was good. Better than good. God knew, Bluey, his second-in-command, had been swimming since birth. The senior lifeguard's rescue rate was the second highest in the country after his own, but —like Ven—Patrick had an uneasy knot in his gut today.

Unlike Ven, Patrick's sense of disquiet had nothing to do with a supposed attack from an unknown "thing" and everything to do with the large number of people enjoying the famous stretch of beach.

Ven existed in the inhuman, paranormal world. Patrick didn't. On a day like today, there were close to forty-thousand human souls on the sand and in the water and that equaled roughly forty-thousand possible drownings, shark-attack victims, blue-bottle stings...

Patrick's gut knotted again. No matter what bizarre threat Ven's paranoia created, he couldn't leave work.

But he's not being paranoid. You know that. And you know exactly what threat—

Shutting down the unwanted thought, Patrick scanned the surf before him, zeroing his focus down on a group of three tourists bobbing ignorantly close to Backpacker's Express. If the beach's notorious and infamous rip took them into its embrace, they'd be out to sea and two miles south before they even realized they were no longer in Bondi waters. It would take at least four lifeguards to round them up, leaving seven to keep the rest of the beach's visitors safe. Seven people to deal with any emergency on the mile-long stretch. His team couldn't do that without their boss, no matter how good they were.

He bit back a frustrated sigh. Just a typical day at work. Danger and death lurking everywhere. He couldn't pack it all in just because his brother thought he was in danger. Besides, it was the middle of the day. What type of paranormal nasty attacked in the middle of the bloody day? And on a busy beach, no less?

The kind in a black suit, maybe?

The silent question scratched at his mind, but he ignored it, returning his attention to the packed surf instead. It was a glorious summer day on Australia's most famous beach. Perfect, in fact. Blue, cloudless sky, clean five-foot waves, warm seventy-one degree water. If said unseen paranormal attack was going to happen, it sure as hell wasn't going to be today. What Patrick would more likely be confronted with on a day like today, what the knot in his gut was probably warning him about, was the possibility of a careless, over-confident tourist taking their life in their hands by not swimming between the flags. *That,* he could deal with on his own. He didn't need his vampire big brother to save a drowning person. When it came down to it, Ven wasn't up to swimming these days anyway, not during sunlight at least. Picking up his old board for a midnight surf or two, sure...*when* he wasn't trying to protect Patrick from threats from who the hell knows, that was.

Shaking his head, Patrick lifted his phone closer to his mouth. "Sorry, Ven. I'm staying put. Either come get me or go back to sleep."

"Ha, ha," Ven muttered. "Really funny. Will you bloody well listen to reason for a—"

"I gotta go, mate." Patrick cut him off with a shake of his head and a wry chuckle. "I'll call you when I get home."

"But—"

Patrick killed the connection and threw his phone on the counter before him. His brother needed to learn how to relax.

Ven had spent the last thirty-six years hellbent on protecting him from some unknown malevolent entity, and Patrick had spent the last eighteen of those years arguing with Ven the entire thing was ridiculous and unnecessary. Nothing was after Patrick. Nothing.

Nothing however, could convince Ven differently. Thank bloody God the bastard spent his days "sleeping", otherwise Patrick would probably go crazy and shove a stake in Ven's chest just to get some unsupervised personal space.

Who in the hell would be coming after him anyway? He was nothing more than a simple Aussie lifeguard.

You know who, Patrick. You just have to—

"You see that group in Backpacker's rip, Wato?" a slightly raspy voice sounded to his left, cutting across the dark unsettling thought.

Grateful for the interruption, Patrick gave his second in charge a quick nod. "Yeah, I see them."

Bluey handed him a pair of binoculars, concern creasing the sides of his pale blue eyes. "One of them's flounderin'."

He took the offered glasses. "Tourist?"

Bluey shrugged. "Dunno, but he's not one of the regulars. Big bloke. Blond. Looks sunburnt, even from here. Maybe forty, forty-five years old, I'm guessin'. Take a look."

Lifting the binoculars to his eyes, Patrick focused in on the group of swimmers bobbing in the surf's choppy southern swell. Five people moved up and down with the rolling waves, their heads breaching the deceptive water, sinking below the surface and emerging again. Five people thinking they were safe when they were in dangerous territory. Five people who would need to be rounded up ASAP. Five people—

A man burst upward from the water, thinning blond hair plastered to a domed skull, sunburnt face distorted in abject fear. He struggled to stay above the inescapable waves, the sea pouring into his open mouth every time he shouted for help. One flabby arm clawed above the surface to wave, once, twice, before he sank below the surface with terrifying speed. Gone.

"Fuck." Patrick threw aside the binoculars. "He's under."

He moved. Fast.

Ordering Bluey to contact the two guards patrolling the southern end of the beach, he charged from the patrol tower, the needs of rescuing a drowning swimmer second nature to him. Snatching up a rescue tube and his board, he sprinted across the sand, dodging sunbathers and beach volleyballers on his way to the water. It would take approximately six minutes to get to the man in Backpacker's Express. By Patrick's reckoning, five minutes too long.

The high midday sun beat down on him as he ran, the blistering hot sand scalding the soles of his bare feet. He ran, board tucked under his arm, stare locked on the notorious rip, searching the increasing swell for any sign of the sunburnt drowning swimmer.

Shit. There was none.

To his left, he saw Grub and Hollywood weave through a crowd of laughing tourists before sprinting into the surf. The two life-guards threw their boards onto the water and launched themselves through the breaking waves at breakneck speed, heading for the group of clueless swimmers.

He flicked his stare back to Backpacker's Express, picking up his already punishing pace, hot sand peppering the backs of his thighs in stinging pinpricks.

Time pressed on him, as brutal as the sun. Grub and Hollywood were seasoned lifeguards, but neither had extensive experience with the infamous rip, and the middle-aged blond man wasn't the only swimmer struggling in the water. It was a foregone conclusion any number of the tourists would soon realize they were in trouble and make a desperate scramble for the approaching guards the second they saw them. Once that happened, the drowning man would certainly go under for good. If he hadn't already.

Patrick plowed into the surf, his muscles burning, sweat streaming down his temples and chest. The cool water stung like icy needles on his flushed flesh, biting at his focus. He pushed through the chilling pain trying to cramp his legs, positioning his board and dropping onto it in one fluid move. Plunging his arms deep into the sea, he pulled stroke after stroke, powering his way through the crashing waves.

With every crest he rode, he looked for the blond man with the sunburnt face. With each dip, his chest grew tighter. He couldn't see him. Which at this point could only mean one thing. He hadn't resurfaced.

Fuck.

"Have you seen a guy with blond hair out here?" Grub's shout rose above the roar of adrenaline in Patrick's ears and he snapped his head to his left, finding the young guard attempting to communicate with a frantic Japanese tourist in a bright yellow Speedo trying to climb onto Grub's board. "Careful, mate. I've—"

"I can't see him!" Hollywood shouted on Patrick's right, pulling himself into a sitting position on his board as he studied the churned-up water around him. He shot Patrick a worried look and shook his head. "Where did he—"

He didn't finish. One of the panicked swimmers knocked him from his board, wailing incoherently as they tried to scramble from the water, fear and shame turning their eyes into bulging discs.

Patrick bit back a curse. He didn't have time for this. The drowning man didn't have time. Ignoring the fracas—Grub and Hollywood would have to handle it on their own—he scanned the choppy waves, feeling the rip's undercurrent pulling at his legs with menacing force. Backpacker's Express was aptly named. It sucked you out to sea. Fast. If he didn't find the blond man soon, he wouldn't. Not until the guy's body turned up on nearby Bronte Beach, bloated and gray and nibbled on by fish.

No way Patrick was going to let that happen.

Cutting through the waves, he searched the water, tuning out everything but his gut. Nothing existed. No sound. No smell. Just the cool water splashing against his board and body and the tight tug in the pit of his stomach directing his search. The inexplicable instinct he never questioned that helped him save those beyond saving time and again. The enigmatic, uncanny intuition that repeatedly led him to those sinking into the ocean's cool embrace.

With that strange, tight tugging in his gut, he paddled his board south.

The water grew black beneath him. Deep. Cold.

He moved slowly, the *thump thump thump* of his heart a soundless tattoo in his chest, a silent beat keeping time with his progress, charting his search. The water sucked at his arms with each stroke he took, the rip reaching for them, hungry and demanding and greedy. He denied the powerful undertow, refusing to be taken in its hold as he stared into the ocean.

Searching. Searching.

His heart slowed, his breath slowed, his existence shrank until it was just him, his board, and the merciless sea around him. Knowing death waited on his shoulder, salivating. Knowing life depended on his instincts. A life waning. Fading.

Heart almost slowed to complete stillness, he searched for the drowning man.

There.

Plunging his right arm into the ocean, he grabbed a fistful of blond hair and pulled, a grunt bursting past his lips as the man's considerable weight snapped at his shoulder muscles. "Gotcha."

Counterbalancing himself against the violent jolt, he hauled the limp body further from the sea, changing his grip until he had the older, unconscious man lying face down across the front of his board. "Get 'em in," he ordered Grub, nodding toward the still-panicking but at the same time gawking tourists bobbing in the swell to his left. "And give 'em a lecture."

Shifting his position to accommodate the motionless man's bulk, he began to propel his board back to the beach. His job was far from done and time pressed harder on him. He may have pulled the guy from a wet grave, but the old bugger wasn't breathing. Until his lungs were cleared of water, the rescued swimmer belonged to death.

Screw that.

Patrick powered through the surf, ignoring the burn in his shoulders and lungs. A distant part of his mind heard Grub and Hollywood barking at the tourists in the water. An even more distant part noted Hollywood sounded right and royally pissed off, but his main focus was the beach. Bluey waited there, defibrillator and oxi-boot ready.

When it came to saving a life, Patrick refused to concede to death. No matter how long an individual had been underwater.

"Move it, move it, move it!" Bluey's roar reached Patrick before he even made it to the sand. Swimmers, sunbathers, and gawkers alike fell out of the way, mouths agape, eyes wide as the other man barged through the crowd, orange-red hair gleaming in the ruthless sun, face furious, arms cutting a path through the melee. He met Patrick in the shallows, scooping the still lifeless swimmer up from Patrick's board and flinging one limp arm around his own shoulder. "Got 'im."

Patrick hooked the man's other arm around the back of his neck and, heart hammering, gut tight, half-dragged, half-carried him from the surf.

The moment they passed the waterline, they dumped him onto his back, the crowd gathering around them, gasping as one as the man's limp body hit the sand.

Before the displaced grains could settle, Patrick dropped to his knees. He didn't have time to wait for Bluey to pass him a facemask. The *man* didn't have time to wait. Blood roaring in his ears, he tilted the bloke's head back, pinched his nose shut and covered the slack, blue-tinged lips with his mouth.

One. Two. Three. He transferred his breath into the man's lungs, watching his chest rise with each exhalation.

Turning his head, he listened for any sound of inhalation. Nothing.

"Don't you fucking dare," he growled, feeling for a pulse.

Nothing.

One. Two. Three.

Again, nothing.

Rising up onto his knees, he placed his palm heels to the center of the man's chest, left over right, and pressed. Again. Again. Again.

"He's not comin' back, Wato."

Bluey's low rumble lifted Patrick's head. He glared at his second in charge, continuing to compress the motionless man's sternum. "Yes, he is."

Returning his stare to the man's pale, flaccid face, he counted off fifty compressions before clamping his mouth over the blue-tinged lips again.

One. Two. Three.

Nothing.

One. Two. Three.

Nothing.

A hand closed over his shoulder. "He was under too long, mate."

He lifted his head, returning his hands to the man's sternum as he fixed Bluey with a level look. "Get the paddles ready."

Bluey released a long sigh and turned away, reaching for the defibrillator.

Patrick pressed his hands into the man's chest. Again. Again. "Don't you fucking dare," he ground out, staring hard into the lifeless face. "I'm not gonna let you."

He pinched the salt-crusted nose and covered the slack mouth with his, forcing breath into the man's lungs.

One. Two. Three.

One. Two. Three.

Nothing.

"No," he snarled. He rose higher onto his knees and pressed the heels of his palms to the man's chest. "I'm." *Press.* "Not." *Press.* "Going." *Press.* "To." *Press.* "Let." *Press.* "You."

He dropped his head and forced breath into the man again.

One. Two. Three.

One. Two. Three.

Nothing. Still nothing.

"It's enough, Wato." Bluey's voice sounded far away. "He's gone."

"He's *not* fucking gone." He jerked his head up, glaring at his second in charge. "Give me the paddles."

Bluey looked back at him, pale blue eyes calm, face expressionless. "You're frying dead meat, mate. You know that."

"*No!*"

He smashed his palm heels to the man's sternum, compressing his chest in rapid succession.

A hideous, wet *glurk* burst from the man's throat, followed immediately by a gush of hot water and sour bile from his mouth.

"Yes, you fucking bastard," Patrick growled, ignoring the gasps and cries around him as he continued to stimulate the man's heart in steady, forceful blows. "Spit it out. You can't breathe with half of Bondi in your lungs. Get rid of it."

Another *glurk*, this one less wet, less fluidy. More water erupted from the man's mouth, spurting this time from his nose as well. A groan slipped from his lips, weak and raw, the sound almost lost in the sudden cheers from the crowd. Eyelids fluttering, arms twitching, the man rolled his head, a shudder wracking through his body before he slumped still again.

Patrick's heart stopped for a second. Shit. He was losing him. Again. "Give me the paddles."

Face expressionless, eyes worried, Bluey held out the defib paddles. Patrick snatched them from him, the violent action eliciting another gasp from the crowd.

"Charge 'em," he ground out, staring at the motionless man's face. A high-pitched whine cut the thick tension as Bluey charged the defibrillator.

"Charged."

"Clear." He pressed the gel-smeared paddles to the man's unmoving chest.

Two-hundred joules shot through flesh, muscle, bone, and tissue. Two-hundred joules of electric life.

The man bucked, spine bowing, fingers splaying wide.

Mouth dry, Patrick stabbed his fingertips against the man's neck, feeling for a pulse.

Still nothing.

"C'mon!" he shouted, giving the man's fleshy shoulders a hard shake. "I've got you this far. Fight, damn it."

A movement to his left—slight and almost imperceptible—flickered in his peripheral vision. Long legs. Blue denim. Black stiletto boots. A cold breeze blew against his cheek. A hot tightness squeezed his heart. He felt—

"He's breathing!" Bluey yelled, slapping his back. "Fair dinkum, mate. You've done it again! He's breathing!"

Patrick snapped his stare to the once-motionless man's face, unable to control a powerful surge of elation at the sight of two—albeit unfocussed—brown eyes squinting up at him.

"Wh...wh...what happened?"

The man's voice was barely more than a rasp, but to Patrick it sounded like a pure song. He grinned. "You tried to drink half the ocean, mate."

The man coughed, a scratchy, wheezy hiccup. "That...was a bit...stupid...of me." Closing his eyes, he pulled a ragged breath, another cough choking the shaky intake before he could finish.

"Take it easy, mate," Patrick cautioned, pressing his fingers to the man's neck again. His pulse was weak but steady. "The paramedics are on the way. Where's your stuff? Towel, car keys, clothes—"

"No, no." The man shook his head, struggling to sit up. His brown eyes flicked around the crowd, almost nervous. "No ambulance. I'm okay."

Bluey squatted down beside Patrick and placed his hand firmly on the man's chest. "Mate, you were dead. Wato here brought you back to life. You need to go to the hospital."

"No. I'm fine. I'm—"

Another coughing fit claimed the man and he dropped backward, lying flat.

"The ambos are here," Grub murmured, popping his head over Patrick's shoulder to nod at the approaching paramedics running across the sand.

Fingers still pressed to the man's strengthening pulse, Patrick shot the paramedics a quick look. Relief coursed through him. Thank bloody God. Maybe they could talk some sense into the—

A woman leant over his shoulder, slim and dressed in snug blue jeans, a New York Yankees baseball cap shrouding her face in shadows. A chill rippled up his spine and his palms prickled, as if he'd suddenly plunged them into a wasp nest. He felt her gaze skim over his face from behind large, black sunglasses before she extended her arm with absolute confidence and stroked long, slender fingers over the man's fleshy chest.

Absolute terror flooded the man's face, turning his sunburnt skin a sick vomit-orange. His brown eyes bulged. He stared up at the woman, soundless words bubbling from his mouth. His pulse rate tripled. Quadrupled.

And stopped.

Dead.

"What the?" Patrick frowned, ramming his fingers harder to the man's neck.

Nothing.

He jolted to his feet, turning to glare at the woman in the baseball cap.

But she wasn't there. In fact, there wasn't a sign of her on the beach at all.

As if she'd never been there in the first place.

Gut twisting, palm itching, Patrick's frown deepened. Where was she? What the hell was going on?

Death walked away from the lifeguard, the stiletto heels of her boots not even remotely sinking into the soft white sand. The coastal breeze caressed her face and arms and she pulled in a long breath, enjoying its heat even as the blazing midday sun sucked the moisture from the flesh of the humans—oblivious to her existence—around her. Summer in Australia. Hot. Hotter. Hottest. Good thing she'd ditched her normal Grim Reaper's attire. Too damn stifling.

Adjusting her sunglasses on her face, she sidestepped a teenage couple making out on a beach towel, casting them a detached yet curious look. He would live for another sixty-five years before dying in a car accident, she would die in five years of advanced skin cancer.

Death, or as she preferred to call herself in *this* millennium, Fred—after a particularly cute Basset hound she once met—*tsked*, noting the gleaming oil smeared over the girl's bare flesh and the distinct scent of coconut heavy on the air. As if humans didn't have enough to deal with in their short time, they had to go and seek out death any chance they could, all in the name of beauty.

Shaking her head, she followed the waterline away from the commotion still unfolding behind her. The paramedics would not revive the drowned man, no matter how skilled or tenacious they were. All she'd left them was an empty skin-wrapped lump of meat and bones.

The icy tingle in the pit of her belly she experienced after every claiming whispered through her, feeding her magic. It nourished her power, sating the Rider within. Today however, it also felt... wrong. Not because the soul she'd removed from the mortal coil— Richard Michael Peabody—was a closet pedophile who deserved to die. That very morning he'd raped—for the tenth time—his six-year-old niece while his twin sister attended a doctor's appointment.

Fred felt no remorse for Peabody. The human male deserved to have his life extinguished. He most *definitely* deserved the eternal damnation awaiting him. When it came to mortal monsters like Peabody, she enjoyed her job. But today, even with the tingle in her core and the sure knowledge of just punishment about to be meted out, she felt conflicted.

Every soul she claimed, every life thread she severed she did with pride. Her purpose was ultimate. Life could not exist without Death. If she didn't do what she did, humanity would pay the price. That didn't mean however, that she was emotionless. She felt no pity for Peabody, and really, who would? But she couldn't help feel sorry for the lifeguard who'd tried so hard to save him.

She'd seen many EMOs at work, but few were as aggressively determined to thwart her work as the lifeguard. It was as though the very idea of losing Peabody assaulted him. Wounded him. Like it was personal somehow.

Raw energy had poured from him in intoxicating waves as he'd fought to save the vile man's life, almost as powerful and energizing as the sun above.

Being near him had been a surreal, unexpected rush.

Uninvited, an image of the tenacious son of a bitch filled her head and she pulled in a soft, appreciative breath. Not just tenacious, but damn fine to look at as well. Tall, lean, and sinewy with smooth skin kissed bronze by the sun and shaggy blond hair bleached golden by its solar rays. His eyes were a fierce, piercing green, his nose strong and hawkish, his lips totally kissable even when clenched together in stubborn denial.

A soft beat pulsed between her thighs and she took another swift breath, surprised at the reaction. It had been a long time since she'd been aroused by a mortal. The last—an arrogant but brilliant Roman general with a nose just like her lifeguard and a succinct way with words—had dumped her for a snooty Egyptian queen with an asp fetish.

She turned her mind back to the Australian, remembering the way he looked as he ran from the sea with water streaming over his muscular body, the sun highlighting broad, strong shoulders, snug blue swimming shorts hugging narrow hips. It was a good memory. A potent memory.

The heat between her thighs pulsed again and, despite the warm breezes blowing across the ocean, a ripple razed her flesh, pinching her nipples into tight peaks. Something about the lifeguard intrigued her. Not just his fierce battle to deny her, but something else. Something different.

She strode along the sand, a detached, professional part of her mind marking those around her for their time, and thought of Peabody's failed rescue. Like the lifeguard, something about it had felt...what? Wrong?

No, wrong wasn't the correct word, especially to describe the lifeguard.

Yummy. *Yummy* was a good word to describe the lean Australian with the messy blond hair. *Sexy as sin* another one. Well, another three, actually.

Unusual, however, *was* the word she was looking for to describe his rescue attempt. But why?

What was it about the sequence of events?

The lifeguard works on the drowning man's body, pounding against the man's fleshy chest with his palms, the sun turning his smooth muscular back to a bronzed sheen. The subtle heat of the day kisses her arms and neck and cheeks as she watches him battle the inevitable. The sound of the pedophile's perverted, weakening heartbeat vibrates through her core, feeding the familiar tingle in her gut as she prepares to sever his life thread... She leans over the lifeguard to touch Peabody and the salty bite of the lifeguard's sweat threads into her being like mist. She turns her head, for some reason wanting to see his eyes, wanting to see if they burn with the same fierce determination she feels radiating from him. She looks at him...and he looks at her, his soft breath fanning her face.

Fred froze, the sounds of the beach—seagulls screeching, swimmers splashing, people laughing—sucked away by stunned shock.

He looked at *her.*

He could see her.

That's impossible. The living can't see you until the very moment you claim them. Not unless you choose for them to do so and you sure as hell didn't choose for this guy to see you today.

But he *had* seen her. He'd looked straight at her, and it was only now, with the post-claiming buzz fading to a soft tingle, that she realized it.

He'd seen her.

How in all the levels of hell had he seen her?

No, it wasn't possible. The living *didn't* see her. She prevented it. The Deities prevented it.

Wishful thinking? Maybe your starved libido is making you see things?

Before she could stop herself, she turned and gave the lifeguard a long, hard inspection from across the sand.

He sat beside Peabody's inert body, head buried in his hands, broad shoulders slumped. She'd seen this very pose before. The position of a defeated human. But unlike others in this situation, anger radiated from the man.

Not misery, or self-centered contemplation. Anger. Simmering, tangible anger.

Fred cocked an eyebrow, her sex squeezing in base appreciation. *Who* are *you, Mr. Tall, Bronzed, and Brooding?*

Stare locked on the increasingly intriguing man, she tapped into the List of the Living threaded into her very existence, seeking the answer.

But all that surfaced from the never-ending database was a name and date of birth.

She frowned. "That can't be right. Where's his date of death?"

From the moment of conception, the time and cause of death of every living creature with a soul was predetermined. The Order of Actuality demanded it. From the smallest baby to the leader of the free world, their lifespan was locked in a fixed time frame, imprinted on their very genetic fiber.

All, it seemed, except Patrick Anthony Watkins. She knew

when he was born, knew he was currently thirty-six years old, but as for when and how he would die? Nada.

Which made him a...

She narrowed her eyes, regarding him across the busy beach.

The sun beat down on those around her, drawing moisture from their pores, turning the heavily populated strip of sand to a wavering shimmer of silver light and color, yet Patrick Watkins remained sharp in clarity.

Just Patrick. Filling her vision.

She studied him closely, pursing her lips.

"Okay," she muttered, sensing his soul, "so he's *not* a demon. Good." His soul's pure, spiritual presence poured from him, powerful and potent even from this distance: a blazing white essence of life and humanity so strong it made her blood sing and her skin tingle. "But if he's got a soul..."

Frowning, she tilted her head to the side, looking at him through the darkness of her sunglasses. It didn't make sense. Having a soul meant he should have a date of death. So why was she drawing a complete blank?

And why, in the name of the Deities, was she so damned turned on? Did the man's ambiguity have anything to do with it? Or was it just because he was smolderingly sexy?

She shook her head again. She needed answers. And another *closer* look.

Because you want answers, or because you want to check him out again?

The unbidden and way-too-close-to-the-bone thought made her sex constrict in a firm, warm pulse of eager anticipation. She couldn't touch him, but she could look. She could look a lot. She could take her visual fill of him because the living *could not* see her. No matter what her foolish mind insisted it saw.

A tense pressure welled in her chest and, turning away from the sight of Patrick kneeling beside the empty pedophile's body, she released a long, dragged out sigh.

It was a sad fact of her existence she could no longer ignore. She, Death, the Grim Reaper, *El Muerte*, Cronus, Azrael, the Fourth Horseman of the Apocalypse, had become a Peeping freakin' Tom.

Gritting her teeth, she stormed along the high-tide line, fighting like hell to ignore the damp tightness between her thighs. "Fantastic. Fucking fantastic."

* * *

Two hundred tall, thick candles materialized into spontaneous existence, illuminating the dark, cavernous room with a cold, flickering light. It washed the black stone walls pale yellow, throwing writhing shadows against the hard surface and casting a weak glow over the slim man in a black business suit where he stood before a massive, bone-framed mirror.

He studied the room—*his* room—in the reflection of the glass. It suited him, this room. A room worthy of the First Horseman. An entity of the Highest Order could create whatever personal environment they desired within the Realm and his space was *exactly* how he desired it to be. A room of sick death and sick life. A room symbolizing his stature and premier position.

His bed took prominent position in the centre, constructed by over a thousand human bones torn from living bodies. Bones once white and raw, now blackened by eons of waxy smoke. He'd taken many a sacrificial virgin's purity on that bed, all whimpering at his power and inescapable strength. He'd taken more than one demon slut as well. She-demons who knew who he was, who knew, unlike his disrespectful colleagues, how important he was. She-demons who recognized his potential and wanted to taste his seed and bear his spawn.

He slid his gaze from the bed to the towering throne standing on a raised dais under a large hanging candelabra, his prick growing stiff at the sight. Both throne and candelabra were made from human bones, just as the bed, but unlike the bed and candelabra, the bones of the throne were stark white. Each humerus, femur, tibia, and skull still ripe with living marrow and tissue. The throne was older than time, but he made certain it defied time as well. It didn't take much to infuse each bone in its construction with an incantation to preserve its rawness. To touch each one was to touch a bone freshly torn from a living being's body, still slick and sticky with blood and fluid, still thrumming with that on which he fed the most—dying life. Whenever he sat on the throne, which he did often, the pain of the personally selected humans whose lives were forfeited for its creation seeped into his being, making him stronger.

Whenever he fucked on the throne, his seed destroyed the female impaled on his shaft and his orgasm decimated an entire region on the surface of man's world, striking every living creature down with disease, swarms of insects destroying all plant life and crops. Whenever he fucked on the throne it was as though he and he alone wielded the force of the Apocalypse itself.

The Deities had commanded he cease such activities, ordering him to toe the line. His impatience and contempt grew. Fuck them and their timeline and their preordained hierarchy. Who were they to decide what *he* did and when he did it? Did they forget who he was? What he would bring about?

He was Pestilence.

Returning his stare to the mirror, he studied his reflection, pursing his lips as he did so.

He was short for an entity, he knew that. Short and thin, without the typical ostentatious tail and horns and over-developed muscles so favored by other first-order entities. No one would ever accuse him of using steroids, that was for certain. His blue eyes were pale and watery, his dark hair lank, his flesh pale and dull. "Sallow" was a word he'd heard muttered often by his brethren to describe him. "Sickly" and "weedy" two more adjectives used loudly and without secrecy by one of his number in particular.

His eyes narrowed as he let his thoughts turn to the last Horseman.

Death.

He drew her image into his mind, remembering all too easily her condescending rebuke of the proposal he'd suggested. A partnership of greatness. Not just a sexual one, but one to undo the very Fabric, to destroy the Order of Actuality completely. A magnificent, malevolent duo to bring about the very end of existence. A *duo*, not a quartet.

Two Riders, not four.

She'd laughed. At both his sexual advances and his proposition. Laughed in his face and told him to grow up and get a life. "Seriously, you don't still believe in that old wives' tale, do you? Do you see my black horse anywhere? Or my pale one, for that matter? Do you see me strutting around in a pair of chaps getting ready for the big assault?"

Curling his fingers into fists, he thought of Death and the Deities and how *all* would suffer from his wrath.

"I am Pestilence," he murmured, smoothing his left palm over his hair as he stared at his reflection in the giant mirror. The flames of the candles flared brighter at the utterance of his name and the organ between his thighs grew stiff with dark anticipation. "I am the First Horseman of the Apocalypse. The one who brings disease and suffering incarnate. The one who destroys the world of man's crops and stock, their weak and young and feeble. *I* am the one who will bring the end, the one who will bask in the glory of the Apocalypse. Me and me alone." He gazed at his reflected form, cock hard, blood thick and fast in his veins. "And *nothing* or no one can stop me."

His reflection stared back at him, human façade just the way he wanted it to be: deceptive, misleading. "No one," he repeated, hot impatience eating at him, cold confidence feeding its hunger as he stared into his own eyes.

His reflection stared back at him. And, with barely a shimmer, turned into that of the lifeguard's.

"No," he sneered, turning away. "Not even *him*."

* * *

Dark Destiny Available Now

More Romance from Lexxie Couper...

Fire Mates Series

Sera's Dragon
How to Love Your Dragon
Tigress and the Dragon
Scorched Desire

About Lexxie Couper

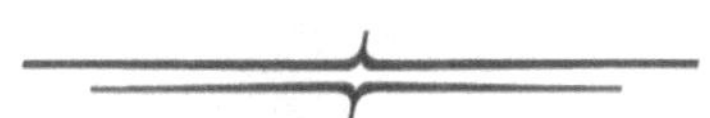

Lexxie Couper started writing when she was six and hasn't stopped since. She's not a deviant, but she does have a deviant's imagination and a desire to entertain readers with her words. Add the two together and you get erotic romances that can make you laugh, cry, shake with fear or tremble with desire. Sometimes all at once.

When she's not submerged in the worlds she creates, Lexxie's life revolves around her family, a husband who thinks she's insane, an indoor cat who likes to stalk shadows, and her daughters, who both utterly captured her heart and changed her life forever.

Lexxie lives by two simple rules – measure your success not by how much money you have, but by how often you laugh, and always try everything at least once. As a consequence, she's laughed her way through many an eyebrow raising adventure. You can find details of her writing at
her writing at
www.LexxieCouper.com